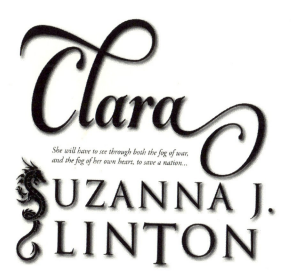

Clara

She will have to see through both the fog of war, and the fog of her own heart, to save a nation...

SUZANNA J. LINTON

Copyright 2016 by Suzanna J. Linton

All Rights Reserved

No part of this book may be copied or distributed without the author's permission.

Other Works

The Lands of Sun and Stone Series

Willows of Fate

The Bookwyrm Series

Part One

Part Two

Part Three

This print edition is dedicated to
Faye Adams.

This character first came alive in her home.

Chapter One

Clara trudged home, the sack of pots banging and clattering against her thin legs. The wind blew against her back, bringing with it the laughter and music of a festival she couldn't attend.

As she walked, she passed fields of peas and beans, the work of her neighbors. She looked at the bright green vegetation with a wistful air as she imagined how the peas would taste after simmering with a ham hock. Clara couldn't remember the last time she'd had something like that. She couldn't remember the last time her father chose tending the peas over visiting the tavern.

Passing a meadow full of playing children, their enthusiasm overflowing at not having to spend a day in the fields, workshops, or among flocks, Clara paused a moment to watch them. One of the girls stopped in her play long enough to yell and beckon. It was the daughter of the local baker. She sometimes slipped Clara rolls after temple-worship. Shaking her head, Clara walked onward to home.

Home was an old cottage in need of new thatching, but it still stood straight and tall. She smiled, feeling proud of herself as she looked at the chimney. Clara had cleaned that herself last fall.

Stopping to catch her breath, she turned to look down the hill. The small, modest buildings of the village sat in the distance, peeking through the green trees. She could see the narrow streets teeming with people and bright, colorful flagging hanging from the homes. Outside the village, in a fallow field, sat the caravan that had arrived the day before, the bright wagons arranged in a loose circle.

Around them all, the broad-shouldered Larkspur Mountains rose. Not for the first time, Clara wondered what it would be like to climb to one of the peaks and look down on her country of Lorst. Would she be able to see the capital, Bertrand?

Hoisting the bag a little higher onto her shoulder, she turned away from the scene and rounded the house to the back. Her mother, a woman with broad shoulders and work-toughened hands, was hanging the laundry.

What took you?" snapped Mama. Da had come home drunk in the early hours of the morning, putting Mama into a foul temper.

"The mender was busy. It's a festival day and he was closing and—"

"Never mind that. Go take them inside."

Clara obeyed, ducking through the low back door and picking her way around broken bits of furniture, farming tools, and other odds and ends. She heard the soft snoring of her father from the corner where sat her parents' bed by the fireplace. She carefully set the bag on the large rough-hewn table, taking care not to rattle the contents.

The sound of many horses' hooves clopping along the road outside the cottage didn't alarm Clara, until she heard them turn, the hooves suddenly softened by the grass surrounding their cottage. She hurried to a window and watched several horses pass as the riders swung around into the back yard. Clara ran to the back door and peered out around the jamb as the riders came to a stop before Lorna.

Mama curtsied and said, "My lord Errol, good day. What brings you?" A thin, nervous smile filled her face.

A young boy of no more than fifteen summers sat on a great black charger, dressed in a green tunic with gold embroidery. Clara's eyes widened. She'd only ever seen him with his father, Lord Brockington, when he rode out to inspect the tenant farms. Errol always hung back, quiet and watching.

Clara's father was one of Lord Brockington's tenants, but the inspection wasn't due until the harvest. What was Errol doing here, alone? And why so early? A shiver danced down Clara's spine.

Arranged behind him in an array of greens, reds, and blues were other boys about Errol's age, cousins from the nearby castle where Errol lived. They grinned at each other as if this was some sort of game.

"My father sends me." Errol stuck his fist on his hip, sticking his chest out, imitating his father's pose. "He says you have not paid your rent or produced a favorable tithe."

"It was a hard season last, Lord Errol. Many of the farms have failed."

"But you haven't paid your rent in several seasons."

"It-it's been a hard several seasons." Mama fiddled with her apron. "Would his lordship care for some ale?"

One of the boys behind Errol snickered, leaning to the side to whisper something to another cousin, who snickered as well. Errol shot a venomous glare at them over his shoulder and Clara clapped a hand over her mouth to keep herself from laughing. Poor Errol looked so put out over his friends distracting the situation from him. He turned back to Mama.

"Father says you have till the end of the month to pay the rest of your rent," he declared, "or you'll be put off your farm."

"His lordship is very kind but you see how hard it is here." She gestured toward the weed-choked field. "Surely we can be given more time." Her bottom lip quivered and Clara didn't need to standing beside her to know that her eyes filled with tears.

Lordling Errol's face softened and he looked on the verge of agreeing, of retracting some of what he said, when the eldest boy in the group—or, the biggest, at least—cuffed him on the shoulder. Errol straightened up in his saddle and scowled.

"No. You have until the end of the month. Good day!" Turning his horse, he trotted away, his entourage close on his heels.

Mama didn't move or make a sound until the noise of so many horses faded into the distance.

"Clara," she screeched. "Come out here!"

Clara scurried out of the cottage to stand beside her mother. "Mama, what are we going—"

"Never mind that now." She was pale and shaking and

Clara almost reached out to hug her. "Here. Help me with the wash."

Silence fell between them as Clara handed Mama clothing from the basket for her to hang. As Mama secured the third shirt on the line, her hands stilled, and a chill swept down Clara's back. Recognizing the sign, she scrunched her eyes against it, hunching her shoulders, but the dream fell upon her like a wave.

She stood at the end of a long, long line, shuffling down a dusty road. Her feet ached and her ankles throbbed as something chafed against them. A chain connected her hands to a boy in front of her. The boy fell, suddenly, dragging Clara down with her and nearly pulling down the person in front of them. A man in chain mail and leathers rode up on a large horse, raising a cane and screaming. Clara was crying but no sound came from her throat.

"Clara!"

Gasping, she jerked into the present. Mama stared down at her.

"What ails you, child?" She looked almost concerned.

Clara shook her head as the tremors passed through her. The waking dreams had never been that strong before.

"I want you to run another errand for me. Go find

Haggard and tell him to come here straight away. Do you understand?"

She swallowed. "Aye, Mama. After I get him, may I go play?"

Lorna glared at her for a moment before her mouth and eyes softened a little. "All right. But Haggard might come get you later. Be home before dark if he don't."

"Yes, Mama."

"Well, hurry on!"

Clara turned and ran away, going full pelt until she came again to the field of children. She stopped and gasped for breath, her side pinching painfully. The walk from there to the village didn't take her as long as it usually did, she walked so quickly.

Vendors lined the streets while jugglers, fire-breathers, and bards entertained wherever there was room to be found. Clara's eyes widened as she caught a glimpse of a man juggling knives.

People pushed against her but eventually she stumbled into a small clearing in the crowd. Twisting her head around, she looked for Haggard, wondering if she should go into the tavern. Two people brushed past her, clearing the way to a small booth selling meat pies. Haggard stood by it, chatting with a pretty maid.

The grizzled old man had once been a warrior, having lost an eye in battle. He covered the hole with a scarlet cloth. Clara liked him very much because he said she was pretty and gave her candy.

"Ah, little girl," he cried as she approached. "And did your Ma give you leave to come to the festival after all?"

"Aye, if I told you to go to her as quick as you could."

"Really? I wonder what your Ma is up to, then." He winked at her, which was more like blinking since it was his only eye.

She smiled up at him. He laughed and patted her on the head.

"You see this child, Kelli?" he asked. "She'll grow up prettier than you, I warrant."

The young woman looked down and smiled, showing only a few teeth. "I can see that."

"Clara, would you like a sweet?"

She nodded eagerly. Laughing again, he took her to a booth selling candy and bought her a stick of taffy.

"Come. Let's see what your Ma wanted."

"She said I didn't have to come back. She said I could play with the other children."

"Did she? Well, I won't stop you, then." He squatted down next to her. "Did you know there's a caravan in town?"

She nodded. Traders sometimes came through the town but it wasn't often they came on a festival day.

Haggard pointed toward the far end of the village. "They're a strange folk, from down South. Steer clear of them, Clara, as no one's familiar with them. They seem like good folk but you never know."

"Aye, Haggard."

"There's a good lass." Tweaking one of her braids, he slipped into the crowd in the direction of Clara's home.

Clara stuffed the candy into her mouth before pushing her way through the crowd toward where the mysterious caravan was camped.

"Lorna, have ya lost your mind?" Haggard stared down at the woman in front of him.

"We don't have a choice," she replied tightly. "It's either this or we lose everything."

"So, this land is worth more than your daughter?"

"We both know she isn't my daughter. All I did was

take in an orphan out of the goodness of my heart and look where it's gotten me!"

He scowled. "What does Egbert say?"

"Egbert won't wake 'til tonight, if not tomorrow."

"He dotes on the girl in his own way, Lorrie. He'll be upset when he wakes up to find her gone."

"Never you mind that. When will I get the money?"

He sighed. "Not in time to meet your deadline, I'm afraid. The end of the month is only two se'ennights away."

"There must be something you can do."

He studied the little woman before him. "You sure of this? I can tell the slaver to keep her out of the brothels but that's no guarantee."

"I don't give two farthings where he puts her. Let her be a whore, for all I care."

"Mother in the Stars, Lorrie! The child is only ten summers!"

Lorna ignored his distaste, only saying, "I need the money soon."

Haggard sighed as he thought. He and Egbert went a long way back, having fought together in many a battle. He owed him his life and to do this would be helping him, partially satisfying a blood debt that never could be really satisfied. Reaching into the purse hung at his belt, he pulled out a gold coin. He held it out for her.

"That ought to take care of your rent with some besides. I'll take the money out of what the trader gives me."

Lorna snatched it from him. "Fair enough."

"When do you wish for me to take her?"

"As soon as you can."

"I'll wait for her to come home. No sense in ruining the festival day for her."

She shrugged as if that made no difference to her, which it probably didn't, dropping the coin into her apron pocket. She walked away, carrying the empty laundry basket under her arm.

☐

Chapter Two

The brightly colored wagons were arranged in a neat circle around a central fire, which Clara caught a glimpse of between the wagons. Men and women in the strange Southern garb (tunics and dresses all in one piece and not in layers like how the Northern folk wore them) walked around the wagons and the center circle, talking and laughing. Music plucked on strings floated on the air to her ears and she wanted to leave the safety of the shop corner where she stood in order to hear better.

But the strangeness of the people frightened her as much as intrigued her. So, she sat down cross-legged, cupping her face in her hands, and watched the people, straining her ears to catch bits of song and lute.

Clara hadn't been there very long before she heard a harsh, "What are you doing?"

Gasping, she jumped to her feet and turned. A thin young man glared at her with grey eyes from beneath heavy brows. His thick dark brown hair was disheveled, as if he had a habit of running his hands through it, and he had the shadow of a patchy beard. He scowled at her. She knew she should be afraid but she was too busy staring at his eyes to be frightened. No one else in her village had eyes of that color.

"Are you spying on us?" he demanded.

"N-no! I was just—"

"I don't care. Go away." He hefted his bag, which made a tinkling sound, in his arms and brushed past her.

Clara watched him for a few minutes, biting her lip, and then chased after him. "Wait."

He stopped and turned. "Why?"

"I want to see your camp."

"Why?"

"Just because."

The boy hesitated, then his face softened a little. "Fine. But stay close. And don't touch anything." He turned and walked off. Clara hurried to keep up.

As they entered the wagon circle, several people greeted the young boy with a, "Ho, Emmerich!"

"I'm Clara," she said.

Emmerich grunted but didn't respond as they approached a bright yellow wagon with rose vines painted along its arches. A silver-haired woman stood by a small cauldron, stirring the contents. As they drew closer, Clara smelled a heady mixture of herbs she didn't recognize.

"Ah, Emmerich, you've returned," the woman said by way of greeting. "And you've brought a visitor." She, too, had grey eyes.

"Her name's Clara," he replied, setting the bag by the back steps of the wagon. "She followed me. Wanted to see the camp. She's one of the villagers."

"My name is Mara, Clara. It's a pleasure to meet you. Would you like to help me make this tonic while Emmerich readies the bottles?"

"But," objected Emmerich. However, Mara silenced him with a look. With a heavy sigh, he sat on the steps and began taking out glass bottles, arranging them at his feet.

"I'd love to help," replied Clara. "What's a tonic?"

And so began a lesson in herbal healing. As the contents of the cauldron simmered, and as Emmerich painstakingly labeled the bottles, Mara outlined the ingredients of the tonic and what it was meant to do, which was cure headaches. Once she was finished, she would sell her product.

"You're an apothecary," said Clara.

"I suppose that's your word for it. But I'm called a healer in the South."

"And a witch at times," interjected Emmerich. He shot Clara a look of suppressed laughter and it made such a change to his features, she almost gawked at him again.

"As well as here." Mara's mouth twisted wryly. "You'd be called a witch, too, Emmerich, if any of those village folk saw you writing right now."

"Where did you learn?" Clara drew close to him and watched him scratch spidery lines on the labels.

"My Da taught me," he said, giving her a funny look, as if he couldn't decide whether or not to tell her to go away. "He's the headman of the caravan."

"That's the elder?"

He grunted and went back to writing.

"How old are you?"

He blinked at her. "Why do you ask?"

"Just because."

"That seems to be your reason for everything."

"It's better than no reason at all."

Mara chuckled. "Emmerich is nineteen winters."

Emmerich being a winter's child made sense to Clara, as he seemed to have an almost melancholic, frosty air about him. Or maybe he just didn't like new people.

"And where's your mother?" she asked.

His hand stopped moving and he bit out, "Dead."

Clara flushed. "I'm sorry."

Emmerich grunted again but didn't look up from his work. Realizing he wanted nothing more to do with her, she moved away and sat at Mara's feet. She plucked blades of grass, tossing them around her. "Why do people call you a witch? You're too nice to be a witch."

Mara chuckled. "Sometimes people call someone a witch because that person happens to have a talent or ability no one else has. Like Emmerich with his writing. Half the people in this caravan can write but very few in your village can. So, to them, we're witches because we can do something they can't."

Clara nodded solemnly. "Like me." Her eyes widened as she realized she had said too much.

"Child, what do you mean?"

"Nothing. It's nothing."

"Probably just bragging about nothing," muttered Emmerich.

His words goaded Clara. Jerking her head up, she blurted, "I know when things will happen before they do. I see them in my mind."

"Oh-ho, so you are a witch. More like a witchling, as you're too small to be a full witch."

"I'm not a witch!"

"Hush, Emmerich," reprimanded Mara. "Like all young men, you speak before you have had a chance to think. And you're not a witch, Clara. Many little ones can do what you do. You'll probably grow out of it. But I suggest you keep it to yourself, just to be safe. There are those who would use you for their own reasons and none of those reasons are good."

Clara nodded and went back to plucking blades of grass. After a few moments of silence, Mara began speaking about herbs and flowers. Clara listened raptly, asking questions and making observations. Emmerich didn't speak again, not even when it came time to pour the tonic into the bottles and some of the hot liquid splashed onto his hand, only grimacing at the pain.

Finally, as the sun began its slant toward the horizon, Mara filled and corked the last bottle.

"Emmerich," said Mara, "I want you to walk Clara home."

Clara half-expected him to object but he only walked

away, calling out, "Come along."

"It was nice meeting you, Mara," she said before turning and running after Emmerich.

"Nice meeting you as well," she yelled out after them.

Clara worked hard to keep up with Emmerich's ground-eating stride. When they reached the edge of the village, he stopped.

"Well, here you are." He gestured at the avenue still full of people. "You're home."

"This isn't my home. I live on the other side and down the road, in the cottage by a stand of sycamores."

He heaved a long-suffering sigh. "Fine then. Come along." But this time, he didn't walk so quickly and he chose a route among the crowd and vendors that was less crowded, keeping within sight of Clara. When going through a dense area couldn't be helped, he took her hand. It was a large, broad hand, and almost seemed to not fit him. A broad scar snaked along just below the knuckles.

Eventually, they left the village and he quickly dropped her hand. The children were gone from the meadow but she could see the places where their play bent flowers and weeds.

When they reached her cottage, Clara was surprised to

see Haggard and his open-topped wagon in the front yard. He leaned against it, smoking his pipe.

"Well, goodnight," she said, turning off the road.

"I'll take you to your door," muttered Emmerich, following after her.

As they reached Haggard, he looked up. "Ho, there, Clara. Who do you have there?"

"This is Emmerich." She felt very proud to introduce her first real friend, albeit a surly one. "He lives in the caravan."

"I thought I told you to stay away from them."

She had no answer for that, so she posed her own question. "What did Mama want?"

Straightening, Haggard reached into the back of the wagon and pulled out a pair of manacles. "Now, Clara, I want you to hold real still."

Like lightning, Emmerich jerked forward and slammed Haggard against the side of the wagon, dealing the man a hard blow to the stomach. "Clara, run! He's a slaver!"

Clara backed up several paces, watching the two men struggle. Fear and confusion grew thick on her tongue. She only knew slavers were bad men and Haggard was not a bad man. He called her pretty and bought her sweets.

"Clara," cried Emmerich again. His bottom lip was bleeding and he struggled to keep Haggard from throwing him to the ground. "For the Child's sake, run!"

The panic in his voice broke the paralysis of fear and she bolted toward the house.

"Da!" she screamed. Da would save her. Da was always there for her.

She heard Emmerich cry out in pain just as she reached the door. It opened and Mama stood there.

Clara stopped, looking up at her with wary, tear-filled eyes. Mama grabbed her by her two braids and dragged Clara back to the wagon.

"Da!" she screamed again. In the falling twilight, Clara could see Emmerich in a heap on the ground.

"Here, take her," said Mama, shoving her at Haggard, who caught her by the shoulders.

Haggard threw her to the ground and held her down with his knee while expertly latching the manacles to her ankles.

"Should we kill the boy?" she asked.

"No," sobbed Clara. Something in her urged her to say, "He's the headman's son."

Haggard gave Mama a significant look. "It'd be folly."

"Then I'll wake him after you're gone."

"It'd be for the best." He lifted Clara in his arms and dumped her into the back of the wagon. "I can't go too far, as it's so dark, but we'll make something of a start."

"Safe travel, Haggard."

He grunted his thanks and climbed into the driver's seat. With a flint, he lit a lamp that hung on a pole. Clucking his tongue, he started his mules, turning the wagon around and climbing up onto the road. Clara crawled to the back of the wagon, using the gate to pull herself up onto her knees.

True night had almost fallen, the last pale pink streaks of sunset fading away, but she could barely make out the shape of the unconscious body in the yard.

"Emmerich!" she cried again, but Haggard twitched the mules into a trot and they soon left Emmerich and the little cottage by the sycamores behind.

Cold water splashed onto Emmerich's face and he awoke, spluttering and coughing. He wiped water from his eyes.

"Get up," snapped a harsh, female voice. "Get up and

be on your way."

He groaned as he sat up. His insides burned and ached. Blinking, he looked up at the woman glaring down at him, an empty water pail in her hand. It took a moment for him to remember why he was laying in the dirt with his side on fire.

"Where did he take her?" he asked, pushing himself to his feet, gritting his teeth against the pain. One hand came up to press against his side.

"That's not any concern of yours," the woman said. "Now get." Turning, she stomped away into the cottage.

As she opened the door, he heard a man's voice slur, "Where's my Clara?"

The front door of the cottage slammed, followed by arguing voices. Gripping his side, Emmerich jogged away. Night had fallen but the festival was still going strong, lanterns and torches lighting the streets as people drank, sang, and made merry. Emmerich shoved his way through them, causing more than one person to protest at the rough treatment.

He staggered into the bright circle of his caravan just as his father was about to ride out looking for him. His Da, Harold, stood by the fire, a group of men gathered around him as he snapped off instructions on how they would search.

"I'm here," Emmerich called as he approached.

Harold turned, eyes widening as he saw his son's bruised face. "What the devil happened to you? Are you hurt?"

"I need a horse," Emmerich said. "A girl's been taken by a slaver and I need to find her."

"A girl?"

"That Clara child?" Mara, who'd been standing with a worried knot of women to one side, came forward. "Is that who's been taken away?"

"Aye," replied Emmerich. He gripped his father's arm. "Da, I fought the slaver that tried to take her but he was stronger. I have to follow her. Please!"

"Do you even know where she's gone, though?" Mara asked.

Harold grimace. "It would be the nearest large town, and that's Pearl Falls. Emm, I know you want to help this girl and that's commendable, but there's nothing you can do. You can't buy her back, we don't have that sort of money, and you can't fight the henchmen a slaver uses to protect his wares. Mother, take Emmerich to your wagon."

"But—" Emmerich tried to protest.

Harold scowled at his son. "The answer is no. Now, go."

Mara took Emmerich by the arm and gently led him away to her wagon.

"I have to find her, Gran," Emmerich said. "I have to. She was really scared and it's wrong."

Mara shushed him. "I know. I know. But you need to rest."

Mara filled Emmerich with a sleep tonic to keep him from running off. Two days passed in a drugged haze. But enough of his head cleared by then so that, on the last night they were to spend in the village before moving on, he only pretended to drink the tonic she put to his lips, spitting it out once she left the wagon.

He waited until the camp settled down for a good sleep before a long day. His side still ached when he breathed too hard (a couple of his ribs were cracked) but he ignored the pain as he gathered some supplies into a pack and went to the few horses. They used oxen to pull the wagons but his father kept a handful of horses for him and a few others to ride.

The rustling of leaves warned Emmerich of the approach of the watchmen and he ducked behind a mare. The pair of men strolled by, talking in low tones about the condition of the road north of them, into neighboring Teir, not noticing Emmerich. He let out a breath once they were gone.

Taking the mare, he led her away from the camp, waiting until he was in the village itself before swinging up into the saddle. With a cluck and a tap of his heels, he started on his way, thankful for the full moon ahead that lit his way. However, the bouncing of a trotting mare did not make his ribs very thankful.

It was a hard ride to Pearl Falls, a little over a se'ennight away further south. Bluebell had the unlucky distinction of being one of the most rural and isolated villages in Lorst. Emmerich's Da liked to joke that the monarchy could fall and be replaced thrice over and most of these small mountain communities wouldn't even notice.

Emmerich pushed as hard as he dared, starting off early in the morning and ending late in the evening. He didn't stop unless he absolutely had to. His aches grew worse as he went and he chewed willow bark to numb the pain.

In his travels with his family, Emmerich had seen villages, towns, and cities alike. He'd seen the sea and the desert. He once saw great beasts called oliphants with tusks longer than his Da was tall, carrying bands of warriors. When he finally reached Pearl Falls, there was nothing to excite his interest. Just dirty streets and tired faces. It looked like any other backwoods town.

He'd dreamed of riding into town just in time to see Clara brought forward onto the auction block. He would ride in, through the crowd, snatch her down, and whisk her away. However, aside from the usual traffic and business, he didn't see a slave market.

Remembering his Da's advice that nothing happened in a town without the tavern keeper knowing, Emmerich rode down the main street until he saw a faded sign painted with a tankard hanging over a door.

The tavern was smoky and ill lit with candles and oil lamps. Several men sat at the long tables over the remains of their noon meals, nursing the ale in their tankards. Emmerich approached the long bar and knocked on it to get the tavern keeper's attention.

"Aye," the man said, sidling over. "What can I do for you, boy?"

"Do you know where the slave market is?" he asked.

"Slave market? Ain't a slave market around here, boy."

"There has to be. I know a slaver was coming here, with a little girl."

The man rubbed his chin. "Little girl, eh?"

"Aye. And the slaver is an old man, with one eye."

"That so?" He gave Emmerich a pointed look.

Grimacing, Emmerich dug into the money pouch at his belt. He hadn't thought to bring much but he did have a few silver coins. He tossed those onto the bar.

The tavern keeper scooped them up. "That slaver came by yesterday. Wasn't here more than a few candle marks and left again, without that girl."

"Who'd he sell her to?"

"There was another slaver here, by the name of Rosch, leading a small band of slaves, but he's already gone, lad. He left about the same time as your slaver."

"Do you know where he went?"

"Not my business to know. Now, you gonna buy ale or are you gonna pepper me with questions?"

Scowling, Emmerich left the tavern, looking around the crowded street as he tried to decide his next move. He no longer had any money and he ran out of food two days earlier. Worst of all, the slaver could have gone anywhere from Pearl Falls, and Lorst was a big country. At that moment, he heard a shout. Turning, he sighed at seeing one of his Da's men, Ivan, coming up to him.

"There you are," Ivan said. "Your Da is worried sick. Had me come chasing after you and I've been a few candle marks behind the whole way. What are you doing here?"

"I need to find her, Ivan."

"Is she here?"

Grimacing, Emmerich shook his head and related what he found.

"Then you've done all you can. Come home, Emm. Come on." Ivan laid a hand on Emmerich's shoulder. "You can't catch up now. He could've gone any which way."

Emmerich stood there a long moment, wrestling with the idea. He hadn't really liked Clara but he hated slavers. And he hated the idea of her ending up dead in a mine somewhere or in a brothel. His skin crawled at the idea of what some men would do to a little girl. But Ivan was right. The trail ended here and, for all he knew, the slaver was bound for Tier or to one of the nomads in the far North. With a sigh, he nodded.

"All right," Emmerich said.

"There's a lad. Come along."

But Emmerich couldn't help one last glance around before following Ivan, as if he half hoped to see Clara, lost in the crowd.

Chapter Three

Thirteen Years Later...

Emmerich strutted down the marble hall, his left hand lying comfortably on the pommel of his sword. A few servants he knew passed by and he nodded at them in greeting. Stopping in front of a pair of large double doors, he returned the salute of the guards standing there.

"Report," he said.

"Princess Monica has retired to her rooms, Captain," replied one of the guards, a swarthy man of Arventi descent named Cassius. "No one has been by save the maids. All is quiet."

"Very good. Carry on."

The men saluted him again as he opened one of the doors and went through, down the hall, to another door. Pausing a moment, he tugged on the red tunic every member of the King's army wore, though his was emblazoned with the double-headed eagle of the Royal

Family's personal Guard. Clearing his throat, he rapped his knuckles on the door.

After a long moment, the Princess's lady-in-waiting, Lady Pauline, answered the door.

"Her Highness is expecting you, Captain," she replied, stepping back. As soon as he entered the room, she picked up a bundle and left, as if doing a late night errand. Lady Pauline always seemed to find a sudden, late night errand to conduct when Captain Emmerich came around.

"Your Highness," Emmerich said as the door closed behind him. "You look well tonight."

Princess Monica set aside the book she'd been reading and stood, smiling. A dark crimson dress hugged the curves of her body and her dark curls were piled on top of her head. Small opals on wire woven into her hair glittered in the lamp and firelight. More opals spilled from her throat. But none of the jewels could compare with her bright blue eyes.

"As do you, Emm. Would you like some wine?"

"I would." As was his habit when he spent evenings with the Princess, he took off his sword belt and laid it on a table to the side. Next to it he slapped down his gloves.

"I saw you practicing with the men earlier today. It was

very impressive." She brought him a goblet of wine.

"I do my best for the Throne." His fingers brushed hers as he took the cup. But, instead of drinking from it, he set it aside and gathered her into his arms. "You're all I've thought about today, though." He began to kiss up her neck, stopping to nibble at her ear.

"Careful. You don't want to be remiss in your duties."

"On the contrary." He started to trail kisses along her jaw, stopping just above her mouth. "I do them better knowing I'm doing them for you." He caught her mouth with his. She tasted like wine and honey and he groaned as his tongue slipped into her mouth to slide against hers.

She sighed as her hands slid up his chest to cup his face. Emmerich's hands worked with the ease of practice as he undid the strings of her gown, sending the fabric to pool at their feet. Breaking the kiss, he lifted her in his arms and carried her to the bedchamber.

Unlike other nights, he didn't take his time in his lovemaking. He was rough, quick, and relentless. When they lay in each other's arms afterward, Monica looked at him with concern.

"Is something the matter, my love?"

The wire beaded with the onyx stones that had been

woven into Monica's hair had come loose and he idly played with one of the jewels. "All is well."

She snorted. "The last time you made love to me like that, you were about to go into battle against the Tierans." She traced a scar on his shoulder with light fingers. "Tell me what's the matter or I'll have you thrown into the stocks."

He chuckled. "You wouldn't dare."

The half-hearted scowl she had mustered dissolved into a smirk. "No. But it's a fine threat, nonetheless."

Chuckling, Emmerich pulled away and climbed out of the bed, going to the washbasin to wash away his sweat. But as he stood there, his smile bled away.

The only sound between them was the sound of water splashing. When he turned, drying his chest, Monica wore a real scowl.

"This is to do with Marduk," she said. "What are you planning, Emm?"

"I'm not planning anything." He tossed the towel to the side.

"You never could lie to me."

He sighed. "You know I love you."

"And I love you."

"I know you do."

"I should hope so, as our affair would risk more than my father's wrath. If the Council learned I had 'sullied' myself with a commoner, we could have a revolt on our hands, and it would ruin any chance of alliance with Tier."

He returned to the bed, sitting beside her. "I only wish you would hear me out."

"I have heard you out. A dozen times over. But Marduk has brought stability and unity among the witches and wizards of the land. The King isn't going to ignore that or set aside the man who's done that simply on the suspicions of the Captain of the Guard."

"My suspicion should be enough!"

She jerked back at the force of his anger. "If you would tell me what those suspicions were based upon, perhaps I could be of more help."

Emmerich looked away, seeing the bloodied and burned bodies of his family in his mind's eye again. But he couldn't dare make himself speak of it. It was his own pain to carry. And he would not have Monica pity him.

After a long moment, Monica threw aside the sheet covering her legs and got out of the bed. "Marduk has been nothing but a boon to this Court. If I didn't know any better, I would say you're jealous."

"Jealous?" He gaped at her

"Yes. And I don't have the luxury of siding with you simply because I care about you. I have to have hard evidence, Emm. I have to think about my people."

"How is this not thinking about your people?" He got out of the bed and rounded it, stopping in front of her. "How is this not looking into their best interests? Marduk is a monster and the longer he stays here, the more he's going to poison those around him."

"Is that why you hired the spy?"

"The what?"

"We both know that Gavin isn't only a bard, Emm. And it was far too convenient that he appeared just when you were beginning to let your sentiments regarding Marduk be made known. You have a lot to learn about politics and espionage, my love."

"Gavin is not a spy. He's here to learn if my suspicions are true and to protect the King."

"That's your job, Emmerich. You are the Captain of the Guard."

"I am doing my job! Getting Gavin into the Court was part of that. And he's close to finding out the truth."

For a long moment, Monica scowled at him, but the scowl slowly melted into a smirk. "No. He's not."

With a flick of her wrist, an invisible force threw Emmerich across the room. He fell against the stand holding the basin and pitcher, sending them crashing to the floor. He stared up at her in shock, his arm bleeding from where the broken porcelain cut him.

She crossed the room, her hips rolling seductively. "Tonight, things change, Emmerich. The King will die. Change your mind about Marduk, and you'll be able to sit in the throne by mine." She stopped in front of him, smiling down at him. "As King."

Emmerich slowly stood, his heart thudding against his chest. He stared at her, confused and in pain. His hand pressed against the wound in his arm. "Monica, what's happened to you?"

"Marduk has been teaching me his magic and I've learned truths you can only dream of. I've seen things you can only imagine. Marduk is going to remake the world, Emm, and it's going to be glorious."

He grasped her shoulders. "My love, listen to yourself. Do you hear what you're saying? You're talking about killing the King, your father, and you wish for me to be a part of that? Marduk has poisoned you. You must—"

Monica shoved against him, sending him sprawling against the wall, and she snatched up the ornamental dagger on the table by them. Screaming, she lunged at him, the blade held high. He didn't even think. Years of serving in the army and then the Palace Guard took over as he caught her wrist, twisted her arm, and slid the blade under her ribs, upward toward her heart.

Her mouth gaped in shock. Slowly, her legs gave way and she collapsed to the floor, the dagger clattering to the ground by her. She choked on her blood as more pooled beneath her.

Distantly, he heard the clanging of bells and shouting. Something else had happened in the Palace. He heard the door leading into the Princess's parlor open and Cassius call for him. Emmerich's heart in his throat, he could only stare down at Monica, who looked up at him with glassy eyes as she shivered with pain and choked on blood.

Cassius approached the curtain covering the archway into the bedchamber.

"Captain!" he cried. "Is all well?"

Monica gave one more shudder and moved no more.

"A moment," Emmerich choked out, stumbling to the

pile of his garments by the bed. "What's happened?" He fumbled with his clothes, his eyes going back to the corpse over and over again.

"An alarm has sounded from the King's chambers. They're saying the King is dead."

Bile rose in Emmerich's throat. He couldn't stay here. "Then, go, man! And take the guards with you. I will attend to the Princess." He swallowed. "She is Queen now and protecting her is a priority."

There was a pause. "Captain?"

"Go! That is an order!"

"Sir!" Boots tromped away from the curtain and, after a moment, he heard the door open and close.

Emmerich, now fully clothed, sat on the edge of the bed, burying his face in his shaking hands as he tried to pull himself together. Gavin was supposed to be with the King tonight. He was either dead or on the run. He had to find him. They had to get away. Go to the North, to the lords there.

Stumbling up, he ran out of the room and away from the nightmare lying in a pool of blood.

Chapter Four

Two years later...

Clara twisted her matted hair and wrapped a short length of rope around it, tying it off with a knot. Fleetingly, she thought of the gowned ladies with long, braided hair, some of it with silk ribbons intertwined with the tresses. Theirs was a style of art - hers, solely utilitarian. She savored a small taste of pride at knowing that word.

"Girl! Where are you?" bellowed the cook.

Scrambling up from her thin pallet, she ran into the kitchen from the tiny room she shared with Cook and two others, adjusting her tunic as she went. Cook, sweaty and breathless, was stirring the morning's porridge in a large hanging cauldron. Her two fellow slaves were working at other tasks.

"I need more wood," she said. "Gerrie didn't bring in enough last night."

Clara rushed into the small courtyard just outside the

back kitchen door. The stink of the compost pile and the bite of the morning air hardly touched her as she jogged around the small rectangles of vegetables and herbs Cook nurtured. Aromatic applewood sat in a neat stack by the wall that surrounded the castle. Scooping up an armload, she hurried back. When winter came, they would have to move the pile closer to the door.

Inside the kitchen, she carefully placed the logs in the fireplace, the greedy flames licking at the wood. The remainder she arranged by the fire and then looked questioningly at Cook, who nodded her head.

"Good gel," she said. "I need ye to begin cutting the fruit now. And wash thy hands first!"

Clara scrubbed up at the sink and began to slice the apples and figs to adorn the lord's table. Her stomach grumbled sharply but she ignored it.

Clara carefully arranged the sliced fruits on a large silver platter. Cook walked by, glanced at it, and grunted her approval. In her own way, Cook was kind. Clara didn't recall being beaten for anything she didn't deserve, like the time she didn't check to see if the milk had soured and almost sent it up to be served at the high table. She still bore the scars from that, but the accident could have killed someone.

With the lord's visitor, breakfast was formal, making the four of them rush from one end of the kitchen to another, preparing the food. Finally, the serving boys, dressed in the dark orange and rusty red of the House of Dwervin, arrived, took up the platters and left. The women collapsed on a bench at the large worktable.

"I cannot wait," said Cook, "for the master to get more cooks. I hear he was lookin' at folk just the other day. Well, time to eat ourselves." She got up and the three girls stood, but Cook impatiently waved for them to sit down.

Cook herself was not a slave, though she never really ventured out much. However, a strange camaraderie had developed between the four of them. The woman returned shortly with a tray bearing small bowls of porridge, bread, and the last of the blackberries. They ate quickly and silently, then stood to clean and prepare for the large and elaborate noon meal. Thankfully, more cooks did arrive.

As Clara scrubbed roots at the sink a few candle marks later, she felt the ominous prickle ripple across her scalp. Terrified, she tried to push it back, but it exploded before her eyes: a man with hair black as midnight and eyes the color of bracken. He sat at a long table, talking to her master. The vision sharpened and focused on the dark-haired man's hand, which reached into his heavily embroidered tunic as if to scratch at a pesky flea.

As he pulled his hand out, he flicked his fingers. Her master, so intent on his conversation, paid no attention, but Clara saw tiny specks of dust flying into his cup. The vision ended and the sink full of roots hazily came back into focus.

Clara leaned against the edge of the table, gasping and shivering.

"What is this?" asked a sharp, deep voice. A hand struck her in the back of her head. "Back to work!"

One of the new cooks scowled at her and she bent back to her scrubbing, trying to ignore the pain in her head.

The visitor is going to poison my master, she thought. *But when? At this meal? Why should I care one way or another, though? He bought me like I was a bolt of cloth for his wife.*

She imagined the ensuing chaos of the lord's death and how she could make her escape. Perhaps she could find a blacksmith that would be willing to remove her slave's collar. However, this was the kindest she had ever been treated, here at the castle. In a sick, twisted way, she should thank him for making her his slave, because Heaven only knew what would have happened to her if she had stayed with her parents or sold elsewhere. That made up her mind.

When she finished her task, she looked around for Cook. The kitchen swarmed with people and heat. Clara blinked the sweat from her eyes. She didn't see Cook and everyone else was too busy to set her a new task.

The serving boys appeared again and began scooping up laden dishes. Clara slipped close to the door. As they left in a neat line, she followed a careful distance behind them as they wound up a flight of stairs to a broad landing.

She hung back, peeking around the corner. The master of ceremonies, a large, rotund man with a smooth face and elaborate embroidery on his tunic, looked at the boys lined up before him. He straightened a tunic here, brushed hair there, and arranged the food on the plates to suit whatever the protocol could exist for food arrangement. Finally, everything seemed to satisfy, and he swept open the door. The boys filed out. Clara got a brief glimpse of an immense hall before the master of ceremonies stepped out, closing the door firmly behind him.

Cautiously, she crept up to the door. Was he standing just on the other side? She became painfully aware of her dirty tunic and undergown, and tangled hair, some of which had fallen from the rope to hang around her face in greasy tendrils. An inner voice demanded to know just what she thought she could accomplish. But she'd come this far. It seemed foolish to stop now.

Taking a deep breath, Clara opened the door a crack and peeked through. She saw the side of the high table. Between her and the table, the master of ceremonies stood with his side to the door, announcing the course. With a gesture, the serving boys began to move down the tables, starting from the lord's and moving down. Chatter filled the massive hall. The rotund man moved a little away and she saw the guests sitting with his lordship, and sure enough, there sat the man in her vision, flicking his fingers.

Before she could let herself think, Clara burst from the door and bolted for the table. People just began turning when she grasped the guest and shoved him to the ground, the chair flying backwards. Wine and food spilled everywhere as he flung out his arms. For a moment, she felt a swift pressure, as if her hair was being pulled, before strong hands gripped her, flinging her to the floor. A boot pressed into her back and she felt the cold tip of blade on her neck above her slave's collar.

"What is the meaning of this?" demanded Lord

Dwervin.

"That child attacked me," cried the man angrily as he scrambled to his feet. "Is this your idea of hospitality, Dwervin?"

"My love, look!" Lady Dwervin pointed at her lap dog. The animal lay curled on the floor by the pool of the lord's wine, convulsing with foam dripping from his mouth.

Silence rippled through the hall. The sword tip removed itself from Clara and calloused hands (now a little more gentle) brought her to her feet. She looked over her shoulder and saw it was one of his lordship's personal bodyguards, decked out resplendently in the house's colors. She swung her attention to the tableau before her.

Lord Dwervin glared at the visitor, who tried to look arrogant and blameless. "Care to explain, wizard?"

A chill ran through Clara as she looked wide-eyed at the man, finally taking in the emerald belt that marked him as a member of the Brethren. The Brethren, recently come to power under the new King, were the arbitrators and dispensers of justice in the land. However, even in the kitchens, Clara heard rumors of wizards attacking people and demanding protection money and extorting them.

What could her master have done to warrant

poisoning?

"I have nothing to explain," replied the man coldly. "It seems that one of your dogs has suddenly taken ill. Perhaps this girl can explain."

Their attention swung onto her. The guard gave her arm an encouraging squeeze. She raised her hands gestured to her head, and then to the wizard. Dwervin stared at her. Her hands fluttered as she tried to think and sweat beaded her brow.

"I know her," whispered Lady Dwervin. "She's the mute that works in the kitchens with Relly."

It occurred to Clara that, until that moment, she hadn't known Cook's real name.

"Well, I'm glad someone knows who she is," her master snapped. "But what is she doing here?"

Desperately, she pointed at the wizard, at the side of his tunic with the inner pocket and then pointed at the wine and the now dead dog. The guard caught on.

He said, "Your lordship, I think she is trying to tell you that Wizard Brellin has something on his person."

"Search him."

Three guards came and grasped Brellin by his arms and shoulders while a fourth reached into the tunic to draw out a small pouch. He opened it, revealing a white powder, which he held out for the lord's inspection.

"I see how His Majesty's favor swings," said Lord Dwervin. "Kill the wizard and we'll send back the head." Lady Dwervin made a protesting noise but her husband cut her off with a raised hand.

The guards forced Brellin to his knees, while the guard with the powder drew his sword. A great boom resounded, knocking everyone to the floor. When they stood, Brellin was gone.

"Find him!" cried the guard who had held (and now helped up) Clara as a panicked babble filled the hall.

Guards rushed to obey as the dinner guests raised voices in alarm and confusion. Such a great din of boot steps and voices arose, she grabbed onto the guard for dear life. The kitchens suddenly seemed like a silent haven.

The lord came and stood before her, and as she only came to his chest she craned her head up to see his face. "How, child, did you know he was trying to kill me?" Closer, she could see he had light blue eyes and a bit of grey in his short blond hair.

Clara pointed to her head, circling around to her eyes.

"You saw it?"

She nodded.

He studied her a long moment before saying, "Orvin, take her back to the kitchens."

"If Relly wants to know where she's been?"

He shrugged. "It's a madhouse down there; I doubt they've noticed her absence. If someone does ask, say that she was caught looking through the service door."

"Gossip travels faster than a race horse, milord."

"Well, let it."

Orvin bowed and pulled Clara away. She finally saw how large the hall was but before she could do more than be amazed, she was back through the service door, going down to the kitchens. The guard said nothing to her at all, only pushed her into the melee before ducking quickly back through the door.

Cook (*Relly*, Clara thought to herself) saw her and cried, "What are ye doing standing there? I need help with this roast!"

Grateful to be amid familiarity, she scurried over to the roasting pit.

Brellin sighed with disgust as he looked at the slit in his

sleeve. He had only just gotten that shirt. Dropping his arm, he carried on down the hall toward his tower room. A page ran up behind him.

"Lord Brellin!" he cried.

Brellin stopped and turned. "Yes?"

"The baroness requests your presence, my lord."

"Let her ladyship know I will be along shortly."

"Aye, my lord." The boy bowed and ran away in the opposite direction.

Brellin turned and stomped on down the hall. Thankfully, he encountered no one and it was a relief to close the door to his room behind him. The large, spacious room contained shelves crammed full of books; tables covered in papers, scrolls, and magical instruments; a bed shoved against one wall and beside it his wardrobe. He shucked off his gloves as he crossed the room to the largest desk. Dropping them by a black globe, he wondered if his Master was available for his report.

Well, better safe than sorry.

Brellin picked up the globe and, cradling it in his palms, he spoke the spell over it. A whorl of flame appeared in the center.

A warm, dry voice said, "Brellin, friend, I trust you are

well?"

"I am, your Majesty."

"And you have news?"

"Yes, your Majesty. I have done what you asked."

"And was it successful?"

"Yes, your Majesty. I've drawn the Seer out. No doubt Dwervin will make her a part of his retinue or some such. And my sources have guaranteed that Emmerich is on his way to take the castle."

"And did you get a medium?"

Brellin reached into his tunic and pulled out a lock of hair. "I did, your Majesty. I will perform the spell tonight."

"Excellent. You have always been my star pupil." The voice took on a hard edge. "Do not fail me, Brellin."

"I will not, your Majesty. Ah. I am curious. I could have taken her, right then. Why must we let her fall into Emmerich's hands?" He didn't fear asking the question. If anything, King Marduk encouraged questions from the ranks, as long as they weren't impertinent.

A soft sigh slid out of the flame. "Because, dear Brellin, she is not ready. I want her in a certain state of mind when she comes to me. Is there anything else?"

"No, your Majesty."

The whorl of flame went out.

Chapter Five

"And just what," Lady Maria Dwervin said, "are you going to do about the girl?"

Dinner was over (mercifully) and the pair sat in comfortable solitude in their solarium. Around them, late autumn sunlight splashed upon the flowers and trees that were slowly falling into their winter sleep. The door leading to the solarium was closed and on the other side stood four guards–double the usual. The late Lord Dwervin said a great dose of caution led to a long life. He would know; he saw his ninth decade before passing.

"What do you propose?" asked Martin. "She's a mute, so she can't exactly function in the outside world. She's been a slave most of her life–?" He looked to her questioningly and she nodded to confirm his assumption. "If I were to give her freedom, what good would that do? She'd end up a whore or just one more beggar. Hell of a way to show gratitude, I think."

"Well, she can obviously see the future. That has to

have some use, with only rumors flying around about the Rebel General's whereabouts. And that was a foolish thing, ordering Brellin's death! You know you just made a traitor out of yourself. We might as well throw our lot in with the Rebellion now."

Martin snorted. "I would rather drink that poisoned wine."

"It's our only sane option. Brellin is going to go running back to Marduk to tell him what happened."

"Aye. And Marduk was the one who ordered my death."

"Not necessarily. Perhaps Brellin has his own vendetta against you or your family."

"My family has done nothing against any magic user. What about you? Does your family have any skeletons hanging about that I need to know about?"

"We have done nothing to incur the wrath of the Brethren."

The two glared at each other a long moment, neither one willing to trust the other.

Finally, Martin said, "Let Marduk come. I have one of the best castles in the North. I can hold him off."

"But with neither wizard or sorcerer, how can we

defend against his magic?"

"I don't know!"

They sat in moody silence for a long moment. Finally, Maria said gently, "All the better, then, to have a Seer. We can teach her how to read and write so that she can tell us her visions."

"Fine. Let it be done. Though if it turns out she was a spy and slaughters me in my sleep, we will only have you to blame."

She didn't ask how the girl would be able to get that close to him in the first place. "And the Rebel General?"

"My family carved our fiefdom out of this valley over the generations. We never made way to anyone and we aren't going to start now. The only reason why we ever bothered swearing fealty to the Throne is because we were always left alone to do as we pleased. We will stand against him."

"And if he should take Bertrand?"

"He'll have his own problems to worry about, then, and not some trifling lord on the arse-end of the country."

She shook her head. "You are being a fool, Martin."

"I have been called worse." With that he stood and walked away to glare at a rosebush, bringing the conversation to a close.

With a sigh, Maria stood and left in a swish of silk and brocade.

Two of the guards detached themselves from the door as she walked away, fuming at Martin in her mind.

Halfway to the kitchens, she caught a page by the arm and ordered him to prepare a bath for one in the lady's maid's bathing room.

"And be quick!" she said sharply.

The boy bowed and scurried off. She sighed and took a deep breath before carrying on.

By the time she reached the kitchens, her composure was restored. Relly, upon seeing her, rushed over and dropped a deep curtsy.

"I want the mute slave," she said.

"The mute, milady?"

"Don't worry, Relly, I'm not going to hurt the child. She's getting a…promotion."

That caught the cook's attention. She kept her questions to herself, though, and gestured to the girl, where she stood at a sink piled high with dishes and cutlery. The girl rushed over wiping her hands on her smock.

Relly said, "I don't know where the slavers picked her

up. She looks Border bred."

Maria studied the girl, seeing the tell-tale signs in the sharpness of the jaw and the slight upward angle of the eyes. Her mousey, dark brown hair, tied back with a rough rope, gave her a very elvish appearance. She decided the child must have come from the Border near Tier. There was much crossbreeding there.

"Come. You will no longer be staying here. Has she any belongings?"

"Only what is on her back, milady."

"Well, she can leave the smock."

Relly untied the offending garment and pulled it off of Clara, who was looking more bewildered by the moment. Underneath it, she wore a ragged grey tunic and undergown.

Turning, Maria left, assured the girl would follow. Sure enough, she heard her light step behind her.

Maria chose not to say anything until they reached her private chambers. There sat her lady's maids, who never followed her to the solarium. They all stood upon her entrance.

"My girls, meet the slave who saved his lordship's life." She put a companionable arm around the girl's shoulders, which only came up to her breasts. How old was this child? "Slave, this is Celestina, Emerald, and Lily."

The lady's maids regarded the slave with interest.

"What is his lordship's will?" inquired Celestina.

"She is to be cleaned up and taught how to read and write until a final decision is made. It also wouldn't hurt to teach her other things, such as embroidery and etiquette." Maria smiled down at her. "Heaven only knows where this young one will end up." She looked back at the trio. "She is a mute, though, so don't expect her to stay up half the night chattering with you."

"She is to stay in our chambers?" asked Emerald.

"Where else? There is a spare room. Lily? You will take charge of her for now. Get her washed and see if there is anything to spare in your wardrobes that will fit her. We'll get the tailor to look at her shortly."

"Aye, my lady." Lily curtsied. "Does she have a name?"

Maria smiled at her naiveté. "Slaves never have names, but I suppose we must call her something." She leaned back a little and studied the slave. "Mouse, I think. Aye. We'll call her Mouse."

"Very well, my lady." Lily curtsied again, and, taking Mouse's hand, led her out of the room.

Maria turned to Emerald. "I want no trouble out of you."

Emerald curtsied low. "Of course not, your ladyship."

Clara followed Lily into a set of chambers across the hall. These were just as lush as her ladyship's. Area rugs woven with flowers and leaves over a green background warmed the cold stone floor. Long tapestries with scenes of unicorns, gardens, and women playing musical instruments covered the walls. The furniture was upholstered in greens, blues, and reds. Five doors surrounded the sitting room. Lily drew her to the door to the right nearest the chamber door.

She opened it and revealed a bathing room. A tin bathtub full of steaming water sat a few feet from a brazier, whose smoke disappeared in cuts in the upper walls. Along the walls were hooks from which hung robes. By the tub on a table sat bottles of lotions, shampoos, and soaps as well as cleansing and drying cloths on a second low table.

"Now," said Lily, "let's get you clean." She began helping Clara out of the ragged clothing, which she tossed to the side with a look of disgust. Looking at her naked body, Lily gasped.

Covering her in thin lines, scars marked Clara's body. On her right forearm, from elbow to wrist, ran a burn scar from grease from an overturned pot. On her legs were the small scars from her forced march, from sometimes having to shove through brambles and thickets. On her ankles were the scars left by the manacles. On her back, hidden from Lily's view, crisscrossed the scars left from the slaver's whips. She earned many of them from using her voice until that vanished somewhere along the dusty roads they had traveled.

Lily shook her head in pity and led Clara to the tub. Carefully, Clara walked up the steps and into the calf-high water, smiling as the warmth penetrated sore muscles. As she sat, Lily unloosed her hair from its rope and attacked it with a sharp-bristled brush. It took a while to undo all of the knots and tangles.

Once all the tangles were gone, she washed it several times in some of the fragrant shampoo, rinsing her hair with warm water from a copper pitcher.

Once the hair was clean enough to suit, Lily directed her to stand, where she slathered her down in soap. She scrubbed her with another brush until Clara's skin turned bright red, working carefully around the slave's collar at her neck. A second copper pitcher full of water was poured over her body, only for her to be scrubbed again and rinsed a second time.

"Sit a moment," said Lily. "I'm going to fetch a dress for you from my wardrobe." She left Clara there, in the semi-darkness of the room and with her thoughts.

Who could have known her snap decision would land her here? Would she remain a slave? The ability to come and go as she pleased, to be treated like a person–her mouth almost watered at the thought. She wondered if she would be expected to look into the future for her master. How could she tell him, though, what she would see? She supposed that was why she needed learn how to read and write.

After a time, Lily returned with clothes draped over her arm. She directed Clara to leave the tub and dry herself. Clara felt a little startled at seeing her body clean. Her skin was a delicate milk-white. As she ran a cloth through her hair, she discovered it fell to her buttocks in silky waves. She immediately thought of the ribbons ladies wore with sudden longing. Would she be allowed to wear them now?

When she dried enough, Lily helped her into the

garments. First went on soft undergarments and a shift of thin cotton. Over that went a light brown linen undergown over which Lily pulled a sleeveless green tunic. All of this was belted with a long cloth belt of light green material embroidered with yellow flowers. Onto her feet went soft, light green slippers.

"Now, I'll show you your room." Lily led her out of the bathing room, up two doors, and into another room. Clara stared with open admiration.

The room was about the size of the bathing room. It had a small stained glass window depicting a woman playing a harp surrounded by roses. The four-post canopy bed was made up in light blue and cream sheets. The coverlet was cream with light blue and light green embroidery. The pillows looked unbelievably soft. A set of steps was pushed against the side.

Directly across from the bed, on the side with the window, sat a small fireplace, in which a servant was laying a fire. Clara resisted the urge to go and do it herself. Rugs of animal fur covered parts of the floor and the walls were decorated with more tapestries. To her right were a large wardrobe and a vanity table complete with a highly shined circle of metal.

"This," said Lily, "is your bedroom." Clara looked at her in disbelief. She pointed at her chest. Lily nodded. "Aye, yours. Now, go sit in front of the vanity while I do something with your hair."

Clara did as she was told. She sometimes caught her reflection in water but this was different. Staring at her, with green eyes wide with wonder, was a young woman. All the baby fat had melted away to reveal an almost too strong jaw with a sharp chin. Her flat cheekbones framed a slender nose under which hung small, pink lips. Arched eyebrows, a little too thick and full, flared over upward tilted, almond-shaped eyes. She had a high forehead. Her hair was a dark brown, and now wildly curling.

Lily picked up a brush and began brushing her hair–again. How often would she have to do that? When it was sort of manageable, she began braiding it in a simple plait then wound part of it at the top of her head like a crown, letting the remainder of the plait fall to just below her shoulder blades. The style accentuated the sharpness of her jaw; Clara wasn't sure she liked it (*it had looked better loose*, she thought).

"There," said Lily. "This is appropriate for an unmarried maiden. Though, you're more than old enough to be married off, I think?"

Marriage? Clara looked at herself intently. Marriage and romance had never crossed her mind. For some reason, she thought of the boy with grey eyes, whose fate she had never learned. She felt, again, the prickle, but nothing came. That seemed ominous in itself.

Her eyes went to Lily, whose hair was also braided, but more elaborately, with ribbons.

"Now, I'm sure her ladyship wants to see you."

They left the room (the servant already gone) and went back across the hall. Her ladyship sat in her couch, her maids arrayed around her. They were chatting gaily as they each embroidered cloth belts.

For the first time, she paid close attention to clothing. Lady Dwervin's dress was of finer materials, as well as darker, bolder colors. The maids were dressed as her only in lighter colors. Her ladyship's hair was the most elaborate. Clara's the plainest.

The trio looked up at their entrance, each of them gasping as Lily gestured at Clara dramatically. Lady Dwervin stood and regarded her with wide eyes.

"She's beautiful," whispered Celestina.

Emerald smiled cynically. "For a slave, you mean."

"That status," Lady Dwervin said sharply, "may change soon enough." Some of Emerald's smile wilted. Clara decided she would have to watch out for her. Her ladyship turned back to her. "Come, Mouse. I think my lord will want to be properly introduced to his savior. Girls."

The three lined up behind her. Clara went to do the same but Lady Dwervin caught her arm and pulled her up beside her. She nodded at the guards, one of whom opened the door. They all swept out, the guards trailing behind.

They walked down to the lord's private audience chamber. A little larger than the kitchens, it was decorated with tapestries depicting war scenes and farming. The lord sat in an elaborately carved chair, looking very bored. Around him stood his steward, the Shire-reeve, guards, and a servant by the lord's elbow holding a carafe of wine. Over Dwervin's head hung his coat of arms.

A farmer (standing a respectable distance away), with a knit cap balled up in his hands, was going on and on about how the rains and cold had ruined the crops. The man seemed distraught, but the lord looked like he was still thinking about his midday meal.

Finally, Lord Dwervin made an imperious gesture with his hand. The farmer fell silent. "Steward Sordin," he said.

A man in a fine tunic and trousers came forward and knelt. "My lord?"

"Are you aware of this?"

"Aye, my lord. We have enough from our good harvests to feed us through the winter."

"But last year's harvest was just as bad!" interrupted the farmer.

Lord Dwervin looked at him disdainfully. "Are you doubting my word?"

The farmer shrunk in on himself a little. "No, your lordship."

"Then, Farmer Earlton, you can go with assurance that your lord is doing all he can."

The farmer bowed and paced backwards a couple of feet before turning and scurrying out. Clara felt deeply sorry for him.

The steward stood and retired to his former post in the corner to the lord's right. Her ladyship came forward before anyone else had the chance to be admitted. Lord Dwervin stood and there was a great show of kissing her hands. For some reason, Clara didn't believe that for one moment.

"My lord," she said, "may I properly introduce you to the slave who saved you." She gestured for Clara to approach. She did, curtsying deeply and keeping her eyes to the floor. "We are calling her Mouse, for the moment."

"Mouse, I am honored to meet you." Then, to her great surprise, he took up her hand and kissed it.

"It is my sincere hope, my lord, that you will show your gratitude to her."

Clara's heart began to race as the lord straightened to his full height and said, "Aye, I would. It is my desire for this slave to learn how to read and write so that she may better serve her realm."

There came a tense moment, as she waited for him to add more to that, but nothing came. Anger, disappointment, and something akin to despair flared in Clara's heart and her eyes lifted, meeting his as he smiled upon her. She suddenly wished she hadn't listened to her dream. She pictured him rolling on the ground with froth falling from those rich, full lips and felt a surge of delight. A part of her warned her that it was bad to think so, but she shoved that thought away, sending it to live with all her bad dreams and memories.

Lord Dwervin began to frown and she realized she had

stared at him for too long. Her eyes drifted back to the floor.

Her ladyship curtsied. "Your lordship is most generous. My lady's maid, Lily, will be her tutor. With his lordship's permission, I would like to retire."

He bowed. There was more curtsying all around and they swept out as they had swept in. Clara's heart, though, sat broken and bitter in her chest.

Chapter Six

Earlton strode away from the castle, the late fall wind snatching at his hair. The cold reminded him to jam his cap tight to his head. He walked without seeing, past the beggars and whores, past the vendors with food and trinkets, and past the shops, taking a sharp turn down into the poor district. The farmer stopped at a doorstep and pounded three sharp taps on the rough-hewn door.

The door opened a crack. Wary eyes regarded him. He made a face and snapped, "It's me, ye stupid git!"

The door swung open and a woman's pinched face scowled at him for ruining the fun of being a fellow conspirator. She stepped back and he hurried in out of the chill, though it wasn't much warmer inside. No one was allowed to cut wood from the lord's lands (though one could buy it at the market for an obscene price) and coal was far too costly for the likes of those that were crowded in the one room hovel.

Four children crouched in the center of the floor,

playing a game of marbles with the smoothest pebbles they could find. The most inventive of the four, a bright-eyed girl named Leah, had painted her pieces. To the far left, the sharp-faced woman, Moira, had gone back to making the black bread she sold at market. Scattered throughout the rest of the room stood or sat men and women who looked desperate and hopeful–mostly desperate.

"Well," grunted a man in a corner, "what happened?"

The farmer heaved a sigh. "The lord didn't even listen. Said the steward was doing all he could. Said there were still supplies from good harvests"

"Hah!" spat a woman. "The steward must have dreamed of those harvests." Everyone nodded in agreement.

A young woman, who sat close to her husband, said, "Then–we'll go?"

Earlton reluctantly nodded. "At this rate, we'll have no food for winter. We'll leave at first light tomorrow."

Leah squealed, scooping up the pebbles she won, her face flushed with triumph, oblivious to the weight in the air around her.

When they returned to her ladyship's quarters, Clara watched dispassionately as the lady sent Emerald on an errand, who left wearing a small, triumphant smile. The two maids and her ladyship returned to their embroidery. Soon, they were chatting as if nothing had happened in the audience chamber. Clara sat in a plain, straight-back chair to the side. She always wondered what highborn people did all day but now she couldn't have cared less.

Perhaps she could run away? A nasty little voice in the back of her mind demanded to know just what a runaway slave, who could not read, write, or talk, could do once "free". Not to mention what would happen to her if she were caught. Clara shuddered at the thought. As far as she could tell, running away would impede her step as much as iron manacles. And what of the collar?

The door of the sitting room opened and Cook entered. Clara twitched involuntarily, wanting so badly to just throw herself into the woman's arms to be taken away and protected. Cook gave her the barest of glances before focusing on her ladyship, who set her work aside and listened as Cook laid out the menu for the night's meal.

"How are we on provisions?" asked Lady Dwervin.

"Fine, fine, though the tribute will be most welcomed."

"No need to worry with winter coming on?"

"Nay—not for us."

That last bit reminded Clara of the farmer. Would he be able to feed his family this winter? Clara barely noticed Cook leaving, so deep in her thoughts. She was not shaken out of them until Emerald returned with a short, bald man.

"The smith, my lady," she said, smiling.

"Mouse," said Lady Dwervin, standing and beckoning for her. Clara obeyed, wondering what this was about. With gentle fingers, the lady turned her to face the smith but his eyes focused on the collar. He touched it gently.

"Still in good condition," he said.

"Then it does not need replacement?"

"Nay. The slavers, they make these for a lifetime." He tugged a little on the collar, sticking a finger between the leather and her throat. "Can't tell when it was last extended. But given her age, she won't need it." Reaching into his pouch, he pulled out a long metal chain. "This will do for the day." He handed it to her ladyship. "I'll have another made for the night."

"But, my lady," said Lily, "won't the leash choke her in her sleep?"

The smith shook his head. "It can be shortened and the

hook will be set close to the bed."

"Then what keeps her from tying herself loose?" asked Emerald.

Clara felt her eyes growing wider as she listened to the conversation, her gaze fastened on the long chain in Lady Dwervin's hands.

"The leash fastens to the collar with a small lock, as it does to the hook. Everything should be ready by bedtime tonight." The smith smiled with pride at his invention.

Lady Dwervin snapped the chain onto the small hoop on the front of Clara's collar. On the other end was a hoop, which she slipped over her wrist. "Smith, I thank you for your help. Be sure to see the Steward for payment."

The smith bowed and left. Tears streamed down Clara's face even as anger began to stoke itself in her gut. Lady Dwervin slapped her. "I have plans for you, slave. Don't waste it with your tears. Now, sit."

Clara turned to return to her chair, but a tug stopped her.

"On the floor, Mouse." she instructed.

Clara hesitated. The lady yanked on the chain, and Clara obeyed.

A small bell chimed. Lady Dwervin set aside her embroidery and stood. The other girls, save for Clara, followed suit.

"We're off to the evening meal, Mouse," she said, tugging at the chain to bid her to stand. "Before we go, understand that you won't be taking your meal at the table. You will sit on the floor. Girls." She slipped the hoop over her wrist as the maids lined up to follow her out of the room.

They left with Clara following behind and to the side of the lady. Several servants tried not to stare as she was led on her leash. Though slaves did wear collars that served a purpose prior to purchase, they became symbols after the owner's purchase. Clara felt herself growing warm with shame.

Lord Dwervin waited for them at the door leading into the great hall. He took Lady Dwervin's arm with a smile and they entered together.

The dining hall was already full of people as they entered. Everyone stood and the maids and the lady took their places at the table. Clara sat on the cold stones at her ladyship's feet.

Lady Dwervin signaled to a server. "Fetch a wooden bowl of broth from the kitchen and a cup of water for this slave."

The server bowed. "Aye, my lady."

"I must admit," said Lord Dwervin in a low voice, "that when you made such a plea for me to get the girl out of the kitchens—"

"You kept her a slave," she replied. "And that is how I am going to treat her so she never forgets. And neither do you."

Later that night, Clara lay sleepless in her bed, half-afraid to sleep. Every time her eyes drifted close, she saw an image of her strangled to death by the metal chain going from collar to hook.

The door creaked as it opened. She sat up, the links of the leash clinking. Emerald, holding a small lamp, entered the room. As she turned to close the door, Clara scooted across the bed as far as the leash allowed.

"You know to be afraid of me," Emerald said, setting the lamp on the bedside table. "Smart girl."

She grabbed the chain and pulled with all her strength.

Clara resisted bracing herself against the bed and using muscles toughened over years of work. Suddenly, Emerald let go of the chain, sending Clara reeling back while her attacker crawled onto the bed.

She grabbed her and pulled her down onto the mattress, pinning her.

"Listen, Mouse," whispered Emerald, "you will do what I say, as I say it. I am the real mistress of Castle Dwervin. Not that stupid cow across the hall. And if you ever see Martin come in late at night, you won't alert the cow in any way. Do you understand?" Emerald pinched and twisted Clara's ear. "Do you understand?"

Clara nodded, too afraid and too angry to do more.

"Good." Emerald let her go and stood. "Tomorrow morning, when Lily comes to get you, you will come and help me dress. You do know how to do that?"

Clara nodded again.

"Good."

She walked around the bed, fetched her lamp, and left, leaving Clara curled in a ball of misery.

Five days after the failure in the audience chamber, the

ragged group, with Earlton as their leader, walked along the small road leaving Dwervinton. Earlton, sighting an ash tree with three slashes high on the bark, signaled for them to come to a halt. He looked up and down the road. Seeing no one, he led the group off the road into the brush.

After walking for three candle marks, a man in green and brown forest garb stepped from behind a black gum tree, what leaves it still had ablaze with color. The man held a short bow with an arrow notched.

"State your name and business," he said,

"My name's Earlton Undersson. These are my friends. We are runnin' from Dwervinton. Your leader offered us shelter."

The archer studied them for a long moment, then approached. From the brush appeared more archers, who kept a wary eye on the travelers and surrounding forest. The first one gave them a closer look.

Satisfied, he said, "Well, come along, then." Turning, he led them into the woods, the other archers melting back into the scenery.

They walked another candle mark and a half. One of the little ones complained of hunger and his mother shushed him. They stepped around a heavy screen of pine and dogwood and into a very small, busy camp. Only one or two campfires were going, as fire was dangerous so close to the castle. Earlton thought, *this is no army.*

The archer led into center of the camp to a large tent. Two spearmen stood on either side of the entrance.

"Is the general busy?" asked the archer.

"Hang on," said on the spearmen, who stepped into the tent. After a few moments, he came back through and held the flap open for them.

The group crowded into the large tent and stared wide-eyed at a man in his third decade standing behind a collapsible table on which laid a map. He looked up and gave a small, crooked smile.

"Earlton," he said kindly, "I see you've taken me up on my offer."

"'Tis just us, General Emmerich," Earlton said apologetically. "My wife, she'd have none of it. Left for Pender's Ford, where her family is."

General Emmerich nodded. "I'm sorry to hear that. These are the friends you told me about?"

"Aye." He introduced them in turn, naming each of their trades. He named the children as well.

When the farmer finished, the general bowed slightly

and said, "This is a scout's camp. We can give you what supplies we can spare but you'll need to add to it with what you can find. We'll be leaving soon to head back to our base camp, where you won't have to worry about food."

The group smiled and sighed with relief. Earlton bowed. "We are full of thanks, milord."

The man shook his head. "I am no lord."

"Ye will be if ye take Dwervinton," said Moira softly.

General Emmerich smiled modestly, then turned to the archer. "Merl, you'll get our friends settled?"

Merl bowed and led the people out. Once they were gone, the general turned back to the map, studying it.

"It's only the start," said a voice coming from a corner. A thin, fair-haired man stood from his seat and came to stand by the general. "If we stay much longer, we'll be flooded with refugees."

For a brief moment, Emmerich thought of men and women crowding a castle yard, crying for help with strange, purple-blue clouds bearing down behind them. He pushed the thought away.

"That's why we're leaving tomorrow," he replied, "before more seek us out. There will be a few, though, to stay behind and point the way to base camp."

"And you'll return in the spring?"

"Aye, if the information you glean for us shows a good weak point. Castle Dwervin is one of the better built ones." He regarded his friend with concern. "And you'll be all right, Gavin?"

"Oh, I'll be fine. No worries there, friend." Reaching under the table, he lifted a pack. "I should be going if I want to arrive before dark."

Emmerich clapped Gavin on the shoulder and regarded him with solemn grey eyes as he left.

☐

Chapter Seven

Gavin paused about a half mile from the village, ignoring the ache in his knees from walking for days prior to this excursion. No houses sat nearby and he heard no one on the road. He looked up at Portent perched on his shoulder, a small merlin he used for messages, and coaxed the bird onto his forearm. Taking away the hood, he unclipped the little leash, and with a smooth motion, tossed the bird into the air. Portent spread his wings and sailed away toward the temple, whose spire rose in the distance over the tree line.

Smiling, Gavin shucked off the gauntlet and shoulder pad and stowed away the equipage in his pack before casually walking on into the village. Several people gave him the probing look given when strangers are a rare occurrence. Most looked too hungry or tired to care about him. The buildings sat tired and crooked along the muddy main road.

He passed the temple, on beyond the buildings, and

then on to the castle itself. He crossed the drawbridge with a jaunty stride into the gateway. Up ahead, the guards were going through a merchant's wares. The merchant, an elderly man with not a tooth in his mouth, watched with detached interest while a young girl (granddaughter? niece?) glared at the two men who both looked equally bored. At least they weren't being rough about the job; just another day's work to them. Gavin patiently waited.

After the merchant drove under the portcullis, one of the guards waved him forward. The other took his bag and searched through it. Nothing but spare clothes and some bread wrapped in oilpaper. He did blink a little at the falconing equipment.

"Had a falcon once," Gavin said. "Had to kill the poor thing."

The guard nodded and stuffed the items back into the pack. Gavin's other item was a case for his lute. The second guard opened the case and delicately examined the instrument.

"Bard, eh?" he asked.

Gavin grinned. "On my good days."

"And what days are those?"

"The ones when I'm not hungry and don't have a

roarin' hangover!" He shared a conspiratorial laugh with the guards, who handed back his things unharmed. "Do ya think the lord will want a bit of entertaining tonight?"

The guard who had admired his lute scratched his bearded chin. "Maybe. Go on into the inner courtyard and go to the doors leading into the main hall. Tell the guard you're a bard and that Lance sent you. Tell him to fetch Bayard."

"Thank you kindly."

He walked on into the throng of people and merchants selling in the inner courtyard. Minor lords and ladies with a sprinkling of baronets, all relatives of Lord Dwervin, were shopping among the vendors. From some corner wafted music. Gavin suppressed the urge to seek the fellow bard out and walked on to the looming doors that led into the castle's great hall.

Four guards stood watch here. They regarded the crowds with bored eyes but their tense shoulders told another tale. Was his lordship expecting trouble? Choosing the closest one, he relayed the message in his best "I'm not from around here but you can't place me" accent.

The guard signaled to a messenger and told him to get Bayard. Gavin decided that this must be a master of ceremonies or "His Holiness the Steward". Stewards answered only to the lord, duke, baron, what-have-you, who were often too busy to be worried over the minutiae of their estates, and tended to be a bit arrogant and stuffy. Though, he had met the occasional good steward. A lot of gullible ones too, surprisingly.

A few minutes later, a man came puffing up to a stop in front of him. *Master of Ceremonies*, he thought. No way would a steward have come to meet him like this. The man gave him a long look, then said, "I am Bayard. We are in need of a good bard. The last one, ah, had an accident."

My, that doesn't sound ominous, thought Gavin. Out loud, he said, "Then rejoice! I'm your man."

"Oh, now? Well, let's hear it."

Gavin dropped his pack and pulled his lute from its case. After a moment of tuning, he launched into a beautiful, courtly rendition of "Roses Falling Down," a popular love ballad. Bayard tapped his foot along as the guards looked past him to the crowd below.

When he finished, he switched to the bawdier version, which left the guards in fits as they tried to keep in their laughter. At the bottom of the steps, a crowd slowly formed. The men of lower class joined in on the raunchier parts while the men of the upper class tried to look as if they didn't enjoy the entertainment. When he finished, the people thundered applause.

Bayard nodded. "I think you'll do but you'll need to get past Steward Warren. Your name?"

"Gavin, sir."

"Well, come on."

He led Gavin into the castle. The main hall was mostly empty. Servants here and there were mopping or cleaning the long trestle tables. On the walls hung tapestries depicting the local lord's military accomplishments. Gavin noted the thickness of the walls.

They climbed a set of winding stairs to the right, a closed door blocking their way at the top. Bayard took out a key on a large hoop and unlocked it. He ushered him into a small room and locked the door behind them. In the room sat a man at a desk. All around him were bookcases stuffed with books, scrolls, and odds and ends. Beyond him was another door and Gavin was willing to bet his lute that the castle's coffers laid behind it. His fingers itched to get to the lock but that was not his purpose here.

"Steward Warren," said Bayard, "I think I have our solution to the bard problem. This is Gavin."

"Oh?" The man (who looked like a stick with clothes) looked up from his papers. He appraised Gavin with cornflower blue eyes. "Well, let's hear it."

Instead of a love ballad, he chose a more serious song about a steward who saved his lord's estate from invaders. He made sure to emphasize how wise and good the steward had been.

Steward Warren pursed his lips when the music ended. "Clever," he said. He shrugged. "I'll pay you to play tonight but his lordship will be the one to decide. And let me say that he is a man of refined taste."

Refined taste translated to more finicky than a rich heiress bent on marriage.

Gavin bowed and said, "Thank you, Sir Steward. I'll do my best."

"Do that." And he returned to his papers in a clear dismissal.

Gavin followed Bayard out, who said, "It's some candle marks before dinner. You're free to come and go before then. Once the sun starts to set, be back here in the main hall. I'll introduce you. You're free to eat in the kitchen."

"And where would that be?"

"This way."

He took him to the kitchens behind and below the main hall. Apparently, the castle sat on a slope.

The kitchens bustled with at least two slaves and four cooks, one of whom was an older woman Bayard introduced as Relly. He explained that Gavin was free to eat whatever was prepared. He thanked the master of ceremonies for his kindness. Bayard nodded in a distracted way and bustled off to do whatever men in his position did when not presiding over a ceremony of one kind or another. Or escorting bards.

Relly led him to a small table by the fire and sat him down. In a moment, she brought him a bowl of stew and some fresh bread.

"Thank you kindly," he said and tucked into the food, which was very good.

"Where ye from, Gavin?" She sat across from him, apparently glad to have an excuse to rest a moment.

"Oh, here and there. Traveled most my life."

"Ye've been to Bertrand?"

"Ah, the capital! Wondrous place! Temples that could touch the sky and women lovely as lilies—such as yourself."

"Oh, tush!" But Relly looked faintly pleased. "We don't get many a visitor around here, being out of the way and all in these mountains. Why aren't ye in Bertrand yourself?"

"Ah, I never could stay in one place long enough. Feet get to itching after a time. 'Sides, it occurred to me one day that I had never been 'round here before. Thought I would come and see."

"Well, glad to have ye." Relly took on a wistful look. "Be nice if—" Then she looked away.

"Oh?"

"Be nice if a certain young maid 'twas here. She'd hang onto your every word."

"That so? Married off, I take it?"

"Nay. They've got her up in the rooms for some reason."

He looked at her quizzically and the woman happily launched into the events surrounding the saving of Lord Dwervin's life. A rumor was floating around that this girl, now referred to as "Mouse," had known of the attempt before it happened but Relly brushed it off. "I think she snuck up there—never been outside the kitchens much—and then saw something to tip her off. Smart gel, she is; always watching the world with those big eyes."

Gavin wasn't so sure himself, but he nodded along. When he finished, he sang a ditty in gratitude and left to go view more of the outside fortifications—that is, sing to more of the locals–before the evening meal.

The hall was half full when Gavin came in that evening. A quick scan told him that the lord had a large extended family and he didn't mind letting his guard eat with him. The oldest son was missing; the lord probably wisely sent him to Court. Bayard spotted him from his place by the high table and came down to meet him.

"Lord Dwervin will be here shortly," he said. He had changed into the livery of the house, the tunic stiff with heavy embroidery. "He will of course want you introduced and to open dinner with a song."

"His lordship is expecting me, eh?"

"Oh, aye. It's been a long time since we've had a bard and the family wants to hear some new songs."

Gavin nodded and mentally ran down a list of the latest ballads. He took out his lute to tune it while Bayard returned to the high table.

Suddenly, the main doors behind the table opened and everyone stood. Lord and Lady Dwervin came in, followed by the lady's maids. Attached to Lady Dwervin's wrist was a chain that led to the collar of a fourth girl, who walked slightly to the side and behind her ladyship. Was this the young woman Relly told him about? She had a blank look on her face, which Gavin noted had Tieran features.

Bayard gestured to him and Gavin rushed up, going down to one knee before the lord.

"Your lordship," said the Master of Ceremonies, "allow me to present Gavin. He has come to petition to become our bard."

"Oh?" Lord Dwervin regarded him. "And who was your last master?"

"Torvin Hunchton, Lord of the Eastlands."

A light of interest sparked in the lord's face. "And what brought you here?"

"Lord Hunchton enjoys the city a wee too much for me, my lord."

"Have you a reference?"

Gavin fished it from his tunic and handed it over. As Lord Dwervin read it, Gavin looked over to catch the slave's eye. She stared at him with a fixed gaze that went through him. The blood fell from her face, making it impossibly pale. Every muscle in his body tensed and a fine layer of sweat covered him in an instant.

A Seer, he thought. *An honest to Mother Seer.*

He suppressed a swear word and slapped on a pleasant expression, looking back to the floor. Lord Dwervin rolled up the reference and handed it back to him.

"Rise," he said, going to his seat, "and stand before us for a song."

Gavin obeyed and swung into a song about a lord and his lady, both madly in love with each other. It had been very popular at Court during the summer. When he finished, those there applauded. The lord nodded his approval. Gavin retired to a corner where he played background music. He took the time to study the family dynamic at the castle. He noticed a few interesting things, among those that the slave seemed to have little appetite, drank from a bowl on the floor (which made his blood boil) and refused to look at him. He fervently hoped no one asked her later if she had any visions recently.

After dinner ended, he found himself entertaining the lord and lady in their solarium. He regaled them with stories and scandals from Court. Lady Dwervin, a shrewish looking woman with light brown hair, peppered him with questions about the latest fashions. Gavin found himself smoothly falling into Court speech. Neither of the nobles seemed to notice or care; it wasn't unknown for a bard to slip from one dialect to another in mid-conversation, as they traveled so much.

When the interview ended, and after an order from the lord for him to go speak with the steward about salary and accommodations in the morning, Gavin walked down the halls as if angling toward the great hall. He was to bunk with the soldiers tonight but he had no interest in sleep just yet.

He walked toward the west wing of the castle. No one stopped him to question his motives for being in that part of the castle, which seemed odd to him. If the lord's life had been recently threatened, then where were the extra guards? He mounted a stairwell and went up several flights before coming out to the likeliest level, strolling easily down the hall.

Finally, he came to a large door with an ivy pattern carved onto it. Across from it stood a plain door. The plain door probably led to the lady's maids' chambers. Gavin paused. How to get the slave on her own? Perhaps this had been a bad idea. Suddenly, the plain door opened and a blonde girl stopped short.

"Oh, bard," she said. "You startled me. Can I help you

with something?"

"I was merely learning the halls."

"Oh. Well. Her ladyship won't like you up here."

"My apologies." Regretfully, he bowed and turned and began to walk away.

Suddenly, the girl said, "Wait." She closed the door without latching it and walked up to him. "I have to run an errand. However, I'm not supposed to leave Mouse alone unchained, but I don't wish to take her with me–"

"The slave?"

"Aye." She smiled faintly. "I know it's a terrible name." She shrugged. "The other two girls are gone. And, well, I think it would be nice if–"

"I stayed behind and entertained her."

"Aye." She smiled with relief.

"'Twould be no trouble, lady."

"Thank you, sir." She curtsied and walked swiftly down the hall.

Gavin turned and went into the chamber, closing the door behind him and facing the empty sitting room. A door sat slightly ajar and he approached it.

"Lady Mouse," he said, stepping in. A girl sitting at a desk jumped to her feet, the chair falling backwards with a clatter. He held up his hands. "I'm not here to hurt you."

She backed away, her mouth half-opened as if she wanted to scream.

"What's your name?" he asked.

Her face crumbled into a mix of fear and consternation. She mimed something with her hands but Gavin couldn't understand what she was trying to say.

"Oh," he breathed, feeling something click. "You're a mute."

She nodded vigorously.

"Then how do you tell people what you see?"

She opened her palms as if they were a book, then with one hand mimed writing on the palm of the other.

"You can read and write?"

She shook her head and pointed back at the desk, where now he saw writing materials.

"You only started learning."

She nodded, beaming widely that he understood her so easily. Gavin scratched the side of his head, feeling as if he had walked into the middle of a ballad without knowing the score.

"I know you had a vision when you saw me."

Her face went carefully blank but Gavin wasn't fooled

easily.

"Are you going to tell your lord about me?"

She shrugged.

"What would keep you from doing that?"

After a long moment, she touched her collar and then mimed taking it off.

"You want to be free."

Nod.

Emmerich trusted Gavin to make deals in his absence and though a Seer slave was quite the commodity, he saw no reason to withhold freedom from her.

"All right," he said. "But only if you tell me what you saw."

Mouse mimed having a sword and fighting with it.

"You saw a battle. Who won?"

She shrugged.

"Well, I suppose it was a little too much to hope that this would be easy."

Gavin scratched his head, idly wondering what his father would tell him right about then. Probably steal the slave and run. Father's solution was always to steal and run. But he had a job to finish.

"All right," he said finally, "here's what we'll do. We'll

pretend this night didn't happen."

That earned another sarcastic look.

"Right. Anyway, I'll help you learn how to read and write. One day, I'll give you a signal that it's time for the attack. I don't know what the sign will be just yet but I'll think of something. But when that sign comes, I need you to go down to the kitchens and hide somewhere. I'll find you. Trust no one but me. Understand?"

Nod.

"It won't happen until the roads thaw after winter, so we have a nice long wait." He started toward the door but paused. "What's your real name, by the by?"

Mouse, looking miserable, shrugged and gestured again at the papers.

"I see. You haven't learned that far yet. I'm sure you'll get there. Now, I'm supposed to entertain you. Why don't we go into the sitting room and I'll sing you something?"

☐

Chapter Eight

Martin frowned down at the map of the valley in his hands. "Is this correct?" he asked.

"Aye," replied his Shire-reeve, Justus.

"Five abandoned villages. Any idea where they've gone?"

"Some we tracked to large towns, bunking with family, but for the most we cannot account."

"And what have you heard?"

"That the Rebel is on his way, my lord."

Swearing under his breath, Martin set the map onto the table and took a deep swallow of mulled wine. A log broke apart in the fire behind him and he turned to stare into the red-orange flames as he rolled the problem around in his mind. Outside, late autumn winds whipped around the castle. The old ones said it would soon snow.

"I suggest fortifying the castle, my lord," went on Justus. "And perhaps sending word to your cousins, if I may be so bold. It is lucky we have already sent the lordling away."

"Luck has nothing to do with it. When that Rebel took Castle Dartmouth, despite that unnatural storm, I knew I would be the greatest of fools if I didn't send Sigmund away. Any word from our spies?"

"Other lords and ladies are fortifying. Some are leaving altogether for Bertrand. Baroness Orlind is trying to hurry her building projects but with the autumn ending, she may have to halt work. Even she can't make the men work when there's a harvest to be brought in. I have had word from three sources, one saying the Rebel army is heading straight for Candor City–"

"Which would be suicide."

"Another says he has retreated to Dartmouth to wait out the winter."

"Unlikely as well. That valley is the last to thaw in the spring and he'll want to get as far south as possible before winter."

"If he intends upon taking Bertrand in the next year."

"From the reports you've brought to me, he is brash and daring enough to do it. What of the third report?"

"That he is heading here but is well-concealed in the mountains."

"We are the last major castle before Orlind."

"And from Orlind he can prepare and then launch an attack upon Candor."

"And with Candor he can control the entire North."

The men stood in silence. Martin looked up from the fire to the painting hanging over the mantle. A rare southern-style portrait of his father looked down upon him with all the disdain he carried in life. Lord Dwervin could only imagine what his father would say to him at that moment.

"My lord," said Justus, "I recommend seeing to our fortifications, perhaps sending away the lady—"

"She won't go. If Lady Maria is anything, it is suspicious and conniving. She probably thinks if I sent her away, I'd never let her come back."

"What do you make of her keeping that slave on a leash?"

"I think it's a lark, personally. But I know she's just throwing the girl's status in my face." He drank the last of his wine. "As if I cared."

"It has been over a month since Brellin's treachery and the Seer has not come forward with a vision. There is the possibility that Brellin—"

"I am quite aware of that. Thankfully, my Steward keeps excellent records and I have a record of a mute kitchen slave being purchased around the time Maria claims."

"But what if Lady Maria is part of a plot?"

Tension filled the room and Lord Dwervin's shoulders tightened. Spluttering, Justus tried to take back his words but Martin held up his hand to stop him.

"You make a good point," he said. "But I am already well ahead of you."

"My lord, if you thought your life was in danger, then why–"

"Didn't I turn to you?" He set the empty cup on the table. "Because I wasn't sure of your loyalty."

"I will always be loyal to you, my lord."

"I know, Justus. Give orders for the walls to be seen to and send out heralds announcing that I am taking young men for my army. Make the usual promises of pay, food, and bunk."

"The barracks can take another hundred men, sire."

"Good."

"Any news from Bertrand, my lord?"

"Nothing new, I'm afraid. The Sorcerer King is still

firmly on the throne and going nowhere. If he has heard about Brellin, he has made no sign of it. Brellin may very well have been working on his own."

"But if he did send Brellin? Can we stand against him?"

"Marduk has enough to worry about than my trying to kill one of the members of his precious Brethren."

"But what about when he defeats the Rebels?"

"We'll worry about it, then. Let us focus on the problem at hand than the problem that may never come. We have no proof, after all, that Brellin was sent by the king."

"There is no proof to the contrary, my lord."

A knock on the door brought Justus' hand to his sword. Martin only smiled as he said, "Enter."

Emerald came in, closing the door softly behind her. Martin gestured for her to come by his side and when she had, he wrapped an arm around her waist. "This, Justus, is my little spy. She has been keeping me informed of all of the lady's comings and goings. You have no need to worry about Lady Maria."

"Aye, my lord."

"Leave us."

Justus bowed and hastily left. As soon as the door

closed behind him, Martin pulled Emerald to him for a passionate kiss. When they broke apart, he asked, "Any news?"

"None, my lord," she said breathlessly. "Lady Maria has been occupying herself with getting the castle ready for winter. She also has been occupying herself with her lover."

"Have you learned who it is?"

"Sir Roland, your weapons master."

"She always did favor the dangerous. It's how I won her." They kissed again. "And the Seer?" He began unbraiding her hair.

"She is learning quickly how to read and write. Lily stays with her all afternoon in the sitting room, pouring over books and scraps of paper."

"Any visions?"

"None that I know of."

"And the bard?"

"Hasn't come near the rooms. It seems he isn't part of a plot."

"As far as we know." He fanned her hair out over her shoulders, running his fingers through the long, silken tresses. "Keep an eye on him, my sweet." His hands went down and began untying her belt.

"Aye, my lord."

Lady Maria sat in her sitting room, her hands busy over a bit of embroidery. Her back straight, hair intricately braided with ribbons, and her clothing expensive and lush— she knew she looked beautiful and powerful. Roland certainly made her feel that way. A soft smile flitted over face at the thought of her lover.

A knock on the door brought her eyes to the candle clock. A full half-mark before she expected her maids back from gathering roots in the woods.

"Enter," she said briskly, setting aside her work. Gavin came in. If he seemed surprised at finding her alone, he did not show it.

He bowed. "My lady. How can I help you?"

"Come. Sit." He started toward one of the armchairs. "No, next to me." She patted the space beside her.

"My lady, his lordship—"

"Minds his own damn business. Come. Sit."

He sat next to her, carefully keeping space between them.

"Tell me. What do you think of Castle Dwervin?"

"It is a very fine castle, my lady."

"How do you compare it with other castles you've seen?"

"It is quite formidable."

"I suppose you've noticed Lord Dwervin has begun reinforcing the fortifications and making improvements."

"'Tis hard not to notice, my lady."

"Do you know why these measures are necessary?"

"Rumor has it that the Rebel General is on his way."

"Aye. Very good. Do they speak of him, in Bertrand?"

"It has been some time since I was last in the capital, my lady. I have no fresh news in that regard."

"Aye, but the Lord of the Eastlands often goes, so it can't be that long ago."

"No. But things change quickly in the Court."

"Of course. But when you were there?"

"There was talk of him. I was not allowed in the more private conversations, my lady."

"I see."

They sat in silence for a long moment. Finally, Gavin said, "Is her ladyship concerned about possible war?"

"Concerned?" Snatching at the dagger she kept at her belt, she lunged forward and pinned the bard to the arm of the sofa, holding the blade to his throat. "Aye. Her ladyship is concerned. I find it awfully convenient that not long after Brellin tried to assassinate my husband, you came along."

"I mean you and your husband no harm, my lady. I swear to that."

"And what of reports that rumors and songs are floating about, leading men and women to abandon farms and seek out the Rebel?"

"I have nothing to do with that, my lady."

"I sent to the Lord Hunchton for confirmation of your recommendation but he is quite conveniently gone away to Court and it will be spring before we receive word from him. Snow has already begun to cover the passes."

"I can assure her ladyship–"

"I care for none of your assurances. I am watching you, bard. You had best be mindful. My husband is an arrogant dolt who thinks these walls will protect him from every danger, but I know better. And I will protect him with everything I have."

"Your ladyship must love the lord greatly."

"I don't give a farthing for the man. What I care for is my position and I am not in a place to take command on my own. So I protect him and therefore my place as Lady of Castle Dwervin and its lands. By any means necessary."

"You make yourself perfectly clear, my lady."

"Good." She sat up and put away the dagger. "You may go."

Gavin stood and bowed, leaving Maria to calmly return to her embroidery.

Late that night, while most everyone slept, Gavin related the confrontation to Mouse, who listened with wide eyes.

"They are mad," he said in a low voice. "Most noble couples have at least a meager respect for each other. Very few actually love each other but at least there is a level of trust." He shook his head. "I will have to be very careful about sending messages to the general." He sighed. "And you? How go your studies?"

She happily showed him a manuscript. On it was a copy from the Sacred Writ.

"Nicely done," he said. "So you know your alphabet fairly well?"

She nodded. Jumping off the bed where they were sitting together, she went over to her bed and dug out a small scrap of paper. She brought it to him.

Taking it from her, he read, "'Clara.' Who is that?"

She smacked him on the arm and jerked a thumb toward herself.

"That's you. That's your real name?"

Clara nodded and smiled.

"That's a very lovely name. How'd you come up with it?"

She snatched the paper from him, returned to the desk and scratched something out on it before bringing it back to him.

He read, "'My mother gave it to me, you dolt.' Oh. Oh, Clara, I'm sorry."

She shook her head and turned away to go stand by the fireplace, in which glowed banked embers. But he caught the tears in her eyes. Gavin got up and went to stand behind her. Reaching out, he put his hands on her shoulders. She jerked away and turned to him, her eyes wide and frightened.

"I'm not going to hurt you. I only want to say I'm sorry. I thought you were born a slave and slaves have no names."

The tears were falling in abundance and this time she let him enfold her in his arms.

"Hush," he said. "Do you want to tell me how–?"

She shook her head and he tightened his arms around her. "All right. You don't have to."

And he held Clara as she silently cried while he cursed himself for his stupidity.

☐

Chapter Nine

Soon, winter settled onto Dwervinton in white flakes. Gavin fell easily into the role of bard, pretending to show no interest in the slave girl Clara and trying to always be around when important news reached the lord, which decreased as the snow mounded. He sent regular reports to his general (always taking care not to be followed) via Portent, who took up happy residence in the belfry of the local temple.

It wasn't long before Lord Dwervin began to receive reports that more of his tenant farmers left to find places with food. He angrily sent out patrols to bring them back but half the time, the families were never found. After a time, the building projects to prepare the castle for attack ground to a halt. Despair began to cling to the air.

The Nativity approached and as parties became more frequent at the castle, the mood there lifted. Gavin dreaded to go into the village because of the conditions. The bodies were being kept in a special charnel house until the ground thawed enough for graves.

"Mouse! Where are you!"

Clara rushed into Emerald's room, ducking automatically as the woman took a swipe at her.

"I need to leave moments from now. And you're too busy reading a stupid book! Hurry, girl."

Clara brushed out Emerald's hair and rapidly began weaving ribbons into the long red tresses. Through a mix of tutoring and trial and error, she had mastered the style she now hated.

After the last tie, she stepped back as Emerald stood. Taking a cloth belt, she tied it tightly around the woman's waist and adjusted her gown around it.

"Very good." Emerald turned to her. "The little Mouse is good for something. Tell me, though, still no visions?" And she laughed, reaching out to give Clara's hair a hard yank.

She swept out of the room with Clara following behind.

Lily approached her guiltily. "I'm sorry, Mouse. Come."

Taking her by the hand, she led her into her bedroom and with practiced ease, chained her to the wall.

"It's just a silly party," Lily said. "You really aren't missing anything." She handed her the book and with a smile, left the room, closing the door securely behind her.

She looked down at the book. Tears obscured her vision and anger welled up in her. Savagely, she threw it away from her, bouncing it off the wall. It fell open to the floor, crushing the precious papers. Lying on the bed, she cried, wishing with all her might she had left the lord to die.

A se'ennight later, Clara began carrying a bit of slate around her neck on a string. She wore at her waist a small bag containing chalk and cloths.

Three days before the Nativity, Lord Dwervin summoned her to his audience chamber. Lily took her.

As they reached the door, a messenger hurried through it, his tunic wrinkled and dirty. He clutched a roll of parchment. The two women entered the room, curtsied low and waited with bowed heads while Lord Dwervin and the Shire-reeve whispered to each other. After a few minutes, the Shire-reeve bowed and left. Except for the guards, they were alone with him.

"Lily," Martin said, "wait in the hall until I call for you."

A look crossed her face but she unclipped the chain and left them. Anxiety knotted Clara's stomach. For a time, the lord only looked at her, as if appraising a commissioned painting.

Finally, he said, "You are looking very, very well, Clara. I see that our care for you has made you blossom."

Taking up slate and chalk, she wrote, "Thank you, my lord." She held it up and, with a small smile, Lord Dwervin waved his hand. She wiped it clean.

"You're very welcome. Tell me, have you had any visions of late?"

She shook her head.

"None at all?" He raised his brows in surprise. Sitting forward, he braced his elbows on his knees, clasping his hands together. "Tell me, how often do you have them?"

"Once every other month or so. It depends on many things."

"Such as?"

"How closely I am involved and how sure the outcome is."

"You mean, if the outcome of a situation is still undecided, you won't see anything?"

"No. I will only have a vague feeling."

"Any 'feelings' of late?"

She considered for a moment, flexing her sweaty hand. If she proved useless, the lord would probably kill her. Learning to read and write was not something a slave normally did and she couldn't think of a single master who would want a slave to have that ability.

Finally, she wrote, "I have been feeling as if something important is about to happen, but I know not what."

"Come now, you must be able to guess."

She wiped the slate with a thoughtful air. Finally, she wrote, "There is a victory in the future."

That made him sit up straight. "Victory in battle?"

"One that will change the course of your lordship's life forever, I believe."

Lord Dwervin sat back with a smile. "My, my, I like that. I'm going to give my servants and guards orders to let you by any time, day or night, so that you can tell me the moment you have a vision what this victory is and when it will happen."

"Aye, my lord." She hesitated a moment and, before she could change her mind, scribbled, "My lord, what if I have a vision at a time when I'm chained?"

"That is a good point." He rubbed his chin. "I'll order

that you no longer need to be chained during the day. Keep the slate at your bedside at night to write down what you may see, and then report in the morning."

Not exactly what I hoped, she thought. "Thank you, my lord," she wrote.

He came down from his dais and stood before her. He tenderly stroked her cheek. "You are very beautiful, Clara."

Her knees began to shake and a cold sweat filmed her forehead. She stared at the tips of his shoes, suddenly wishing the clothing she had donned that morning, thinking it was so perfect, had a dozen extra layers. The lord's look seemed to pierce the cloth and stroke her body in places no man had seen.

Finally, he said, "Don't worry. I won't touch you because I can't risk those stories about a Seer's virginity being true. But if that gift should turn out to be not as profitable as I would like." He smiled. "You may go."

Hastily, she bowed and left before he changed his mind.

A roaring party in the great hall greeted New Year's Eve. Clara listened with a detached air from her seat on the cold stones at her ladyship's feet. When she had been in the kitchen, Relly and herself, along with any extra help, shared a cup of wine and said a prayer to celebrate New Year's. She suddenly wondered why Relly never seemed to go to a family's for celebrations. Not for the first time, she was saddened at how little she had known of a person she'd considered a dear friend.

Both Lord and Lady Dwervin got very, very drunk. It took the lady's maids and Clara all their strength and resourcefulness to pull Maria away from the party to her rooms before she disgraced herself. After seeing to her, the girls retired.

Emerald didn't seem ready to settle down, though. She slipped away after a few moments.

"To see her beau," Celestina said, sniggering. "One of these days, her ladyship is going to catch the two in a tryst and it's not going to end well."

She and Lily laughed and opened a decanter of wine. They invited Clara to join them but she was in no mood to celebrate. The two went into Lily's room to drink and gossip.

One of the rare nights she spent unchained, but little good it did her. Only a fool would try to escape on such a cold night.

She carefully put away her velvet finery and, after washing her face and brushing her hair, dressed in a soft nightgown. She stole into the sitting room for one of the precious volumes kept in a case. She drew out one on a favorite holy man and went back to her room.

Clara was barely into the story when something scratched against her door. She slowly got out of bed and went to the door, easing it open.

"Merry New Year's," said Gavin. He held up a flagon and two wooden cups. "I thought we would toast."

Frowning, she pointed downward and cocked an eyebrow.

"Lord Dwervin is frolicking with a certain maid. I don't think he'll notice me gone."

Smiling, she stepped back and let him in. Gavin sat at the fire, setting the drink and cups next to him. Reaching into the deep pockets of his tunic, he took out cheese and bread.

"I noticed you barely touched your food. Will the lady join me?"

Smiling, she fetched her slate and chalk before sitting across from him and taking a cup. Gavin poured her and himself some wine.

Holding up his cup, he said, "To our esteemed general. May he hurry the hell up."

They touched cups and drank. She smiled shyly at him, setting hers on the floor. He grinned at her as he cut the bread and cheese, giving her a portion. They ate in companionable silence.

"Nice to see you unchained," he said. "I suppose everyone is too busy celebrating."

She nodded.

"It won't be long now, you know. If you ever hear me sing the peasant's version of the Hymn to Light, then you know it's time to hide in the kitchen gardens." He took another sip of wine, studying her over the lip of the cup. "Clara, I've noticed you have seemed worried. Is everything all right?"

Her face fell a little. Taking up her slate, she wrote, "Lord Dwervin wants a vision. But I have had only one and if I tell him, your general's plan is ruined."

"Then lie."

She shook her head. "Lying is a sin." She didn't need to add that lying slaves were also executed.

"Aye, but you're intention is to do good."

She shook her head and just pointed at her last sentence

more emphatically.

He sighed. "Clara, you're being naïve. If you don't prove yourself of worth to Dwervin, he will find other uses for you. And you won't like those uses. The only reason why he hasn't done that yet is because a Seer's ability goes when her virginity does. Or, at least the stories say so."

Clara flushed as fear stabbed through her. "What should I say?"

"Tell him… Tell him you saw a summer battle. Tell him you saw a blue and white banner drenched in blood."

"What does that mean?"

"My general's colors are blue and white. Trust me, Dwervin will know what that means."

"And you're certain it will work?"

"Oh, aye. Very."

They sat in silence for a time. Finally, Clara picked up her slate and wrote, "Where did you grow up?"

He shrugged, taking a sip of wine. "All over. My da was in charge of a troupe—" A sheepish smile creased his face. "I'm so used to giving the usual lie. My da was head of a band of thieves. My ma was very good at gaining the confidence of wealthy people, only to take their money. She died when I was just a boy." He shrugged. "When I was old enough to strike out on my own, I did. That's when I met Emmerich."

Her body jerked as if stung. Gavin frowned and asked, "You know that name?"

On her slate, she wrote, "There was a boy in a caravan that came through my village before I was sold. His name was Emmerich."

"He did say he was raised as such." He shrugged. "Could be the same, or not. You'll get your chance to see soon enough. But, back to my story, Emmerich caught me stealing from a wealthy merchant in Bertrand. You see, I tried for quite some time to earn an honest trade as a bard. But it's hard to unlearn upbringing. Emmerich was in the Guard and caught me as I was climbing down from a window.

"Actually, it was more like he was waiting for me. He knew who I was. Seemed to know everything about me. He wanted me to infiltrate the Court. He said he knew about…" A bleak look filled his eyes. "He said he knew there was a man named Marduk who was going to take the throne and he had to be stopped. But we were too late. Things had been set in motion long before our conversation on the darkened street. By the time I had figured out the knot of things, it was too late. And now a sorcerer and a murderer sits on the throne."

The crackling of the fire filled in the silence as he watched the flames dance. Clara almost didn't want to ask but had to. Taking a cloth, she wiped the slate clean, and wrote, "What happened then?" She touched his arm gently.

Turning, he looked at the slate. "Ah. Well. There were more than a few Guards and soldiers who didn't want to see a sorcerer king. But there wasn't the usual last surviving Heir to rally them. No, Marduk was quite crafty in killing off anyone who could claim a Blood Tie. But Emmerich rallied them. We went north and over the past two years we have gathered an army."

She hurriedly wrote out another question. "What happened to Emmerich's family?"

"I don't know. Emmerich doesn't talk much about his family."

"What happened to yours?"

"Da and the others went to Tier. He talked about crossing the sea but Da has a penchant for talking up something and then never doing it. What about you? Can you tell me?" He poured himself more wine.

Clara took a deep breath and wiped the slate clean. She

stared at it a long moment, then wrote, "My parents couldn't afford to pay their rent. So, they sold me. Eventually, I was brought here. There isn't much else to tell." She held it up for him, thinking how the last line wasn't true, but she couldn't think of a way to describe the horror of those days on the road, how her voice dried away to nothing.

"Well," said Gavin, "I am glad you're here."

Gavin had given her a lot to think about over the next two days. When a vision startled her awake (blood and screams and a man in spiked armor striding into an empty hall, cries of victory in his wake), she laid in her bed for a long moment, staring at the ceiling as she wondered what the truth would cost her. The chance for freedom? A flogging?

She had no choice but to bring the lord news, because he was running out of patience. But the truth? Remembering Gavin's words regarding intention, and the need for her to be free, she slowly sat up and wrote the exact opposite of what she saw.

After Lily unchained her and she dressed, Clara rushed

down to the audience chamber where she knew Lord Dwervin was preparing for the day's audiences.

As she approached, she heard, "Get this man out of my sight!"

Clara winced from the bellow. The audience room door flew open and two guards dragged away a servant. She watched them go and turned, looking into the room. Lord Dwervin, face red from anger, stood in the room's center.

"Well?" he demanded. "Come in!"

Two days after New Year's, the lord still suffered from a hangover.

Clara scurried in and the guards closed the door behind her. Martin jammed his fists on his hips and glared at her.

"What do you want?" he demanded.

Trembling, she held out her slate, which he snatched from her hand. As he read the vision, the anger drained from him and his shoulders relaxed. The scowl relaxed into a cocky half-smile.

He looked up at her. "Very good. You've finally earned your keep." Taking out his handkerchief, he wiped the slate and handed it to her. "There isn't much detail in that, but, no matter." He reached up and touched a wisp of hair dangling by her cheek. "Though I have to admit to feeling a little disappointed."

Turning, he gestured to the steward and they began to talk about the remaining rations. Realizing she was dismissed, Clara hurried out.

Chapter Ten

Marduk looked up at the sound of the door opening. A wizard in a dark robe and wearing the emerald belt of the Brethren entered the study and knelt.

"Your Majesty," he said, "the Sisters have sent a new candidate."

"Just the one?" Marduk rolled up the parchment he had been reading and handed it to the page standing at his elbow. "Take that to Emerson, dear boy." The boy bowed and left at a quick trot.

"Yes, your Majesty," the wizard replied. "A young man. They also send their apologies but it has been a difficult month, what with the new plague that has broken out in the poor section."

Marduk grimaced. "Send the Sisters my deepest sympathies—and our best Healers. We need that plague cured before it enters the City proper. Or, better still, before it kills more people in the poor section."

"Yes, your Majesty."

"Where is the candidate?"

"Just outside, my liege."

"Bring him in and then you may go."

"Yes, my liege."

The wizard stood and went to the door, gesturing for the man to enter. The candidate was short (most likely from years of malnutrition) and his hair was an unnatural rust red. His small, dark eyes darted around the room as he entered. Stopping a respectful distance from the desk where Marduk sat, he sank to his knees. The ratty clothing hanging from his thin frame stood in stark contrast to the opulence surrounding them.

"What's your name, boy?" Marduk asked, his voice gentle.

"Patrick, your Majesty," came the soft reply, barely above a whisper.

"You don't need to fear me. Come. Sit in one of the chairs." He nodded at the two chairs in front of the desk. "Are you hungry? Shall I order some food?"

"If-if it pleases the King." But the mention of food brought a wild, hungry look to his face, which he barely suppressed as he stood and sat in one of the chairs.

"It does." Marduk rang the hand bell on the desk. In a

moment, the servant door opened and a maid entered, curtsying. "Bring whatever is ready in the kitchens for our friend here."

The maid curtsied again and left, casting a fearful glance over her shoulder at the young boy. After the door closed, no one said anything for a long moment. Marduk evaluated Patrick, while he covertly looked around the room, not meeting the King's eyes.

"Be at ease," Marduk said, finally. "You're not in any trouble. What did the Sisters tell you before they sent you?"

"They, they said I was chosen for something."

"Did they give any indication of what that something was?"

Patrick shook his head.

"Well, then." He sat forward and clasped his hands on the surface of the desk. "I'll tell you, then. When I became King, I swore the Sacred Oath. Are you aware of it?"

Patrick shook his head again.

"The Sacred Oath is sworn by every Sovereign who takes the Throne in Lorst. We swear to take care of our people, to make sure they are clothed and fed and safe. Not all Sovereigns take that Oath seriously. But I took it after our beloved King Tristan and his daughter were murdered.

The whole city was in chaos. Fear ran rampant in the streets. Do you remember those days?"

Marduk's earnest tone drew Patrick's eyes up and he nodded. "I do, my liege. Those were horrible days."

"Yes, they were. We were betrayed by those we trusted most. We were struck to the core by those who were supposed to protect us. In the midst of all of that, the Council came to me and begged me to take the Throne. Not only because there wasn't anyone of the Blood left, but because they knew I had a vision." He stood, clasping his hands behind his back as he walked around the desk to stand at the corner nearest Patrick.

"A vision, my liege?" asked Patrick, looking at him with wide eyes.

"Yes. A vision of a better Lorst. A strong Lorst. A Lorst that doesn't have to fear its enemies any longer, or fear a knife in the safe confines of its borders." He smiled. "A Lorst remade. And, one day, a remade world. One where we are all safe and free."

Patrick swallowed and slowly looked down. "I don't know how I can be of help, your Majesty."

"Now that is where you're wrong, my friend. You are perfect. We need you, in fact. We can't do it without you."

The boy's eyes returned to Marduk. "Me, your Majesty?"

"Yes. You." At that moment, the servant door opened and the maid returned with a laden tray. "But, first, let's get some food in you and then, I'll take you to where you'll be of the greatest help."

He smiled brightly as the tray was set on the desk in front of him. At an encouraging nod from Marduk, Patrick dug into the food with a messy glee. Marduk's lip curled a little but he quickly hid his disgust.

"I'll be back in a moment."

The boy only grunted in response as Marduk walked away, opening the door and whispering to the guard outside, "Fetch me Captain Jarrett."

"Yes, your Majesty." The guard saluted and quickly strode away.

Marduk returned to his desk and went back to looking through papers while the boy ate and drank to his heart's content. Finally, after what felt like an age, the door opened again and Jarrett entered.

"You called for me, your Majesty," he said, stopping behind Patrick's chair and bowing.

"I did," replied Marduk. "We have a new candidate. I

thought you would escort us."

"It would be my pleasure, your Majesty."

"Are you ready to go, Patrick?"

The boy greedily slurped down the last of the wine and nodded, belching. His already dirty tunic sported new stains. He wiped his face with his sleeve as he stood. Marduk also stood.

"Then, this way."

If Patrick was nervous about entering an underground complex, he didn't show it. Instead, his eyes slowly took on the glassy stare brought on by the drugs in his wine. Jarrett supported him as his feet began to drag against the floor.

They entered a menagerie of strange beasts, passing cages where too-intelligent eyes watched them. Across the room, something gave a coughing growl. They passed tall cages filled with trees, where something bright blue darted among the leaves, on their way to a small door. Marduk ran a hand over the door, muttering.

With a shudder, the door swung open, revealing a small, round chamber hewn roughly from the bedrock. A circle of braided gold and silver was set into the center of the rough, rock floor. In the middle of the circle sat a small chest on a pedestal. Though the room was lit by several of the smokeless lanterns, the shadows in the corners were thick and impenetrable.

On the walls were painted in blue and black wards and other sigils of containment, interspersed with precious stones.

A wizard awaited them.

"Erin," said Marduk. "Is everything ready?"

"It is, my liege."

"We're going to try something new today. Jarrett, if you will."

Jarrett shoved Patrick, sending him stumbling into the circle. He dropped with a heavy grunt onto the floor. Jarrett drew his sword.

"You won't need that," said Marduk.

"If it's all the same to you, your Majesty, I would like to be prepared."

Marduk shrugged in answer as he took a book from Erin. "Very well. We all need our good luck charms."

"Thank you, your Majesty."

He opened the book and began to chant while Erin set some herbs in a bowl to smolder. For a moment, nothing happened. Then, slowly, the shadows in the room deepened and a cold, damp chill stole across the air. A pale blue light exuded from the box, reaching out to the boy and engulfing him.

Patrick twitched and moaned. Marduk picked up the pace of his chant, sweat beading his brow as he concentrated on the image in his mind. Patrick screamed as his flesh rippled. The wet sound of joints popping filled the room as his body contorted unnaturally. Cloth tore as fur rippled over him and the light intensified until it hid him.

Slowly, Marduk's chant wound down and the light lessened, easing back into the box. In Patrick's place laid a mound of shaggy, rusty red fur which slowly shifted as the creature stumbled to its six feet. It looked like a bear but it had long fangs protruding over his lips and his eyes were blood red.

The creature made a coughing noise, its mouth working. The eyes rolled in panic as it looked down itself. A blood-curdling scream erupted from its throat. Jarrett twitched but Marduk and Erin smiled.

"Isn't he beautiful?" shouted Marduk over the second scream, watching the creature turning in a circle and shaking, as if trying to wake from a nightmare.

"Very, your Majesty," replied Erin. "But rather loud, I think."

"Silence!" barked Marduk.

The creature quieted, wincing away from Marduk.

"You will go with this man," the King said, pointing at Jarrett. "Jarrett, take the creature to its cage. I'm sure you know where the strange bears go."

"Yes, your Majesty," replied Jarrett, sheathing the sword. "Come along."

He opened the door and stepped out, the creature following. As it got to the door, it tripped over its feet and sprawled to the floor.

Marduk laughed. "Isn't that precious? Like a newborn learning how to walk."

The creature groaned, stumbling up. Tears tracked down its muzzle.

"Come on," repeated Jarrett.

"Be gentle, Captain. He's new, after all." Marduk laughed again.

Jarrett left the menagerie feeling the desperate need to clean himself. But he had other duties to perform. As he entered the Academy, he smiled at the children in the halls. Many of them stood in clumps and talked with eager voices. They were between classes and were waiting for the next bell. Jarrett nodded at a few youngsters he knew who also served as pages in their off time.

After going down a few corridors, he entered a laboratory, where a wizard wiped down a slate board.

"Bruin," he said in greeting. "How go classes today?"

"As they usually do, I suppose. Those that aren't bored with tears pepper me with questions they should already know the answers to."

"Oh, it can't be that bad."

"So says the man who's never taught in a classroom."

"I teach self-defense to some of the noblewomen."

"Not the same thing, I fear." He tossed his rag aside. "What brings you?"

"The King wishes to know how the translation is going."

"Slowly. But we're making real progress. I'm sure we'll crack it by the time the lady arrives."

"Good. Good." He looked at Bruin significantly.

The wizard raised his hands and they glowed softly as he spoke a few words under his breath. Slowly, he lowered his hands. "Now. What brings you?"

Jarrett sighed and leaned against one of the tables. "He remade another one today."

Bruin grimaced. "That's the third this week."

"He needs breeders. No doubt the poor thing is rutting with every female he can get to."

"And those females will gestate at an alarming rate, give birth, and it'll start all over again. Do you know where he's shipping them to, once the offspring are trained?"

"I think he's stationing them in different places over the country, in preparation for the Rebel army forming in the North."

"And you're sure Emmerich is the general?"

"Absolutely. All the spies agree."

"And you're sure he didn't murder the Princess in cold blood?"

"I know Emmerich, Bruin. He's a good man. And, for all his faults, he was involved with the Princess. He wouldn't have just killed her. No. The only solution is that she attacked him and he defended himself."

"So you say."

"You doubt me?"

"Much happens under the fog of war that rational men

would not do at any other time."

Jarrett grimaced and rubbed his jaw. "I'd rather not think like that."

Bruin sighed. "I'm sorry, Jarrett. You have to watch Marduk make those creatures and here I am, filling your mind with doubts."

"It's all right. You have a right to have such concerns."

"Hmm."

They didn't say anything for a long moment. Finally, Jarrett said, "Have you discovered yet why Marduk wants the lady?"

"Not from what I can discover. I'm not even sure what's in that damn chest. He's broken that spell up among different members of the faculty, sworn each of us on our magic to maintain secrecy save to our contact. And everyone has a different contact. With the information so scattered, there's no telling what the purpose of the spell is supposed to be, and how it relates to the Lady Seer. We only know she is integral."

Jarrett swore under his breath.

"I concur."

"Do you think she can be brought over?"

"I don't think we should approach her until we know

she's safe. Who knows what sort of enchantment Marduk will have her under when he brings her here?"

"Can you arrange something?"

"Like what?"

Jarrett gave a little half-smile. "I'll let you know when I think of something."

Bruin chuckled. "You do that. You know I'll do anything for the Rebellion. Just keep your spirits up, Jarrett. We need you." He walked up to him and clasped his shoulder, looking into his eyes. "Don't give into despair."

"You don't see them, Bruin, after the spell. They know they've become something different. Some embrace it. Most don't. But they all scream at first." He shook his head. "Curdles a man's blood."

"It'll be over soon."

"I hope so, my friend. I hope so."

☐

Chapter Eleven

As winter waned, the snows let up and melted. Dwervin's building projects restarted. Scaffolds sprung up on the sides of the walls as men repaired chinks in the mortar while others saw to reinforcing the drawbridge and adding sharpened stakes to the sides of the moat. The grey walls and surrounding grounds crawled with sudden life.

As the first shoots of spring began to struggle from the ground (and the first of many funerals began), the people of Dwervinton began to half-heartedly celebrate the many weeks of Carnival, leading to the season of penance. If one looked closely enough, men stood in knots during the evening festivities, growing quiet if a soldier walked by.

At the castle, servants and slaves cleaned the halls and corridors of the castle. Maids aired out linens and freshened wardrobes with new bunches of herbs. Gavin took in these signs of spring with a heart struggling around a core of lead. Nothing pleased him about battle.

Mud squelched under his boots as he walked through

the town to the temple. Poor merchants hawked their wares with an almost desperate vigor. The bones of more than one face stood out in sharp relief. It had not been an easy winter.

The temple sat empty, the presbyter gone to officiate yet another graveside service. Up the stairs to the belfry, his falcon Portent waited for him patiently perched on a sill. Gavin gave him a soothing stroke as he unhooked the latest message from his talon. Portent looked at him almost disdainfully before preening his feathers.

The message read, "All is well. We will be there on schedule."

He rolled up the little slip of paper and regarded the village below him with a somber gaze.

The final night of Carnival came in splashes of color and noise. Men and women dressed in costumes danced and roamed the streets and alleys as children ran through the crowds, shrieking with joy. Musicians congregated in the square as vendors sold food and drink. In the castle, Gavin entertained the nobility along with a troupe of performers who had come in the night before. The state of their bodies and their clothing saddened him.

At the tables, food and drink washed down gullets liberally. People laughed loud and often. As the night edged closer to its middle, Gavin hopped onto the performer's dais and held up his hands for silence.

"Lords and ladies! Soldiers and wenches! Let me regale you with a small bit of country piety on this, a holy night." And he launched into the Hymn of Light. After a few lines, those of slightly lower classes began to sing along, albeit a little drunkenly. He noticed Clara watching him with serious, dark eyes before slipping away, the chain (forgotten by Lady Dwervin) wrapped around her hands. No one at the tables noticed, too drunk and too happy to care if a little slave girl took herself to bed. After the song, when he felt no one watching him, he too slipped outside, going up to the parapets.

One of the guards over the east wall gave him a bored, lazy wave as he approached. "Come to entertain us, Gavin?"

"More like to get a breath of good, clean air."

He chuckled. "Aye, lords and ladies are not always good at washin'."

Gavin patted him on the shoulder as he nonchalantly

strolled along. He lazily swung around to the front, approaching the portcullis. Another guard greeted him. In the far distance, he saw a light flare, then douse.

The guard grunted. "Wonder what—" An arrow pierced his throat, blood gushing down the front of his chain mail. His knees buckled and he fell. Gavin dropped to his knees as, below, in the town, screams erupted. He stared at the man, feeling the bile rise in the back of his throat. His name had been Percival.

"Raise the bridge!" cried the captain of the guard. "Get his lordship to safety!"

A horn winded. Gavin crawled to the stairs and rushed down them into the gatehouse. Two soldiers cranked the wheel as quickly as they could. He crept up to the first and struck him over the head with the hilt of his boot knife. The other guard turned on him, shocked.

"Gavin? What is this?"

Without a word, he shoved the soldier away, sending him sprawling, and kicked the lever. Outside, the bridge fell with an earth-trembling crash. The soldier, a new recruit whom Gavin had been teaching to read and write, stared up at him.

Gavin said, "Do you love your lord?" The boy shook

his head. "Then leave! Take off your livery and hide, because soon you'll get a new lord who isn't going to let you starve!"

The boy tore off his tunic and ran away. Gavin followed, thinking about a scared slave in the kitchen gardens.

Clara burst into the kitchens. The cooks, sitting at their private feast, looked at her in surprise. Relly got up.

"Why, Mouse! I haven't seen you in so long!"

Clara ran up and grabbed her arm, tugging her in the direction of the gardens. The other cooks gawked at her.

"Child, what is it?" she asked gently.

Taking up slate and chalk, Clara wrote, "An army comes. We must hide!"

The older woman shook her head sadly. "I canna read, me girl." She looked at the other cooks, who only shook their heads, looking at the girl as if she had lost her mind.

Sighing, she ran out into the gardens to a corner and hid behind the only non-utilitarian plant: a rosebush Relly loved like a child. She heard the woman say, "I best go up to her ladyship and let her know about Mouse."

A man's voice said, "Don't worry yourself. They'll come fetch her, soon enough."

And that's when the screams began. Images bombarded Clara, suddenly, over and over. Men fighting. Guts falling from opened bellies, the smell of rot making her gag. Limbs severed from trunks to fall, twitching, onto the ground, only to be reattached as the men replayed the fight but with a different ending. Her lying dead and broken under the angry glare of her betrayed lord. Her kneeling before a new one. The images blended together until she couldn't tell one from another. Blood. So much blood and death and fear. Sunbursts of pain blinded her.

Hands shook her roughly. "Clara! Clara! Damn, girl, what is wrong?"

The voice faded. There was only pain and the dark.

When she awoke, Clara found herself in her bed. Her head ached terribly. Rolling slowly over onto her side, she saw Gavin sleeping in a chair by the bed. It occurred to her that he was handsome. The beginnings of a beard shadowed his cheeks and chin. His long fingered hands spread out on his knees as his head lolled back. He snored lightly.

She sat up, then froze. Her hands flew up to her neck. Her bare neck. Tears welled in her eyes. She gingerly walked over to him, every part of her aching, and she wrapped her arms around his neck.

Gavin woke with a start and she pulled away.

"You're awake," he breathed.

She tapped her neck, then hugged his again. Slowly, he returned the embrace.

"Aye," he said, "the General gave you your freedom. The least he could have done, really, as you kept the truth a secret from Lord Dwervin. He's still alive, you know." Clara jerked back and looked at him. Gavin frowned. "Emmerich will be passing judgment on him soon enough, once he's healed from his wounds. Lady Dwervin died, however, which wouldn't have happened if she hadn't foolishly tried to attack my friend. Don't worry, the lady's maids are alive. Emmerich sent them packing to a nearby convent." He stood.

"Emmerich," he continued, "wanted to see you when you awoke. I, ah, think you need to get dressed first." He gestured to her shift. "I'll leave you to that." He turned, then paused. "What happened that night? In the garden? It was like you were having a seizure of some kind. Dove, you've been asleep for two days now. We were afraid you weren't going to wake."

She looked away and began trembling. He reached for her but she stepped back. After a long moment, he let his hand drop.

"I'll wait for you in the sitting room."

The castle felt very empty as the two walked down to the audience room. No maids bustled through the corridors. No messengers running on errands. No baronet having a tryst in a corner. Clara suppressed a shiver as she tugged on her sky blue tunic.

In the audience room, gaggles of attendants and officials stood about in groups talking, holding sheaves of papers and making gestures. A very strained Steward Warren was speaking with a man in his third decade with black hair, who stood with his back to them and his sun-browned hands clasped at the small of his back. He wore a forest green tunic over black shirt and trousers. From a plain leather belt hung a sword in a battered sheath.

As they approached, the man turned—and Clara saw

again the boy with eyes like clouded silver, whose fate she had always wondered about. The boy—man, she corrected—studied her with a bemused expression. She beamed at him, incredibly happy, as if the world all of a sudden righted itself. She noticed a blue and white starburst embroidered on his chest.

"General Emmerich, allow me to introduce to you Clara," said Gavin in introduction. "She claims to remember you."

Hurriedly, she wrote, "You were the boy who came to my village in your father's merchant train. You had a tinker named Merton. I helped to make the tonic you bottled. You fought the man who took me." She couldn't bear to spell out Haggard's name.

Emmerich read the message then looked her over again, recognition dawning. "Why, the little witchling. I often wondered what happened to you. But couldn't you talk then? What happened to your voice?"

She reddened a little and shrugged.

"No matter. You'll still come in handy against Marduk." Emmerich turned back to Gavin, saying, "Things went better than expected. The villagers gave up, no questions asked. I noticed the soldiers did more standing to the side than anything else."

"It looks like your storytellers helped."

"Aye. As did your songs."

Gavin shrugged off the compliment, his face dark. "I think I need to take Clara to the kitchens for some food."

"Oh. Well, come back when you get a chance. This is one of the best castles in Lorst. We were damn lucky, Gavin. Damn lucky."

With that, he turned back to Steward Warren and resumed the conversation, which seemed to be about grain supplies. Gavin took Clara's elbow but she pulled away.

On her slate, she wrote, "I wish to see Dwervin." She reached out to grab onto Emmerich's tunic, but Gavin snatched her hand away.

"General," he said, "Clara has a request."

Emmerich turned and, reading the message, raised a brow. "Why?"

"I wish to speak to him," she jotted out.

He considered her for a long moment and then nodded. "Gavin will make the arrangements."

Emmerich watched them as they left, still feeling a little shock over meeting the fiery little girl (young woman, he corrected) after all this time. He remembered the gruff mother and mysterious one-eyed man who had left him pissing blood for a few days. The old anger stirred but he pushed it away to continue his conversation about rations.

In the kitchen, a lone Relly cooked. She dropped her ladle when she saw Clara, and scooped the girl up in a vigorous hug.

"Oh, child, ye tried to warn us, didn't ye! Oh, I'm so happy." She glared at Gavin. "And ye knew! I can't believe I let ye take me for a fool."

"You're not a fool, Relly."

"I ought to chase ye right out of my kitchen." She clutched protectively at Clara.

"There's a war going on and Dwervin was on the wrong side. It wasn't anything against you."

"War? I haven't heard of a war!"

"Well, I can't help that." He sighed. "Could you please feed Clara? Then I can explain everything properly."

"Clara?" She turned to the former slave. "That is ye name, gel?"

She smiled at her and nodded.

"And ye are no longer a slave?"

She shook her head.

Relly studied Gavin for a moment, then let go of Clara. He took Clara's arm and led her to a small table. After a moment, Relly brought them steaming bowls of vegetable soup. She also set down crusty yeast rolls and joined them.

As they ate, Gavin told Relly about the war and Marduk. The conversation lulled and, being done with her bowl, Clara took out her slate.

She wrote, "Why would General Emmerich want this castle?"

"The valley is entered by a small pass, making it easily defended. It's isolated, which means it would take time for Marduk to mount an army to come out here. It's small and unimportant, it's only claim to fame being its proximity to Orlind, which means it'll take a while before he'll care enough to do so. This is the perfect base for Emmerich's needs before launching against Orlind. And Orlind is the victory that matters."

Relly snorted. "Makes me wonder how it was so easy for him to take."

"Well, I was here to open the gate and the people were so tired of Lord Dwervin that many let Emmerich's band of warriors approach without stopping him or sending word. The soldiers met along the way were incredibly easy to bribe."

"I canna believe this!"

"Do I look like I can help that?" He stuffed the rest of the bread in his mouth. "Finished?"

Clara nodded and they stood. Relly got up and said, "I think she'll be staying. You go along now, Gavin."

"Why don't we let her decide? Clara?"

She looked puzzled at being asked. Then, she wrote, "I need to go. Thank you, Relly, for your kindness."

Gavin read the slate aloud. Relly, tears brimming in her eyes, embraced her for a long moment.

As they left, he asked, "Did you mean it, about seeing Dwervin again?"

She nodded.

"Well, let's get it done."

Clara hesitated and the healer raised a brow, as if asking, "You sure you wish to do this?"

She did. She couldn't explain why, but she did. Stepping into the room, she looked up at the healer, who whispered, "I will be just outside, if you need me. Don't be afraid. He's too weak to do anything." He left and the door latched closed behind him.

The small bedchamber must have belonged to a minor cousin. A woman, if the pale yellows and greens of the tapestries and floor coverings were any indication.

The once great, self-assured Lord Dwervin lay on the small bed, looking small and insignificant with a pretty green and blue quilt drawn over him. Sweat beaded his ashen face. He opened his eyes when she came to his bedside, her eyes traveling to the blood-flecked cloth covering his chest.

She looked up to meet his gaze and almost winced away from the hate contorting his features.

"You," he hissed. "You knew. You knew all along. And now you've killed me."

She shook her head. No. No, she had just chosen a side. Wasn't it right of her to choose the side that gained her freedom?

"Aye. You did. Even if I get off this bed, I'm still a dead man. All because of you. You could have warned me." He could barely speak above a whisper, but, from the force of his words, he might as well have been shouting.

She shook her head again, numb.

Suddenly, Dwervin's hand clamped over her wrist as his eyes bulged. "The healer," he choked. "My heart." He clutched at the cloth with his free hand, his mouth gaping in a silent scream.

The anger, which had been lying dormant in her gut, flared in a fine fire. She snatched her arm away. He, who had bought her like she was a hunk of meat, who was willing to watch her be treated like an animal, who would have raped her if given the chance, who denied her freedom after saving his life—he wanted her to save him once again?

Clara blinked away the tears of rage and only stood there. He bucked and writhed, his arm flailing impotently. The motions slowly became feebler until they stopped. A low rattle rushed from his lips, his chest stilled, and the light left his eyes.

Lord Dwervin, scion to a long lineage of mountain lords, died. It took less than five minutes.

Turning, Clara walked out of the room, passed a surprised Gavin and burst into a run. She didn't stop until she reached her room. Falling onto the bed, she wept.

"We'll be making our move two se'ennights from now," Emmerich said. "The neighboring fiefdom of Baroness Orlind will be able to provide plenty of supplies for the final push towards Castle Newfound and Candor City." He unrolled a map and studied it.

They were in the (now late) lord's chambers, which Emmerich had taken up for his own. He stood at a map table to the side while Gavin lounged by the fire.

"Are you going to take the title?" asked Gavin.

"Of Lord Dwervin? I don't see how I have much of a choice. But the steward will be doing most of the tending and ruling and such. He's not half so bad, especially since he's absolutely terrified of me." The expected laugh did not come and Emmerich looked up to see Gavin staring into the fire. "All right. What is it?"

"It? Nothing." He looked at him with wide, innocent eyes.

"I really do think I'm the only one you can't lie to. Tell me what it is or I'll have you thrown in the dungeon or the stocks or something equally reprehensible."

"How can a soldier know a word as big as reprehensible?"

"I like to read." He walked over and sat across from his

friend. "What's wrong?"

Gavin sighed. "The healer on duty thinks Clara may not have gotten help for Dwervin when she could have."

Emmerich's clasped his hands and looked down at them. "What do you think?"

"I think that would have been beneath her."

"But it is possible, or you wouldn't be upset about it. After all, by your account, she had every reason in the world to hate him."

"I just can't imagine Clara doing that."

"People are capable of all sorts of things." His voice softened. "You and I should know that better than anyone."

An uncomfortable silence filled the pause. Finally, Gavin said, "You could have been happy to see her, when I introduced you."

Emmerich sighed in frustration. "Gav, I met her once over ten years ago. It's not like we were long-lost lovers." He made a face. "She wasn't even near womanhood, in fact."

"Aye, but didn't you see how disappointed she was? I read the message on the slate, Emm. I know you tried to rescue her from slavery."

"What did you want me to do? Dance a jig? Propose marriage?" He laughed.

Gavin sighed and shook his head. "Never mind."

"When did you start caring, anyhow? Besides, I'm sure she's gotten over it." Emmerich regarded him for a moment. "Do you like this girl?"

He looked away. "Does it make a difference? Look, Clara has lost all her old friends and family. You were the last thread that held her to her past."

A dark look crossed his face, gone as soon as it came. "The past is gone and dead. No use in hanging onto anything that happened in it."

"Right. That's always been your guiding star."

Emmerich looked at him sharply. "What's gotten into you?"

"Nothing, nothing." He stood and started to leave. "I'm going to bed."

"Come and sit back down. We have to talk about our plan of attack. I always think better when you're around to ridicule me."

Gavin hesitated at the door. Looking over his shoulder, he said, "Good night, Emmerich."

And he left.

Chapter Twelve

The next morning, Clara awoke with a start. The familiar prickle danced along her scalp and down her spine. She jerked upright, pressing her knees against her forehead as the vision fell upon her.

She saw a woman standing on a parapet overlooking a mountainside Clara did not recognize. Her white hair was piled on her head in an intricate knot and a long silver chain with a round disc pendant hung on her neck. The ruby in the pendant's center caught the light as it laid against the deep blue of her velvet tunic. At her left stood an armored man holding a map. He said something but Clara did not hear him. The woman turned to the man on her right. Clara recognized him as the man who tried to poison Lord Dwervin. The woman said something to him and he laughed.

The vision dissolved. Sweat beaded her forehead and her whole body trembled. Nausea flowed over her. She turned, leaning over the side of the bed, and vomited into the piss pot.

The door to her bedchamber opened and Relly entered. She set a breakfast tray on the bedside table.

"I thought ye'd be hungry," she said. Her smile faded. "Somethin' the matter, girl?"

Clara flung the coverlet off her and dashed to the wardrobe. She pulled out the first tunic her hands landed on (a dark red) and then pulled out an undergown of pale cream.

"Ye need help?" asked Relly.

Clara shook her head and gently pushed the Cook out of the room.

"Something the matter?"

Clara nodded.

"Ye need to hurry to the new lord?"

She nodded again.

"I'll get out yer way, then." And the door shut in her face.

Clara gulped down most of the food to make Relly happy, then pulled on the clothes. She brushed her hair and braided it. When she came out, the cook stood from the couch but before she could speak, Clara was already running as hard as she could to Emmerich's chambers. It wasn't until she was halfway down the hall that she realized she forgot to put on slippers.

Emmerich and Gavin shot to their feet when she burst into the room, with two guards close behind. Her hands went to her slate–but she had forgotten it. She looked around in a panic as the guards clamped hands onto her arms and shoulders.

"It's all right," Emmerich told the guards. They released Clara and, saluting, returned to their posts, closing the door behind them.

"I got you, love," said Gavin. On the map table, he laid out paper, pen, and ink.

They watched as Clara furiously scribbled out her vision. When she was finished, she stood back, smiling triumphantly. Emmerich picked up the paper and the two men read it.

"This noblewoman," said Emmerich, "did she have on a silver necklace? With a large pendant?" She nodded. He looked at Gavin with a frown. "The Baroness."

"Looks like she has a wizard in her employ. And the wizard that tried to assassinate the late Dwervin, no less."

"I hate wizards. Why didn't the Grand Temple just burn them all?"

"Because the Grand Temple swore to not interfere with government anymore and the first thing the wizards did was make themselves indispensable to the sovereigns." Gavin shrugged.

Emmerich sighed, then looked to Clara. "Thank you, Clara. Tell me, can you call up these visions on your own?"

She shook her head. Taking back the paper, she wrote, "I can feel them coming, though. I can never stop them."

"Well, please don't try!" His hands gripped her shoulders. "This information was vital."

Clara felt disturbingly aware of the warmth of his hands flowing through her clothes. She took a slow step back, giving a half smile as a sort of thanks, though waves of nausea were beginning to wash over her again. Perhaps she shouldn't have eaten that breakfast so quickly.

"Is it possible that the Baroness sent Brellin to kill Dwervin? There was much fear that he was working for the Sorcerer King," said Gavin.

"Well, there's always been a rivalry between Dwervin and the Baroness. A wizard will do anything if you pay him enough."

"That is true, but it still troubles me." Gavin looked over at Clara, who had collapsed into a chair at the table.

"You're pale." He came over and felt her forehead. "Your skin is like ice. I think she needs mulled wine, Emmerich."

"I'll have the kitchen bring some up. If this is how visions affect her, then it would be best to not overly rely on her." He pulled a rope hidden by a tapestry. In a moment, a manservant entered and Emmerich directed him to fetch the wine. "Now," he said, "we'll have to figure out how to get around this. Ah, I think she'll be all right, Gavin."

Clara felt very embarrassed that the general's right-hand man, now kneeling by her feet, seemed more interested in coddling her than giving advice. She smiled at him reassuringly.

Taking up the paper, she wrote, "I am still tired from what happened in the gardens. Visions don't always affect me this way."

"What did happen in the garden?" asked Gavin.

"Aye. I've been curious about that myself," broke in Emmerich.

She wrote, "I've had time to think about this. I think I saw the multiple endings of the battle and it was more than I could bear."

"Then maybe we'll keep you from battlegrounds, then,"

said Gavin. Emmerich snorted and he gave him a harsh look. "It nearly killed her, man."

The bard moved her to a seat by the fire. Closing her eyes, she tried to shake the feeling as if there was more to know. The feeling often came to her after a vision, as if she hadn't seen everything. Eventually, the manservant returned with the wine. She sipped it, letting the warmth seep into her. The two men were talking about tactics but she found herself not caring. Soon, she fell asleep by the fire.

When Clara slowly awoke, she heard two low voices arguing.

"A campaign is no place for her," whispered Gavin.

"She's no good to me a hundred leagues away," Emmerich replied.

"We can use Portent."

"I know you think highly of that merlin, but this is too serious. What if Portent was shot down, and the message fell in the wrong hands?"

Silence fell for a long moment.

When Emmerich spoke again, his voice was gentle. "We're almost through, old friend. But in order to lop off the snake's head, we have to do things we're not comfortable with. You spent all winter here. I'm sure soldiers died who you wished you could have warned."

Gavin drew in a deep breath and let it out slowly. "Those soldiers had a choice whether or not to fight. They heard the rumors of you. I even spread a few of my own. But why do I have the feeling you aren't going to give Clara much of a choice?"

"She's going to get a choice; I just already know her decision. Think about it. She's been a slave most of her life. She probably has never set foot outside of Dwervinton in that whole time. Do you really think she's going to stay behind?"

"She could just choose to strike out on her own."

"If she has any sense, she'd realize how suicidal that is. Even in the best of times a lone woman can't hope to wander around unmolested."

A pause. Clara could picture Gavin frowning. "Maybe she will find a willing partner."

The air grew taught with tension. "Are you that willing partner?"

"No. You know I'll see you to the end."

"Good."

Finally, she couldn't stand it any longer and opened her eyes, yawning. She sat up straighter, wondering how much of the day had passed.

"Look who's awake." Emmerich smiled at her from where he and Gavin sat by the window. "I trust you slept well."

Gavin sat in a chair next to her. "You've been asleep for about a candle mark. Do you feel all right?"

She nodded. Emmerich came to kneel before her. "Clara, do you want to come with us?"

She looked at Gavin, whose face had hardened and he gave his friend a poisonous look. "It's a hard road," he said. "We'll understand if you don't want to go."

"But it's a road out of here," Emmerich interjected. "You will be using your gift for a great cause, Clara. Marduk needs to be stopped and the rightful person, a better person, put on the throne. You could play an important role in this. You'll have bodyguards, of course, and we'll keep you away from battlegrounds. And, ah, whatever else you want is yours: fine clothes, servants. Does that suit you?"

She paused and looked from one man to another. Gavin only wanted to protect her. However, Emmerich offered a way to have her own life. She nodded and smiled reassuringly at Gavin, who scowled.

Chapter Thirteen

The next day, Clara took her place at Emmerich's left hand at the table for the evening meal in the great hall. She looked down the tables where the other soldiers sat (the family either dead or sent somewhere to be held as prisoners) and smiled faintly at the camaraderie in their laughter and conversations. She heaved a happy sigh.

The servers came forward and dishes were laid out before them. Emmerich cut her a portion of the large trout and gave it to her with a nod. She reached for her slate to ask him a question but he had already turned to address to Gavin.

The other captains talked around her. None addressed her. She wondered if they knew who she was.

"The latest reports," one began, but was silenced by a cough from Gavin. His eyes cut to her.

Emmerich frowned, looking to Gavin a moment before saying, "Let it wait until the meeting, Captain Turin."

Her eyes went back to her plate, feeling as if she might as well be sitting on the floor again.

Clara stepped out of the chapel after the evening prayers. Bowing, she accepted the presbyter's blessing and began to walk down the hall to the stairwell. Spying Gavin up ahead, she raced forward, the sound of her running drawing his attention.

"Clara," he said, stopping. "Did you enjoy evening prayers?"

She nodded. Taking out her slate, she quickly wrote, "I need to ask you a favor."

"And I'll try to comply." He nodded at a couple of soldiers who strolled by and saluted him.

"I need to get into the meetings General Emmerich has with the captains."

"It's not your place, Clara. The less you know, the better you are."

She glared at him, swiped her slate clean, and wrote, "I need to be a part of this. How will I understand my visions if I don't know what's happening?"

"No."

"Why have you been keeping me from overhearing anything at the table? Why are you acting like this?" Her chalk slapped into the slate with each word, her hand shaking.

After he read what she wrote, he put gentle hands on her shoulders. "To protect you." He gave her a swift kiss on the forehead and walked away, leaving her confused and angry.

Five days before departure to march on Orlind, Clara hid behind the tapestry in the meeting room beside Emmerich's quarters. She thanked the Child that Emmerich had started giving her an allowance. It took a lot of money to bribe the one literate scullery maid into divulging the time and place of the meetings but after a se'ennight of spying on them, it paid off.

The army that came to take over Dwervinton was only half the actual force. The other half had gone to the port of Seasong, on a peninsula called the Knob, which lay to the northwest. The fighting there had been a little more spirited there than at Dwervinton, but after the installation of a lord sympathetic to Emmerich, those men were returning to meet them at Castle Orlind. Emmerich hoped to take Candor City, which would wrest control of the Northern part of Lorst away from Marduk.

But what worried everyone was that Marduk wasn't

sending out the forces they expected to stop them. It made everyone uneasy, filling many a discussion with speculation as to why.

"Something more important may have his attention," Emmerich had said once, to which the other captains nodded in agreement, their eyes shadowed with concern as to what they could be.

When Gavin came to visit with her in the evenings, she tried to get more information from him, but he always changed the subject.

Emmerich's entrance knocked her out of her reverie. She watched him through a tiny slit in the tapestry. Today he wore a black tunic and shirt with grey pants. He looked very handsome, though the steel in his eyes detracted from his looks. Gavin followed behind.

"We still have a while before the others arrive," he said, sitting at the table's head. "You know, I'm going to miss this castle living."

Gavin snorted, taking his seat. "You say that now, but wait until this is all over. You'll be stir crazy by the time winter comes."

"Aye, and I'll come riding up to your front gate, demanding for you to come on some harebrained adventure."

"Wasn't that how all this got started?" Emmerich snorted a laugh in reply. "But," Gavin continued, "I don't think you'll find it so easy, when this is over, to oust me from my comforts."

"Oh, now? Got your eye on a pretty lady? A pretty lady who happens to be a Seer?"

Gavin shot him a look. "I'm getting tired of this sort of thing. I want a place to settle."

Emmerich leaned forward, clasping his hands as he pressed his forearms onto the table. "The truth, now. Every evening, I turn around to ask for a song, or a riddle, or some sort of decent conversation, but you're never about. I ask around and I'm told you've snuck away to Clara's quarters. How long have you been bedding her?"

Clara clasped her hand over her mouth to muffle the gasp.

Gavin stared hard at his friend. Finally, he said, in a low, dangerous voice, "Slander her again and I will defend her honor."

"Easy, friend. You know I meant no such thing."

Gavin stood and paced up and down the room, going in and out of Clara's field of vision. After a long time of silence, Emmerich spoke up.

"Gavin." His voice was soft and gentle.

"Her parents sold her! That—harlot treated her like she was less than human!" Gavin cried. "They kept her chained all the time and made her sit on the floor to take her meals in the hall. It was a miracle that Lord Dwervin didn't rape her. But he tried to break her and for that I should have killed him immediately."

"Well, he's dead now. Clara avenged herself nicely."

"I still don't think she just stood there–"

"I think you should give her more credit. I also think you may believe it, or it wouldn't trouble you so."

The words stole away Clara's breath. She clasped her shaking hands together. They knew. Or, at least speculated, and that was nearly as bad.

"I see the look in her eyes some days, Emmerich. No man will be able to hold her and have all her heart because she won't be able to trust him."

"But?"

"But, I would like to try."

The scrape and thud of boots and the creak of leather announced the captains' arrival. Gavin returned to stand by his seat and Emmerich stood to receive his subordinates.

Clara was glad; her mind swirled with emotions and thoughts. She would have to find somewhere quiet to sort them out. Pushing them aside, she listened closely to the meeting.

After reports on men and supplies she only half-understood, Emmerich announced that he had just received word from a spy by way of the merlin Portent that revealed Castle Orlind's weak point.

"From what our spy says, there is a weak spot on the south end of the castle. The thawing snow has weakened the foundations and there's a chance of the wall caving in."

"How far along are they on repairs?" asked a captain. Clara could never remember their names.

"Not very. It'll take them the rest of the spring and into summer to fortify the wall." He paused significantly. "They had to drain the moat and build a scaffold over it."

Several captains let out a breath. One whooped.

Emmerich stood and began to walk around the room. "Gavin, has our little fount of information come up with anything new?"

"No, but I'm sure she'll come up with something. It's not exactly a precise art."

He came to stand by the tapestry. Clara pressed her

back to the wall and tried to think invisible thoughts. Suddenly, the tapestry swept back and Emmerich glowered down at her.

Chairs scraped back as the seated men jumped to their feet. Steel hissed as they drew their swords, except for Gavin. He stood, tensed, shock and dread coloring his face.

"Well," said Emmerich, "I don't remember extending you an invitation." He gently took her arm and drew her out so the others could see her. They sheathed their swords at a wave of his hand.

Taking up her slate, she wrote, "I deserve to know!"

Emmerich frowned at the written outburst. "Gavin told me you weren't interested."

She looked at him, shocked. Gavin said, "It was for your own good."

Clara opened her mouth, as if she could yell at him. She let out a harsh breath and stamped her foot. Emmerich watched her with an almost-amused look.

"Gavin," he said, "we'll discuss this later. Gentlemen, allow me to introduce to you Lady Clara, our very own Seer." The men bowed as he led her to an empty chair beside his, going as far as pulling it out for her.

"You can't let her stay," cried Gavin.

"Sit, Lady Clara."

Startled at the title, she sat.

"Gavin, do you need to be dismissed?"

Gavin's face mottled, his hand dropping to his sword. The other captains tensed and the moment poised on the edge of violence. Finally, he shook his head and sat.

And Emmerich unrolled a map as if nothing happened.

After the meeting, Emmerich said, "Gavin, you may go. I'll escort Lady Clara to her rooms."

With a curt bow, he obeyed, leaving the door open behind him.

Emmerich worried about him. He wasn't the same person–anxious and worried, not carefree at all anymore. He felt it was time to separate the two a little bit.

Emmerich turned to her and offered his arm. She cautiously slipped her hand over his forearm. "You don't need to fear me. I suppose not many people show you courtesy, my lady."

She seemed surprised and a little pleased. Together, they left the room and went up to the old lady's maids' chambers. No one could persuade Clara into taking late

Lady Dwervin's quarters.

They entered the sitting room, and here, Clara's body language changed. She grew tense and began playing with her belt. She edged away from him and sat in one of the armchairs, her back rigid.

He sat across from her, in another armchair, leaning forward with his elbows on his knees and hands clasped. "Are you worried I'm going to discipline you for sneaking into the meeting?"

She nodded with downcast eyes.

"Well, I won't. And don't worry about Gavin. I suppose he means well. Anyway, I think it's time for you to stop skulking around me as if afraid of me. I can be a harsh man but I need you to be able to come to me. I wish you had come to me with your request to be at the meetings. Gavin and I aren't always of one mind." He sat back. "You showed a lot of fire tonight. You really want to be a part of this war?"

She took her slate off and looked down at it. Some of her hair had fallen loose from her braid. It hung around her face in wisps in a pretty way. Taking up her chalk, she slowly wrote and held it up. It read, "I have no choice but to help you."

"That is true. A lone woman wouldn't last on the roads. You could stay in the castle but I don't think you would want that."

She shook her head and they sat in silence for a long moment. The way she sat up straight and proper, intelligent eyes lost in thought, reminded him of someone else. He scrubbed his jaw to distract himself. Finally, she wrote, "Is this why you wanted to talk to me in private?"

"Well, that and I was wondering if you'd be interested in learning how to fight? I mean, I'm not expecting you to become a master swordswoman or something. Just, to know enough to protect yourself."

"Why were you taunting Gavin earlier?"

The sudden question surprised him, turning the conversation down a much too personal route. He stood. "I'll leave you to your rest. If you want to learn how to fight, meet me by the stables at first light. That will be my only free time, as it's when I usually practice anyway."

Clara nodded but, before she had a chance to write anything on that blasted slate, he left.

Chapter Fourteen

Clara dressed with nervous, cold fingers, the fire casting large, malformed shadows onto the walls. On her table sat the remains of a light breakfast.

"His lordship told me to bring it, as well as to wake you," the maid had whispered. She set out her clothes with a look of disdain. Clara found out why quickly enough: they were a dark brown boy's tunic, shirt, and trousers. She managed to find suitable boots in the bottom of her wardrobe.

Outside, her breath puffed white vapor as she crossed the flagstones in the early morning light, the sun barely cresting the tree line. She walked with long strides to the stables, ignoring the stares of servants and soldiers, and found Emmerich already at his sword exercises. Holding his sword carefully, he slowly worked through forms and stances, then repeated them more quickly, over and over, until he became a blur and his blade sang through the air, the sun glancing off the metal. She watched with awe.

When he finished, he turned to her. "You're late," he said. Today he wore the uniform she first saw him in and the way the sun cast its light around him made her feel shy and exhilarated all at once. But remembering what he said of her yesterday tossed cold water on her feelings.

She reached for her slate, only to find that once again, in her excitement, she left it in her room. She settled for a glare.

He grinned and waved her over, sheathing his sword. When approached, he held out a wooden practice sword. "We'll start with this."

She held it as if she expected it to bite her. With a sigh, Emmerich came up behind her, reaching around her to arrange her hands and fingers on the hilt. She tensed.

"Clara," he said softly, "I am your teacher this morning. When we meet at this time, that is what our relationship is: teacher and pupil. You have no reason to fear me. Now. Part of fighting is being loose. You have to be relaxed; it makes it easier to respond. Take a deep breath. Fill your lungs. That's it. Now, let it out. Again. Take in your tension. Now, let it out with your breath. Again. Good."

He smelled like leather, soap, and musk. Clara would admit to herself much later that it was mostly his smell that made her stomach unloose and her shoulders relax. But that morning she only credited his good teaching skills. He placed his hands lightly on her hips and turned them slightly.

"Bring your right foot back. No, too wide. Your feet can be no wider apart than your shoulders. Good. Bend your knees a little. Very good." He reached up and tilted her forearms up. "This is your defensive stance. Now, I'm going to guide you through some forms."

They worked until the sun came over the tree line. Steward Warren interrupted them with a cough. Emmerich frowned, but let Clara come out of her stance. Her legs and back ached. She thought longingly of the bathing room.

"We'll meet here tomorrow at the same time," he said. Turning, he strode away, the steward hurrying to keep up.

"I think you did well," said a voice suddenly. Clara whirled, jerking the sword up into a defensive pose without thinking. Gavin leaned against the stable wall. Blinking, she smiled shyly and dropped the pose.

"I don't like that you need to learn this," he continued, "but you did well."

He straightened and walked away. Clara opened her mouth, trying to make herself call out to him, to ask him if he really did think she was learning well, to perhaps explain everything he said yesterday, but nothing came. She watched helplessly as he turned the corner out of sight.

Low clouds cast red light at dawn as the army assembled outside the village. Clara felt unsteady as she perched sidesaddle on her bay gelding. She looked enviously at Gavin's trousers. Sitting with one leg on either side of the horse seemed so much more stable. And it wasn't as if she had had much practice. The day before, when she admitted she'd never ridden before, Emmerich all but threw her into a saddle and wouldn't let her go until she could ride one circuit around the paddock without falling off. She rubbed a bruise on her shoulder.

Emmerich cantered up the line of soldiers and supply wagons. He stopped beside her, looking quite dashing in his dark green tunic and trousers as he turned in his saddle to give the line one more look. Over his chest he wore a heavy leather vest with the blue and white starburst worked into it over the heart, and from his hip hung his sword.

He faced the road and held up his hand. The trumpeter raised his horn and, when the general dropped his hand, winded a long note, which was repeated along the line. They lurched forward. Clara grinned nervously at Gavin, who smiled back. Before her may be war and blood, but behind her was the place of her captivity. She felt she had a reason to smile.

That night, they camped in a large fallow field. Men erected Clara's tent between Emmerich's and Gavin's. As they did so, with Gavin overseeing, Emmerich casually strolled up.

"When you have a moment," he said, "gather a few soldiers to act as the lady's guard."

"I already have some men in mind."

"Good." He clapped his friend on the shoulder and walked on, barking orders at someone.

Gavin walked away in the opposite direction, angling for a company of men on the far side of the camp. Four soldiers laughed and bantered as they set up their tents. One of them saw Gavin approach and greeted him with a friendly, "Hullo, Gavin!"

The other three turned as he came to a stop before them. "I have a job for you all," he said. "Guard duty."

"Ya need someone to watch yer back?" asked a redhead with his front teeth missing.

"No, Lorne. This is for a lady named Clara. She's staying in the tent between mine and General Emmerich's."

"Must be a mighty fine whore," spoke up a bald man with a scar bisecting his scalp. The others snickered until they caught Gavin's glare.

"What she is," he said, "is none of your business. She's very important, though, and she needs constant guard. You four can split it up however you like; I just need two of you with her at all times, starting this evening. Understand?"

The men saluted half-heartedly and he left to tell Clara about her new shadows. He found her helping the horse master. He paused to watch her.

Mud and dust stained her dark red riding dress and her hair fell loose from her braid. A little dirt smudged her cheek. Fatigue slumped her shoulders but a small smile curved her face as the horses bent to eat the hay she sprinkled before them.

He came up beside her and touched her arm. "You don't have to do that anymore," he said gently.

She looked up and formed a question with her large eyes and sweet mouth. He took the food from her hands and scattered it in a quick motion.

"You're not a slave, anymore," he said. "Neither are you a servant. You are a free woman." He lowered his voice. "In fact, you're the general's Seer. You are the most important of his advisers. You can tell him to not pitch a battle and, unless he's feeling really stubborn, he'll follow your advice. Such a woman does not scatter hay for horses. Come." He took her hand and led her back to her tent. "We really ought to get you a lady's maid and a title of some kind, so that no one will doubt your purpose."

She took up the slate and wrote, "But I like to help. I like to work."

"It's all you've known. How can you say you like it? You don't know anything else to know if you don't. Like it, that is."

"When I was with the lady's maids, I did very little besides sew and I spent most of the time being bored." She tripped a little as she wrote and Gavin steadied her.

"Appearances have to be kept up. No one will know what to think of you if Emmerich holds you in high esteem but you help the horse master. But let's not argue about this. I've found guards for you." Her eyes widened in surprise. "You're very important and we can't risk something happening to you. They'll come by in the evening; they're good men and I trust them with my life. You'll be safe with them."

She nodded slowly, then wrote something quickly on her slate. She held it up and it read, "You worry about me too much."

"Sweetling, I wonder sometimes if I don't worry enough." As they approached her tent, he noticed the four bodyguards were already there. "Ah, your guards are here. Perhaps they wanted to take a look at you before later this evening. Let me introduce you. They're all good, loyal men."

But before they got much closer, one of the men turned around, and Clara stopped dead in her tracks.

"Something wrong?" he asked, laying one hand on her arm.

The man, a new recruit with one eye named Haggard, took a tentative step forward. "Clara?"

Clara turned and ran away as fast as she could. Gavin yelled her name but she ignored him. He took off after her with the bodyguards close behind.

Her lungs and legs burned as she pelted through the tents at full speed, fear burning in her gut. Some of the soldiers shouted, wanting to know what was the trouble, and she collided into one, knocking him down and scattering the supplies he carried. Catching herself, Clara kept going. Up ahead, Emmerich conversed with the horse master. He looked over when he heard her coming, his hand falling automatically to his sword when he saw her face.

She stopped in front of him, shaking and gasping, tears rolling down her face.

Emmerich put his hands on her shoulders. "What's wrong? Have you had a vision?"

She shook her head. Behind her, she heard Gavin cry, "Clara!"

A fresh surge of fear drove her behind Emmerich, gripping the sides of his left arm with both hands as she looked around him. He brought his left hand back to hold her side as he faced forward. His right hand clenched the grip of his sword.

Gavin stopped in front of them, the four guards coming to a huffing stop with him. Those standing around watched with interest.

"What the hell is going on, Gavin?" Emmerich asked.

"I don't know," he replied. "I was about to introduce Clara to her guards when she ran."

"I can explain," said Haggard, his voice rougher than she remembered. "But perhaps we ought to talk in your tent, my lord?"

Emmerich turned toward Clara. "Is that all right with you?"

She slowly nodded, feeling safe with Emmerich standing there. As they walked toward the tent, he put an awkward arm around her shoulders. She kept a healthy distance from touching his side with hers.

Emmerich's tent was sparse and utilitarian. Boxes and bags sat against one cloth wall. Opposite from it stood a small cot and in the center stood a larger folding table. He stood in front of the table with Clara at his side. The three other guards lined up next beside the entrance while Gavin and Haggard stood before them.

"All right," he said. "I'm listening."

Haggard looked down and away. For Clara, now that some of the fear had leaked away, a great amount of rage filled her. She had the sudden fantasy that Emmerich, on hearing the story, would summarily have Haggard executed.

Clara felt a good bit of pleasure at the thought.

"My Lord General," Haggard said, "'bout a dozen or more years back, I was friends with a man who couldn't provide for his family. He was about to be forced out of the land he had worked for seasons and seasons. His wife came to me. Said she wanted me to sell her child so they could pay the landlord his rent. I didn't want to do it was trying to get out of the business, myself. But she was desperate. And I thought–"

"You thought," Gavin interjected, his face going cold, "that she would have a better life somewhere else."

"Aye. Told the slaver not to sell her to a brothel or anything like that."

"Well," said Emmerich, "he didn't. He only sold her to one of the crueler bastards this part of the country has to offer. You said you don't deal with slavery, any longer?"

"No, sire. Young Clara was my last sale."

"And you'd be willing to swear that before a presbyter?"

"Aye, sire. A thousand times over."

"Gavin?"

Gavin looked at Emmerich with more than a little anger in his eyes. "You can't possibly be still considering having this man guard Clara."

Clara turned to Emmerich, who studied Haggard closely with a clenched jaw. Finally, he said, "Clara, would you be willing to let this man guard you?"

She gaped at him. This was the man who sold her into slavery and he wasn't going to have him killed? Or at least beaten?

Emmerich said, "Leave us."

"Emmerich," Gavin choked out.

"Must I begin repeating myself with you, Gavin?"

For a long moment, the two men sized up the other. Finally, Gavin said tersely, "No, my lord."

The men left, leaving Clara and Emmerich by themselves.

"You really hate him," said Emmerich. His hands dropped away from her.

Taking her slate, she wrote, "Wouldn't you?"

"Aye. I would. Do you know why I accepted an old, one eyed man into my army?"

She shook her head.

"Because he is one of the best swordsmen I have ever seen. Aye, he's old and his reflexes aren't what they were. But he has taught my men more about the sword in the last month than most have learned in a lifetime. I trust him. I ask that you do the same."

Clara glared up at him and then down to her slate, writing, "He sold me into slavery." To her horror, tears filmed her eyes.

"He did. But that was a long time ago. I'll have the other guards keep a close eye on him but I don't think he'll be bothering you. And he'll only guard you during the day. Not at night. However, if you don't want him, I'll get someone else."

She stared at her slate for a long time. If she said no, would Emmerich be disappointed in her? And to have his good opinion spoke volumes about the person. Finally, she wiped it clean and in slow, careful letters, she wrote, "He may remain."

"Good." He paused, as if about to say something else, but changed his mind. "Come. Let's let them know what we decided."

More like what you decided, she thought, but she took his arm and let him lead the way.

That night, a figure was seen slipping into Haggard's

tent. The next morning, his one good eye sported a bruise and he favored his left side. No one asked any questions.

Clara began to hate traveling. She ached in places she didn't know existed. The general's fighting lessons left her exhausted before the day even begun. After a time, she began to stink of sweat, horse, and leather and there was no way for her to bathe properly. It would take too long to heat water and the thought of bathing in a stream near a camp full of men made her blush red all over. So, she settled for sponge baths in her tent.

A few days before arriving at Orlind, the morning lesson ended with Clara being tossed into the mud. She glared up at Emmerich as he offered her a hand. She was very tempted to smack it away. Grimacing, she took it, and he pulled her up.

"Apologies," he said. "I didn't mean to be so forceful."

And for the first time since the incident with Haggard, Clara looked at him more closely. Dark circles smudged the underside of his eyes, and his hair, usually neatly brushed, was tousled as if he had just rolled out of bed and shoved his hands through it. Forgetting they were in full view of everyone else in the practice area, she touched his arm, forming a look of concern with her eyes.

Emmerich hesitated for a moment before pulling away. "I'm fine. Only anxious."

Clara didn't believe him but nodded anyway.

He took a deep breath and let it out gustily. "Would you like to have dinner with me, tonight?"

She raised her brows and gestured toward the large dining tent where the people of rank gathered.

"Aye, I know. We eat together in the evenings but, what I mean is, would you like to dine with me in my tent? We haven't had a chance to really, ah, talk."

He looked so uncomfortable, Clara wished she could laugh. Smiling, she nodded her acceptance.

"Well, then." He saluted her with his sword and walked off, Clara watching him as he went.

Clara dressed with a little more care than usual before dinner. She put on a pale green undergown and a yellow tunic, belting it with a brown cord. The gown had small, trailing sleeves and a heart-shaped neckline, which the tunic matched. She honestly didn't know what to do with her hair, so simply plaited it as usual. She was just pulling on her slippers when one of the guards called, "Lady Clara, Sir Gavin to see you."

With a plunge of her heart, she heard again Gavin's desire to have her heart, something she had been avoiding thinking about since hearing it in that meeting. Snatching up her writing things, she went to the entrance and pushed aside the flap.

"Oh," said Gavin, when he saw her. "What's the occasion?"

Blushing, she wrote, "General Emmerich wants me to dine with him."

And, as if on cue, Emmerich came out of his tent and looked toward them. He had changed clothing as well. Instead of his travel-stained uniform, he wore all black, with the starburst embroidered on the left side of his chest. The color made him more severe, but Clara liked it.

"I see," said Gavin, his tone almost strangled. One of the guards snickered and he shot him an ugly look.

Clara started to write an apology but Gavin waved his hand. "No. I understand." He walked off just as Emmerich came to stand beside Clara.

"It's all right. He'll get over it," said Emmerich. He

offered his arm. "Ready?"

Slowly, Clara slipped her arm through his and let him lead her to his tent, all of five feet away.

Once inside, he said, "You look very lovely."

She smiled her thanks. A small table had been set with the night's meal. A candelabrum burned in the center and two place settings were out. Because it was Emmerich, being the general, all the items were fine gold, silver, and porcelain. How they transported the stuff without injury, Clara had no idea.

Emmerich gallantly held out her chair before sitting across from her. A servant came forward and poured wine.

"I thought," he said, "that is, ah. How are your guards working out? I'm sure they obey you."

She wrote, "They're fine. I don't like having Haggard, though."

"I know. But I trust him. I ask that you do the same." He shifted a little.

Anger bubbled up in Clara and she sipped wine to cover her grimace.

"If he really does bother you, I can get someone else. But, I would really like for you to give him a chance. Will you do that for me?"

Clara studied him for a long moment before nodding a grudging yes.

The meal advanced in awkwardness. If making conversation had ever been Emmerich's strong suit during his days at Court, he had lost the knack from lack of use. Somehow, they managed to spend an hour talking without actually saying anything.

As the dessert was set before her (blackberry jam cake), Clara's impatience got the best of her. Taking up her slate, she wrote, "Why did you want to have dinner with me like this?"

"Ah. Well. I wanted to see how you were doing."

She fiddled with her chalk as she considered her next words. "What did Gavin mean, about trying to have my heart?"

Emmerich grew still as he read her words. For a long moment, he said nothing, only ate some of his cake. Finally, he said, "He cares about you. He probably wants to eventually ask for your hand in marriage."

Clara set down her fork as she took that in.

Emmerich cleared his throat. "Would you accept him?"

Would she? Could she? Slowly, she shook her head. She barely knew him, really.

He nodded and looked away. "You should probably tell him that." He carried on eating.

After a moment, she picked up her fork.

After seeing Clara back to her tent, Emmerich retired to his own, feeling like a fool. While he felt both glad and selfish that Clara held no real interest in Gavin, he almost wished she had. Because then she would be less of a distraction. He was on campaign, for the Child's sake. He had no business becoming interested in a woman.

But that night, the old dream came back of blood and accusation and when he woke with a start, his first thought was of a name he hadn't dared to utter in a long time. And he knew that the only reason why he thought of it at all was because of Clara.

Chapter Fifteen

In the darkness before dawn, Clara sat up in her cot, her eyes adjusting to the gloom. A fire flickered outside her tent, throwing a little light through the small gaps around the flap; she could barely make out the shadowy outlines of her guards.

Garments sat neatly folded on a nearby trunk, laid out by a servant just last night, and she got out of bed to put them on. More and more people began moving outside her tent as she dressed and she distantly heard orders being snapped or shouted. If she hadn't wakened on her own, the noise would have roused her.

Once dressed and her hair braided, she scooped up her slate, chalk and a bag, and stepped outside. The two guards bowed to her. Pointedly ignoring Haggard, she gave a smile to the other guard, whose name she hadn't caught. The flap to Gavin's tent was folded open and she went inside.

Gavin stood in the center of his tent, two men buckling on a combination chainmail and plate armor that covered his chest, shoulder, arms, and legs. The links made soft chinking noises as the men tightened straps and adjusted. Gavin, his arms spread as if he were about to take flight, stood patiently under their hands.

Clara came to stand in his line of sight, forcing herself to smile at him. She had been awkward around him ever since that night with Emmerich, but it wasn't only that. Chainmail made her nervous. She scribbled a good morning on her slate and held it up for him to read. He responded with a tight-lipped smile.

Digging into the bag, she took out a spare handkerchief. The men, their work done, stepped back. Gavin swung his arms, testing for anything too tight or too slack. He nodded to the men and they left.

Stepping forward, she proffered the handkerchief. He took it. "Is this a favor?" he asked, a smile beginning to tug on his lips.

Shifting uncomfortably, she gestured for him to unfold it.

He did so, revealing a small, round medal with the image of a sword-bearing archangel. "Ah." Some of the humor went out of his face. "A good luck charm."

She shrugged, not wanting to give words to her fear

that he might not come back and therefore needed protection.

"I will bring it back to you."

She shook her head and pushed his hand toward himself, indicating he should keep it.

He refolded the cloth around the medal and tucked it behind the chainmail shirt. With a nod, he turned and began pulling on the spiked gloves lying on the table. "I think Emmerich wanted to speak to you. You should go to him now. I have to make sure the Captains are getting everyone lined up. We'll be quick-marching to Orlind. Hopefully, we won't be too ragged by the time we get there." He gave her another smile as he left.

Feeling vaguely as if she had done something wrong, she left the tent and crossed over to Emmerich's, trying to ignore the two guards following her. Emmerich's tent bustled like an overturned anthill. Several men stood around, taking turns lobbing requests and information at him while more men outfitted Emmerich in his armor. She felt lost in the clamor and watched as two men buckled on the general's chainmail and armor.

Gavin's had been elegant in its simplicity and showed obvious signs of repeated mending. Emmerich, however, was resplendent.

Highly polished, the pieces caught and held the light. Gauntlets with spiked knuckles and forearms were pulled onto his hands. Spiked greaves went onto his shins. Even the boots bore deadly steel toes. On his shoulders and arms went plate armor embossed with swirling details. His face grave and solemn during the process, he calmly issued orders, answered questions, and took in information with all the ease of an experienced lord planning a dinner party. But a look of calm fierceness filled his eyes and his body contained a violence controlled by cunning and discipline.

He had become death.

His eyes fell on her and Clara shrank back without thinking.

"My lord," said a servant.

The moment broke and he turned to take his sword from the servant. He buckled it around his waist with practiced ease. The well-worn and familiar belt and scabbard seemed to anchor him in the present and Clara saw some of the Emmerich she came to know over the last se'ennights. But the Death-Man still shimmered just beneath the surface.

Another servant held up his helmet, which he took, and

that seemed to be the signal for all the men to disperse, bowing. Clara stood to the side while they left.

"I see you rose early," he said after the flap closed behind the last one.

She nodded, holding her slate and unable to think of something to write. "Good morning" suddenly seemed inadequate.

"Have you seen Gavin?"

Another nod. She hurriedly wrote, "He's gone to check on the Captains." She held up the slate.

"Come closer. My eyesight isn't that good."

She did, stopping barely a foot away as memories of her time with the mail-wearing slavers skirted around her mind.

"Ah. Good."

She lowered the slate and eyed the armor again, trying to convince herself it was only Emmerich.

"I'm told the ladies find this equipage dashing. What do you think?"

She shook her head.

"You look afraid."

Clara shrugged, not wanting to talk about it.

He reached out and she tensed. Slowly, he cupped her chin and lifted her face. Her heart sped up as he looked at her.

"Never fear me," he said. He started to lean a little closer and her stomach tightened.

But he hesitated, the moment passed, and he carefully dropped his hand away. Hand shaking, Clara reached into her pocket and pulled out her other handkerchief. She held it out to him.

"What's this?" he asked, taking it. He unfolded it, revealing the same medal she gave to Gavin. "Oh. Where'd you get this?"

"The presbyter," she wrote.

"Thank you. It's been a long time since a lady gave me something before battle. Not since–" He shook his head, folded the cloth and tucked it behind his mail. "Do you mind helping me into this blasted helmet? I usually manage fine by myself but I don't mind a little help."

She hung her slate back around her neck and took the helmet from him. Spikes crawled in a line over the center and swirls were etched on the plates curving around to protect the face. He bent as she lifted the helm and pushed it onto his head. He reached up and helped. It fitted tightly. Standing so close to him, she felt awkward and clumsy but the stupid piece eventually slid into place. She buckled the chinstrap.

Only his eyes, nose, and mouth were visible. More chain mail hung to protect his neck. Something alien and strange looked down on her now and Clara had to remind herself that it was only Emmerich. Emmerich who swore he would never hurt her. One day she would believe it. Maybe.

"Clara," he said, taking her hands and holding them, "I've left orders for you and some men to go to a camp a day's ride from the castle, separate from here, in case a raiding party comes or something like that." He must have seen the mutiny rising in her eyes because he gently squeezed her hands. "I only want to protect you. Gavin will come fetch you when this is over."

The flap behind her rustled and he let go. She turned. Gavin, wearing a plain helm, came into the tent.

"All is ready, Emmerich," he said.

"Good." He walked out without sparing Clara another glance.

Gavin said, "Emmerich told you about the arrangement?"

She nodded.

"Good. Your things are being packed now." He walked

up to her. "Can I have a kiss for luck?"

Blushing, she gestured toward where he had put the handkerchief and medal.

"Aye, I have that, but I would rather have a kiss." He pulled the helm off.

Why didn't Emmerich ask? she suddenly wondered. Pushing the thought aside, she leaned forward to give him a quick peck on the cheek. At the last moment, he turned his head and stole it from her lips. When he pulled away, she wasn't sure whether to smile or hit him.

"Just in case," he said. "A man finds he doesn't want to leave behind any regrets, before he rides into battle." He cleared his throat. "You mean a lot to me, Clara."

Turning, he walked out and she trailed behind, stunned. The men were bustling around as they arranged in neat companies outside the circle of tents. Gavin jogged over to saddle up with them, yanking on his helm as he went. The sun was just beginning to crest the horizon, throwing pale, watery light over the tree line.

Clara joined the throng of those staying behind and watched as Emmerich and Gavin hauled themselves into their saddles. Gavin gave her another smile as silence descended upon the army. Finally, Emmerich raised his hand, horns blew, and the army marched out. Clara stood and watched until they were all gone.

The chosen hiding place was a secluded dell and the men pitched her tent on the lee side of a boulder. A knot of worry gnawed a hole in her stomach but when supper came, she forced herself to eat. It could have been poison for all she tasted it.

The apprehension only grew and Clara slept fitfully that night. She woke several times, body tensed and drenched in sweat, listening for something. What, she didn't know.

Finally, somewhere near dawn, she woke as waves of tingling sensations swept over her body. Sitting up in her pallet, she suddenly Saw, as if through a misted glass, Emmerich giving the finally orders to the captains. As the men turned away, he touched his chest, where the medal laid by his heart.

She saw the men lining up in their ranks. She saw the trumpeters raising their horns. It felt as if her body was only a bottle of thin glass and her spirit pressed against the stopper.

Half-blind to her surroundings, she stood and stumbled

out of the tent in her shift. The men breakfasting by the fire stared at her. She ignored them, dropping to her knees.

The flames of the fire leapt up and surrounded her, consuming her, becoming her. Heat filled and flushed her, breaking the bottle and she soared up and up. She came to stand in a sun's center. But that even faded and she rode pillion with Emmerich as he crossed the field on his black battle charger, her hands gripping his sides. The edges of his chainmail bit into her skin and she could hear his labored breath. She could smell his particular scent: horse and leather, sweat and musk. Men roared like the ocean and rushed like waves to slam against the opposing force meeting them outside the walls.

Only for the scene to turn on itself and the force was smaller, then it was bigger. Another shift and Emmerich rode a white horse. But didn't he mount a black just the other morning? She squeezed her eyes shut but she still Saw.

Beside her, Gavin went down with a cleaved skull only to stand and fight again. Emmerich died a thousand times in her arms (arrow in the eye, battle axe to the chest, dagger to the throat) and lived a thousand more. The wizard, from his tower, killed hundreds that lived again, and he died many times only to strike out once more. Blue tongues of magic rent the air. She was drenched in blood one moment only to be clean another.

Screaming soundlessly, she fell back, reaching for darkness, but even there she did not find solace. Even there she Saw.

"Sire," said Haggard, "there's something wrong." He scowled up at Gavin as he dismounted.

"What is it?"

"She won't come out." He gestured to the small tent. The other five guards stood around it with grim looks.

"What do you mean?"

"She started havin' a fit of some kind and when she came out of it, she went into her tent and won't come out. She hasn't eaten, either."

Frowning, he strode over to the tent and swept into it. Clara looked up at him from where she sat in a corner, in a soiled shift, hugging her knees against her chest. She studied him with wide eyes, which, after a moment, drifted away to something else. She rocked slowly back and forth.

"Sweetling?" He knelt in front of her. "Can you hear

me?" She squirmed away when he reached for her. "It's all right. I'm not going to hurt you." He eased closer to her, keeping his hands visible. "Let me hold you." He tried again. This time, she let him pull her to him. "You're trembling. It's all right." He made soothing noises as he hugged her close to his chest.

For several minutes they sat there as he stroked her hair and whispered sweet assurances. Slowly, the tremors eased from her body, though her eyes still stared vacantly. Continuing to whisper to her reassuringly, he stood and carried her outside.

"Take down the campsite," he directed the men.

"My lord." Evan, the tallest of the bodyguards, approached him. "There's still a bit of breakfast by the fire."

"Thank you."

He sat her next to the fire and went about trying to get her to eat from the porridge pot. She wouldn't have it, though, and he let them throw it into the woods.

Emmerich looked up from his maps as Gavin came in. "A messenger rode up not too long after you left. Marduk is sending forces to help defend Candor. Hopefully, once Asher arrives, we'll be strong enough to take the city regardless of the force Marduk sends." He stretched gingerly, wincing at bruised ribs. "How does our little Seer like her new apartments?"

"Couldn't tell you." He poured a goblet of wine and took a large swallow.

"What's the matter?"

"Clara's in a state of some sort. Looks like we didn't keep her far enough away from the battle."

"What is she doing? Or not doing?"

He took another swallow. "I think you better see." He set the goblet down, turned on his heel, and walked quickly out with Emmerich on his heels to the late Baroness' apartments. They took the stairs two at a time.

The sitting room sat empty. He heard soft footsteps and softer humming in the large bedchamber, whose door hung ajar. Both men hesitated.

"Clara?" Emmerich called, brushing past Gavin.

He pushed open the door as he stepped inside. She stood, wavering a little in the corner, with Gavin's cloak draped over her shoulders as she stared at the corner. He started when he realized the humming came from her: a tuneless melody that barely came above a whisper.

"Clara?" he said, stepping toward her.

She turned and, ignoring him, walked past him to a tapestry of ladies in a garden. With a tentative hand, she traced the woven threads. The hum became more solemn and soft.

He stepped up behind her and laid a hand on her shoulder. She twisted away violently, her mouth open in a silent scream. She fell to the ground and covered her head with shaking hands.

"You're all right," he said, kneeling by her. "You're all right. I'm not going to hurt you." He pulled her arms away from her head. "Clara, I would never, ever hurt you."

Her eyes, though, looked beyond him, to something else. She began to rock back and forth, her hands trembling and her fingers working uselessly as she made a soft wailing sound. A chill went through him.

He slapped her, knocking her to the floor with a solid thud.

"Emmerich!" Gavin cried. He took a few steps forward but Emmerich stopped him with a raised hand.

Her eyes snapped open and focused on them, filling with recognition. She began to tremble and tears spilled over her cheeks.

He awkwardly gathered her into his arms, letting her cry. Dry sobs wracked her body, driving Emmerich half-mad. He hated when women cried.

When the sobbing slowed, he lifted her and laid her onto the bed. He asked, "Can you tell us what happened?"

She hesitated, and then nodded.

"Where is her slate, Gav?"

It lay in a corner. On it she had drawn a circle containing sigils. Gavin held it up for Emmerich to see, who only shrugged and looked to Clara. She shrugged and gestured with her hands, as if to say she had no explanation. Gavin wiped the slate clean with his handkerchief before handing it to her.

She wrote slowly, pausing often as if to consider the best words. After a time, she gave it to Emmerich, who read aloud, "It was like I forgot myself. In a single moment, I saw all of the horrible things that could have happened in the battle. You dead. Gavin dead. So many soldiers dying in different ways. Then, I wandered in a fog with people calling from a far distance. I couldn't see where I was or to where I was going. And then, there was shouting, and it was over. Where am I?"

Gavin said, "You're in the apartments of the former Baroness of Orlind."

"Aye," Emmerich said. "I, uh, they will be a nice place for you to stay. And we will be staying here for a time." He related what he told Gavin.

She slumped back against the pillows, the slate slipping from her fingers onto the bed. Her face was ashen with fatigue.

"You were humming earlier," Gavin said.

Clara looked at them in surprise, cautiously pointing at herself.

"Aye. We both heard you. Can you talk now?"

The question turned her face into a mask and she slowly shook her head.

After a long moment, Emmerich said, "Are you hungry?"

She nodded.

Gavin found the bell pull and while they waited for the servant to appear, Clara's eyes drooped closed and she slipped away into sleep. Gavin tugged on Emmerich's sleeve, nodding toward the sitting room. They went in together, Emmerich closing the door behind them. A servant came through the chamber door and Emmerich instructed him to bring some food for the lady.

After the servant had gone, Gavin said, "You shouldn't have done that."

"Shouldn't have done what?"

"You shouldn't have struck her."

Emmerich scowled. "I guess I should have just left her there to rock herself back and forth until Doomsday, then."

"I would have found her help. She's been horse shit on the bottom of everyone's shoe and now you treat her like she's some battle-shocked soldier who just needs a swift slap across the face? Not like she's a person, a woman, with needs and feelings?"

"The Healer would have done the same thing. I did what I knew needed to be done."

"Oh, because what you decide is always best."

Emmerich took a quick step back, as if struck. "There's something more going on here than your infatuation."

"I'm not infatuated." He scowled. "I'm not the one who invited her to a private dinner in my tent, after all."

He blinked, having not quite expected that. "What's going on, Gavin? You were fine when you left for Dwervinton. What happened there?"

"What happened? What happened?" His voice rose to a

pitch and Emmerich waved at him to keep it down, glancing over at the bedchamber door. Gavin jammed his fists over his hips and lowered his voice. "You know what's wrong with me? I'm sick of this whole damn war. Those men died, Emmerich, and I knew it was going to happen all along."

"Well, that's disheartening, as this war has hardly started. Aside from battles, Gav, what–"

"You know damn well what I'm talking about. Those spy missions I conducted for you, to learn what the Brethren was doing. Those assassinations. The spreading of your propaganda. And then—that, that lie."

"And then you met her. And now you don't want a part of it because you want to take her to some neat little hiding spot, cower in a dark corner, and hope everything ends soon and well."

"It's not like that. We aren't fighting cleanly, Emmerich."

"Cleanly? Cleanly? War is not clean. You do what you have to do to get the job done."

"At the expense of being human?"

"I did what I felt was best for my men."

"Really? By hiding the truth?"

"When has the truth ever helped anyone?"

"I guess Monica taught you that one."

Emmerich grabbed Gavin, pinning him against the wall, his arm shoved against his throat. "Never mention her name in my presence," he hissed.

Gavin glared at him, the anger coming off him like waves of heat. Emmerich stared back for a long moment before letting him go and stepping back.

Silence stretched between them. Distantly, birds twittered. Emmerich's right hand twitched, his whole arm suddenly remembering the feel of dagger parting soft flesh.

"I need you to check the rations," he said huskily.

"Can't your stewards do that for you?"

"Aye. But you also need to clear your head."

Gavin snorted before turning on his heel and striding out.

Chapter Sixteen

Gavin's and Emmerich's sightless eyes stared into her own, their blood soaking the ground, and Clara tried so hard to scream. If she screamed or called their names, everything would be all right. They would wake up. Emmerich would rib Gavin over something and Gavin would ignore him and everything would be all right.

But she couldn't make a sound. It felt as if a horse stood on her chest and all the while, the eyes stared and stared.

Clara jerked upright in her bed, panting. Light streamed through the tall arrow slits of her room. Every muscle in her body ached and fatigue sat in a snarled bundle of pain just behind her forehead. Slowly, she eased herself out of bed and rubbed her eyes as if she could rub away the images of her nightmare.

It was so late in the day. Why hadn't anyone woken her? And then she remembered Emmerich's order that she spend today in rest. Well, the day wasn't going to be spent in bed.

Opening the wardrobe, she sifted through the clothing hanging there. Much of it was her own garments brought from Dwervinton. A few pieces, however, she did not recognize. Had they belonged to the baroness?

It struck her, suddenly, that she spent last night in a dead woman's bed and the thought made her skin crawl. It seemed like a horrible sort of invasion. What had the baroness been like? Kind? Or like Lady Maria, all caprice and contrariness?

Pushing aside the thoughts, she took out an unfamiliar midnight blue gown, in the Southern style, that is, all one piece with a full skirt. The morning light caught the small silver stars embroidered on the hem, collar, and cuffs. She thought it rather pretty, though she couldn't really picture herself wearing it. Holding it up against her, excess material pooled at her feet. The baroness had been at least three inches taller than her. Laying it aside to hem later, she reached for the familiar gowns and selected a dove grey gown with a pale blue tunic. She took a dark blue belt from a drawer.

Setting these beside the blue gown, Clara took her time washing up and fixing her hair before pulling on the clothing. She was tying on her slippers when she heard someone come into the sitting room. Hastily grabbing her slate and chalk bag, she left her room, only to freeze in her tracks.

Haggard stood beside the breakfast table on which laid a tray of food.

"I brought you some breakfast," he said. "Thought you might be up by now."

She watched him carefully, body tense as she waited for any sudden movements.

"I'm glad you're better. Gave us quite a scare yesterday." He smiled weakly, showing he was missing an eyetooth.

She nodded a thank you but made no move to take up her slate or come closer.

He started to walk toward her but stopped when she took a step back closer to her bedchamber.

Haggard held up his hands and said, "I'm not going to hurt you, lass. I'm... I'm sorry for what I did. But, it seemed like the best thing at the time. And now look where you are now, in this place, with fine clothes!"

Her hands balled into fists as tears blurred her vision. She longed to make him feel what she had felt over the years—the pain, the cold, the hunger, the loneliness and despair. She wished she could cram it all down his throat. She reached up and rubbed away the tears. When her vision cleared, she jerked back. Haggard had come closer, standing near enough to touch her.

"Easy, Clara," he said. "I want to... I can't go to the other children I've helped to sell but I can do this for you and maybe it'll make up for the others."

He drew his sword and for a brief moment, Clara wondered wildly if she would be able to make it to the main door or if she could alert her guards someway. But then he knelt and turned the sword to offer her the hilt.

"Take it," he said.

She slowly reached out and took the sword, raising her eyebrows at the weight. It weighed no more than a small basket of apples or a large tin of sugar.

"My lady," he said, "my sword is yours. My life is yours. Do with them what you will." And he bowed his head, exposing the back of his neck.

Clara's pulse quickened as the moment stretched in silence. She could kill him, if she wanted. Surely Emmerich and Gavin would know this ceremony, ritual, or whatever it was. They wouldn't blame her. A voice in her mind hissed,

"You let Dwervin die. Would this be so much harder? Just let the blade fall. What did Emmerich say one day? It doesn't take that much strength to kill a man."

She wanted to do it. The fire of anger roared through her. She could hear the blood pounding in her ears. But then she pictured their faces when they saw what she had done, how disappointed they would be in her for killing a man offering her his life. It was like water on the fire and she suddenly felt cold and empty.

With her free hand, she tapped him on the shoulder. When he looked up, she offered the sword back to him as he had offered it to her. Haggard stood and took it, sheathing it.

"This means I'll do anything to protect you," he explained. "Just say the word, and I'll even kill for you, my lady." He bowed. "I'll leave you to your breakfast."

And he left.

Gavin rubbed his left shoulder. "Good match," he said.

"Aye," Ivan said, "but you seemed a little distracted, if you don't mind my saying, my lord."

"A lot on my mind." With a wave, he left the weapons

master to have at his next victim—that is, sparring partner.

He entered the main hall of the castle. Sighting the maid that attended Clara's rooms, he said, "Hello, you there." The maid stopped and waited for him to approach.

She curtsied. "Aye, my lord?"

"Do you know if the lady is awake?"

"I don't, my lord. One of her guards took her breakfast and I haven't been called to her rooms."

"When was this? The breakfast."

"One or two candle marks ago, my lord."

"Ah. All right." He nodded to her and continued on his way.

After stopping by his rooms to wash and change, he went to Clara's. Two guards, one of which was Haggard, stood on either side of her door.

"Which one of you brought her breakfast?" he asked.

"I did, my lord," said Haggard.

Gavin frowned. "The Lord General gave you strict orders not to address her."

"Only wanted to make peace, my lord."

"Did you?"

"I think so, my lord."

Gavin found this a little hard to believe. He entered the

sitting room. It sat empty but the door leading to the balcony stood open. Crossing the room, he went out onto the balcony. Clara sat in a chair, hemming a blue gown. She made to stand but he waved a hand.

"Please, don't," he said. "You need your rest."

She shrugged and went back to her work.

"That must be one of the baroness'. Emmerich and I thought you would like some of her clothes. I thought that color would look especially good on you."

Picking up her slate, she wrote, "Thank you."

"You're welcome." He sat in the other chair and watched her for a few moments. "You look quite beautiful in the sunlight."

She gave him a slight smile.

He shifted a little and said, "Haggard said he spoke to you. I hope he didn't bother you."

Clara set her work down again and, picking up her slate, wrote out a reply: "He did this ceremony where he gave me his sword and said that his life was mine, to make up for what he had done."

He raised his eyebrows. "That's very serious. That means you could ask him to do anything, and he would be obligated to do it." Gavin paused, thinking about that. "He must be truly sorry."

Clara nodded, her eyes filled with thoughtfulness, and she picked up her work again.

The warmth of the sun, a lack of sleep, and the sparring session eventually took their toll and Gavin drifted to sleep, his head lolling onto his chest.

He walked down a wide Great Hall. Wind pounded on the stones outside like a giant's fists, sending tremors through the floor. Torches lit the hall but the shadows in the corners moved and shifted.

A hand touched his shoulder.

Yelling, he whirled. Men, women, children, presbyters in cassocks, and soldiers in armor stood behind him, filling the once-empty hall. The stench of decay rolled off them and he gagged. Open sores on their faces, necks, and arms oozed puss and blood.

"Why?" whispered their voices. "Why?"

The hand shook him again and he turned, lifting his hands to defend himself–

And he was on the balcony, Clara standing in front of him and watching him with wide, fearful eyes. She reached for her slate but he said, "I'm fine. I'm fine."

He stood and turned away from her, looking out over

the gardens. Servants tended the neat, square beds. He felt a soft touch on his shoulder. Looking down, he reached up to cover Clara's hand with his.

"There are things I have done that still haunt me, I'm afraid," he said. Turning, he faced her, taking both her hands between his. "Clara, there is something I must know. Did you let Dwervin die?"

She jerked her hands away and stepped back, staring at him with an unreadable expression.

"I wouldn't judge you, if you did. We've all had to make...hard decisions. I wish I could just walk away from all this, but I can't."

She nodded and looked down.

He cupped her face in his and lifted it so he could look in her eyes, which were full of fear and anguish. For him, perhaps? "When this is over," he said, "I do not want to see you spirited away into Emmerich's court. You are the only thing that's making any of this bearable, sweetling. I hate to see you bound up in this, but I don't think we have a choice. Maybe you see the battles as you do because your fate is entangled with ours, too much so to just sever.

"I love you, Clara. Please say you will be mine always."

Her mouth opened, making a little "o" of surprise. To

Gavin, time seemed to stop as he waited.

"Lord Gavin?"

Looking up, he saw Haggard standing just inside the parlor. Scowling, he asked, "What is it?"

"The Lord General wishes to see you in the audience chamber."

He nodded, sighing, and the guard saluted before retreating. Gavin looked back down at Clara. "I'll be back, my love. You can give me your answer then."

Gavin's heart didn't stop pounding until he reached the hall leading to the audience chamber. He hadn't meant to propose to Clara. The moment had just felt right. As soon as Emmerich was done with him, he would race back upstairs to hear her answer.

She'll say yes, he reassured himself. *Even though she's been spending time with Emmerich, she formed a bond with me first. Surely she feels it, too.*

The captains were assembled in the chamber when he entered, clustered around Emmerich, who stood in front of the baroness' chair with a map in his hands.

"Gavin," he said, "I have a mission for you."

He felt his heart drop a little as he came to stand before Emmerich. "Aye?"

"I need eyes inside of Candor."

"What about our spy?"

"He fled. Apparently, everyone is getting out of there right now and he's found reason to do the same." He rolled up the map. "I want you to leave as soon as possible."

The thought of leaving Clara made him sick to his stomach. He didn't fully trust Haggard and the memory of Emmerich striking her still made his blood run cold.

"Gavin?"

"I need to speak with you in private."

Emmerich frowned but nodded. The captains left, glancing at them over their shoulders.

Once the door closed, Gavin said, "Let me take Clara with me."

Astonishment filled Emmerich's face. "You must be joking. You know I can't do that."

"Any visions she has, I'll report to you."

"She's safer here."

"I can protect her."

"Gavin, this is madness."

"I've asked her to marry me."

His friend blinked. "What?"

"I've asked her to marry me."

For a moment, he didn't respond. "And she's accepted you."

"Not yet. Your message interrupted us."

Emmerich rolled up the map and set it on a table. "Do you think she'll say yes?"

"I do. We've been spending a lot of time together."

"So have she and I, but you don't see me making marriage proposals."

"I love her, Emmerich."

"Does she love you?"

"What does it matter to you?"

Emmerich turned away, rubbing his jaw. "It's a fair question. She may accept you just out of gratitude."

"It's no concern of yours."

He looked back at him. "You're my friend, Gavin. Of course it's my concern."

Gavin squared his shoulders. "I'm taking her with me."

He stared at him a long moment. "If she accepts you, then many blessings, but I cannot let you take her."

"And if she wants to go?" He braced himself, ready for a fight.

"Well, then, I can hardly stop her, but I would want to talk to her about it first."

"So you can persuade her as you did when talking with her about coming with us at all?"

Emmerich ignored the jab. "Go. Learn her answer. If you wish to wed before you leave, we'll make the arrangements. I'm sure there's a presbyter or two wandering around here somewhere."

"Emmerich—"

"Go, Gavin. You're wasting the daylight."

Marduk signed the document with a flourish and handed it to the courtier. "Anything else?" he asked, looking around. The other courtiers and statesmen nodded and muttered negatives.

"Then I think we'll call it a day," he said. "You all may go."

The men and women bowed and left until only a man robed in red, wearing the emerald belt of the Brethren, remained.

"You have a report, I hope?" Marduk asked, standing.

"Brellin is dead, your Majesty."

He sighed. "What a pity." He sat in silence for a moment, staring into nothing. "He was the only man who could beat me at chess, you know. Well, I'm sure others could, too, but he was the only one with the guts to do it. And what a sense of humor and honor. He'll be greatly missed. Have you informed his wife?"

"I have, your Majesty. She's arranging a memorial service. She wishes for you to attend."

"Of course." He poured himself a goblet of wine. "Care for a drink?"

"Thank you, your Majesty."

Marduk gestured for him to help himself and he turned to admire the cityscape. The wizard joined him presently, goblet in hand.

Marduk raised his cup. "To fallen comrades, Erin."

"To fallen comrades."

They drank in silence for a moment. Erin said, "Do you know if he completed the spell, your Majesty?"

"I have every confidence he did, but I will be testing it tonight."

"And…if he didn't?"

"Our spy has proved to be most helpful, so it won't be the end of the world if it doesn't." Marduk took a deep breath. "We live in exhilarating times."

"Yes, your Majesty."

Chapter Seventeen

Clara dropped back into her chair, feeling numb.

Gavin loved her? He wanted to marry her? Her heartbeat gained speed and she balled the dress in both hands.

Did she love him? Did she want to spend the rest of her life with him?

She stared out over the railing of the balcony, imagining a life with Gavin, perhaps even having children, which she couldn't scold or tease or soothe. She couldn't cry out for help if Gavin hurt himself in the field or on horseback. She couldn't look across the table and ask him about his day. She looked at the slate on the table beside her, wanting to smash the thing into a million pieces. A poor substitute it was for a voice.

"Clara?"

She jerked at the soft voice and turned, seeing Gavin standing in the doorway. Standing, she wondered for how long she had been daydreaming.

He came to stand in front of her. "Emmerich is sending me to Candor City. He's forbidden me to take you with me but I'm willing to tempt his wrath. Will you come? As my wife?"

Clara's heart broke as she stared into his hopeful, grey-green eyes. Slowly, she shook her head.

He gripped her shoulders. "You don't have to stay for him. We can send your messages by way of Portent, my falcon. You don't have to stay."

She shook her head and pulled out of his hold.

Making no move to follow, he let his hands drop to his sides. "Don't you love me?"

Clara clenched her eyes shut, shook her head, feeling the hot tears sting her cheeks.

"Is it him?" Gavin's voice was husky and low. "Is it!"

Opening her eyes, she furrowed her brows and reached for her slate.

Gavin snatched the slate away, and, grabbing her, pushed her until he had her pinned against the balcony railing. "Is it Emmerich? Is he the one you love?"

Terrified, her mouth opened and closed uselessly. Why did she have to love someone else? Couldn't it just be that she didn't love him?

After a long moment, he let her go. Gavin turned away from her, returning the slate to its place on the table, and reached into his belt pouch. With a slow flick of his wrist he dropped a folded handkerchief onto the slate before leaving her shaking on the balcony.

She waited until the door to her chambers closed behind him before she went to the table. Unfolding the handkerchief revealed the medal she had given him before the battle. Tears slid down her face as she dropped into her chair.

Emmerich stared out the window of the audience chamber and didn't move when he heard the door open behind him.

"Well?" he said. "Did she accept?"

"My lord?"

Turning, he was surprised to find a servant standing the doorway. "Oh. Nothing. What is it?"

"Lord Gavin has left."

"What?"

"He ordered for his horse to be saddled and rations to be brought before leaving along the south road."

"Did he have anyone with him?"

"No, my lord."

"Ah, thank you."

"Does my lord require anything?"

"No."

The servant bowed before stepping out, leaving Emmerich alone with his thoughts.

That evening, Clara did not come down for the evening meal, though Emmerich had sent a servant to call her down. He spoke little during the meal and his men knew his mood well enough to not address him.

After the meal, he went to his chambers, where he sat by the fire and brooded.

She told him no, he thought. Because she didn't love him? Because she felt it important to stay here? Or had she said yes and they were going to wait for his return? And why hadn't she come down?

Why did he even care? Hell's bells, he should be concentrating on the war, not a woman.

Throwing himself out of the chair, he paced the room for a time. Finally, unable to help himself, he turned and left. He would talk to her about it. Surely there wouldn't be anything untoward about that.

Clara did not touch the plate of food given her but left it on the table. Tired, she undressed and went to bed, sleep coming upon her quickly.

She dreamed of a meadow edged in a thick fog, the grasses and flowers at her feet wet from heavy dew. Birds sang in the hidden forest.

Clara…

She turned, trying to find the source of the voice.

Clara…

It was a man. His voice was soothing and calm. A desperate desire to find him gripped her.

Clara.

With an easy stride, she walked into the fog in search of the source of the voice.

Emmerich entered the sitting room without knocking, so deep was he in his thoughts. He stopped the moment he realized it was dark in the room with only the banked fire throwing a feeble light. He was just about to turn around when he heard the bedchamber door unlatching.

"Clara?" he called. "I didn't mean to disturb you. I just…" The words died in his throat as he watched Clara, dressed only in a white shift, walk out of the bedroom toward him. As she drew closer, he saw her eyes were rolled into the back of her head.

"Clara?" Was this a new sort of vision? He shivered as he stared at the whites of her eyes. "Clara, can you hear me?"

He reached out to touch her shoulder as she started to pass him but she slapped him away.

"Wait." This time he grabbed her arm and pulled her away from the door.

Clara hissed at him, driving a fist into his gut. Grunting, Emmerich wrapped both arms around her and wrestled her to the floor. She kicked and clawed at him, making small grunting noises. He gritted his teeth as he tried to hold her down.

"Guards!" he cried.

The two guards burst into the room, swords drawn, their faces going blank with surprise at seeing Emmerich trying to hold Clara down.

"Get some rope," he gasped. "One of you, grab her legs."

Just as one guard knelt down by her feet while the other ran out of the room, she went limp.

"Clara," called Emmerich, reaching out to touch her neck, letting out a sigh of relief when he felt her pulse beating beneath his hand.

Her eyes opened and she frowned when she saw him. Looking around, her face crumbled in confusion.

"It's all right. You were sleepwalking."

She sat up and he helped her stand. Clara looked down and, seeing she wore only a shift, wrapped her arms around herself.

"You can go, Norne," Emmerich said. "I think the lady will be all right now."

Norne saluted and left, closing the door firmly behind him.

"Are you all right?" he asked.

She nodded, though she didn't look very certain.

"Come. Sit down."

He gently took her by the arm and guided her to the couch. Emmerich was glad it was so dark in the room. The sight of her, vacant and fighting him, rattled him almost as badly as the first time. And there was something different about this second time, other than her eyes. Last time, she seemed lost. This time, she seemed intent on going somewhere.

"Where's your slate?" he asked once he got her seated.

She pointed to her room. On his way to the door, he pulled the bell pull for a servant. Clara's bedroom looked much tidier than his and her own special scent of lavender and soap filled his nose. He took a deep breath, appreciating it despite himself. The slate lay on the bedside table and, on his way out, he scooped up a robe left lying over the back of a chair.

A grateful smile lit up Clara's face when he handed her the robe and she was just belting it when the servant came in.

"Two goblets of mulled wine," he directed.

The servant bowed and left. Emmerich took the tinderbox and flint from the mantle and began lighting lamps around the room. Once that was done, and he couldn't honestly think of anything else, he sat in an armchair beside Clara's spot on the couch.

"We'll just wait on the wine," he said.

She nodded and they lapsed into silence. Emmerich

looked at her from the corner of his eye. Clara sat straight and tall, the slate on her lap and her hands folded over it. Her eyes were downcast and her hair, usually carefully braided, fell in silky waves down her shoulders. She looked tired, drawn, and absolutely beautiful.

He made himself look away, suddenly thinking of another dark-haired beauty.

Monica. When would she stop haunting him?

They sat in silence until the servant reappeared with a tray bearing the two goblets. He set them on the table and asked, "Is there anything else, my lord?"

"No."

The servant bowed and left. Emmerich handed Clara a goblet. "Drink some of that and then tell me what happened, if you can."

She took a slow sip and some of the color went back into her face. Her eyes flicked up to him and he suddenly noticed redness around them, as if she had been crying before going to bed. He looked away to pick up his own goblet. They drank in silence for a time.

Finally, he couldn't stand it anymore and said, "Gavin told me about his proposal. I take it you didn't accept him?" He looked at her.

Clara shook her head.

"Don't be hard on yourself. He'll get over it." He cleared his throat. "You may even change your mind."

She lowered her eyes and didn't answer.

"Clara, can you tell me what happened?"

Setting the goblet back onto the tray, she took up her slate and wrote on it for a few moments before handing it to him. It simply read, "I was dreaming that I was looking for someone."

"Anything more?"

She shook her head.

"Clara, please think—"

She abruptly stood and went to the closed balcony door, looking out its small, barred window.

Something within Emmerich broke. He strode up to her and turned her around. She looked up at him with solemn, sad eyes.

"I only want to protect you," he said. "I only want to help you. Dammit, if there is something happening to you, you will tell me, won't you?"

She nodded, looking down.

"I want to post more guards, in case you sleepwalk again."

She nodded again.

"Look at me. Please."

She raised her eyes.

"Clara." He cupped her chin in his hand. "Do you trust me?"

The question seemed to surprise her and she nodded adamantly.

"Good." He dropped his hand away, though the feel of her skin still pressed against it like a memory. "I'll let you rest." He forced a cocky grin. "Be dressed and ready for practice tomorrow morning."

And he left before he gave into the urge to kiss her.

☐

Chapter Eighteen

The next morning, Gavin saddled his horse, letting his hands do the work for him.

She had said no.

Why? He had done so much for her.

Was it for him? Was she in love with Emmerich?

Emmerich, the bastard who let whole villages die. Emmerich, the man who murdered the Princess. Emmerich, who sent Gavin on assassination missions to other lords when they were first building their army.

An image of Clara in Emmerich's arms flashed through his mind and he had to stop what he was doing, taking deep breaths against the tide of anger welling within him. He had to focus on the mission.

But, for all Gavin knew, the mission was just a ruse for Emmerich to get closer to Clara.

He shook his head. No, now he was being ridiculous. Emmerich may have tried to move in on Clara, but Gavin knew him well enough to know he wouldn't go through with anything. Though he killed her in the end, he had loved Monica. That wasn't going to make moving onto another girl easy. Gavin remembered Emmerich inviting Clara to his tent for dinner. Besides, it was obvious his good friend wouldn't wait for him to be out of sight.

No, he had to finish the mission. The sooner they took Candor, the sooner he could return to Clara.

And set about changing her mind.

Three days after their strange conversation, Clara was awakened by a young woman with dark red hair and pale blue eyes.

"Good morning, my lady," she said as Clara sat up. "My name is Cassie. I'm your new lady's maid."

Lady's maid? Clara blinked, suddenly remembering Emmerich making mention of that the previous night.

"I can read, my lady, so I should be able to help you in whatever you need."

Clara nodded and gestured toward the clothes laying on a nearby chair.

"Oh, I'll leave you to get ready for your practice session." Cassie curtsied and walked out.

Once the door closed, Clara scuttled out of the bed and, in a flurry of cloth, dressed. When she entered the sitting area, Cassie was laying out breakfast things. She stepped back and gestured at the table with a smile.

Clara nodded and sat. While she ate, Cassie moved about the room with ease, straightening a pile of books Clara had started reading through, rearranging pillows on the couch, and other little things Clara hadn't even noticed were out of order.

When she finished her meal and stood, Cassie said, "Are you ready to go down, then, my lady?"

Clara nodded and, strapping on her practice sword, headed out. Looking over her shoulder, she saw not only Cassie but her (now) four guards following. She turned away with a frustrated sigh, feeling like the whole stupid castle was starting to follow her around.

Down in the practice yard, Emmerich watched her approach with a barely-concealed amused look.

"I see you met Cassie," he said. "Do you like her?"

Clara nodded curtly. Unable to help herself, she took up her slate and wrote, "I can take care of myself."

Some of the humor went out of his face. "I know. But your rank demands it. And it's just in case."

They hadn't really talked about her strange episode. Clara didn't like to think about it. She had the strangest feeling, ever since, that there was something not quite right. Sometimes, she found herself scanning a room as if looking for someone, though she didn't know for whom she searched. It deeply unsettled her.

"I have something for you," he said, bringing her attention back to the present. "You've made so much progress over the se'ennights, I thought you earned it." He turned and picked up a sheathed sword leaning against the fence. "Take off your practice sword."

She did and he took it from her, dropping it in the dust at their feet. Stepping forward, he deftly buckled the new sword around her waist. She raised her eyebrows at the weight. It was lighter than Haggard's sword.

"Draw it," he said, stepping back.

Clara did, and admired the etching on the blade: twin ivy vines winding around each other along the length. The pommel was a small dark blue stone and the grip wrapped in black leather. The cross guard was etched with more ivy leaves.

"About time you had your own sword, I think," said Emmerich, a strange look on his face. "And, this to match." He held out a sheathed dagger.

Sheathing the sword, she took the dagger and drew it, admiring the identical pattern.

"You can wear it on your waist, or in your boot. I would suggest your waist."

She nodded, feeling gratitude well up in her.

"Well, come on. Today we're doing archery." He turned and walked away before she had the chance to write a thank you on her slate. After fumbling with her belt to slide on the dagger, she jogged after Emmerich to the practice range.

Emmerich began by showing her the different parts of the bow and arrow, filling her mind with archery terms. He was just beginning to notch an arrow when a messenger ran up to them in the field.

"My lord," said the boy, bowing low. "A message for you." He held out a rolled missive.

Emmerich unrolled it and Clara stepped close to read it around his shoulder. It was from the mysterious Captain Asher she had been hearing about. It read:

All is well. Will be arriving in a few se'ennights' time. Have amassed enough men for another company.

Emmerich grunted and nodded at the messenger, who

left.

Clara touched Emmerich's arm and, when he turned to her, wrote, "When he gets here, we will march onto Candor?"

"Aye."

"And will you hide me away again?"

"Clara, you can't ride into battle. Not with your condition. And you sure as hell can't go ahead to join Gavin."

The fierceness of that last statement surprised her and she did not try to continue the conversation during the remainder of the lesson.

Chapter Nineteen

A se'ennight after leaving Orlind Castle, Gavin waited in the long line streaming into Candor City. Castle Newfound reared from a hill in its center, its tall spires piercing the air.

The largest walled city in the Northern fiefdoms, and their touted "capital", it sat on an island where the River Braddock, coming down from the icy mountains of the far North, split into River Lance (which turned west on into the Plains) and River Lyn Tone (which traveled south, through Bertrand, easing east and on into the ocean). From the rivers sprang numerous tributaries and smaller rivers that watered the fertile swampland of the Far South.

Every bit of trade going south to Bertrand went through Candor. Every bit of trade coming up from Bertrand went through Candor. It sat like a giant purse on a rich man's desk, begging to be stolen.

Many had tried. The vast majority of invaders had failed. So, quite naturally, while some residents (including the spy) had left, many a merchant were streaming into Candor to avoid the–

"Damn rebels," muttered the mercenary standing in front of Gavin.

"You're just sore you ain't lying warm with Aimee," replied his companion.

"She could have come."

"But she didn't." His friend looked over at him. "I'm sure she's not warming someone else."

The first mercenary growled a low curse.

"It'll go right over us," continued the friend. "No one has been able to take this place."

"They took Orlind."

"Orlind was a pile of rubble."

"I heard the Baroness had a sorcerer."

"And I heard their leader is a two-headed monster, but that don't mean I believe it."

"Well, whichever, if it weren't for him, our employer wouldn't be making us stand in this bloody long line."

His friend sighed. "Can't really argue with that."

They were silent for a while. Thunder rumbled in the distance, eliciting groans all around. Gavin gratefully urged his horse forward a few dozen steps with the line as one more caravan was let through the main gate.

The first mercenary spoke up again. "Though, I can't help but cheer him on."

"Oh?" The second turned to look at his friend.

"Aye." He looked at his friend. "You've heard the stories coming out of Bertrand. If half of them are true—"

"Probably aren't."

"But if they are, I may not be so quick to draw on any of his soldiers if they come knocking on the front gate."

"Our employer would like to know that."

The first mercenary's shoulders tensed. "And will he?"

His friend smiled. "Ah, hell, no, Bert. I'm right there with you."

"Damn straight."

The crowds within Candor vibrated with more energy than ever. There seemed to be more of everything since Gavin's last visit. More vendors lined the narrow street. More people shouted at the top of their lungs to be heard by their companions. More animals brayed, neighed, whinnied, and defecated. Gavin felt like he was trapped in a tiny room with a hundred unwashed bodies all yelling at the same time.

He finally pushed his way toward the residential eastern side of the city. Here, where guards in blue livery patrolled, things were calmer than the streets close to the city's center and the castle. Houses hid behind walls and carefully sculpted trees and hedges. A few dogs barked but otherwise, it remained quiet. And deserted. Not even children played in the streets.

After a few blocks, he approached a modest gate. Dismounting, he pulled on the clapper. A few moments later, an older man wearing purple and grey approached.

"Can I help you?" he asked.

"Aye," Gavin replied. "I'm here to see Master Elbert Wigginson."

"And you are?"

"Terrence of Brill."

"I shall tell him you're here." He turned on his heel and walked back up the path into the house.

Gavin waited, tapping his foot on the flagstone. A pair of guards strolled down the sidewalk on the other side of the street. He looked casually away. Finally, the servant returned and, opening the gate, bowed him in.

"If you will follow me, sir," he said, locking the gate

and leading him to the house, where Gavin hitched his horse at a post before going inside.

Decorated in the Southern style, rich red wood paneled the walls, and tables held artfully arranged trinkets. On the walls hung religious paintings and portraits of merchants and their wives. The servant led Gavin down the hall to the study.

He opened the door, stepped in, and said, "Terrence of Brill, sir."

"Thank you, Lawrence. That will be all." A stocky man with grey hair stood from behind his desk.

Gavin came in and the servant took Gavin's bag and left, closing the door behind him. The two men studied each other for a moment before Elbert broke into a broad grin. Coming around the desk, he held his arms open wide.

"Terrence, my old friend."

The two men embraced.

"Sit, sit," Elbert said, drawing him to the two chairs arranged before the fireplace. Gavin sat gratefully while his host poured them wine at the sideboard. "I would ask what brings you to Candor, but that's hardly necessary."

"Aye," said Gavin. "The streets here are silent compared to the center and by the gate. Thank you." He accepted the glass of wine. He sipped and raised a brow appreciatively.

Elbert sat across from him. "That's because most of those homes you saw are empty. It's rather amusing, actually. The merchants outside Candor come here seeking refuge while those within run for Bertrand or Tier or even across the sea."

"Like rats off a sinking ship."

"Don't insult rats, my friend." He sipped his wine.

"His coming is delayed, by the way. Our friend? He's decided to wait for the rest of his party to join him."

"Doesn't like to travel alone?"

"In this time? With the rebel mob on the loose? Hardly."

Elbert chuckled. Slowly, though, the laughter bled from his eyes and his face settled into grave lines. "Our other guests are only a se'ennight's journey away. Probably less."

"That so?"

"Aye."

"I hope that it isn't a large number."

"Oh, large enough to fill Lady Perth's mansion."

They sat in silence for a little longer. Finally, Elbert continued, "Some new plans are being drawn up for the summer home."

"Sounds delightful."

"Oh, it is. Trouble is, my architect wishes to surprise me. Won't let me even get a peep out of him."

"I hate it when that happens."

"Who doesn't?"

Silence filled the room again. When the wine was gone, Gavin set the empty glass on the table with a small clink. "I hate to intrude on your kindness—"

"Feel free to wander the house while my maids prepare your room."

"You are too kind, old friend."

They stood and hugged again. Gavin walked out of the room and turned right to go up the servant's stairs. He went up, all the way to the attic. Opening the dusty door, he smiled to see Portent perched just inside an open window.

Sitting next to the bird on an old trunk, he took out a small scrap of paper, an ink well, and a pen. He added a little water to the well, shook it, and, dipping the pen in, carefully wrote in code, "Expect about 300 extra men. Will be here in one se'ennight from this sending. Beware. Marduk is planning something unknown."

Sprinkling a little sand on the words to dry them, he looked out the window onto the rooftop of the neighboring house. He wondered how Clara was doing. Had it really been just a se'ennight since the last time he saw her? His heart clenched a little.

Portent stood patiently while the message was being tied onto his leg. Holding him around his body, Gavin leaned out of the window and tossed the bird into the air. The falcon opened his wings and soared up into the sky.

Gavin awoke. Outside on the street, several drunks sang and a few carriages rattled by. Soft moonlight filtered into his room through the drapes. Sitting up, his eyes scanned the dark bedchamber, the space between his shoulder blades itching with suspicion.

Kicking off the coverlet, he rolled out of the bed and lit the bedside lamp. Warm yellow light flooded the room. He was alone.

Scooping up yesterday's trousers, he jerked them on and fastened on his sword. He carefully lifted the lamp and approached the bedchamber door, straining his ears for any sound. Hearing nothing, he opened the door and eased into the hallway.

From the stairs floated up the muffled sounds of conversation. Elbert having a late night visitor? Gavin's stomach cramped a little as he walked silently up to the landing and looked over the railing's edge. Flickering light spilled into the hallway from the parlor. Keeping to the wall to avoid creaky stairs, Gavin came halfway down the staircase and blew out his lamp.

"The price has doubled," Elbert said.

"You should be grateful," replied a smooth, accented voice, "that you are getting your life, much less coin."

"I'm not asking for more coin. I'm asking for the release of my nephew and his family."

"Done."

"How can I be sure you will?"

There came a long pause and, then, softly, "You doubt the word of the King?"

"No. No. Not at all."

"It sounded like you did. I speak for the King. Any deal we strike is the same as if you made it with him."

"Aye. Of course."

"Where is he?"

"Upstairs, second bedroom to the left."

Gavin tore off the glass shade of the lamp and held the wick to a lit candle in a sconce by him. As the first soldier came through the parlor door, he flung the lamp as hard as he could. It shattered on the expensive wooden floor at the soldier's feet, flaming oil splashing everywhere. The soldier took most of the oil in his face and fell, screaming, as the conflagration spread in the hall.

Elbert yelled, "What's happening?"

Gavin dashed back to his room and snatched up his pack. Not bothering with anything else, he ran to the servant's stairs and took them two at a time, coming out in the kitchen. Men were yelling and cursing by the parlor as they tried to put out the flames. From overhead, he heard running feet.

Gavin's hand grasped the knob of the backdoor when he heard, "Nowhere to go, spy."

Whirling, he drew his sword but his attacker was already on him, punching him in the gut and stomping on his foot. He lashed out with the blade but the man caught his wrist and twisted. With a cry, Gavin dropped his weapon. The man struck him on the head with something heavy and Gavin sunk to the floor, unconsciousness swallowing him.

The first thing Gavin smelled when he woke again was horse dung. Next, he felt a hard floor beneath him and tight ropes binding his arms painfully behind him. His hands were numb. A cloth covered his eyes and a raging headache pounded his skull. Below, he heard a horse snort and stomp.

Groaning, he sat up. Whoever tied him hadn't bothered with his ankles.

"Ah, you are awake."

The speaker jerked the blindfold off of Gavin's head and bright sunlight pierced his eyes. Blinking rapidly, he focused on his captor, seeing first an emerald belt reflecting candlelight. Gavin brought his eyes up to the wizard's face.

The man was short and swarthy. Black hair chopped closely to his head, he had large, expressive black eyes over a short nose. Someone could have called him handsome. That was not the first word to spring to Gavin's mind.

"What do you want?" Gavin asked.

"No preamble?" He spoke with a heavy accent, possibly Arventi, but the words were the dialect of Bertrand's High Court. "No begging for your life?"

"You're going to kill me in the end. So why bother?"

The man nodded. He sat in a chair across from Gavin. "I have a few questions."

"I'm not terribly surprised. You want to know how big General Emmerich's army is? How many siege machines he has? What his plan of attack on Candor is going to be? You're going to have to kidnap someone else, because you aren't learning any of that from me."

"We already know all of that."

Fear, like a lump of ice, lodged into Gavin's heart. "Is that so, now?"

"It is."

"And how did you come by this information?"

"Well, obviously, we have eyes and ears in the Castle Orlind. But let's not waste time on such trifles."

"Why have you kidnapped me?"

"Tell me about the Seer, Lady Clara."

"I don't know who you're talking about."

"You're lying. Eyes and ears, remember? So, tell me about her. Everyone has a story. What is hers?"

"Go to Hell."

The humor drained from the wizard's face and his eyes became flat, black, and cold. "Tread carefully, bard. I can make your blood boil without killing you, and I can make flesh-eating beetles appear under your skin. Answer my question."

Gavin spat toward him.

"Not very original," he said. "But I give you full marks for spirit."

Casually, the wizard raised his hand and Gavin's flesh began to melt from his bones. Liquid pain flowed over his body and he began to scream, over and over, as skin bubbled and boiled and slid off of bone, muscle, organ, and tendon. Blood and melted skin splattered on the floor in large drops. The air felt abrasive as it touched the exposed tissue. He felt the air whistle past his teeth as he screamed.

The wizard waved his hand again and the pain stopped. Blinking and gasping, Gavin looked at his body: unmarked and whole.

"Someone will hear me," he said hoarsely, trembling.

"That's what spells are for, my friend. Let me ask again. What is Clara's story?"

"No."

Every bone in his body began to vibrate and, one by one, break. His leg bones shattered, his ribs fractured, his hips broke, and his fingers contorted into unnatural angles.

The scream ripped from his voice as he fell to the floor, his spine crunching loudly. The pain left. Gavin turned onto his side and vomited.

"I'm not," he gasped, "telling you anything."

The wizard sighed. "It's going to be a long day, I think."

Beetles crawled up his legs and tore at Gavin's body, gulping down greedy bites. It felt like a small, hot knives slicing into him over and over as the beetles worked their way up. Gavin squeezed his eyes shut.

It's only an illusion, he told himself. *Only an illusion.*

"I will return soon," said the wizard as he stood. "Torturing is thirsty work." He climbed down the ladder into the main part of the stable, leaving Gavin writhing on the floor in a world of pain.

Candle marks passed as the beetles slowly worked their way up. He whimpered and twisted, rubbing his body against the rough boards until his skin tore and bled as he tried to scrape away what really wasn't there.

As the beetles reached his neck, panic flooded his mind and he began to scream over and over. The beetles reached his jaw. He felt their antennae brushing his bottom lip. Tears streamed down his face as his voice gave out. One sane part of his mind wanted to know if the information was really worth this price?

The pain stopped and Gavin stared up at the wizard as he shook and cried, mucus from his nose running down his chin.

"I just realized," said the wizard, "that I never introduced myself. My name is Gennadios. I apologize for interrupting. Allow me to–" He raised his hand.

"No!" rasped Gavin. "No."

"My friend, I have to keep doing this until you tell me what I want to know."

"Why do you want to know?"

Gennadios knelt beside him. "Whether you like it or not, King Marduk will capture Clara. It will go easier with her if he knows something about her. Seers are fragile. If he pushes her the wrong way, it could break her. It could kill the gift. Could kill her. It is very important that we know who she is. What she is like."

"She will be treated well?" Tears and mucus covered his face as he turned his head to the floor to muffle the sobs leaking up through his mouth.

"Hush." Gennadios stroked his back. Gavin flinched away. The wizard shifted his weight and sat on the floor. "Yes. She will be treated well."

"I will tell you everything I know."

"Good. Good. Begin with her childhood."

Gennadios stomped down the ladder. His two companions looked up from their game of hnefatafl.

"How'd it go?" asked Barsabbas.

"He's broken," Gennadios said, dropping heavily into a nearby chair.

"You look tired, Genna," said Norton.

"I am. That was not an easy one."

"How long did you leave him in that last illusion?"

"Three candle marks."

The two men made appreciative noises. Norton said philosophically, "If he cares for her, then it's natural that he should hold out for so long." He moved one of his pieces against Barsabbas.

"Do we have any wine left?"

"Oh, plenty." He stood and fished out a flagon from their luggage. He passed it to Gennadios, who drank greedily from it.

Barsabbas moved a piece. "Did we learn anything useful?"

"Oh, we did," Genna replied. "It seems that the lady is rather wounded."

"The wounded ones are the easiest."

They sat in silence for a few moments. Barsabbas beat Norton. Switching sides, they began the customary second game.

Norton asked, "What are we to do with him?"

"We aren't supposed to kill him," said Barsabbas. "He goes back with us."

"Why?"

Barsabbas shrugged as he made his move. Norton gave Gennadios a questioning look.

"I do not know either, Norton," he replied. "His Majesty has his reasons though, long may he live."

"We leave at first light?" asked Barsabbas

"Yes," said Gennadios. "Emmerich and his band of would-be rebels will be here in two or three se'ennights. It would be best to put as many leagues between us and them as possible."

The two men nodded as they carried on with their

game.

☐

Chapter Twenty

A few days after Gavin's departure, five men rode up to the gate of Orlind Castle. When asked for their name and business, a flag bearing the Tieran King's crest was waved. A messenger was immediately sent to summon Emmerich, who ordered for the emissaries to be allowed entrance. He also sent for Clara, who met him in the audience room of the Castle.

Clara sat in a small chair to his right, with Cassie standing beside and behind her, while his captains stood to his left.

The door of the room opened and the five men entered. They wore black trousers with dark yellow tunics over chain mail. Their swords were lighter and more elegant than what the Lorst men wore on their hips. Their hair was also long and tied back with silver clasps. One man led them while the four walked behind in a wedge.

The men stopped and bowed. Emmerich was immediately struck with how similar they looked to Clara:

the same almond eyes with the upward tilt, and the same sharpness of the face. They were also small, like her, perhaps half the height of an average Lorstian man.

But Emmerich had enough experience with fighting Tieran raiders to know they were fierce and not to be underestimated.

"Greetings," said the leader, "from King Precene. We come bearing gifts and offers of peace and support."

"Your offers are appreciated," Emmerich replied, "and I offer you and your men the hospitality of our castle."

"Thank you." The man gave a slight bow. "I am Lord Theseus and these are my men. I come from the Provence of Praula, which is on the border with Lorst. This is why his Majesty sent me to treat with you."

"We are well-met, Lord Theseus. These are my captains." Emmerich gestured to his left. The men bowed to each other. "And this is Lady Clara, my Seer."

From the corner of his eye, he saw Clara stiffen a little at the attention being drawn to her. She drew herself to her full height as Theseus and his men turned to her.

"Well-met, my lady," said Theseus as he bowed. "My lady may already know this, but an empty chair is kept by the throne in Aphos, our capital, for any visiting Seer who wishes to use it, in honor of Lady Persephone, who with her visions saved our people."

Clara glanced at Emmerich before giving a deep nod of her head.

"Her ladyship," said Emmerich, "appreciates your words. Please forgive her for not saying so herself, but she doesn't have the ability to speak."

"Interesting," said Theseus and Emmerich could see he wondered how Clara fulfilled her role.

"What tidings does your king send?"

Theseus turned and gestured. The men brought forward the ironbound chest they had carried between them. Kneeling, they opened it, revealing gold coins, more than enough to finance the army for the rest of its campaign. Provided that it was a short one, that is.

"This," said the Tieran lord, "is only a taste of what King Precene offers."

"Does he offer men as well?"

"Three full companies, to be sent to wherever you desire, as soon as I can return word to him of a successful end to our negotiations."

"And the captains in charge of those companies?"

"They will obey your command, of course."

"What does His Majesty wish in return?"

Theseus drew a scroll from his belt and held it up. Emmerich gestured and Herne came forward to take the scroll, handing it back to Emmerich. He broke the heavy seals and unrolled the parchment. Clara leaned over to read it and, for a moment, he was distracted by the clean scent of her.

Forcing himself to focus, he read the terms.

"These are steep terms," he said after reading them.

"I am in full authority to make amendments to it."

Clara was staring in the distance, her eyes wide and vacant. Suddenly, she shook herself and began scratching away on her slate. He glanced at her a moment before turning back to Theseus. "You wish for us to send a tithe to your king. That is not what allies do. That is the behavior of vassals to an overlord."

"It is merely trade."

"Interesting, then, that there is no stipulation of what he will send in return."

Clara touched his sleeve and he bent to read the slate. It read, "If you agree to these terms as they stand, there will be blood between Tier and Lorst."

Emmerich nodded and looked back at Theseus. "My

Seer warns me that there will be conflict. Therefore, I will not agree to these terms. As they stand, of course."

The emissary looked from Emmerich to Clara and back again before forcing a smile. "Of course. Who agrees with everything that is written at its first presentation?"

Clara touched Emmerich's sleeve again. He hadn't even noticed her writing. He read the slate and looked at her questioningly. When she nodded, he turned back to the lord. "Here is my suggestion. For the most part, there is nothing wrong with these terms. However, let us drop the tribute, as well as the petition to return the border city of Klaress. In their place, I offer open trade between our countries as well as a country-wide festival, to be held annually, to honor the help Tier extended."

Theseus drummed his fingers against his belt as he considered this.

"Also," continued Emmerich, "a law will be passed to protect your caravans and Klaress will be declared neutral territory between us."

This seemed to do it for the emissary and he readily agreed.

That night, a banquet was thrown for the emissaries and Clara found herself sitting next to Lord Theseus.

"My lady," he said, "if I may be so bold, but you seem to have inherited some of the look of my country."

From the corner of her eye, she saw that Emmerich had turned to listen to the exchange.

"Pray, who was your father and mother?"

Clara fidgeted. As far as she knew, both of her parents had been Lorstian, and she wrote as much on her slate.

Theseus's eyes went from her writing back to her face. "If the lady says so. But, I must admit, your eyes remind me of someone I met once, though I cannot place who."

Flustered, she bowed her head and turned back to her meal. Emmerich looked at her with interest for a moment before asking Theseus a question about a Tier-made blade he had won on the battlefield. Clara, though, barely touched her food as she wondered if there was something about herself she hadn't known all along.

The next day, they saw off the emissaries after Theseus promised that the companies of men would be sent to Candor City.

"I expect to be in possession of it in a month's time," Emmerich said.

"Your confidence does you great credit," said Lord Theseus. Turning, he took Clara's hand. "It was a pleasure to meet you, my lady." Bending, he kissed the back of the knuckles before releasing her and, with a final bow to Emmerich, walked down the steps of the Great Hall. He mounted his horse, waved, and trotted out of the courtyard, his companions riding behind him.

Emmerich turned to her and said, "There was no vision, was there?"

She smiled up at him and shook her head.

"But you realized that the Tierans put a lot of stock in Seers, when he told you about Persephone's chair."

She nodded.

"So you knew if you faked a vision, it would make the emissary more pliant."

Another nod.

Emmerich chuckled. "That's quite devious. What inspired you to do so?"

She took out her slate and wrote, "Sometimes, a little deception is necessary. A friend taught me that."

A dark look crossed her face and Emmerich could

imagine who that friend was. Instead of answering, however, he turned to walk into the shadowy depths of the Hall.

Chapter Twenty-One

When Clara woke the next morning, she was glad to see that Cassie had yet to arrive. Cassie was a sweet girl, and sometimes tried to draw her out in conversation, but Clara felt suffocated by all the people surrounding her.

Getting up, she dressed quickly in the riding clothes, strapping on her sword. Much to Emmerich's amusement and chagrin, she had taken to wearing it all the time. She eased open her door. The room was dark except for a guttering lamp, which threw off weak light. She trimmed the wick, bringing more light into the room, and crept up to the door. Opening it, her four guards turned to look down at her. She held up her slate, on which she had already written, "I would like to go for a ride."

"This early, my lady?" asked one of them, a normally quiet man named Reid. He was the only one who could read.

She nodded.

"Do ya wish for us to get your maid?"

She shook her head.

Another guard spoke up. "Won't be right, my lady."

She gave him a hard look and stepped out into the hall, closing the door behind her. With long strides, she walked away, forcing them to follow. One of them whispered about turning back but Reid said no.

"It'll be all right," he said.

"General isn't going to like this."

Clara glared over her shoulder before picking up her pace.

Outside, dawn was only just beginning to break up the darkness of night. The soft air carried the barest edge of cold; it would be autumn before long. Clara wondered if they would winter in Candor. Surely Emmerich wouldn't try to force his way further south when the snows came.

The stables were warm and sweet smelling. Usually, she liked it, but something about it gave her a bit of unease. She paused, expecting a vision to come upon her, but nothing happened. Shrugging, she went to her horse's stall and reached for the door, but a guard stopped her.

"Let me, m'lady," he said.

Scowling at him, she opened the stall and set about tacking up her horse herself while the guards scurried about getting their own horses ready. A sleepy groomsman came around to investigate.

"Need some help, m'lady?" he asked.

She shook her head.

"Off for a bit of a ride, eh? I hear the southern path is quite nice."

She smiled up at him as she tightened the girth.

"You have a good morning, m'lady." He bowed and left her.

Once her horse was ready, she led him out, swung up onto the saddle, and took off with the guards barely behind her. She galloped toward the front gate, waving wildly. Soldiers yelled for the gate to be opened and men scrambled to pull the lever. The doors groaned open and the drawbridge fell just in time for her to dash through.

A few moments later, she heard the thunder of her guards' horses. She turned to go down the southern path, which was a leisurely trail used by the Baroness on her pleasure rides. But as soon as she was hidden by a stand of trees, she jerked the reins and changed direction.

The woods were more open on that side of the castle and she was able to navigate around the trees easily. She grinned wildly as the wind whipped over her. Before long, she came out into a clearing and she stopped her horse. Listening, she heard the distant shouting of men as they called for her. Clara looked up toward the castle before digging in her heels and galloping on.

After more trees, she came out onto another path, one she didn't recognize. Clara slowed her horse and went down the path at an easy walk. Taking a deep breath, she listened to the silence of the forest as the sun began to fill the world with her rays.

"My lord!" Haggard burst into the room.

Emmerich, who'd just started breakfast, jumped to his feet. "What?"

"It's Lady Clara. She's run away."

"What?" He blinked. "Why would she do that?"

Haggard shook his head. "I don't know, m'lord. Me and the other men went to relieve the night watch and they were comin' in, saying she'd run off and they couldn't find her."

Emmerich felt like he was going to be sick. Hadn't he given her everything she'd asked for? Why would she do such a foolish thing?

"Saddle my horse," he ordered. "I want six men to go with me."

"Aye, my lord." Haggard bowed and ran out.

Emmerich strapped on his sword and belt knife. After a moment's hesitation, he added his boot knife as well. Running fingers through his hair, he dashed out and down to the stables, where a flurry of men were getting ready.

He saw Reid and grabbed the man's arm. "What the hell happened?"

"I don't know, my lord. She wanted to go for a ride and wouldn't let us get her maid. As soon as she was saddled, she bolted for the gates and got away before we could catch her."

"Which way?"

"South, but there was nothing that way. We think she changed directions."

Nodding, Emmerich mounted his horse, waiting barely long enough for the rest of the men to saddle before pelting out of the castle. He turned and headed toward the southern trail but as soon as he came around a stand of trees, he held up his hand, coming to a stop.

Emmerich looked carefully at the ground. It had rained the night before and the ground was still muddy. It wasn't long before he saw it: hoof prints turning westward. Turning his own horse, he led the men into the woods.

Birds twittered all around her as Clara went deeper along the forest trail. Above, the sunlight began to pour more strongly. Looking down, she saw that tall grass filled the trail. The sign of disuse made an uneasy prickle dance down her neck while it also excited her. Maybe she would find a secret place she could escape to whenever she needed?

A twig snapped in the woods to her right. Stopping her horse, she gazed into the shadowy woods. Another twig snapped to her left. The horse danced uneasily. Looking around, she saw no one. Shrugging it off as animals, she carried on.

Rounding a bend in the road, she found her way blocked by a log with brush piled over it. Clara eyed the obstruction. Emmerich hadn't shown her how to jump a horse and she wasn't sure if she wanted to give the exercise a try.

Something crashed through the woods on either side of her and birds erupted out of the treetops. Turning, she felt the blood drain from her face as men came out of the woods on foot. Dirty and wearing patched clothing, they carried swords, knives, and maces. There were eight in all. Clara's hand landed on her sword hilt.

"Good morning, m'lady," said one of the men. "Comin' from the castle?"

Cold sweat broke out over her forehead as she worked her mouth, trying to summon words or even a guttural sound.

"Cat got ya tongue?" He laughed and the other men joined in. "Why don't ya come down, pretty lady? We've been quite lonesome."

He approached her while his friends hooted and whistled.

"Maybe ya belong to the new lord? Maybe he'd pay to have ya back." He grinned nastily as he reached for her ankle.

Drawing her sword, she slashed at his arm, cutting deeply.

The man swore at her, clamping a hand over the deep cut. "Get her!" he cried.

The other men swarmed toward her, yanking her down to the ground. The horse neighed loudly, rearing, and one of the men grabbed his reins to hold him steady. Clara swung her sword again but it was yanked from her. Hands groped over her clothing, pulling at her hair. She felt one grimy hand slipping under her skirt to grab her thigh.

Suddenly, she heard underbrush crashing and the men backed away from her. Looking up, she nearly wept at seeing Emmerich, followed by several men, dashing up the path. The brigands broke away from her and ran into the woods.

"Should we follow?" asked Haggard.

But Emmerich ignored him as he fell out of the saddle and raced up to Clara, who was slowly sitting up.

"Are you hurt?" he cried, gripping her shoulders. "Are you hurt?"

She shook her head.

He yanked her to her feet. "Get on your horse."

Shaking, Clara found her sword and fumbled as she sheathed it. She eventually mounted up and Emmerich and the other men escorted her back to the castle. The whole way, he did not speak to her. Chancing a glance at him, she quailed at seeing the firm set of his jaw. The last time he looked so angry was when he came upon a deserter from their army. He had the man whipped.

Once they were back in the castle courtyard, with many curious people milling around, he stopped and dismounted. She did the same and flinched when he grabbed her arm.

"Captain Herne," he barked.

The captain in question came forward. "Aye, my lord?"

"Gather a squad of men. Go southwest of here; there's a band of brigands in the woods. Find them and kill them all. Have the bodies hung and left in the trees to serve as a warning."

"Aye, my lord."

As Emmerich pulled her toward the castle, he bellowed, "Everyone get to work!"

The crowd dispersed as he led her up the steps of the main entrance. She tried to pull away but he only gripped the harder. They said nothing until they reached his audience chamber, where his steward already waited.

"Out," he ordered, "and make sure we are undisturbed."

The steward scurried out, closing the door behind him. Emmerich locked it. Clara watched him. He stood for a time with his back to her before slowly turning around.

"Did you know?" he asked, his voice dark and dangerous. "Did you know those men would be there?"

She shook her head, shocked that he would think such a thing.

"Why did you do it? Were you running away? Were you going after Gavin?" He began to walk towards her.

Frantic, she began to back away, her hands scrambling for her slate. But it wasn't there. She must have lost it in the struggle. Tears pricked her eyes as she wildly shook her head. Her back pressed against the wall.

Emmerich grabbed her arms. "Then why?"

She shook her head, feeling the tears come down her face. His hands tightened and she gasped at the pain.

Emmerich let go, suddenly, and took a step back. "I have given you everything you could possibly want. And this is how you repay me?"

Her mouth opened and closed, but fear clogged her throat. She couldn't have spoken even if she wasn't mute. The rage in his eyes set something off within her and she trembled.

"You are not to go anywhere without your maid and your guards, do you understand?"

Clara nodded.

"I will find a replacement for your slate."

She nodded again.

"You may go."

Slowly, she walked past him, but barely got another step when he grabbed her again, pulling her against him. He wrapped his arms around her in a tight embrace.

"Never do that again," he said softly. "Please."

She nodded, her cheek rubbing against his chest.

After a long moment, he released her, and she fled the room.

Emmerich watched her leave. He took a deep breath and turned to look out the window, his hand raking through his hair. He had come so close to kissing her. He gripped his hands to keep them from shaking.

"My lord?"

Looking over, he watched the Steward hesitantly enter the room.

"Aye?" he asked.

"I have a new missive from Gavin, my lord."

He took it from the man, who gratefully bowed and fled. Emmerich frowned as he read the message. Three hundred men? It was a good thing Asher had a new company.

Rolling up the paper, he left the room to go upstairs when a soldier came running up to him.

"My lord," he said, bowing, "Captain Asher is coming."

"How far off?" he said.

"He will arrive in the late afternoon, my lord."

"Assemble the captains."

"Aye, my lord."

The soldier bowed before running off again.

Emmerich returned to his rooms, where he penned a very quick reply to Gavin's missive, and then went up to see if Clara was in her quarters. Guards stood at the door.

He knocked and after a moment, Cassie answered. "I wish to see her ladyship," he said.

Cassie curtsied. "She is ill, my lord."

"Ill?" Had one of those men hurt her after all?

"Aye, my lord. I don't think she will be down today."

"Tell her I require her presence later this afternoon. Captain Asher will be arriving."

"I will try my best, my lord."

He nodded and left her.

Chapter Twenty-Two

Emmerich stood at the top of the steps leading into the Great Hall. The captains stood arranged around him. Other soldiers and servants waited in the large courtyard below. Movement behind him made him turn. Clara came to stand just behind and to the side of him, wearing the Baroness' dark blue gown. Her eyes were red and her cheeks pale. Guilt went through his heart and he turned away.

Slowly, the sound of hundreds of clopping horse hooves, bits of tack jangling, and the stomping of men's boots grew louder on the air. The chatter in the courtyard died away as Captain Asher rode over the drawbridge and entered the courtyard. Behind him, his men marched, stopping just on the other side of the bridge. Emmerich felt excitement welling up within him at the thought of finally marching out to Candor.

Asher stopped his horse at the base of the stairs and dismounted. Coming up the steps, he knelt and said, "My lord."

Asher looked every inch the noble. Tall and slim, he had sharp features, pale blue eyes, and curly blonde hair that spilled down to his shoulders.

"Rise," Emmerich said. "Come and give your report."

He turned away, hearing Asher give instructions to his lieutenant concerning the men as Emmerich held up his arm to Clara.

"Shall we?" he asked gently.

At first, he thought she would refuse, but she slowly took his arm. He led her into the Hall with the captains falling into step behind them, going upstairs to the map room. Servants with wine waited for them but after everyone was seated and served, he dismissed them.

"Captain Asher," Emmerich said. "You may begin when you're ready."

The captain stood, putting his hands behind his back. "My lord General, fellow captains." His eyes traveled over to Clara and surprise flitted over his face before he bowed toward her. "My lady."

"This is Lady Clara," Emmerich explained. "She is our Seer."

"It is a pleasure to meet you, my lady."

Clara nodded back, not meeting his eyes.

Asher straightened his shoulders and said, "Seasong was in good condition when I left it. If the residents there are not entirely loyal to our cause, they are at least happy with what improvements have been made since they were conquered." He grimaced. "I have also learned that many of the rumors coming out of Bertrand are true. At least, the ones about Marduk's experimenting on people.

"I met several products of Marduk's experiments. From what we can tell, he's trying to use magic to invent an aquatic people to use as weapons. The end results are men and women with fish appendages, some of whom cannot leave the water or they will suffocate. Most want to die and when I took Seasong, many ended their lives. What few are left are loyal to you, my lord Emmerich. However, they cannot stand freshwater, so I don't see how we can use them. Though, the idea of using them is distasteful to me.

"Those that could still speak talked about other creatures Marduk is trying to create: people who have been stolen away to be transformed into giant cats or dogs or winged creatures. It is said there is a complex underneath the Palace where he works on his experiments." He paused as his listeners absorbed his news.

"I have brought," he continued, "with me a company

of men ready to take on Candor and who are more than willing to march all the way to Bertrand. They wish to make Marduk pay for his atrocities." With that, he bowed toward Emmerich and took his seat.

No one said anything for a long moment.

Finally, Emmerich said, "I think it's safe to say we know now what's been keeping Marduk so distracted; why he hasn't been sending his army to the north after us. He's busy preparing an army of unnatural creatures."

The other captains stirred in their seats, speaking low murmurs at this.

"We will linger in Candor, then," he continued, "to gather more men before the final drive."

"It is not an easy march to Bertrand," spoke up Captain Wilhelm. "Should we consider wintering in Candor?"

"I would like to avoid that. Now, we must choose a captain for this new company."

The meeting continued on as they discussed the new captain as well as other logistics. Emmerich noticed Clara listening intently, her eyes straying often to Asher. Jealousy flared in him.

When the meeting adjourned, it was already late afternoon, nearly time for the evening meal. Emmerich ordered for food to be brought to them so they would not have to go to the Hall.

As he discussed the new captain (an impressive lieutenant from the Southern lowlands called Owen) with Wilhelm and Herne, Emmerich looked over and was surprised to see Asher speaking with Clara. Clara, who still had no slate yet, nodded and tried to smile as she listened.

"Never mind that, my lord," said Herne, noticing the direction of his gaze. "Asher always has to make nice to the ladies."

Emmerich glared at the captain. "I'm well aware of that. Send for Owen and have him join us."

Herne bowed and Emmerich turned away from him to join Asher and Clara.

"My lord," said Asher, bowing slightly. "I was regaling her ladyship with stories from Seasong. From what I understand, her ladyship has never seen the sea."

She shook her head, not meeting Emmerich's eyes. She gestured toward the door and curtsied.

"You aren't staying?" asked Emmerich. "Surely you're hungry, especially after this morning."

He knew it was the wrong thing to say the moment the words flew out of his mouth. She shook her head and left, still not meeting his eyes.

"I apologize, my lord," said Asher, frowning, "if I spoke out of turn."

"No. It's nothing you've said. Come. I want to look at a few maps with you."

Clara gratefully stepped out onto her balcony after escaping from the meeting. She had cried for most of the day after facing Emmerich's anger and now she felt tired and hollow.

She closed her eyes and raised her face to the soft evening breeze. Someone stepped out onto the balcony behind her.

"M'lady," Haggard said.

Tensing, she turned, her hand falling to her hip but she wore neither sword nor knife.

He held up his hands. "M'lady, I was just checkin' on ya."

Clara studied him for a long moment. His sheath hung empty at his side. His sword laid on the floor several steps behind him. Slowly, she relaxed and nodded. He came to join her at the railing. She edged away from him, putting a safe distance between them.

"I'm sorry," he said, "that ya got yelled at. But, it was scary, you runnin' off like that. But I understand it. It's hard, having people around you all the time."

She looked out onto the mountains, not responding.

"And mayhap Emmerich shouldn't've yelled at you, as I know he did. He's got a temper on him, everyone knows that. But you must not let it happen again, lass. Ya have to do everything he says. Makin' him mad, that's what got–" He stopped himself.

Clara turned to him, raising her brows. The old warrior shook his head and the real fear in his eyes frightened her.

"You don't need to be hearing rumors, m'lady. I jus' came here to check on ya, give you some advice, not to gossip."

She gestured with her hand for him to continue.

"You really want to know?"

Clara nodded.

"Well. Everyone knows Marduk killed the king. And people figure he got the Heir, too. But he didn't. Rumor among some of us soldiers is that Emmerich killed Princess Monica, because she wouldn't stand up to her father and make him boot out Marduk. Rumor is that Marduk killed

Emmerich's family way back when and when Marduk turned up at Court, Emmerich wanted nothing of it. He was the Captain of the Guard, and the Princess's personal Guard, but they were lovers, too. And, one night, after nights of arguing, he lost his temper, and killed her. It just so happened it was on the same night Marduk killed the king."

Clara shook her head. Emmerich wouldn't ever do such a thing.

"I know it's hard to believe, m'lady, but think on it. He's got a temper. I bet he came close to hurtin' ya? I saw the anger in him, when we got back to the castle. Almost followed ya, if I hadn't been sent to find the brigands." He took a step closer. "Please, Clara. Don't make him angry again."

The argument replayed itself in Clara's mind as horror mounted in her heart. She stubbornly shook her head.

"What are you doing here?" Cassie's sharp voice cut through the air. She stood in the doorway, holding a tray containing Clara's meal. "His lordship expressly forbade you from speaking to her ladyship."

"I–"

"Leave. Now."

Haggard bowed and walked out, pausing long enough to retrieve his sword. Cassie set the tray on the table before coming to stand in front of Clara.

"Are you all right, my lady? I'll have him removed from your guard."

Clara nodded, grateful that she no longer had to deal with Haggard's presence. But her mind still spun with what he said. Was it true?

"Would her ladyship like something to eat?"

No, she didn't, but Clara sat at the table anyway.

The setting sun streaked gold and pink along the mountaintops, the clouds to the west aflame with mauve and scarlet. Haggard paused a moment to enjoy the sight before crossing the small courtyard outside the barracks. Most of the men were in the main Hall, eating, but a few slept or dozed in their bunks before taking late night watch shifts.

He walked down the long, narrow barracks to the storage room at the end, lit only by the fading light of the setting sun. Once inside, he wedged a chair under the latch to keep anyone from interrupting him. The room was crammed full of swords, pikes, daggers, crates of them, along with uniforms, armor, and the like.

Making his way around the precariously perched crates, he went to the very back of the room. Lighting the candle in a lantern hanging nearby, yellow light allowed him to see as he knelt and pulled a small bowl from bag hanging at his side, along with a clump of herbs. Water from a skin on his opposite side he poured into the bowl and crushed the herbs onto the water's surface.

Holding the bowl in both hands, he chanted soft words in a low voice. The candle suddenly shivered and guttered, though there was no breeze in the stale room. The herbs moved, drifting in a spiral as if stirred by an invisible finger.

"What is it?" spoke an impatient voice.

"I have news," Haggard said.

"Go on."

"The lady, she ran off today. Not sure why but Emmerich was livid when she got back. Saw it as my chance, so I told her what the king wanted her to hear."

"And how did she react?"

"Shocked. Not sure if she believed me. But the thought is there."

"That's all that we need. You've done well, Haggard."

"Well enough for you to let my daughter go?"

There was a pause. "We'll discuss that when your mission is complete. Anything else?"

"Only that we should be moving on Candor soon. Not sure when."

"Very good. Contact me again when you know more."

The herbs in the bowl went still but Haggard didn't move for a long few moments, staring into the bowl, a look of sorrow and determination painted on his fingers. Outside, the sun slowly slipped away and night covered the valley.

☐

Chapter Twenty-Three

Light glinted off and refracted through dozens of crystals hanging on long strings from the ceiling. Broken bits of rainbow danced on the floor as the crystals swayed gently in the breeze that wafted through the tall, open windows of the circular room.

Marduk lifted his face to the breeze and took a deep, contented breath. He stood from his seat on the floor, feeling the gentle energy of the room thrumming through him. A page stood quietly behind him, paper and charcoal in hand. Marduk stepped up to the nearest crystal, peering into it.

"Archer's Glen," he said. "A boy named Tanner." He moved on to the next crystal as the page furiously scratched out the names. "Summerwind. A girl named Alissa." And on he went, going through the room, pausing at every other crystal to peer into its depths and name a place and a child.

Finally, he came to a crystal that was different from the others. It sat nearest to a window and a gold wire had been wrapped around it. Gently, he cupped the crystal with both hands, feeling a soft smile tug at his lips.

In the depths of the crystal formed the image of a young woman with long brown hair bound in a tight braid. Her large eyes were sad as she nibbled at her meal. She wore a beautiful blue gown, in the Southern style, but she plucked at the fabric every so often, as if she weren't used to it.

Clara. His Seer. Over the years, he had kept watch over her, keeping her safe as much as he could. And now, it was almost time. The apple was nearly ripe.

He looked over to the page. "That will be all for today, my boy. How is the book I gave you?"

"It's very good, your Majesty."

"Have you gotten to the part where the hero forces his way into the tower?"

The boy's face split into a large grin. "Oh, yes, your Majesty. But I had to put the book away right after."

"Well, run along, then, and finish it. You can tell me what you think of the end tomorrow."

"Yes, your Majesty. Thank you, your Majesty."

"Don't forget to take that list to the Finders."

"Yes, your Majesty." The boy bowed and left.

The door had barely swung closed when it opened again. Erin stepped into the room.

"Your Majesty," he said, bowing. "I hope I'm not interrupting you."

"No. No, not at all. In fact, come here."

Erin crossed the room, carefully avoiding the crystals swinging slowly on their strings, and came to stand beside him.

"Look," said Marduk. "Do you see her?"

Erin leaned forward, squinting. "Yes. I do."

"Lovely, isn't she?"

"Very much."

"I saw her when she was still a small child. Have I told you this story?"

"No, your Majesty."

"Ah, well, my master loved to invent new spells and he charged me one day to invent a spell that would let me find those with strong abilities and aptitudes. It took me a long time but I perfected it. She was the first of such that I ever saw."

"And is that why you chose her, your Majesty?"

"Partially."

"It is an exquisite spell. It allows us to find more

apprentices and make sure the Rebels don't get their hands on them. Truly brilliant. But if you've watched her over the course of her life, why do you need the bard?"

"Divide and conquer, my friend. You'd be amazed at what an ounce of broken trust can do, both to others and yourself. Her emotional turmoil and sense of abandonment are exactly what I will need."

They stood in silence for a long moment. The shouts and laughter of children floated up through the windows. Marduk glanced at a candle clock and saw it was time for afternoon session to end at the academy.

"She looks sad," said Erin, suddenly.

He sighed. "She does." He dropped his hands. "She certainly does. Did you come to admire my crystals, my friend?"

"No, your Majesty, not just that. I have the report from the menagerie."

"Oh?"

"Yes. The last batch of aerials is ready for flight."

"Excellent. Schedule them for their first test in the morning. And make sure the Keepers aren't expecting me. I like surprising them."

Erin smiled. "Yes, your Majesty."

"Any other news?"

His smile slipped a little. "The Keepers are reporting a disturbing trend among the aerials."

"What sort of trend?"

"They aren't as docile and easily controlled as we would like. And they are incredibly intelligent. The Keepers fear they may be developing minds of their own."

Marduk frowned, considering this. "We'll watch them a while longer. They are beautiful creatures. I'd hate to have to destroy the whole breed."

He started to weave through the maze of crystals, Erin falling into step behind him.

"Anything from our spy?" he asked.

"Yes, your Majesty. He expects them to be moving to Candor soon."

"How soon?"

"He's not sure."

He nodded as they reached the door. "Put our men in Emmerich's camp on alert. They will need to be ready to go at a moment's notice."

"Yes, your Majesty."

Marduk looked one last time at Clara's crystal. "She'll be home soon. Make sure her room is ready."

"Yes, your Majesty."

A new slate sat beside her breakfast. Clara stared at it through one eye as she rubbed sleep from the other.

"His lordship," said Cassie, "sent that up." She looked her over, worry creasing her forehead. "Perhaps her ladyship should skip today's practice?"

Clara shook her head as she picked up the slate. Sleep eluded her last night. Every few moments, it seemed, she woke, staring into the dark as if searching for a face or answers. But now, in the bright, sane light of day, she couldn't hide in her chambers.

Walking away from the table, she started for the door.

"Don't you need to eat?" Cassie called after her but Clara was already out in the hall and striding away. Her guards hurried to catch up with her and she noted that Haggard wasn't among them. A small bit of angry joy bubbled up in her.

When she reached the practice area, she was surprised to find not Emmerich, but Captain Asher waiting for her.

"My lady," he said, bowing. "The General has asked me to take up your practice sessions. He's drilling the new company and overseeing its new captain. Otherwise, I'm sure he would be here." Asher smiled ruefully. "I know I'm a sorry substitute, but if her ladyship permits, I would be happy to teach you."

She stared at him, feeling her plans for interrogating Emmerich fall apart. But there would be time later, she was sure. Straightening her shoulders, she nodded, and he led her into the nearest practice ring.

Asher was a much gentler tutor than Emmerich. She always had to watch out for any dirty tricks with him. He seemed to delight in leaving her sprawled in the dirt. But Asher's style was more gentlemanly, though his footwork was a study in chess and he quickly put her into positions that left her unable to defend herself properly.

At the height of the practice, with anger and blood singing in her ears and her limbs trembling from fatigue, she thrust, over-reached, and Asher knocked her to the ground. Clara, from her place on the ground, glared up at him as she gasped to catch her breath.

"Her ladyship is very good," he said, grinning, looking barely out of breath. "Shall we try again?" He reached out with his hand.

Scowling, she took it. The moment his skin touched

hers, light filled her eyes, blotting out everything. She raised her hands to block it out but the light shined through them. When it faded, she stood beside a bed in a chilly room.

The fireplace sat cold and empty and from outside came the cawing of crows. Turning, she looked down at the bed. Emmerich, pale and still, lay on top of the thick quilt, his hands crossed over his chest.

No.

She reached out, tentatively, and touched his cheek. It felt like ice.

No.

Light flared again and she stood in a grand throne room, grander than any Great Hall she had seen. Marble columns soared to an arched ceiling and giant red and gold banners fluttered in the cold breeze. A crowned man in a long, ermine-trimmed cape stood before her. He began to turn around and she wanted to scream for him to stop. She did not want to see because she knew who it wasn't.

"Clara."

Emmerich's voice wafted over her and she nearly burst into tears. Turning away, for the first time in her life, she wrenched herself out of the vision. Later, she wouldn't know how she did it, only that the pain tearing through her was more than she could bear.

Clara blinked her eyes open. Emmerich knelt over her, his hands on either side of her face.

"Clara," he repeated. "What did you see?"

Sitting up, she pushed away from him, stumbling to her feet. He stood, letting her go. She barely noticed Asher and other men standing around them in a loose circle. The air felt hot and heavy and she shook and gasped under its smothering weight.

"Clara." Emmerich's sharp voice cut through her encroaching panic. His hands grabbed her shoulders and squeezed tightly.

She squirmed, trying to break his hold.

"Hold still, girl. What did you see?"

Clara brought her arms up, quickly, breaking his hold. Before he could react, she ran, barreling through the men. Emmerich yelled after her but she kept running. She didn't stop until she reached her rooms, going through the sitting room and out onto the balcony.

Bracing herself against the railing, she breathed deeply until the shaking eased. The day, though hot, felt lesser so than it did down in the ring. Staring out over the forest and toward the mountains, she could almost believe what she had seen had been a mistake.

The door to her chambers opened and closed and she heard familiar footsteps cross the room out onto the balcony. She didn't need to turn around to know it was Emmerich.

"I brought your slate." He set it on the railing.

She took it and looked down at the smooth black. They didn't speak for a long time. He was the first to break the silence.

"What did you see?"

Her eyes slowly rose to meet his. He stared at her dispassionately, his mouth set in a hard line. Taking out the chalk, she wrote, "Did you murder the Princess?"

Shock flooded his face as he read her words. "Who told you that?"

She pointed at her question.

"Who told you?" he shouted.

Clara winced, but kept pointing.

Some of the anger went out of him and an emotion she couldn't describe filled his eyes. It looked like sorrow and regret and hate rolling together into some black and ugly.

"Aye," he said. "I did."

Shocked, unthinking, her mouth moved and formed the

word, "Why?" Breath gushed from her lungs and nearly voiced it.

He stepped closer. "It doesn't matter. What did you see?"

She stared up at him, feeling herself shattering and going numb under the weight of this truth. Fumbling, Clara pulled out her handkerchief, scrubbed away her question, and wrote, "I saw your death."

Setting the slate on the table, she walked away. He didn't try to follow.

☐

Chapter Twenty-Four

Days passed. Emmerich didn't try to make Clara come down from her chambers and when her maid tentatively asked for bolts of cloth and patterns, he granted the request without thinking. Later, he ordered for books and writing utensils to be sent to her rooms. Maybe he shouldn't encourage her self-imposed exile but he didn't want to be the one to break it.

What little camaraderie existed between him and the other captains faded. Even Asher seemed distant.

A se'ennight after the incident, Asher pointed out that they hadn't heard from Gavin.

Guilt stabbed through Emmerich. He should have noticed. But he had thrown himself into getting the army ready to move out. That was what he told himself, anyway.

"We have to assume, then," Emmerich said, "that he's been captured. Or killed. This changes none of our plans, however."

"My lord," spoke up Captain Owen, "we should send a

spy to Candor and learn what has happened."

"No. We'll just risk another man. Asher, how soon can we move out?"

"In three days, my lord," came the reply.

"Then let's prepare."

Cassie came to stand by Clara as the lady worked on a new dress at her table. The lady had not left her rooms except for late evening walks in the gardens. Cassie worried for her mistress. Something had happened between her and the Lord General. But she would not speak of it.

"My lady," she said, "I have received word that the army will be moving out to Candor. His lordship requests that you come with them."

Clara made no move to acknowledge her words. Her fingers moved with confidence over the seam of the undergown.

"What shall I tell his lordship?"

Clara's hands stopped. After a moment, she picked up her slate and wrote, "I must have an answer to my question, first."

"My lady, I assume he knows what you mean by that?"

She nodded.

Cassie, feeling confused, curtsied and went to the soldier that waited outside the room. She relayed the message before returning to sit by the fire. As she watched Lady Clara, Cassie reflected on how this all began when Haggard visited her. She wondered if she should bring that to his lordship's attention.

After a long while, someone knocked on the door and Cassie answered it. It was the soldier. He handed her a rolled bit of sealed paper.

"Thank you," she said. "Does it require an answer?"

"No," the soldier replied.

Cassie took the paper to Clara, who broke the seal and read it.

"Are we going to Candor, my lady?" she asked after a moment.

Clara stood, laid the paper on the table, and shook her head before going into her bedchamber, closing the door behind her. Cassie, who had never before pried into the private affairs of her mistresses, picked up the paper.

It simply read, "It does not matter. What is done is done."

When Emmerich left Candor, he did not look back. He did not turn to see if a familiar figure watched him leave. He did not send one last message to bid farewell. He mounted his horse, gave the signal, and led his army down the long stretch of road to Candor City.

But that night, when he undressed in the privacy of his tent, he took a folded, sweat-stained cloth from where it had been tucked against his heart. Unfolding it, he stared down at the round medal that caught the lamplight like a promise.

☐

Chapter Twenty-Five

Gavin listened to the wails of the tortured and imprisoned as he stared at the grimy stone wall across from him. Long scratches and furrows marked the stone and he knew, if the light was strong enough, he would see blood in the deep cuts where people tried to claw out of the room. People, driven mad by torture or listening to torture, had dug at the walls to find a way out. He wondered how far he was from that himself.

I betrayed her.

The thought echoed through his mind and he tried not to shudder. He had been captured before, but this was the first time they possessed something he actually cared about. Marduk was a monster, but if Gavin cooperated, Clara would come to no harm. And if Emmerich defeated Marduk, then it would all end well. In the end, he hadn't betrayed her, but protected her.

Or so he kept telling himself.

Heavy boots tromped down the hall and he looked

over as they came to a stop at his cell door. Keys jangled and the lock clanged. The door opened to reveal Erin, Marduk's right hand and Headmaster of the Academy, as well as several guards.

"His Majesty wishes to see you," said Erin.

Gavin stood as guards came forward to unfetter his feet and lead him out. They took him up several flights of back stairs and down a narrow servant's corridor. Stopping at a door, Erin opened it and stepped inside the room.

"Your Majesty," he said. "I have brought the prisoner."

"Bring him in," came the soft reply.

He was brought into a spacious room Gavin recognized as the study King Tristan liked to use for his daily business meetings with guildmasters and tradesmen. It looked exactly as Gavin remembered.

Marduk sat at the large desk, papers scattered in front of him. At his elbow stood a young page and to the side were several men in rich robes.

"You may go," Marduk said to them. The page and the men bowed and left the room, one of them glancing back as he passed Gavin.

Silence enveloped the room when the main door closed. Marduk looked much the same as Gavin remembered. A man of average height, he had dark brown hair dusted with silver, which he wore tied back. His eyes were dark brown, his face was broad and his nose slender, and his palms were wide with long fingers. He wore rich red robes. When he stood and came around the desk, Gavin saw he wore an elaborate emerald studded belt.

"Gavin, how are you?" asked Marduk, coming to stand in front of him. One expected a rich, velvety voice to match the face and Gavin always felt a tiny bit of surprise at hearing a soft tenor instead. "I wanted to thank you for the information you gave us about Clara."

"I don't want your thanks," Gavin replied.

Marduk smiled. "I have something more to ask of you. In return, I will not execute you. When Emmerich is defeated, I will simply exile you. And Clara with you."

Gavin stared at him a long moment. "Why would you do that?"

"Why wouldn't I? I have no need for a Seer save to end this war. Once the war is over, and my position secure, I have no need for her."

Gavin thought about that, letting the ramifications roll through his mind. "And if I don't do this?"

"Then not only will I kill you, but I'll slit her throat in

front of you beforehand." He said it as pleasantly as a greeting.

A chill swept over Gavin. "What do you want, usurper?" he asked.

A guard punched him in the gut, making him double over. "Don't talk to his Majesty in that manner," the guard said.

Straightening, he coughed. "I'm only speaking the truth."

"The truth," said Marduk, "as you see it. But it is truth that I came to speak to you about. When Clara comes here, she's going to be full of questions. You're to answer them."

"You honestly want me to do that?"

"Honestly? When Clara arrives, she's going to want to know about the Princess and Emmerich and perhaps a few other things. I want you to make Emmerich the hostile party. Given his temper, and choices, that won't be difficult. The story is already there. You have only to leave out a few details."

"You want to be the hero of the story?"

"No. Not the hero. Just a man doing his duty. Most of all, however, I want Clara to doubt. You're a bard. You can do that."

"Why? What's the purpose?"

"You don't need to worry about that."

He frowned. "And we'll be free to go? After the war?"

"I give you my most solemn word."

Gavin knew he couldn't trust Marduk, but the thought of Clara dying ate at him like fire. If there was any way he could protect her, he had to take it. Besides, maybe he could hint to her that something was wrong. Or maybe he could escape and take her with him.

"Very well," he said. "I'll do it."

"Good man."

The main door opened and a page approached them, stopping a respectful distance away. Marduk watched the boy bow and said, "Yes, Thomas?"

"A message for you, your Majesty. From the Farseers." Thomas walked up to him and held out a rolled missive.

Marduk took it, unrolled the paper, and read it, a small smile teasing around the edge of his lips.

"Very good. Thank you, Thomas." After the boy bowed and scampered out, he turned to Gavin. "Now that we're done with generalities, let's get down to the specifics of the story you're to tell."

It took a little over two se'ennights before they reached Candor City, making camp under star and torchlight in one of the large fields used for the annual spring fetes held outside the city walls. A sudden storm that washed out part of the road had slowed them and there were rumors that rain further south had obliterated more roads. To top it off, a few platoons were ill with a summer fever.

"All the more reason, my lord," said Captain Asher, "for us to remain at Candor for the remainder of the year."

They stood in Emmerich's tent, gathered around a folding table on which laid maps of Candor City and the countryside.

"He is right, my lord," said Captain Herne. "We can make it to Bertrand before the winter snows, aye, but there's wisdom in recuperating here. And the men will have time to come to trust the Tieran King's reinforcements."

"What does the Seer say?" spoke up Captain Wilhelm.

Emmerich looked up from the small map in his hands. "She has had no visions of our impending battle."

"Why hasn't she ridden with us, though?"

The tension in the room tightened.

"The men are beginning to talk," said Captain Owen.

"They blame the roads and the fever on the Seer's absence. They say she knows we're going to lose and that's why she wouldn't come."

"The Seer," said Emmerich, "chose to stay behind because the journey from Dwervinton to Orlind was too hard on her. She is resting and will join us in Candor City."

The captains nodded but looked unconvinced.

"But what we must focus on now," he continued, "is how we're to gain entry into Candor. Still no word from Gavin?" He looked at Asher.

Asher shook his head. "It's a safe assumption, my lord, that he is either dead or captured. But we have no word of either."

"Any chance of us sneaking in a last minute spy?"

"Our scouts report that the lord of Candor has sealed the city."

"Damn."

"We could offer terms of surrender," said Owen.

"Asher, are you familiar with this lord?"

"The Northern lords do not often come to Bertrand, Lord General, save for one or two, and if this one ever did, I never met him."

"But what did people say about him at Court?"

"They considered him as backward and barbaric as all the other Northern lords." Asher shrugged. "I find it difficult to believe that he will surrender to us. Candor has withstood many invading armies. No doubt he believes he can simply wait us out. He has a nearly unlimited supply of water, thanks to the rivers, and large stockpiles of food, not only ones he has collected but also what wares fleeing merchants have brought."

Emmerich stared down at the map, Clara's prediction of his death rankling in the back of his mind. Death had always been this vague concept, something that happened to everyone but wouldn't happen to him. At least, not yet, that is. He still had so much to do.

"Send a rider," he said, "in the morning with terms. I leave you to write them, Asher. Bring them to me for approval, of course. But we must still discuss a plan of attack. As Captain Asher points out, the lord will most likely choose to wait us out." He grimaced. Gavin was supposed to have been their way in again, and, like a fool, Emmerich didn't bother to make a back-up plan. Gavin had never failed him before. Worry and fear roiled in his gut.

"What are these?" asked Owen, pointing to hash marks

on the map of Candor's perimeter. "These can't be gates. They're on the river."

"Those are the water gates leading into the ports. Candor has two, for either side. The lord of Candor has no doubt had the gates closed now that we're here."

"And I suppose the gates go all the way down to the riverbed?"

"Aye, I–"

"Actually," said Asher. "I don't believe they do. Not this one, at least." He pulled the map to him and pointed at the gate on the far side of the city.

"What makes you say that?"

"I have a cousin who worked in Candor's ports some years ago. He said they had constant trouble with that gate jamming. The teeth would go just under the water's surface, but not all the way down."

"That was years ago, though. How do you know they haven't corrected the problem?"

"I don't, my lord. But it wouldn't be difficult to send one or two men to check it out."

"Do it. Any other ideas?"

The men studied the maps in silence for a few minutes. Emmerich glanced over at Asher, who looked away when their eyes met. However, for a brief moment, he saw concern there.

Herne said, "Our greatest concern is what will happen when the men get on the bridges. They'll be sitting ducks, vulnerable to whatever the Candor army decides to drop on them. We can order for shields to be raised to guard the ram bearers but that will only offer marginal protection."

"Our best option," said Captain Turin, "is to get men on the ramparts as soon as possible. Make that a priority over the ram, in fact. We can try the catapult but the distance between the city and the riverbank will be a major problem. We should get a tower on the bridge."

"That's a disastrous idea," interrupted Owen. "The tower is wooden. If the enemy sets it alight, we won't be able to get past it to the city."

"They aren't going to set something like that alight so close to their walls."

"It's still a mad idea."

The other captains began to speak up and the meeting dissolved into a shouting match.

Emmerich banged his fist on the table and shouted for order. When the men quieted, he said, "Prepare the tower and the ram. Have the men work all night if they have to.

Captain Asher, send the spies. This meeting is adjourned. Captains Asher and Herne, remain behind."

After the men left, and it was just the three of them, Emmerich went to a small chest and from it took a rolled parchment. He brought it back to the table, laying it flat and pinning down the edges with small stones.

"Asher, Herne," he said. "This will be our most difficult battle. It would behoove us to be prepared for every eventuality. With that in mind, I wish to appoint Captain Asher as my successor and, Herne, for you to be witness to it."

"My lord, I can't-" began Asher.

"You cannot be serious-" said Herne.

"I am very serious," Emmerich said. Taking out an inkwell and pen, he signed the document. "This is certifying that I am appointing Asher as successor and heir." He held out the pen to Asher.

Asher looked from the pen to Emmerich. "My lord, I'm sure you will live through this."

"As am I. But we need to be prepared. I didn't expect to lose Gavin, after all."

Slowly, he took the pen. "I'm not worthy, my lord. I'm just—"

"What? The son of a minor baron?" Emmerich cracked a small half-smile. "I'm the son of a wandering trader. If anything, you're the more proper choice."

Asher smiled faintly, hesitated, and came around, dipping the pen in the well and signing with a flourish.

"Now, Herne, as witness."

Herne, without a word, signed the document, bowed and began to leave.

"Herne," said Emmerich.

The captain stopped and turned, his expression unreadable.

"You will keep this to yourself."

"Of course, my lord," he replied. And he left without another word.

"They're all fearing disaster," said Asher. "Gavin's gone. Lady Clara refused to come with us. And now you've just appointed me your successor?" He grimaced. "My lord, what did the lady see, that day in the practice ring?"

Emmerich turned away, sprinkling sand over the ink to dry it. "It isn't important."

"I believe it is, my lord. As your successor, I feel that I should have a right to know."

His hands stilled in the process of tapping the salt off

the parchment. Silence filled the tent as he thought about Asher's words. He trusted Asher as much as, if not more so, than Gavin, though not even Asher knew all he had done.

"She saw my death," Emmerich said.

"Did she say when?"

"No."

"Then it may not be tomorrow."

"No. It may not."

"We all die, my lord."

"I'm aware of that." He rolled up the parchment. "But I'd be a fool to not be prepared, aye?"

"Very true, my lord."

They fell quiet as Emmerich placed a wax seal over the roll. When he had done that, and carefully placing it aside to dry, he turned back to Asher.

"That doesn't explain it," he said.

"Explain what?" Emmerich asked.

"It doesn't explain why she didn't accompany us."

"I gave the reason at the meeting."

"She seemed more than fine when I sparred with her, my lord."

"You don't need to concern yourself with that."

For a moment, he thought Asher was going to argue. But the captain only studied him a moment longer before bowing.

"I will go see to my tasks, now, my lord." And he left without another word.

☐

Chapter Twenty-Six

Emmerich had been gone barely a day when Clara was more than ready to leave her rooms. She had tried to keep herself occupied with sewing but found quickly that her newfound knowledge refused to leave her alone.

She was pacing the balcony, wringing her hands, when Cassie came to her after taking the breakfast tray downstairs.

After watching her for a moment, Cassie said, "My lady, I wish you would tell me what troubles you. Why have we not ridden out with the army?"

Clara stopped, looking out over the forest and to the mountains beyond.

"Does it have something to do with what that soldier, Haggard, said to you?"

She hunched her shoulders but made no move to answer.

Cassie came to stand beside her. "My lady, whatever troubles you, I am sure it will all come out right in the end."

Clara smiled bitterly. Taking up her slate, she wrote, "I doubt that."

"Why? My lady, please tell me."

Clara looked at her, feeling the need to talk to someone, anyone, about the truth that was burning a hole through her heart. Finally, she wrote, "What do you know of the Princess' death?"

"Princess Monica? I heard what everyone else has, that Marduk murdered her. Is that wrong?"

"Haggard told me that Emmerich killed her."

The blood drained from the woman's face. "No. That can't be true. My lady, Haggard must have-had to have-been lying to you."

"He warned me to not do anything to anger Emmerich, or I could meet the same fate." Her hands shook as she wrote the words.

Cassie grasped her hand, as if to keep her from writing more. "My lady, I have known many men in my life, but Lord Emmerich is a good man, he–"

Clara wrenched her hand away and wrote, filling the slate, "Emmerich said it was true."

She shook with the need to cry, to scream, to throw something to let out the pain shoved deep inside of her.

Emmerich was going to die, leaving her with the irreconcilable images of the good man she thought she knew and the murderer.

After a long moment, Cassie asked, "Did he explain why?"

Clara shook her head.

"That was the question, wasn't it? On the day before they were to leave? You were asking him why."

She nodded.

"My lady, I can't imagine why, either, but there has to be a reason. Lord Emmerich is a good man. You must see that."

Taking her slate, Clara cleaned it and wrote, "My deepest fear, Cassie, is that more has been hidden from me, that I have not been on the right side after all. But how can I know the truth?"

They stood in silence for a long moment. Clara blinked away tears. She had cried enough over the last dozen days.

Cassie said in a low voice, "I think her ladyship has been indoors for too long. Perhaps you will care for a walk in the gardens?"

Numb, Clara nodded and followed her maid out of the room, barely noticing her guards falling into place behind them. As they walked, she idly watched servants and soldiers going about their daily business, nodding whenever someone bowed or curtsied as she passed. It seemed so strange, how accustomed she had become to such courtesies.

As they entered the Great Hall, they heard, "Damn cur!"

The Steward slapped a young boy, knocking him to the floor.

"You will scrub this floor again!" he cried.

The boy, whose face was already purple from an old bruise, covered his head with his arms as the Steward kicked him.

Clara didn't even think. She strode up to the Steward, grabbed him by the arm as he swung his leg back for another kick, and, twisting her body, threw him to the floor.

The man scrambled back to his feet, raising his fist, but stopped when he realized who she was.

"M-My lady." He bowed. "I apologize. I didn't realize. How may I help you?"

She scowled at him before bending to help the boy to his feet. Touching his cheek with gentle fingers, she turned back to the Steward and raised her brows.

"I'm afraid I don't—"

"Her ladyship," spoke up Cassie, coming to stand beside Clara, "wishes to know why you have abused this boy."

"Oh." A slight flush began to creep up his neck. "He's lazy, my lady. I was simply applying discipline."

Clara looked around the hall. The floor gleamed. She bent again, swiped the wood with her hand, and, straightening, held it up.

Cassie said, "Her ladyship does not find anything wrong with the floor. It appears that the boy has done his job well."

Taking up her slate, Clara wrote a few lines and gave it to Cassie, who read, "You will not strike another servant or slave again. If you feel that punishment is necessary, then bring the matter to me."

"Her ladyship," said the Steward in an overly patient tone, "is very kind, but it is my duty, as the one left in charge of his lordship's household, to dispense discipline as I see fit."

Anger rose up in Clara and she snatched back her slate. After writing on it again, too furious to feel embarrassed at the small crowd gathering around them, she handed it back to Cassie.

"Then," read the maid, "from this moment, I shall assume the role as lady of this demesne until such a time as when his lordship returns or when I go to join him. And when I leave, I will choose someone to take my place."

"Lady Clara, forgive me, but you are not Lord Emmerich's wife or betrothed. This is not proper."

Cassie handed over the slate but as Clara wrote, the Steward began to walk away. One of the guards grunted, blocked his path, and grabbed him by the arms, turning him to face the women.

"What is the meaning of this!" he cried. "Release me."

"Her ladyship," said the guard, "ain't done speaking yet."

Clara smiled smugly as Cassie read her new message. "Neither is it proper to heap punishment where it is not deserved. I understand the day-to-day duties a Steward performs while the lord and lady are in residence, and you may assume those, but I will make the final decisions, including those regarding punishment, as is proper for a lady of the demesne. If you feel you must fight me on this, I will go to the falconry to send word to Lord Emmerich, and you may explain to him why he was disturbed with domestic troubles while on campaign."

The Steward stared at them in disbelief and, for a moment, Clara thought he would call her on it. But he bowed as best he could. "Of course he should not be disturbed, my lady. I will gladly cede to you these responsibilities. I will inform the Cook and head maid."

She nodded at the guard, who released him. The Steward bowed again and walked away.

Taking her slate back, wiped it clean and wrote one last message. Cassie glanced at it before turning to the boy and saying, "Tell the other servants and slaves that they may come to me—ah, to Lady Clara—with any grievances they may have. She will always treat you fairly."

"Thank you, m'lady," he said, bowing.

Clara smiled at him and waved at him to dismiss him. He grinned at her as he gathered up the bucket of dirty water, taking it outside to be dumped. Slowly, the crowd began to disperse.

"Well, then, my lady," said Cassie as she gave back the slate, "we seem to make a fine pair, if I may say so."

Clara grinned, wishing she could laugh.

Emmerich slept fitfully, waking every few moments as if someone had called his name. His dreams were muddied and confused. One moment, he would be in Monica's chambers, and the next, standing over Clara's bloodied corpse. Other times he dreamed of fire and screams.

Finally, he got out of bed, yanked on his trousers from yesterday, and went to the front of his tent, throwing back the door to let in the cool, early morning air.

His guards saluted him, which he returned absentmindedly. The camp was already busy with preparations. At the edge of the camp, men were putting final touches on the siege tower.

Spying one of the captains, Emmerich called out, "Owen!"

Owen jogged up to him and bowed. "Aye, my lord?"

"Has Captain Asher sent the terms yet?"

"The messenger left barely a candle mark ago, my lord."

"Thank you, captain."

"My lord."

Emmerich returned to his tent and sat down with a sigh at the table. Reaching out, he took the handkerchief laying there, unfolding it to reveal the medal. He regretted, suddenly, not telling her everything. But did it really matter? He had murdered someone he claimed to love and there was no explaining that away. Explaining wouldn't bring Monica back, wouldn't undo his crime. Yet, he had never cared before what others thought, but now it pained him to think Clara was away from him and thinking him a monster, no matter how true that may be. No matter how much he may deserve it.

A rustle behind him caused him to turn and he felt a bit of surprise at seeing Captain Asher.

"Captain Owen," Asher said, "told me you were awake."

"Aye. Sit down. It's too early in the morning for ceremony."

Asher sat across from him at the table. "Then I'll be bold enough to say that you look awful, my lord."

"I didn't sleep well."

"Is there anything you wish to speak about?"

"No." He tried to smile to take the bite out of the word. "But thank you for the inquiry."

"The men I sent to look at the gate have returned."

"What have they learned?"

"The gate is still jammed."

Emmerich closed his eyes in relief. "Gather six men who can swim. I will lead them myself."

"My lord—"

"No arguing. You will lead the charge against Candor."

"The men will need to see you, my lord. Send me. I can swim well enough."

"I will not put my successor in that sort of danger."

"Be as that may, the men will still need you for morale. There are already doubts because of the Seer's absence."

Emmerich thought about that.

Asher took his pause as opportunity to continue. "I can choose someone else to lead the squad of men. It doesn't need to be either of us. But I believe it to be essential that you lead the charge."

Emmerich nodded reluctantly. "Very well." He scrubbed his face with his hand. "Any other news?"

"We stopped a caravan last night, on its way to Candor."

"Oh?"

"They had news of Lord Gavin. One of the women claims she saw a man matching Gavin's description, wearing chains and a collar, being taken by three wizards to

Barlow's Crossing."

Emmerich sighed. "There's a portal there."

"He is definitely in Bertrand, now, my lord."

"Where he is either dead or being tortured for information."

"Do you think he will break, my lord?"

"Everyone has a breaking point, Asher. The question is whether or not Marduk will find Gavin's breaking point."

"How much did he know of your plans for invading Candor and Bertrand?"

"Gavin was the lynch pin in the plan for taking Candor. And we didn't speak of a secondary plan, so there's no information in that score. We'd gone over several plans for entering Bertrand but we never settled on anything for certain."

"That's still a lot of information."

"Aye. It is. But I can't imagine Marduk capturing him only for that."

"You believe that he's at work on something else?"

"I do. I have a gut feeling that says there is more he's cooking up besides unnatural creatures."

"Soldiers have been sent to fortify Candor."

"True, but it has the feeling of a consolation gesture, as

if he's pretending to care."

"Perhaps his experiments have his attention. Or he believes it makes him invincible."

"It's a possibility but my gut says it's otherwise."

Emmerich pondered the problem, feeling like there was something he was missing. After a moment, he shook his head. "I think I need some breakfast in me before trying to guess the motivations of a madman."

"I will fetch it for you, my lord."

"No, no. I can walk to the dining tent to get it. Go about your duties. And you're my successor now. In private, please call me Emmerich."

"Very well, Emmerich. I will let you know when the messenger has returned."

"Thank you, Asher."

Several se'ennights after the incident with the Steward, Clara awoke knowing the army prepared to attack Candor. She could see, like a haze over her eyes, Emmerich being dressed in his armor. She could see the army forming and the giant spire that was the siege tower. She could hear the horses whinnying and the stomp of boots. The sharp musk of leather and horse pierced her nose.

Squeezing her eyes shut, she tried to push it away, as she did that day when she saw Emmerich's death. But it refused to move; she could not turn away. Distantly, she heard Cassie come into the room and speak to her. But she could not answer.

I have to get up, Clara told herself. I have to hear the court cases today.

Breathing in and out, she pushed at the images, twisting and pulling away from them as they tried to hold on to her mind. To her shock, they began to ebb away until they were in the background, like three or four people standing directly behind her and murmuring in low voices.

Cassie looked at her with concern. "Are you all right, my lady?"

Clara nodded, getting out of bed.

"Today is the day of attack, isn't it?"

Another nod.

"Perhaps you should remain in your chambers, then, my lady. Lord Emmerich warned me—"

Clara shook her head as she walked to the washbasin. Splashing water onto her face and rubbing vigorously, she tried to ignore the image of Emmerich mounting his horse.

As Clara went through the motions of dressing and eating breakfast, the future and the present mixed and melded in the back of her mind. She stopped every few minutes to breathe and focus on each task as she completed it. But time still managed to slip from her.

In fact, she almost jerked with surprise when she found herself standing in the audience chamber, a crowd of peasants waiting to be heard. The room was silent as they waited for her to give the signal for the Steward to begin the proceedings. Clara, trying to not shake both with nerves and the force of the visions, sat in the oak chair and nodded.

The Steward read the first case from the scroll (a dispute between two merchants) and she focused so hard on judging the case, she gave herself a headache.

(They were making the final approach. She could see, one moment, a soldier bolting forward early and, the next, the gates opening wide and welcoming Emmerich with open arms.)

The next case involved a woman and her inheritance. The brothers wished for a share but she demanded that she had the right to keep it all.

(Emmerich sat tall and strong on his horse while a messenger shouted down at him. One moment, Emmerich ordered the attack

while, in another, the men cheered, the gates opened, and the city surrendered.)

Three boys were caught stealing. The merchant wished to press charges. But the boys were obviously starving and had only taken a little bread.

(Now the siege tower was being pushed along the bridge. Fire was being thrown only for boiling oil to be thrown in its place moments later. Men swam under a gate into a cavernous port below the city, defeating the men guarding the port, only for them to die in the water seconds later.)

Cassie whispered Clara's name into her ear to bring her back to the moment. A man was accused of beating another man, seriously injuring him. But the accused claimed he had been goaded into it by the victim.

(Bloody battles waged on bridges leading into Candor City. Emmerich fell from his horse only to rise again. Asher died only to live again. Arrows blackening the sky; this was the only constant.)

The cases ended. Clara felt as if she had missed something. She looked to Cassie, who whispered, "You judged fairly, my lady. Have no fear."

The peasants were filing out and the Steward was outlining the business of the day. The end of summer was approaching and they had to prepare for the harvest.

(A horn was winding. The images were fading. Someone won. They had won. The vision almost overwhelmed her but she saw the men pouring into the city. There was looting one moment and none the second. The siege tower toppled to one side and suddenly did not. But there was one constant: Emmerich's black stallion stood riderless.)

"My lady?" Cassie asked, alarmed, as Clara sunk to her knees. "My lady, do you wish to return to your chambers?"

She almost let Cassie lead her away. But the open fear in the Steward's face made her shake her head and stand. If it was true, if the end had finally come for him, they could not know. Not yet, at any rate.

☐

Chapter Twenty-Seven

That evening, Clara went to her room exhausted. A headache pounded in her head and the niggling feeling of disaster still rode her shoulders.

"I will prepare a hot bath," said Cassie.

Clara nodded and sat on the couch, leaning against the arm and closing her eyes. She had waited all day for a messenger to come with something brought by pigeon or falcon. But nothing had come. Could she dare to hope that, for once, she had been wrong?

A muffled shout from the corridor made her open her eyes. She could hear the scuffling of boots and the clang of steel upon steel. A rush of adrenaline pushed away her fatigue and she scrambled to her feet. Clara ran to her bedchamber just as the door behind her opened.

Turning, she saw a man, in the blue and white uniform of the soldiers, bloody sword in hand, followed by five men, enter the room. Cassie came out of the bathing room. When she saw them, she opened her mouth to scream but he reached out and hacked off her head, leaving it to hang by a few pieces of sinew. Blood fountained as her corpse fell to the floor.

Horrified, Clara ran into her room as the other men gave chase. She slammed the door closed behind her, locking it, and snatched up her sword from beside her bed. Unsheathing it, she faced the door.

There was no way out. No secret passages (that she knew of) and no one was coming for her. She opened her mouth, trying to force a shout, but the resulting panic almost made her throw up as something heavy began to slam repeatedly against the door. Adjusting her sweaty grip, she raised the sword and planted her feet.

There was only one thing for it.

With a squeal of breaking metal and shattering wood, the men gained entrance.

"She needs to be alive," cried the leader as Clara stepped forward to meet them.

The first man hesitated in trading blows with her and she took advantage of the first opening by slicing open his gut. Intestines rolled out onto the floor and she gagged even as she turned to meet the next man.

But she was unprepared for two men coming at her at

once. One met her sword while the other clubbed her in the back of her head. She fell to the bloodstained floor and blacked out.

When Emmerich awoke, he laid in a strange bed and his side felt as if it were on fire. He tried to sit up and grunted as the pain lanced through him. Something moved in the room and a lamp was lit. A very tired Asher looked down on him.

"It is good to see you awake, my lord," he said.

Emmerich fell back onto the pillows. "What happened?"

"You were injured in the battle. We nearly lost you several times, in fact, but the healers here are quite good. They saved you."

"I take it we won?"

"Aye. I accepted the sword of office as lord of Candor in your stead. I hope you don't mind."

"Well, you can keep it."

Asher grinned. "I don't think I can do that, my lord."

"How many times do I need to tell you to call me Emmerich?"

"One more time, I think, my lord."

He snorted. "How many men did we loose?"

"Thirty deaths, twenty are wounded."

"Not that bad."

"Especially since we took the un-takeable city."

"What turned the tide?"

"The squad we sent to slip in through the water gate. They opened one of the main gates."

"Excellent. I must have fallen shortly before then."

"You had, my lord. You took a spear in the side. It really is a miracle that you are alive."

"Has word been dispatched to Orlind that all is well?"

"I've sent men to go fetch her ladyship. But I will dispatch a pigeon on the morrow. It is night, now, my lord."

Emmerich shot him an angry look. "You should have spoken to me about sending for the Seer first."

"The men need the Seer here."

"They won this battle just fine without her."

"Aye, but do you think they'll remember that when we reach Bertrand? I'm sorry, my lord, but this was a decision I made for the good of our men."

Emmerich wanted to argue but he could see the logic in

Asher's reasoning. He nodded grudgingly. "Very well. Any other news?"

"None worth reporting, my lord." He stood. "I'll leave you to rest." He turned to go.

"Wait. When I was undressed, did anyone come across a handkerchief with a medal?"

"Aye."

"Where is it?"

Asher opened a drawer in the bedside table and took it out. Emmerich held out his hand Asher placed it in his palm.

"Thank you."

"Do you require anything else, my lord?"

"No. No, that is all."

"Then I will leave you to your rest." Asher bowed and, after turning down the flame of the lamp, left Emmerich in near-darkness, holding the handkerchief to his chest.

When Clara woke, it was to the sound of water slapping the sides of a boat and to the sight of stars gently gliding by overhead. Her hands were bound behind her back and her feet were also tied. Rolling to her side, she pushed and wiggled until she managed to sit up.

Torchlight illumined the small riverboat. A man sat at the rudder, guiding them down the river, while other men sat around quietly talking. They had changed from their uniforms to the neutral tones of peasants. The leader, on seeing her awake, came to kneel beside her. When he came close enough, she swung her legs out as hard she could and caught in the side of the knee.

Grunting, the man dropped to one knee and, quicker than she could see, slapped her.

"None of that," he grunted. "You do that again, and we'll tie ya t' the mast. Understand?"

Slowly, she nodded.

"Now, d'ya know where we're takin' ya?"

Clara could very well guess but she shook her head.

"To the Tieran capital. To King Precene. How's that sound?"

Clara blinked. The Tieran king was Emmerich's ally. Why would they kidnap her? She scowled at him, remembering suddenly how he had slain Cassie. Sweet, brave Cassie, the only real friend she had ever had. At that moment, she was so full of rage, her sight almost ran red with it.

"Don't look at me like that, girl," he said. "I didn't have a choice. The King has my family. It was either you, or I'd ne'er see 'em again. What would you have done?"

Fight, she thought. She would have fought. Unable to contain herself, she spat into his face, and braced for another slap.

But it never came. He wiped his face with his shirtsleeve. "I suppose I deserve that." And he stood and rejoined the others.

Clara looked back up at the stars and tried not to cry.

Asher finished reading the newly received missive and looked up at Emmerich, whose eyes were dark with rage and pain. Beside Asher stood Owen and Wilhelm.

"Kidnapped," Emmerich whispered.

"A soldier is on his way to give a fuller report," explained Asher, "but her guards, lady's maid, and one of the traitors were all found slain and Lady Clara missing. They believe she was taken away by boat in the nearby Braddock River. We believe they must be heading for the portal at Barlow's Crossing, which is ten miles north of here. It's been several days, so they are close to reaching it, if they haven't already."

"Send men there, immediately. Perhaps we still have time."

"Aye, my lord."

"Does the missive say who was the leader of the traitors?"

"No, my lord. The soldier should give us more information."

"Could there be more traitors, here?"

"It is a possibility, my lord. I have hired bards and asked friends among the soldiers to keep an ear out for dissension."

"Good."

Emmerich fell silent, his face a stony mask. Asher had never seen him like this and it frightened a part of him. Suddenly, Emmerich hissed and clutched his side.

"My lord?" asked Captain Wilhelm. "Should we send for the healer?"

"No," he gasped. "No, I am fine. Asher, go and send the men. Every moment they aren't on their way is a moment wasted. And be sure to subdue Barlow's Crossing. It seems we may have missed something when we passed near there."

"Aye, my lord." He licked his lips. "There is a chance of recovering her, my lord."

"If she makes it to Bertrand, there may be nothing to recover. Go. All of you."

Chapter Twenty-Eight

They reached a small town on the river just as the sun crested the tree line. The boat docked next to similar riverboats, though some twice as long as it. A large ferry bearing livestock slowly drifted across the wide river while, on the docks, men loaded and unloaded boats. A faded wooden sign by the road leading away from the docks read "Barlow's Crossing".

The leader walked over and, untying Clara's feet, he grabbed her arm and hauled her to her feet. With rough hands, he buckled a slave's collar around her throat. Clara glared at him but made no move to resist.

"Come on," he said, latching a lead to the collar and pulling her along behind him as he stepped from boat to dock.

As they came down to dry land, a squad of scarlet-clad soldiers stopped them.

"What is this?" demanded one.

"Jus' a slave, lieutenant," said the leader. "Takin' her to

the market today."

"Just the one? Shouldn't you have a boat full?"

"It was a slow se'ennight, lieutenant."

Some of the men found that funny but the lieutenant ignored them. "She's very finely dressed for a slave."

"She was sold to me, fair and proper."

"I would like to see that paperwork."

The man hesitated before bellowing, drawing his sword, and attacking the lieutenant. The soldier jumped back while drawing his own sword and then met him with a clash of steel. The other men escorting Clara drew their swords as the scarlet-clad soldiers surged forward. Clara, seeing her chance as the men fought, ran down the road, her lead rope trailing behind her in the dust. She tripped and fell, knocking the wind out of herself.

"Hey, now!" a man shouted.

Looking up, she saw her captors were subdued and two soldiers came running up to her. They pulled her to her feet and she twisted, trying to get away from them.

"Hold on," one cried. "We're trying to unloose you!"

Clara stopped, staring at him with surprise. The soldier made good on his word and untied her hands while the other got the collar off. She was rubbing life back into her hands as the lieutenant came walking up, his clothing torn and bloody.

"My lady," he said, "are you all right?"

She nodded, trying to not look intimidated, as if large men in scarlet tunics over chainmail addressed her all the time.

"What happened, my lady? How did you come to be in these men's company?"

Clara worked her mouth uselessly, looking around for anything to write upon.

"My lady, can you hear me?" the man shouted.

Shooting him an exasperated look, she nodded.

"Then, you are mute?"

She nodded again and gave up any hope on finding a slate or paper in the near vicinity. Seeing a stick on the ground, she smiled and snatched it up. On the ground, she wrote, "I was kidnapped from my home."

"Where is your home, my lady?"

Clara felt the blood begin to fall from her face as a suitable lie failed to come to mind.

"My lady, are you the Seer we were sent to meet?"

She looked up at him, her mouth falling into a little "o" of surprise.

"His Majesty the King sent us to meet you. His Farseers had a vision, it seemed, that you would be here. If her ladyship will come with me, we can depart for Bertrand immediately. There are wizards waiting by the portal as we speak."

Clara twirled the stick in her fingertips, trying to make sense of this new development. Could she run, right then? Aye, she could, but how far would she get? Where would she go? She immediately thought of Candor, which had to be nearby, but then remembered Emmerich, who had lied to her. Besides, she wasn't sure if Candor had been taken. And what if she had been on the wrong side, all along? After all, she had only the word of others to go upon. Sadly, she realized she couldn't even trust what Gavin had told her because he obeyed Emmerich.

Clara returned to her original question: should she run?

Slowly, she ran her hand over the dirt of the road, smoothing it, and wrote, "And if I don't wish to accompany you?"

"Then we will gladly escort you to anywhere you wish to go. His Majesty expressly forbade forcing you to go anywhere."

That did it for her. She wrote, "I will go with you." And

she tossed the stick to the ground and brushed her hands off.

"Allow me to see to these brigands, my lady, and we will be on our way."

The lieutenant saluted her and returned to where his men were trussing up her captors. He said something, which caused the leader to struggle as they took them away. He began to yell her name and say something, but a soldier punched him across the mouth. They dragged him, half-dazed, to a nearby wagon into which the soldiers loaded him and the others.

The lieutenant returned. "Is her ladyship ready?"

She nodded, wondering what the brigand was going to say.

"Then right this way."

They walked up the dirt road into the town proper. Barlow's Crossing was busy with its daily business, even though it was still quite early in the morning. People watched them only to look away if Clara noticed them.

They turned down a side street and on to a small stone house. The lieutenant opened the front door and they came into a spacious hall.

"Through here, my lady," he said, gesturing toward the

parlor at their left.

The parlor was bare except for an intricate pattern painted onto the wooden floor. It was a large circle with knot work spreading out from it in a sunburst. Two wizards awaited them.

"My lady," one of them said and they both bowed low. "I will be escorting you to Bertrand while my colleague activates the portal."

She nodded as if she expected that.

The wizards began lighting the thick candles set into sconces around the room. After that, the wizard that hadn't spoken to her began to thumb through a large book on a stand while the other approached her.

"I am Wizard Bruin," he said. "And I will be your liaison with the King and the rest of the Court during your stay with us. Her ladyship looks as if she's had a hard journey."

She nodded as she began to slowly feel more ill at ease. Was she making the right decision?

Suddenly, the front door banged open and a soldier jogged into the room. "Men from Candor, sent by the Rebel, are coming. They will be here in a candle mark."

"Then we have to hurry. My lady, if you will come with

me into the circle."

For a brief moment, she had a moment of doubt as she thought of Emmerich's face. *But he murdered the Princess and won't say why*, she thought. If Marduk was the enemy, she had to learn for herself, but she feared she had been with the enemy all along.

Clara followed Bruin into the circle.

"Excuse my forwardness," he said, taking her hand, "but it's best this way. In fact, you may want to close your eyes." He smiled. "But you don't have to. The first time is always the most disconcerting, though."

The other wizard began to chant and white light snaked through the lines on the floor. Outside, she heard shouts and the clang of steel. The lieutenant turned to the door, his sword in his hand, ready to face the threat.

The light flared and Clara felt herself tip forward into the brightness. She gripped the wizard's hand as the light shifted into a multitude of colors and she continued to feel as if she fell, her skirts flapping around her. The colors spun and swirled, and she couldn't decide if she felt joy or pain as wind whipped over her skin. Suddenly, the light faded and she dropped to her feet.

Swaying, she nearly fell but Bruin caught her.

"Easy, my lady," he said. He smiled at her. "Did you close your eyes?"

She shook her head, grinning up at him.

He laughed. "I didn't close my eyes on my first trip either. And I threw up when we landed. But you seem to be fine."

Clara nodded, looking around. They stood at the top of a great tower and at their feet spread a gorgeous city, the morning light glistening off the alabaster and ivory of towering monuments, curved roofs of basilicas, grey stone and red brick of other buildings, and the haze of wood smoke overhanging it all. In the distance, light gleamed on the waters of the Lyn Tone River. Wind whistled around them and she gripped his hand tightly. Up above, a strangely shaped bird with a too-long tail flew.

"My lady," said Bruin, "welcome to Bertrand."

The man who had led the men that brought Clara to Barlow's Crossing slammed against the door of the prison cell.

"Let me out! We had a deal!" he yelled, kicking the door.

A few moments later, he heard men coming down the hall and he backed up. Keys clanged as the door was unlocked and Lieutenant Martinson stepped into the room.

"Hey, I want–" the man began.

"Shut up," replied Martinson. "Did you tell her you were taking her to Tier? And she has no idea King Marduk sent you?"

"Aye, that's right."

"Then why did you try to warn her back at the docks?"

"I thought you were double-crossing me. But, aye, the girl has no idea."

"And Haggard? Is he still loyal to our cause?"

"Aye. He's on his way to Candor right now to handle Emmerich."

"Then our deal is done."

Martinson stepped to the side and an executioner came in, bearing an ax.

"What are you doing?" He started to back away.

"Paying you your wages before Emmerich's men arrive," said Martinson.

Two soldiers dragged the man to the floor. He kicked, yelled, and struggled, but nothing prevented the whistling fall of the executioner's ax.

"One of the men returned from the Crossing, my lord," said Asher. "They were too late. Lady Clara is at Bertrand now."

With an oath, Emmerich threw his cup and it shattered against the wall, tonic spilling everywhere. Groaning, he clutched his side. Asher licked his lips and looked down.

"What do we tell the men, my lord?" he asked.

"The truth. They'll learn it eventually." Emmerich panted, his forehead beaded with sweat.

"Shall I gather a rescue mission?"

Emmerich hesitated. "No."

Asher blinked in surprise. "No?"

"I need every man to march on Bertrand."

"But, my lord–"

"I will not be swayed in this, Asher."

The captain stared at his general, trying to comprehend this. He had never said it to anyone, but it had been his opinion that Emmerich saw Lady Clara as more than a tool in his fight against Marduk. He had half-expected Emmerich to try to throw himself into a saddle to go after her. "My lord, I'm afraid I don't understand."

Emmerich stared at him for a long moment. "We can't use the portal so it will take se'ennights of travel. There won't be anything left of her, by the time our men reach Bertrand."

Asher nodded slowly, remembering the creatures at Seasong and the rumors of the tortures Marduk inflicted. "I understand, my lord."

"The best thing we can do is end this war."

"Aye, my lord."

But Asher wasn't so sure.

☐

Chapter Twenty-Nine

Bruin led Clara down the tower and several flights of stairs into a grand corridor. The pink marble floor gleamed and delicate white statuary of birds, deer, and lithe women stood in niches along the walls. Men and women laughed and talked as they walked, pausing to bow or curtsy as she and Bruin passed.

One wizard stopped them. "Are you going to the audience chamber to see His Majesty, Bruin?"

"I am."

"He's not in there. Check the courtyard."

"Ah. Thank you."

"Who is your lovely companion?"

"Oh, forgive me. Lady Clara, this is Wizard Trevor. Trevor, allow me to present Lady Clara."

"Charmed," said Trevor, bowing gracefully. "I would love to accompany you but I have a class to teach." With another bow, he walked by.

"Trevor teaches applied magics at the Academy," Bruin

explained as they continued on.

Clara arched a brow and rolled her wrist to ask for more information.

"Applied magics is taking theory and learning how to use it in a day-to-day setting. For example, a student may be familiar with the theory of earth magic. In applied magics, he'll learn how to take that theory and use it to clear out collapsed mineshafts or fill in sinkholes."

She pointed at him, raising her brows.

"What do I teach? Ancient linguistics and alchemy. I know, it's a strange combination, but I enjoy it."

They descended a short set of steps and turned left. The shouts of children echoed down the hall.

"Looks like Trevor was right."

They rounded a corner and came out into a cloister walk. Stopping, Bruin looked to his left. "There is His Majesty."

Clara's mouth dropped open. The King of Lorst, the sorcerer king, the usurper no one wanted, darted around the courtyard, kicking a dirty ball as his red robes streamed behind him. He laughed loudly as pages in their red tunics darted around him, trying to get the ball back. Finally, one succeeded, kicking the ball away and to the opposite end of the courtyard. Another boy jumped forward and sent it flying between two tall vases overflowing with ivy.

"Good shot!" cried the king breathlessly, clapping.

As the boys cheered, Marduk looked around and saw her.

"Looks like it's time for me to go," he said. The boys whined and the king chuckled, patting the heads of a few as he strode up to the cloister walk.

Bruin bowed lowly as the king approached. "Your Majesty, allow me to present to you Lady Clara."

"My lady," said the king, reaching them. He took her hand with both of his and kissed her knuckles. "It is an honor to finally meet you."

Without thinking about it, she dropped a curtsy.

He let go of her hand and she rubbed it with the other, her fingers tingling.

"Bruin," said Marduk, "why don't you make sure her ladyship's room is prepared?"

"Yes, your Majesty." He turned to Lady Clara and bowed before bestowing a deeper bow toward the King and leaving. She almost grabbed his arm to make him stay.

"Now, if her ladyship will be so kind as to accompany me." He proffered his arm.

Clara slipped hers over his and he led her down the walk.

"My Farseers told me you would have gone on a rough journey and they appear to be correct. Have you eaten?"

She shook her head.

"Then we will see to that first. Ah, you there." Marduk signaled at a passing servant, who stopped and curtsied. "Have a breakfast sent up to my private study."

The servant curtsied again. "Yes, your Majesty."

Marduk led her away. They walked without speaking and Clara looked around constantly. They passed open doors into lavishly decorated rooms as well as groups of people who laughed and talked and their smiles did not fade as the king passed. The decorations were superb and exceeded anything Clara could have dreamed or had ever read about in the books she'd sneak into her room at Dwervin.

They reached a large door flanked by soldiers, one of whom opened it for them.

"Thank you, Andrew," said Marduk as they entered.

Clara sucked in a gulp of air at seeing the study. Bookcases so tall a catwalk ran along the middle of them reared up toward a vaulted ceiling. A spiral staircase in a corner led up to the walk. Comfortable chairs were arranged before a fireplace and several desks were scattered around the room. One particularly ornate one had two chairs arranged in front of it.

"Do you like it?" he asked.

Clara nodded.

"It's one of my favorite rooms. I could spend hours here, if I could. Come and sit."

He led her to a table in front of a giant window overlooking expansive gardens. He pulled out a chair for her. Clara sat, feeling more overwhelmed by the moment. Marduk took the seat at the head of the table, folding his hands in front of him.

She took the moment to really look at him. Handsome, with fair hair and pale green eyes, he appeared to be just passing the prime of his life. He did not seem to be a murderer or a madman. He did not fit the picture painted for her by Gavin and Emmerich. If anything, her world was feeling even more deeply rocked.

"Do I please you?" he asked, running a hand through his hair.

Clara blushed and looked away.

Marduk chuckled. "That was childish of me. I

apologize. Ah, I'm very glad my soldiers got to you in time. When my Farseers came to me, we had mere hours to pull men together. I did not even know that Emmerich had a Seer in his ranks."

She glanced at him.

"My lady, please do not be afraid or worried. I'm not going to force you to do anything you don't wish to do. But those of us who are touched with the ability to do more, to see more, than the average man must look out for each other. I couldn't just let you be taken to Tier."

A soft knock on the door interrupted whatever he might have said next.

"Enter," he called.

The door opened and the servant from earlier came in bearing a tray. She set it in front of Clara.

"I will leave you to eat," said Marduk, standing. He started to leave but stopped. He turned back to her. "I have in my custody Gavin. Would you like to see him? I don't know if you were at all close to him while in the Rebel camp."

She nodded, her heart suddenly leaping to her throat.

"Then I will have him with me when I return." He bowed. "My lady."

She watched him leave before turning back to her breakfast. She had come to Bertrand on almost a whim, at the bare thought of finally getting the truth. Why, then, did she feel so uneasy?

"She's here," gasped Bruin. He had run all the way to the barracks and now he leaned heavily against the doorway of Jarrett's quarters.

"You saw her?" asked Jarrett as he buckled on his sword belt. He had been on night duty and dark circles smudged the underside of his eyes.

"Saw her? I was on duty at the portal at Barlow's Crossing. I escorted her. She's in the King's private study right now."

He ran a comb through his hair, trying to get it under control. "His Majesty is going to send for me soon, then."

"I imagine so. But don't be surprised if he won't let you see her until tomorrow."

"Give her time to get settled, to relax."

"To think she's been on the wrong side all along."

"Yes." He grimaced. "What's our move, then?"

"She's a mute, Jarrett. I don't know if that's because

she's soft in the head or if there's some other cause. The King told me she would be a mute, but he didn't explain why."

"He wouldn't."

"No, I suppose not. But can we trust her to see what's wrong with her own eyes?"

Silence fell as the men pondered the problem. Finally, a small half-smile tugged on Jarrett's lips. "Lets see what happens when she sees the truth on her own."

"Jarrett, you can't reveal yourself to her. Not until we're sure it's safe."

"I'm the Captain of the Guard, Bruin. And I know the King is going to put me in charge of her personal security. I don't need to reveal myself."

Clara ate most of the breakfast, surprising herself as she had had very little appetite since Emmerich left, and began perusing some of the papers on nearby desks. Equations and diagrams covered dozens of sheets of parchment. None of it made any sense to her. Finally, she turned to the bookshelves. The first few cases contained more volumes on magic but eventually she hit upon one containing books of saints' lives, fairy tales, romances, and legends. She pulled down a large red volume and began to page through it, pausing in wonder at the colorful illustrations. At Dwervin or Orlind there had not been anything nearly so fine.

The doors opened and she hurriedly stuffed the book back into its place. Turning, she put her hands behind her back. Marduk smiled at her as he entered.

"My apologies, my lady," he said, "but I should have made it clear." He gestured around the room. "You are free to look at whatever book you like."

Clara nodded her thanks. Movement behind Marduk caught her eye and she felt her heart thud heavily. Gavin, chained, filthy, and thinner than she remembered, walked into the room, accompanied by several soldiers. His shoulders and head slumped heavily.

Clara ran forward and flung her arms around him, squeezing him tightly as tears pricked her eyes.

"Clara," whispered Gavin, his voice rough and low, full of joy and longing and something else she couldn't identify. She wanted to call it sorrow.

"You must have much to discuss," Marduk said when Clara stepped back. "There is a desk with writing utensils over here that you may use." He indicated the desk nearest the fireplace. "Forgive me, but I must have the soldiers remain here as guards. I have a matter to attend to and will return shortly."

He left the room, closing the double doors behind him.

Clara took Gavin by the arm and led him over to the desk. The soldiers followed at a respectful distance, spreading loosely around the room in a semicircle.

"Clara," whispered Gavin, "how did you come here? Were you kidnapped?"

Taking one of the pieces of parchment, Clara scribbled a summarized version of her adventure over the last few days. Gavin shook his head sadly.

"I don't understand that, either, sweetling. The King of Tier has long courted an alliance with Emmerich. Perhaps he has begun to lose patience. What of Emmerich? Is he well?"

What little happiness she had drained away.

"What is it?" He gripped her free hand. "Is he dead?"

Clara shook her head.

"Is he going to die?"

She wrote, "I believe so."

Gavin swore. They stood in silence for a long moment.

Finally, she wrote, "You told me Marduk killed Monica, but I've learned that Emmerich did. He confirmed it to me himself. Why did you lie?"

He sighed, his shoulders drooping. "I never liked hiding it from you to begin with. Monica and Emmerich were in love, that's the truth. But when Marduk arrived, Emmerich became jealous. He thought Marduk was trying to court Monica away from him. He wasn't of course, but Emmerich had lost everything. I suppose he was afraid of losing her. And, aye, he never spoke much of his family but it doesn't take a genius to figure out they're all gone.

"He also believed that Marduk was a part of a plot to overthrow the King. That was what he had me looking into, but I could never find enough evidence. There was a plot but it always seemed the conspirator was three steps ahead. I couldn't confirm who it was. Emmerich tried to get Monica to force King Tristan to dismiss Marduk. She refused. Repeatedly. He lost his temper and killed her. Emmerich blames Marduk for her death."

"But what of King Tristan?"

"An assassin. Whoever the conspirator had been hired one to slip into the king's chambers the night Emmerich murdered Monica. Marduk had a premonition but by the time he got to the king, it was too late. He immediately went to Monica's chambers and that's when he came upon Emmerich over her body.

"I went with Emmerich because I was sure of Marduk's villainy as well, that he had been the conspirator all along. But we've done things, Clara. There were Northern Lords he had me assassinate in their beds so we could claim their men. There were coffers we raided so that we could house and feed his growing army." He took a deep breath. "Now I'm not so sure if perhaps Emmerich hadn't been the conspirator all along and had merely hired me to direct attention from himself. But Marduk's quick actions that night foiled whatever plan he had, if it had been him all along." He looked down. "Emmerich's the one who's been spreading the rumor about Marduk experimenting on people. He told Asher to lie in his report, that they came across such creatures."

Clara looked at him, feeling as if the world was breaking apart under her feet. She could not reconcile this Emmerich with the one she had thought she'd known. Then, she remembered him screaming in her face and that horrible moment where she feared for her life, and, so, she wondered.

Finally, she wrote, "You haven't explained why you lied."

"When I reported to Emmerich there was a Seer in Dwervin's household, I was instructed to befriend you."

Clara flinched in horror.

He took her hands as best as his manacles would allow. "But as I grew to know you—"

She snatched her hands away and backed away from him, refusing to meet his eye.

"Clara," he said, "as I grew to know you, you began to mean more to me than anything. Believe me when I say I do love you. I asked you to marry me that day because I truly do love you. Once we were on the road to Candor, I was going to tell you the truth and we were going to run away together. But Emmerich guessed my plan and that's why he forbade you to go with me."

Clara's mind flew back to that evening, when she mysteriously sleepwalked, and when she thought Emmerich was going to kiss her. She remembered his eyes, dark and intense. She remembered the feel of his hands on her face. Clara reached up and touched her cheeks, feeling her heart begin to break. How could she, a Seer, have been wrong all this time? But, could Marduk be forcing Gavin to lie to her?

Her mind swam with the possibilities.

"Clara." Gavin was in front of her, reaching for her, but she turned away, shaking her head. Turning to one of the guards, she pointed at him and made wild shooing gestures. She didn't care if she looked like a madwoman. She only wanted Gavin out of her sight.

None of this can be true, she insisted to herself. But as she looked again at Gavin, whose eyes seemed to pity her, she felt her faith in him and Emmerich shrink even more.

Two of the guards took Gavin by the arms to lead him away. He went without resistance. She turned away from him, staring at the surface of the desk as she listened to them leave.

But just as she heard the doors open, Gavin called over his shoulder, "No matter what happens, never doubt that I love you."

After shuffling of chain and feet, the doors closed and with a voiceless gasp, Clara began to cry. She pressed both hands to her mouth as she shook with sobs.

The doors behind her opened again and after a few moments, someone turned her around and enveloped her in an embrace. The person rubbed her back in soothing circles. She pulled away enough to look up.

Marduk looked down at her. "My dear, are you all right?"

Horrified, she stepped out of his embrace and rubbed her tears away even as more sobs threatened.

Marduk started to say something but changed his mind at the last moment. Licking his lips, he said, "Your rooms are ready. You must be very tired."

She nodded and took his arm when he offered it.

He didn't speak as they walked, going through two or three wings and up flights of stairs. In a dim part of her mind, she felt amazed at the immensity of the Royal Palace.

Finally, they came to a set of large double doors, decorated with carvings of roses and lilies. Four guards flanked them.

"These are your rooms," Marduk said as two of the guards opened them.

They stepped into an opulent sitting room. The floor was grey-white marble overlaid with rugs woven with pinks, whites, pale greens and lavender. The walls were painted in beautiful murals depicting forests, streams, and waterfalls in which frolicked unicorns, nymphs, sprites, and fairies. The furniture was done in the same colors as the rugs only a few shades darker and plump cushions were scattered on the couches and chairs.

To her right was a large archway in which hung rose-colored curtains tied back with golden ropes. Beyond the archway stood a canopied bed finer than even the one in Orlind. To her left was a closed door and she could only assume it led to the bathing room.

"These are only part of your rooms, actually," said Marduk. "Several rooms are yours, forming a private wing of sorts, for as long as you choose to stay here."

Clara stared at him in disbelief. What need did she have for an entire wing?

"But, I'm afraid it isn't entirely ready. Your library isn't finished, for example. But that's if you wish to stay, of course. You don't have to decide yet." He dropped her arm, though he seemed reluctant. "I will leave you to rest now. I've given strict orders that you be not disturbed. This evening, I will send a woman to act as your lady's maid. Will that suit you, my lady?"

Numb, Clara nodded.

"Then until tomorrow, my lady." He took her hand and kissed it before leaving.

The sound of the door latching seemed loud in the lush room. A wave of fatigue washed over her and she stumbled into the bathing room. It, too, was beautifully appointed in creams and blues, but she barely noticed as she stripped off her grimy clothing and washed in a basin.

A thick white robe hung from hook. She wrapped herself in it before leaving the room to go into the bedchamber. Clara rarely slept in the nude but she felt so tired, suddenly, that she didn't care as she shucked off the robe, climbed the steps, and rolled in between the coverlet and thick feather mattress, falling asleep almost immediately.

Chapter Thirty

When Clara woke again, daylight streamed through the bedchamber window. She watched motes of dust floating in the shafts of light, feeling well rested. She must have slept all the preceding day and night, which seemed odd but she put it down as stress. Sitting up, she found she was still naked and she pulled the cover up over her chest against the chill of the air.

A footfall in the archway drew her attention and she saw a young woman, with hair the color of straw, standing there.

"My lady," she said, "my name is Katerina. I am your new maid." She curtsied. "Are you ready to rise, my lady?"

Clara nodded, though she made no move to get up. She looked around for the robe from the day before.

"Allow me to choose your clothes for today, my lady, and I will help you dress."

Katerina went to a large, white wardrobe and selected a bright blue gown, laying it on the bed. She selected several undergarments, including the corset so popular in the South, and laid those out.

"Does this color please you?" she asked, indicating the dress.

Clara nodded and slowly got out of the bed. As Katerina began to help her, she said, "My lady, though I know you must still be tired from your ordeal—you were sleeping very soundly when I came here last night with these clothes—the king has ordered for the Royal Tailors to attend you. The clothing in the wardrobe was given by ladies of the Court who did not need them, but her ladyship will need a suitable wardrobe of her own.

"Then, his Majesty has requested the pleasure of your company at the noon meal. Please, take a deep breath and hold onto the bed post."

Clara wrapped her hands around the wood and took a deep breath.

As soon as she did, Katerina tightened the corset, tying it tightly.

"Is that too tight, my lady? You may release your breath. I'm told the corset is not generally worn in the North."

The corset was quite tight but Clara thought she could

manage. She shook her head and stepped into the dress as Katerina held it open for her. More strings were tied in the back.

"After the noon meal, her ladyship is free to do whatever pleases her. Perhaps a tour of the gardens?" She came around to stand in front of Clara and adjusted the bodice of the dress. "There also has been proposed a ball, to be held in your honor. Won't that be lovely, my lady?"

Clara looked around for something to write upon, since she had no idea what a "ball" was.

"I believe you are searching for this?" Katerina picked up a slate and piece of chalk from a nearby table.

Clara took it with a smile of thanks and wrote out her question.

"A ball, my lady, is a formal gathering where people eat, drink, and dance."

"I don't know how to dance," she wrote.

"I'm sure we can find someone to teach you. Balls are so wonderful. I know you will like it."

She felt skeptical but nodded.

"If her ladyship will follow me, there is a breakfast laid out for you in the parlor."

Clara found herself to be just as hungry as she was

yesterday and ate every crumb of what was put before her. The dishes were cleared away and a servant called to remove them to the kitchens.

"If her ladyship will come with me," said Katerina.

Clara gathered up a handkerchief, the slate, and chalk and followed her maid out of the room. She looked around with avid interest as they left the wing. Glancing over her shoulder, she was elated to find no guards followed.

They passed people who made no acknowledgment of her, going down into the lower levels of the Palace where there was more traffic. They came into a wing where they passed rooms where people were being fitted for shoes, seeing hairdressers, and meeting with tailors.

They came into the very last room, where several men in matching scarlet and white garb awaited them.

"Lady Clara," said Katerina, "the Royal Tailors."

And so began one of the strangest mornings Clara had ever endured. She was shown dozens of bolts of cloth in a variety of shades, patterns, and kinds. Every inch of her was measured and re-measured, with and without her corset. When the tailors learned she enjoyed riding, a whole new set of bolts were brought out. Her mind swam with it all and, in the middle of choosing cloth for her ball gown, she thought, *But I might not even stay here.*

After the tailors, they visited the cobblers and hairdressers. The hairdressers cooed over the length and thickness of her hair and they intricately styled it, piling it in braids on her head. By the time Katerina led her away, Clara was sick of the whole idea of clothing and appearance and wouldn't have cared if Marduk turned her out into the street wearing nothing but a potato sack.

She also felt hot and out of breath. Her back pained her but she tried to show no discomfort as Katerina led her down the hall, chattering about something.

The hall tilted, all of a sudden, and Clara felt lightheaded. The floor rose up to her meet her but strong arms caught her around the waist.

"My lady," cried her maid, coming to kneel beside her. "Are you all right?"

"She looks ready to faint," said a masculine voice. "Is there a couch nearby?"

"Right this way."

The man lifted her in his arms and followed Katerina back into the wing, going into an empty fitting room. He laid her on a fainting couch and the incline helped her breathe a little better. The man, who she saw now was a soldier from his scarlet tunic and mail, knelt beside her. A golden double-headed eagle covered the chest of the tunic.

"Are you all right, my lady?" he asked.

She nodded and smiled at him.

"This is Lady Clara," said Katerina, "newly arrived. His Majesty rescued her from men trying to sell her to the Tieran King."

"I have heard of her." The soldier took her hand and kissed it. "My lady, I am Captain Jarrett, of His Majesty's Royal Guard, and I've been apprised of your situation. In fact, I came here searching for you, to speak with you on the particulars of your personal guard. My lady, if I may be so bold, but you are of the North, yes?"

Clara nodded. Jarrett smiled, laugh lines crinkling around the corners of his lips and eyes. He had tanned skin, white teeth, and black hair.

"Then, my lady, it's safe to say you aren't used to the, ah, Southern fashions?"

He means the corset, Clara thought, and she shook her head.

"Katerina, I believe you may need to make some adjustments for the sake of her ladyship's health."

"Yes, thank you, Captain Jarrett." Katerina frowned at

the soldier but he ignored her.

"I will be waiting in the hall, then, my lady." Jarrett stood, bowed, and left, closing the door behind him.

Katerina helped her to her feet and neither of them spoke as she loosened the corset.

"I am sorry, my lady," she finally said after tying up the dress and coming around. "I should have realized it needed to be looser."

She looked upset and Clara gave her a little hug to show she was forgiven. Katerina looked surprised but returned the embrace before opening the door, allowing Jarrett to come in.

"My lady," he said, "I understand you're to meet the king for the noon meal. It is nearly that time. I will be happy to escort you, and we can talk along the way." He offered his arm and Clara took it.

As they left the wing and walked down the hall, he said, "As I said, as Captain of the Guard, I am in charge of your personal guard, my lady. If you feel threatened or frightened at any time, please tell me. I'm afraid you'll have to tell me or one of my lieutenants when you plan to leave the Palace, so I can make the proper arrangements. As things stand now, you will only have guards at your chamber door."

They entered a large hall in which milled exquisitely dressed people. Conversations echoed against the marble walls and pillars, creating a cacophony of sound. As they weaved through the crowd, it seemed as if Jarrett hurried her. Behind them, Katerina protested but he didn't seem to hear as he pulled Clara along.

Finally, they came out of the other side and Jarrett, glancing over his shoulder, said, "We seemed to have lost Kat. Before she finds us, I must ask, my lady, have you had any of the wine here?"

It was a strange question and she shook her head.

"I would firmly suggest you avoid the wine. It would not be to her ladyship's liking."

Frowning, her hand reached for her slate to ask what did he mean by that, when Kat emerged from the crowd.

"There you are," he said, smiling as if nothing odd had happened. "I was afraid we had lost you."

"As had I," she huffed.

"His Majesty's private dining room is just through here, my lady." And he led them on.

Jarrett left her with a bow in front of the closed door leading into the room.

"Pardon my forwardness, I would be wary of him, my lady," said Kat. "He is well-known as an incorrigible flirt."

Clara didn't think Jarrett had been particularly flirtatious but only nodded to show she had heard the maid. One of the guards flanking the room opened the door and stepped inside. Clara faintly heard him announcing her.

The guard stepped back out and held the door open for them. When Kat failed to follow Clara, she looked back with a crooked brow.

"His Majesty," said Kat, "wished to have this time alone with you, my lady."

Apprehension clenched her gut, but before she could reach out to drag the maid into the room, the guard closed the door. Realizing there was nothing for it, she turned to face her fate.

The small room was large and sunny, with bright rays pouring in through tall windows. Through the windows was a vine-covered terrace, small white blossoms waving in the wind, and beyond the terrace sloped a clipped lawn. Bertrand gleamed in the distance.

The room itself was painted in rose and creams and

matching rugs were scattered on the floor. King Marduk stood by a small cherry wood table by one of the windows.

"Lady Clara," he said, "I'm so glad you could join me."

His bright smile and easy manner gave her a vague sense of vertigo, as if she had stepped through a mirage.

She crossed the room and sat in the chair he held for her. When he sat across from her, a servant stepped forward and lifted away the silver covers over their plates. Another servant stepped forward with a decanter of wine and, after filling Marduk's glass, went to fill hers.

Suddenly remembering Jarrett's warning, she put her hand over the top of the glass.

"Does her ladyship not like wine?" Marduk asked.

She shook her head and pointed at the beaker of water on the table. Marduk nodded at the servant, who set down the decanter and filled Clara's glass with the water.

"I hope you enjoy the food. I wasn't sure what you liked," he said, cutting a piece of meat and sticking it in his mouth.

They ate in silence. Clara looked out the window, watching the odd carriage clatter by. The room appeared to be situated near the main drive leading up to the Palace. The Palace itself was on the tallest hill in Bertrand. She wondered if the city extended around them on all sides.

When they finished and the dishes cleared away, a servant set dishes of pudding in front of them. Clara glanced at the servant and jerked in shock, thinking it was Asher. But a heartbeat later, she realized he only had the same curly blonde hair.

"Everything all right?" asked Marduk.

She nodded, smiling sheepishly, and began to eat the dessert.

"Have you enjoyed your morning thus far?" he asked.

She nodded again.

"Has Captain Jarrett contacted you yet?"

Another nod.

"He is a good man and you can feel free to trust him completely. And Katerina? Has she served you well?"

Clara nodded, sipping the water, feeling no need to talk about her near faint in the hall.

"That's lovely." Marduk patted his lips with a cloth. "I suppose we should transition to more important, serious matters then. The first matter, and I am sorry to ask this, involves General Emmerich."

What good mood Clara had been in faded away. She felt her face go solemn as she looked at the king.

"First, I must ask, was he in good health when you were taken away?"

She nodded.

"I only ask because my sources within Candor have said he's made no public appearances since the fall of the city. All of the day-to-day duties and taking control of the city has been handled by his first Captain, Asher." Marduk watched her carefully as he continued. "Captain Asher who, I believe, was appointed to be his successor?"

Clara shrugged. Emmerich had made no mention to her of appointing a successor.

"Hmm. Still, I think it might be safe to assume Emmerich is either ill or dead?"

Looking down, she made no move to reply.

"I understand if Emmerich became a friend of yours during your, ah, tenure with his army. If he is dead, you have my most sincere condolences."

She nodded. On impulse, she wrote, "What's to become of Gavin?"

He sighed. "Gavin is a traitor, even if he was misled. I'm afraid I cannot change the law in this regard. There is only one punishment for treason: death."

Her mouth dropped open as tears filled her eyes.

Vehemently, she shook her head.

"I'm sorry, Lady Clara. I have no choice."

The chalk scrapped loudly on the slate as she wrote. "Can't you keep him imprisoned for life? Or exiled? Please? For me?"

He sighed, his fingers idly playing with a fork. "I can bring it before the Council, but I can make no promises."

Seeing that there was nothing more she could say, Clara cleaned her slate even as she fought back tears.

He fell silent for a time as he finished his dessert. She had lost her appetite. A servant cleared away the bowls and refilled their glasses. Once they were alone again, Marduk leaned forward, clasping his hands on the table in front of him.

"My lady, I want you to know that I will not force you to do anything you do not wish to do. But, now that you know the truth, I ask that you consider being of service to the country of Lorst and help me to stop Emmerich."

Slowly, Clara wrote, "Did you ever catch the assassin that murdered King Tristan?"

"No. I'm afraid we never did find the man. Nor were we able to locate the conspirator behind it. Whoever it was—and, yes, I believe it was Emmerich—he was very skillful in keeping himself hidden."

Clara slowly wiped her slate clean again, trying to ignore the bitter taste in her mouth.

"My lady, you need not make a decision right away. You've been through a lot in these last few days alone. Rest. Explore the Palace and Bertrand. When you have made your decision, let me know."

She wrote, "Katerina told me about a ball in my honor?"

"Ah, that. Well, if you choose to leave, it will be your going away ball. If you choose to stay, it will be your formal introduction into the Court. If you have yet to make a decision, it will be simply a ball." He laughed. "Courtiers don't care for the reason to make merry as long as they have the opportunity."

Clara smiled weakly as she let that sink in, gazing out through the window once more. Finally, she wrote, "I will try to give you an answer soon."

"That, my lady, is all I ask."

Chapter Thirty-One

The afternoon stretched before Clara after leaving the King's dining room and she didn't know what to do at first.

"Why not a drive through Bertrand?" suggested Katerina as they strolled away. "We can visit one of the basilicas, if you like, or a bazaar."

She considered that for a moment and then nodded. She obviously wasn't a prisoner, so why not enjoy herself?

"I shall inform Captain Jarrett immediately. If her ladyship will wait here." Katerina walked away, leaving Clara in the hall full of the glittering, beautiful people.

Suddenly feeling shy, she stood by a pillar and tried to blend in. Listening to the surrounding conversation, she didn't hear anything about the Rebel Army, or Emmerich, or anything of greater importance than the latest fashion or next garden party. Clara felt confused. Didn't courtiers help run the kingdom?

It seemed to take a long time for Katerina to return. "If her ladyship will follow me," she said.

Katerina led her down the hall and out onto the front steps. A black coach with the royal arms emblazoned on the door awaited them. Mounted guards in scarlet garb, with the double-headed eagle on their chests, awaited them as well. Two stood before the carriage and two were behind.

Clara bit her bottom lip. Was this really necessary?

Katerina saw her hesitation and said, "The King doesn't wish for any harm to come to you. And Captain Jarrett has taken his job very seriously ever since..." She cleared her throat, looking away. "Ever since he succeeded his predecessor."

They descended the steps and a footman opened the carriage door, setting out a footstool. Clara climbed in first, surprised to see Captain Jarrett already there.

"If the ladies don't mind, I think I will accompany Lady Clara on her first outing," he said.

Katerina hesitated in the doorway. She looked from Jarrett to Clara. "Does her ladyship object?"

It seemed like nothing and she shook her head. She rather liked Jarrett, despite his cryptic warning. Katerina climbed in and sat next to Clara. The door closed and, after a moment, jerked into motion.

No one spoke as they went down the winding drive. They passed through the Palace gate and down into a residential section.

"This is the High Circle," said Jarrett. "The most noble of the families have their homes here. Cousins of the Royal Blood also stayed here but, unfortunately, they all mysteriously died. An illness peculiar to them, I believe, wasn't it, Katerina?"

"It was," she said coldly, giving him a hard look.

He chuckled. "Kat here thinks I'm uncouth for bringing that up."

"It certainly isn't fit for polite society."

"If her ladyship isn't offended, why should you be? Are you offended, Lady Clara?"

Clara smiled and shook her head. Jarrett's manner reminded her of Gavin's. She liked hearing him speak.

"See? Lady Clara, if I should offend you, feel free to brain me with that slate." He laughed at his joke and turned back to the window, pointing out some of the houses and talking about their inhabitants.

Soon, they left the High Circle and passed two more residential sections before entering the commercial section of the city.

"Would her lady like to take in one of the markets?" asked Jarrett.

She nodded excitedly, having forgotten for a moment that she should be worrying over Emmerich and the fate of Gavin.

Leaning out the window, Jarrett yelled at the driver to stop at the next market. It was a cloth and jewel market. Many soldiers milled about, keeping an eye on the more expensive wares. Jarrett got out first and helped Clara and Katerina out. He took Clara's arm and led her through the crowd, Kat following close behind.

They went from vendor to vendor, looking at the beautiful cloths and jewelry. Clara paused to examine a bolt dyed a deep purple.

"Does her ladyship like it?" asked Jarrett.

She nodded and mimed sewing.

"You can sew? Would you like to use that to make a dress?"

She nodded but patted her waist, where a money pouch would have hung.

"No worry, my lady." Going to the vendor, he began to haggle for the cloth. Clara tried to stop him by pulling on his arm but he only patted her hand.

"Her ladyship is right to protest, Captain," Katerina interrupted. "It's not proper for you to buy her such an expensive gift."

"Kat. You worry too much over what's proper." He winked at Clara and turned back to his negotiations.

"I do wish you would stop calling me that."

Clara grinned as she turned from them, looking across the courtyard. Something green caught her eye and she froze, staring. A young boy in tattered clothing stood at the mouth of an alleyway. He stared back at her. From beneath his tunic swung a large green tail.

Their eyes met for a long moment before he turned, disappearing into the darkness, the tail whipping behind him. Clara tugged on Jarrett's sleeve again and pointed frantically.

"What's the matter, my lady?" he asked as he handed the merchant some coins.

Taking out her slate, she wrote, "I thought I saw a boy with a tail."

When he read that, he covered the slate with his hands before Kat (who was distracted by a nearby necklace) could see. In a low voice, he said, "I would keep such remarks to yourself. Quick, my lady, erase that. And do not speak of it again. Not even to His Majesty."

His cold, serious look frightened her and her hands shook as she scrubbed the slate clean. When Kat turned back to them, she frowned.

"Are you all right, my lady?" she asked. "Do we need to return to the Palace?"

Clara nodded again, wanting to get away from the strangeness that surrounded her.

The bolt of cloth was delivered to her rooms but Clara didn't have the heart to work on it. Instead, she directed it to be taken to a room she would turn into her workroom. It had lots of natural light and several tables. When she found it after returning from the market, it made her feel at home while also frightened her that Marduk could guess her hobbies.

The rest of the day was spent with her wandering through the wing, looking at the rooms. Katerina's presence became so annoying, that she ordered the maid to leave her be until she needed her. It was something Lady Maria would have done, but Clara needed solitude. Finding a barren room that hadn't found a purpose yet, she stayed in there, staring out the window, until she heard Kat searching for her. It was time for the evening meal and the King again requested her presence.

Feeling bold and moody, she sent word that she was ill and could not attend him. After poking at the meal brought to her, she washed and went to bed, only to toss and turn for several candle marks. The image of the strange boy with the tail, as well as Jarrett's words, would not leave her.

Giving up on any hope of sleep, she climbed out of bed and dressed in one of the lighter dresses, foregoing the corset entirely. Rudely plaiting her hair, she shoved her feet into the first pair of slippers she came across and opened her chamber door. The hall was quiet and dark. To her left stood the doors of the wing itself, on the other side of which stood the guards.

But perhaps it wouldn't be unusual if she went for a late night walk? She couldn't very well climb out of a window, so going through the entrance seemed her only option.

The guards turned to her in confusion when she pushed open the door.

"Is all well, my lady?" one of them asked.

She nodded and pointed down the hall. With two fingers, she mimed walking.

"One of us should go with you, my lady. Captain Jarrett wouldn't—"

"The Captain," interrupted another, "instructed us to let her go whenever she pleased, even without escort. In case she had a vision." The guard looked at her squarely. "Have you had a vision, my lady?"

Catching on, she nodded.

"All right," said the first reluctantly. "His Majesty will no doubt be in his observatory." He gave her directions to it. Clara nodded her thanks and scurried away.

The candle mark was very late and she came across no one in halls or stairs as she traveled to the ground floor, save for the odd soldier. No one tried to stop her.

Going out onto the grounds in the front, she tried to decide her next move. Seeing a footpath that went around the Palace, she followed it, looking around with interest. The only sounds were her footsteps, crickets, and the occasional owl. After what seemed an age, she rounded a corner and stopped short.

A dark shadow slipped through a cellar door in the side of the Palace. It seemed an odd place for a cellar door and, after the shadow disappeared, she approached it. The door sat ajar slightly. She pushed it open to reveal a downward slanting hallway lined with smokeless lanterns.

As she descended, the door swinging closed behind her, a feeling of foreboding grew within her. Her skin crawled and it was everything to keep her from bolting. She forced herself to focus on her gait.

At last, she came to another door. Two guards stood there. Horror filled her as she saw they had catlike eyes. They regarded her for a moment.

One of the said in a sibilant voice, "The King bid us to let you pass when you came, my lady." She glimpsed fangs as he spoke. "Please let us know if we can be of any assistance." He opened the door for her and they bowed her through, the door creaking closed behind her.

She stepped into a large room lit by a giant witch light burning overhead. The room was full of cages and tanks. Creatures shuffled and moved in them. Something large snorted in the one to her right and she jumped, turning.

A giant boar stared at her. Shaggy fur edged its throat and spikes crawled up its spine. Hard plates like scales covered its sides. Giant tusks protruded from under the snout. But what sent a shiver through her were the eyes. The eyes gazed at her with all the intelligence and sorrow of a person. The eyes looked right through her.

Turning, she found a second boar to her left. To get away from their uncanny gazes, she moved on.

Each cage contained another animal. Some looked like great cats while others resembled dogs. A few were equine in appearance. But they were all two or three or even four times the size of their natural counterparts. All of them had spikes and shaggy fur. All of them looked upon her with the same soulful eyes.

She came to some large tanks and she gazed into them. Seaweed grew from a dirt bottom and normal fish swam by. It seemed serene enough. But something moved in the murky depths. Slowly, Clara stepped closer, placing her hands on the glass.

A blue-grey blur shot out of the murk toward her, swimming past at amazing speed. She jerked back as the creature twisted, returning to float just in front of her.

It had the long tail of a fish, with a fin growing out of its back. The hands were so webbed as to barely deserve the name. More scales covered the stomach and chest. But the shoulders and head were like a person's. The eyes were large, round, and black. There was no nose. Gills opened and closed along the neck. The mouth opened, revealing rows of sharp teeth.

Shuddering, she backed away.

At the very back of the room were tall cages that stretched all the way to the ceiling. Trees had been made to grow, though how the wizards kept them alive, Clara couldn't even begin to guess.

She stood and gazed into the leafy darkness but nothing moved. She remembered the strange bird she had seen on her first sight of Bertrand and turned away. She didn't want to see anymore. She couldn't bear to see anymore.

Turning, she fled, but in her panic she turned down the wrong pathway. Stopping, trying to get her bearings, a grunt drew her attention to the side.

In cages filled with rocks and on the rocks, shaggy, giant-footed men slept. The size of their feet in comparison with the rest of their bodies was almost comical and Clara wondered how they managed to walk. Dark stains covered their feet. It reminded her of the stained feet of the men and women who stomped grapes for wine.

Jarrett's warning rang in her mind and Clara gagged, backing away. She remembered, suddenly, Asher talking about the sea people. Her shiver threatened to become a shake and she clasped her hands together. Gavin had lied to her–again. Why? To protect her? To aid Marduk?

The door at the entrance suddenly opened and closed. Spinning, she listened to boots tromping along nearby. Was she supposed to be down here? If Captain Jarrett was a part of the Rebellion, then he made sure she would be down here, which meant there was something she needed to see.

Turning, she raced away, her slippers barely making a sound on the stone floor as she slipped down yet another pathway. There were more sad-faced creatures—no, she corrected herself. There were more sad-faced people. Clara gulped back her bile as she tried to move silently.

She stopped by a cage and listened. Two men were speaking but she didn't recognize either voice. The voices drifted past them along a different pathway and she edged down the aisle. Taking a moment to get her bearings, she found an aisle that bisected the room and eventually found her way back to the entrance without encountering the guards or wizards or whoever they were walking among the cages.

The catlike guards turned to her curiously as she came out.

"Are you well, my lady?" asked the one who had addressed her earlier.

She nodded and, before they could ask another

question, she walked away as quickly as possible. Later, Clara barely remembered her walk back to her rooms. But when she entered them, she immediately went to the bathing room and dry heaved over the hole in the floor meant for such refuse.

What have I done? she wondered.

It was some time before Clara's stomach settled and she splashed water onto her face. She had to leave. She had to escape. She needed to get back to Emmerich before–

Someone walked up to the door of the bathing room. Turning, she looked frantically for a weapon when she heard Jarrett's voice say, "Lady Clara?"

Her knees going weak with relief, she went to the door and opened it.

He stared down at her, the dark shadows the room making deep wells under his eyes. "The menagerie is horrible, isn't it?" he said.

Slowly, she nodded.

"I think you need to sit."

Clara wasn't going to argue that. She let him lead her to the couch, where he sat her. "I would have taken you, but one of my partners objected. So he disguised himself as the King and ordered the guards to let you through if they saw you. And he cast a spell over me so I could follow you, see your reaction. I think it's safe to assume you aren't in the King's employ."

She shook her head, feeling disgusted with and hating herself. Whether or not Emmerich killed the Princess seemed suddenly irrelevant, knowing that Marduk was a monster.

"All of those creatures," he continued, "were once people. But Marduk changed them. He will use them in battle, when Emmerich gets here. There's a chest that he uses to do it. I've seen him use it." He grimaced. "How it works, I don't know. We know he's working on some project that needs you, Lady Clara, but we can't guess how or why. Either way, he needs to be stopped."

She nodded, feeling her emotions beginning to settle and a strange calm stealing over her. She looked up at Jarrett.

"Will you help us, my lady?"

Clara nodded. A question suddenly occurred to her. She pointed to him, then downward, cocking her head and frowning.

"Are you asking me about the menagerie?"

She shook her head and pointed at him emphatically

and pointed downward.

"Uh. How did I come to be in here without raising suspicion?"

She nodded.

"Grappling hook. I climbed in through the balcony." He nodded at the open door, which, in Clara's earlier panic, she hadn't noticed.

Of course he did. That struck her as funny and she shook with silent laughter. If she had a voice, it would have sounded hysterical, she was sure.

☐

Chapter Thirty-Two

Asher, exhausted, dropped into the chair, propping his feet up on the footstool. Leaning his head back, he breathed a deep sigh of relief to once again be back in his chamber.

Though his status as Emmerich's First Captain allowed him to take a larger chamber, or even a whole set of chambers, he chose to room on the same floor as the other captains. His chamber was small but adequate. And since he had no lady to keep him warm at night, the small size of the bed was no problem.

The thought of women reminded him of Clara and he hoped the young Seer was all right. Though he had barely known Clara, he recognized a strength and resilience in her quite like that of his own sister, who awaited his return to Seasong. It troubled him that Emmerich wasn't willing to at least send a spy to ascertain her condition, but he understood the wisdom behind it.

At least, that's what he told himself when he defended

the general to the other captains. Emmerich had been acting strangely ever since Clara had been taken. More and more of the responsibilities of bringing Candor under heel had fallen to him. In fact, he went all day that day without noting anything down to ask Emmerich, as he had done in the beginning. He knew that if he were to go see the General right then, he would be staring into nothing, morose and silent, unwilling to answer his questions beyond monosyllables.

He must have loved her, Asher suddenly thought. He sat up more in his chair, suddenly feeling even more sorry for his general. It hadn't ended well the last time he had loved someone.

Someone pounded on his door. Groaning, Asher got up and opened it. "Aye?"

A soldier saluted him. "Captain, Haggard has just arrived."

"Haggard? He must have ridden night and day to get here so quickly."

"We believe he did, my lord. His horse died as soon as he dismounted."

Asher frowned. Any misuse of an animal detested him and he decided he would take Haggard to task for that.

"Where is Haggard now?"

"He was taken directly to General Emmerich."

"Thank you. You may return to your duties."

The soldier saluted again and marched off. Asher tugged on his tunic, ran a hand through his hair, and walked down the hall to see what news Haggard had brought.

Someone knocked on his door and Emmerich slowly opened his eyes. He had been dozing and half-dreaming about Clara. He almost expected the mute Seer to walk in after he croaked, "Enter," but it was only Haggard, grim and travel-stained.

"I've come to give my full report, my lord," he said. He had his hand on a pouch at his waist, and he shifted his weight.

A prickle danced over Emmerich's scalp and he struggled to sit up. The wound in his side pained him, causing him to fall back into the pillows.

"Well," he said roughly, "go on."

Haggard came closer to the bed, though he had not been bidden to do so. Again, there was that feeling of unease and warning, and Emmerich slipped a hand under his pillow, where he kept a dagger.

"M'lord," began Haggard, "it was a group of Captain Terrence's men. We think they may've been actin' under his orders." His hand slid into the pouch.

"Haggard, what do you have there?" He heard a commotion in the hall outside his door.

Haggard lunged at him.

Asher was halfway to Emmerich's chambers when Captain Wilhelm came running up to him.

"Asher!" Patrick cried. "The spy, he's been found."

"What?" Asher grasped Wilhelm's shoulders as the captain came to an unsteady stop before him. "What are you talking about?"

"The spy we thought had fled?"

"Aye."

"He hadn't. He was imprisoned in a house near the Red Quarter."

"Who had captured him?"

"Conspirators against Emmerich. They're Marduk's men."

"Was their leader there?"

"No. The conspirators were killed but the spy was able to tell us everything. There was a plot, to kidnap both the Seer and Emmerich."

Asher felt the blood leave his face. "And did he know the leader's name?"

"Their leader is the old swordsmaster, Haggard."

Asher swore and began running down the hall, yelling for guards.

Wilhelm followed hard on his heels. "What is it?"

"Haggard is with Emmerich now."

They climbed the last set of stairs, taking them two or three at a time. He yelled at soldiers in the hall to follow him. The guards flanking Emmerich's chamber door drew their swords in surprise.

"Is Haggard in there?" demanded Asher.

"Aye," a few of the men answered but he was already dashing past them. He heard the tramp of nailed boots following him as he slammed open the bedchamber door.

He was just in time to see a flash of light, then only an empty bed where Emmerich had laid.

The portal opened in a burst blister of blue, depositing

two figures onto the stone floor.

The Rebel General, Emmerich rolled off of Haggard's body, a bloody dagger clutched in his hand. The old warrior gurgled as he choked on his own blood and Emmerich smiled grimly the sound.

Erin gestured and black-robed wizards converged on Emmerich. He caught one in the groin with his foot as he twisted, rolled, and gained his feet. His teeth bared in battle rage, ignoring the wound at his side. Blood began to stain the white bandages. Emmerich raised the dagger, bellowing a challenge. But one of the wizards threw the sleeping dust into his face.

He gagged on the air as his lungs constricted. Slowly, Emmerich sank to his knees, then slumped to the ground, unconscious.

Erin smirked as he came forward. One of the wizards checked Emmerich's throat.

"He sleeps," he told Erin.

"Good." Turning, he nudged Haggard with his toe. "What of this one's brat?"

"The White Sisters are tending her."

"Have her taken to the menagerie. His Majesty has been wanting to experiment on children."

"Aye, my lord."

When Emmerich woke again, he lay on a comfortable bed, dressed in new clothes, and he heard the distant twitter of birds. The room was small and the walls were stone. A fireplace sat to one side. He was also tied down with padded restraints.

A maid was standing beside the bed, rolling soiled bandages.

"Where am I?" he asked.

The maid jumped. "Oh, my lord, you startled me."

"Where am I?"

"You are in the Palace in Bertrand. King Marduk will be here shortly."

The maid gathered up the cloths and a basin of red water and left Emmerich. As soon as the door closed behind her, he started to pull at the restraints. But they were tightly tied and strong. He stopped when a sharp pain lanced through his side and across his chest.

Looking around, Emmerich began to feel a little excitement. If he was in Bertrand, then he was near Clara. If he got free, he could find her and they could flee. Just as he started to pull on the restraints again, the bedchamber door opened and Marduk swept into the room.

"Old friend," he said. "I'm so glad that you've come to be my guest. And you gave me a guest-gift without meaning to do so! Ordering Haggard's death would have been annoying and you saved me the trouble."

Emmerich froze, feeling the old hatred stir in his heart. "Traitor," he spat.

"That, friend, depends entirely on what side of the battle you're on: the winning side, or the losing. From this side, I would say you're the traitor." He picked up a cane bottom chair from where it sat by the wall and brought it over by the bed. Sitting, he crossed his legs and folded his hands over one knee. "Are you resting comfortably?"

"Where is Clara? What have you done with her?"

"Your Seer? All I've done is provide clothing, an entire wing for her use, a very well-trained lady's maid, and a heavy-handed dose of kindness from myself."

"She isn't some simpering whore you can pay off to do your bidding."

"No." He bared his front teeth in an approximation of a smile. "No, she isn't that. What she is, though, is hurt, confused, and just about ready to believe anything I tell her.

And she was that way before she even got here! I usually have to manipulate people into believing me. But she came here already made, like a Nativity gift. All she lacked was the bow."

"You manipulated her plenty, I'm sure."

"Well. A little. I am the one responsible for dropping the knowledge in her ear that you killed Monica. I told Haggard to be fuzzy on the reasons why. And, there were other things but they hardly matter." Marduk smirked as he took in Emmerich's expression and he made a tut-tut sound with his tongue. "Still with the anger issues, eh?"

"Let me out of these restraints, and I'll show you anger issues."

"You're acting like I slaughtered your whole family. Oh, wait! That's because I did." He chuckled. "I suppose they should have helped my master when they had the chance."

Emmerich shook with fury and the need to strangle the sorcerer with his bare hands.

"You should be proud of yourself. Not every man starts a war over the desire for vengeance." He made a show of adjusting the cuff of his right sleeve, smoothing the fabric before rejoining his hands over his knee. "You haven't asked me about Gavin yet."

Emmerich choked back enough of his anger to say, "You haven't given me a chance to, yet."

"Well, I beg pardon, then."

"None given."

"You are a hard man, Emmerich. But, anyway. Gavin is well. Or, as well as anyone living in my dungeons can hope to be. He isn't being tortured. No, I got from him what I needed. When I've achieved my goals, he'll get what he deserves: a long drop and a short stop. Or maybe I'll tie him down on the ramparts of one of my castles and have his guts exposed for the ravens to eat?" He sighed. "I can't decide."

Emmerich knew if he kept Marduk talking, he would tell him everything. The man was egotistical, that way. "What have you gotten out of Gavin?"

He snorted. "A promise to help me."

"I don't believe you. He would never—"

"You're right. He would never. Except he fell in love. And when men fall in love, they do things they would never do. Now, enough about me. Lets talk about you."

"I have one last question."

"Just one? Oh, all right. I'm in such a generous mood today."

"What are your goals? You have Lorst. What more can you possibly want?"

A dark, hungry look filled Marduk's eyes and Emmerich shivered at the evil that suddenly peered down at him. "Oh, why should I tell you when you will very shortly see for yourself? You're a big part of my plans, dear friend, and I'd hate to ruin the surprise. Now, ask me why I brought you here."

Emmerich glared up at him for a long moment, thinking about telling him where he could put that smirk. But he swallowed back the urge. "Why have you brought me here?"

"Because Clara must be free to choose. And in order for that to happen, you must be dead." He stood. "Goodbye, dear friend."

Marduk walked away but stopped at the door and turned around. "Monica was my best apprentice. I swore I would get my revenge upon you, Emmerich. And today I will. Just as you took something precious from me, I take something precious from you."

He left the room and a moment later, two wizards entered, one of whom carried a small chalice. Emmerich began to struggle wildly against his bounds but it was no use. As the wizards closed in, he thought of Clara.

☐

Chapter Thirty-Three

Asher stared at the place where General Emmerich had laid.

"I'll have the city searched," said Captain Wilhelm.

"No need," Asher replied. "Emmerich is not here. No, he's in Bertrand now, at the mercy of the usurper."

The soldiers behind them exchanged looks and low mutters. Asher knew it wouldn't be long before news of this spread to the entire camp, even if he ordered the men there to secrecy. He turned to Wilhelm.

"Assemble the captains," he said. "We will meet in the council room."

"My lord." Wilhelm saluted and left.

Asher reassigned Emmerich's guard and dismissed the other soldiers who had followed him before walking to the council room. He didn't wait long once he arrived.

"What is going on?" demanded Herne. "Wilhelm is babbling about Emmerich being kidnapped."

The other captains gathered in a loose circle around

him and Asher.

"He has been," Asher confirmed.

A shocked silence filled the room.

"We should leave immediately," spoke up Owen. "We cannot leave Emmerich in his hands."

The other men chorused their agreement but as the voices rose, Asher let out a piercing whistle, silencing them.

"No one can guess the actions of a madman," Asher said, "though I think it makes it more likely that Emmerich is well on his way to being dead now. We know that a long-standing feud was between the two, though none of us spoke of it or inquired into it. But we followed Emmerich because we wish to free Lorst from a sorcerer who would twist and pervert nature herself. And despite that feud, Emmerich has led us well.

"Now, if we are to continue to serve him as he deserves, we must complete what he started: ousting Marduk from his throne. Herne, have we any recent news from the Tieran king?"

"A rider came in last night, my lord. King Precene congratulates us on our victory and assures us his men are on the way."

"We need not inform him of Emmerich's capture as of

yet. The Tierans are superstitious people and will take this as a bad omen."

"No doubt, my lord."

Asher took a deep breath. Lorst had an uneasy peace with Tier. It hadn't been that long ago since their last war together and many people still distrusted them. Hopefully, Precene wouldn't learn of his hiding the truth and take it as an excuse to go to war with them.

"We have two months," said Terrence, "before the snows come and make it impossible to leave the north."

"Two and a half, more like," said Herne. "We're far enough south to risk waiting later."

"Winter is still a bad time for war," pointed out Owen. "By the time the Tieran men get here, it may be too late to press our cause. We may have to winter here."

They fell silent as they considered the possibility.

Finally, Wilhelm said, "What if we pushed on without the extra men?"

"Marduk's army is large," responded Asher, "and though it pains me to use them, the Tieran companies will have magic users among them who can help us. I would rather we won this without resorting to magic but we may not have that luxury any longer. The fact that Marduk could so easily send men here to snatch away both our Seer and our General means we will need all the help we can get."

He flexed his hand, thinking all of this over. Finally, he said, "I need a map."

One of the captains grabbed a map from a cubbyhole in the wall and unrolled it on the large table. They held down the corners with rocks and candlesticks. Asher bent over the map to study it.

"How long," he said, "would it take for us to get from here," he pointed to Candor and then drew a straight line down with his finger, "to here?"

"At least a month," said Herne, "since there is a major city between us that we would have to subdue."

"We could bypass it. Use the river rather than the roads for as far as we can.

"And risk going without stores?"

"Aye."

"Then three se'ennights at the least if we push it. What is your plan?"

"My plan is to have the Tierans meet us here, on the plain that lies to the west of Bertrand." He pointed to the spot on the map.

"It's risky. They may not make it in time."

"But they could. Perhaps the Tierans will have spells to quicken their travel."

"Aye, but do we want to risk our men's lives on that?"

Asher looked around the table. "Are we?"

The captains looked one to another. Terrence said, "It's foolhardy and mad."

"On the one hand, we should be cautious, but Marduk has struck our core. We must strike back, and I fear if we put it off until next spring, he will have grown too strong to defeat. We have all heard the rumors that something has his attention."

Silence fell in the room again. Finally, one by one, the men nodded their acquiescence.

"There is the matter, now, of First Captain," said Owen. "With Emmerich gone, you're now the Lord General."

Asher sighed. "Of course. Herne?"

"Aye, my lord?"

"You have the position, if you want it."

"There are more experienced men than I, my lord."

"I would have none other than you."

"Then I accept."

"Good. You can choose your replacement later. But,

now, I have a letter to a king that I need to write."

Marduk paced his chambers. Early morning sunlight glided through the wide windows and the city outside glistened. Normally, he would be enjoying the view, but he couldn't hold his mind still long enough for it.

Finally, someone knocked on the door.

"Enter," he said.

Erin swept into the room, coming to a stop before Marduk and bowing. "The potion has finished taking affect."

"Excellent." He clasped his hands together, as if to keep himself from flying apart in excitement. "I was concerned he would be too hearty. I need to keep Clara off-balance and we couldn't afford to wait overly long. Where is our little Seer?"

"I believe she is still in her chambers."

"Good. Good. Go and fetch her. Bring her to Emmerich's room. I will be waiting there."

Clara stared down at the hoop of embroidery, trying to

gain some interest in weaving the colored threads through the cream fabric. Beside her, Katerina hummed softly as she worked.

A knock on the door brought a much-desired interruption and Clara set aside her "work" as the maid answered the door. A wizard she had often seen in Marduk's company came into the room. He bowed.

"My lady," he said, "my name is Erin and his Majesty has sent me to fetch you."

She stood, gathering up the bag that contained her writing utensils, and followed Erin out. Whatever was wrong caused the wizard to walk quickly and she had to stretch her legs to keep up. She gasped against the corset and feared another fainting episode by the time they finally reached the top of a tower on the Palace's far side. Marduk waited for them outside a door.

"My lady, are you well?" he asked when they reached him.

She shook her head as she tried to catch her breath.

Marduk gave Erin a hard look. "My apologies for Wizard Erin's zealousness. Do you need to sit or lay down?"

Clara shook her head. Her heart had finally slowed and

she could breathe easily again.

"My dear." Marduk took her hands in his own and stared down at them, sorrow creasing his face. She fought the urge to snatch her hands away, remembering the creatures. "My dear, as you may have guessed, I have spies in the rebel army. It's a necessity. I wouldn't be surprised if Emmerich has—had—sent spies to my own court." He looked up at her. "I also devised a plan to use one of my spies, my most trusted spy, to bring Emmerich here. I gave him a passing stone. Do you know what that is?"

She shook her head.

"It's like a portable portal. It only works once and will bring those who activate it back to the place where it was made. I gave Haggard such a stone."

At the name of Haggard, Clara looked down to keep Marduk from seeing the hatred and disgust that filled her eyes. Of course it had been Haggard. Who else, but that slaver?

"The plan was to hold Emmerich as a captive, which isn't as bad as it sounds, in order to end this conflict. But Haggard was too late. Emmerich was badly hurt in the last battle and though we tried to heal him here, our best efforts came to naught. He died, Clara."

She stared up at him, into that handsome face she wanted to smash beneath her boot heel. She wanted to pluck out the eyes that gazed at her with sympathy. Tears misted her vision and, in horror, she covered her face with her hands. It could be a trick. It couldn't be Emmerich.

"Would you like to see him?"

She nodded, dropping her hands and letting him see her tears.

Marduk opened the door to his left and gestured for her to enter. "I will be out here."

And Clara stepped into the room from her vision. She looked around, recognizing every stone in the floor and wall, every cold coal in the fireplace. Crows cawed. And there Emmerich lay, on the bed, hands folded over his chest, just as she Saw.

Clara walked over to the bed, wishing this wasn't true. She stared at the body, willing for there to be a flicker, a momentary haze, to reveal the illusion. But nothing happened. Reaching out, she caressed his cheek. It was cold and very much real.

With a sob, she dropped to her knees by the bed and laid her head on his side. If she had gone with him to Candor, maybe she could have prevented this. But he was a murderer. Didn't he deserve what he got?

It didn't matter, though. She didn't know the Emmerich of then. All she knew was the Emmerich of now was gone.

Raising her head, she looked at him and felt rage and grief consume her. No more, she swore. I am through with merely passing through this world. I will avenge his death.

Standing, Clara leaned over Emmerich and kissed him. A bitter taste, like a tonic, touched her lips. She grimaced, wondering at the taste. Was that the poison Marduk had used to murder him? Turning, she spat onto the floor and rubbed her lips.

Looking down at Emmerich, with tears streaking her face and rage and grief warring in her chest like dragons, she forgot to be afraid of her voice. Everything narrowed down to this moment, this place, and nothing else mattered.

She said, "I love you."

Her voice croaked and cracked. Clara cleared her throat and swallowed, wishing there was water in the room. A tremor of fear snaked through her but she called upon her anger to suppress it. Again, with more confidence, she said, "I love you, and Marduk will pay for what he's done."

Leaning down again, she kissed Emmerich's forehead. She turned and left the room, closing the door behind her.

Marduk, Katerina, and Erin stood on the landing outside, watching her. Erin's face was guarded while Katerina and Marduk regarded her with open sympathy.

"Are you well, my lady?" Katerina asked.

Reaching into her bag, Clara took out her chalk and slate and wrote, "I will be well. Where will he be buried?"

"I cannot give him a large funeral," said Marduk, "but I can arrange a private, secret service tonight."

"Thank you," she wrote. Taking a deep breath, she continued. "I want to help you end this war. I wish to join your Court as its Seer."

Marduk smiled and it looked like the sun coming from behind a cloud. "My lady, your services will be most greatly appreciated it. And, I must confess, the thought of you leaving grieved me greatly. I've gotten used to having your beauty and friendship gracing my halls."

Clara forced a smile, all the while imagining sliding a dagger's blade across Marduk's throat, the crimson blood spilling down his chest.

Chapter Thirty-Four

Jarrett rolled his shoulder, grinning at his opponent. "Good blow," he said. "But you need to be careful about blocking your left side."

"Aye, Captain," said the soldier.

"Captain Jarrett!"

Turning, Jarrett spotted one of the young pages. He saluted his sparring partner before walking over to the boy. "Yes?"

"His Majesty demands your presence."

Jarrett tossed the practice sword into the barrel with the others and followed the boy from the yard, passing many other mock battles and training in progress as he tried to knock some of the dust from his tunic.

The boy led him into the king's private study, where Marduk was laughing over something his lackey, Erin, had said.

"Jarrett, my friend," he said.

Jarrett bowed low and knelt onto one knee. "Your

Majesty."

"Rise, rise. Would you care for some wine?"

"No, your Majesty." He stood.

"Ah, yes, like most of my men, you prefer ale. I suppose I should start keeping the disgusting stuff on hand."

"Whatever pleases his Majesty."

"Hm." Marduk regarded him for a moment with shrewd eyes. "Lady Clara is going to become a fixed member of the Court as our Seer. I understand you've only been recruiting men as you need them?"

"Yes, your Majesty."

"I want you to gather your best men whose sole job is to protect her. She cannot go anywhere without at least two guards with her. Double the guard at the entrance of her wing. I expect you to be present at each of her Court appearances. Do you understand?"

Oh, she's not going to like this, he thought. "Yes, your Majesty."

"You may go."

Jarrett bowed and left the room, going immediately to Clara's chambers, wondering what had changed to make Clara accept her new position. It was time to call the

Rebellion leaders together. The guards saluted as he approached.

"Is the lady in?" he asked.

"Yes, captain," one of the guards replied. "She looked ill, sir."

Frowning, he entered the wing and went to the chamber door, knocking. The door opened and Katerina shook her head upon seeing him.

"Her ladyship is not well," she said.

"I must speak with her immediately."

"She has received some terrible news and is in no condition–"

The door yanked open the rest of the way and Clara looked up at him with reddened eyes. She gestured for him to enter.

"My lady," he said, bowing and entering. "I've come to speak to you about the particulars of your guard, now that you're to be a permanent member of the Court."

She nodded and gestured toward the couch and chairs. Once comfortably seated, Jarrett began to run through what Marduk had instructed him.

"I will take the first watch with the new guard tonight," he said.

Clara nodded and he stood, surprised she hadn't fought him over the order for her to be constantly accompanied.

"If there are any problems, please let me know." He bowed. "If you'll excuse me."

Something was wrong, he could feel it. Something had happened that deeply upset Clara and, tonight, he was going to find out what.

Clara lay awake in her bed, unable to sleep. Every time she closed her eyes, she saw Emmerich's body and rage coursed through her again. She heard the slight creak of the door leading onto the balcony as it opened.

Getting out of the bed, she pulled on her robe and pushed back the curtain to step into the sitting room. Three dark figures were entering the room.

"Clara?" asked one of them, revealing it to be Jarrett.

In answer, she turned to the table at her right and, using the flint and tinder there, lit the lamp on the table. Warm yellow light pooled around her in the room. Looking up, she was surprised to find the other two figures were Wizard Bruin and a spindly old man she did not recognize.

"Clara," said Jarrett, "I'm sure you've met Bruin. He's a

member of our resistance. And this is Tanner, one of the leading guild members."

Tanner and Bruin bowed.

Swallowing, Clara took a deep, shaky breath. Now that the moment had arrived, she felt nervous and afraid. "Good evening," she said.

The men looked at her, stunned, for a long moment. She clasped her hands behind her, trying not to shake. She had been practicing that phrase in her mind all afternoon but the fear that now shook her upon saying it nearly knocked her over. Finally, Tanner broke the moment by saying, "We were led to believe you were a mute, my lady."

"I-I am. Or, I-I was. Um." She swallowed again. "This is hard to explain."

"Well," said Bruin, "we don't have much time."

Taking a breath, Clara slowly and haltingly spoke about what had occurred that morning. "I-I have always been t-terrified to speak."

"Now your anger is greater than your fear," Bruin finished for her.

She nodded.

"It's a phenomenon they teach about in the Academy. People are crippled not because of an injury of the body, but of the mind, and sometimes it takes an event to undo the crippling."

"This is all well and good," said Tanner, "but the news of Emmerich's death is most distressing."

"I-I haven't heard of a r-rebellion in Ber-Bertrand," said Clara.

"Marduk has laid enchantments over the whole of the city. They prohibit any treachery to leave. Trust me when I say we've tried sending messages and representatives. The results were not pleasant."

"But it doesn't keep treachery from occurring within the city," said Jarrett. The light cast deep shadows under his eyes and his voice held a rough note. "Marduk relies on a network of spies to keep him informed. That's why the rebellion leadership is not very large. Those sympathetic to the rebellion, that's another story. We've been waiting for Emmerich to draw close before trying to do anything. Now it seems we have to choose a different tactic."

"The K-King of Tier is sending troops," said Clara. "Th-that should be of great help."

"Yes. But who is leading the army now?"

"C-Captain Asher." Feeling terribly thirsty, she went to a nearby sideboard and poured herself a glass of water, which she sipped, letting the cool liquid soothe her throat.

"I know Asher," said Tanner. "He's the son of a minor baron and served in the army, when that army held its allegiance to King Tristan. He's a good man."

"We should try to assassinate the king," spoke up Clara, her words ringing clear and unhindered.

The three men stared at her. Finally, Bruin said, "What you suggest is foolish and more than a little mad."

"Why?"

"Marduk doesn't surround himself with wards and enchantments because he's so strong. He can deflect nearly any attack on his own power. If I cannot get near Marduk, I don't see how you can."

"He thinks I am-m easily man-n-n-nipulated and u-u-used. In a few d-d-d-days is the b-ball to welcome me as Court Seer. I will make my m-m-move then." She lifted her chin. "I swore I would av-venge Emmerich."

"If you fail, you could bring about the downfall of the whole rebellion, simply because of everything you know."

"Mard-duk says there are s-s-spies in Emmerich's army. I know nothing that he c-c-couldn't learn through them."

"Except you've seen us. You know about us."

"But Marduk d-doesn't know that.

Bruin shook his head. "I do not like this." He looked to Tanner.

Tanner sighed. "The rebel army is still a ways off. Though I admire Asher, I don't know if we can succeed without Emmerich. This may be our only way."

The two men looked at Jarrett, who drew himself to his full height. Clara gazed at him, not saying anything, only waiting for him to speak.

Finally, he said, "I don't like it, either, and it's a desperate move. But these are desperate times. I will make sure what soldiers are in line with us are ready, Lady Clara. Only, do not let your dagger—or your courage—fail you when the time comes."

"No," she said, "it will not." And the anger and hate throbbed in her heart like an open wound, as if in agreement.

☐

Chapter Thirty-Five

Warm sunlight fell across Emmerich's face. For a moment, he was a little boy waking up after a long fever to find the sun shining and his grandmother humming a lullaby while she sat next to him. He could almost hear the clacking of her knitting needles as she made a scarf.

When he did open his eyes, though, he didn't recognize the pale green walls around him, and no grandmother sat next to him. To his left, a large window admitted the sunlight. He slowly sat up, grimacing at the pain in his side, and looked out the window. A garden full of late summer flowers and vegetables rippled in the wind. Several women in white dresses and veils tended the beds.

Emmerich looked around the room. It was small and simple. A small wardrobe stood to one side and beside it was a stand containing a pitcher and basin. The walls were bare. Rugs of cream and green lay scattered on the floor. The bed was small. Looking down, he realized he wore only trousers. Fresh bandages were bound tightly to his side.

It came flooding back to him: his conversation with Marduk, the dark-robed wizards, the bitter drink. For a moment, his mind wanted to catch hold of a memory, of a rough voice speaking from far away. But the memory slid away as soon as his mind touched it, leaving him feeling as if he had forgotten something terribly important.

Growling in frustration, Emmerich threw off the quilt covering him and swung his legs over the edge of the bed. His side protested the movement but he ignored it. He took a deep breath and stood slowly.

Muscles too long unused pulled and pained him. The wound in his side burned. He gritted his teeth and slowly walked to the wardrobe.

Opening it revealed a collection of trousers and simple Southern-style tunics (sleeved and not requiring an undershirt as in the North). He grabbed one of the tunics and carefully pulled it on. It didn't fit quite right: it was too tight along the shoulders and gaped around his waist. He saw no belts, so decided to live with the deficiency.

By the wardrobe sat a pair of slippers. Emmerich frowned but knew if he tried to yank on boots, he'd pass out from pain. He shoved his feet into the slippers and slowly walked to the door.

It opened when he tried it and he felt a little uneasy at finding it unlocked. The hall was bright, a green and white runner tracing a straight line down the hardwood floor between white, unadorned walls. He heard the sound of women talking and laughing softly.

Emmerich carefully walked down the hall, trying to not jar his side. He wrapped the arm of the opposite side around his waist, pressing his hand against the wound.

Two large, spacious rooms opened off the hall. To his right was what appeared to be a sitting room, decorated in more green and white, with touches of fawn and palest blue. To his left was a simple kitchen. In front of him was a set of stairs, no doubt leading to the quarters of the women he saw in the garden.

The back door sat open and it was through that the voices drifted.

For a wild moment, Emmerich thought about walking out, stealing a horse, and, well, that was where his imagination failed him. But it seemed, for a moment, a better plan than finding the women. A hot lance of pain shot through his middle and he realized he wouldn't stay upright on a horse, much less gallop on one.

Grimacing, he shuffled through the kitchen and out the

back door into the garden. Six women worked among the flowers and vegetables. One of them looked up and, seeing him, burst into a wide smile. She put down her basket and rushed over to him.

"I am so glad you're awake," she said on reaching him, "but you should not be out of bed."

"Where am I?" he asked.

"You are at a House of Healing of the White Order, on the far outskirts of Bertrand." She gestured behind her and Emmerich could see the distant Palace on its hill, its four towers catching the morning sun. "But many people simply call us the Sisters."

"How long have I been here?"

"Only two days. My name is Sister Rose."

Emmerich looked at the woman, trying to remember what little he knew of the White Order. They had been organized not long after Marduk's arrival to Bertrand, and though there had been no overt, obvious connection, Emmerich never could shake the feeling that there was. But the White Sisters never did anything other than provide assistance to the poorest of Bertrand's poor, hence the location of the Healing Houses: they all sat outside the Old Wall that separated the high from the low.

"His Majesty," said Sister Rose, "sent you here so that you may rest and recuperate. Come. Let's get you back to bed."

Emmerich thought about protesting but, despite the coolness of the day, sweat beaded his forehead. His knees shook and the pain was slowly becoming overwhelming. He let the sister lead him back to his room. By the time they reached his bed, he leaned heavily against her and gasped for breath.

He sank into the bed with a sigh of relief.

"I'll get you a tonic for the pain," Rose said, turning away.

"Wait." He caught her hand.

"Yes?"

"Did Marduk say why he brought me here?"

Rose looked at him like he was daft. "So that you may be healed, of course. He said you must be in fine form for the ball in a fortnight."

"Ball?"

"Yes. The ball to welcome the Lady Clara, the new Court Seer."

A bitter feeling rose up in Emmerich. He let go of Rose and turned his head away as she left.

Chapter Thirty-Six

Jarrett hunched his shoulders against the bitter wind as he crossed the street to the tavern. Pushing open the door, he entered the smoky, loud room. Men crowded around tables and at the bar, drinking and talking. Two bartenders and several barmaids were busy taking drinks and food to customers. They barely noticed him as he came in, working his way through the crowd to the stairs in the back.

The stairs led up to the second floor, where rooms were rented for the night, or the candle mark, whichever was required. Jarrett went down the hallway to the middle door on the right and, after a repetition of raps, opened it.

Tanner, Wizard Bruin, and three other people stood around the room. They turned to look at him as entered.

"You're late," said a sour-faced woman.

"My apologies, Lady Dinar, but I was held up by the king." He closed the door behind him.

Bruin raised his hands, which glowed softly for a moment before he lowered them. "We may speak freely now," he said.

Jarrett nodded his thanks. "I have called a special meeting to discuss our current situation." He related to the three people about Clara's plan.

When he finished, another of the leaders, a young man with white-blond hair, shook his head. "Madness," he said. "She can't hope to succeed."

"Thirst for revenge will drive a person to achieve great things. But, yes, there's a strong possibility she will fail."

Lady Dinar said, "You should have tried harder to dissuade her."

Bruin shook his head. "She would not be moved. We could have all argued with her until the sun rose, but it would not have changed her mind. Emmerich's death, it seems, has enraged her past all reason."

"So, then, what shall we do? There's no way she can hide you three's identity from Marduk. And if Marduk finds you, he finds the rest of us."

"Our intelligence suggests that Captain Asher will make a hard push toward Bertrand, if he hasn't started already. There's a good possibility they will be here in little over two or three se'ennights."

"That will do us little good if we're dead."

No one could think of a way to argue that. Jarrett adjusted his cloak as he mulled over his next words.

"We know nothing of this girl," said the sixth person, an old man sitting in the corner. "We only know that Marduk is captivated with her, that Emmerich had used her, and that she is deeply affected by Emmerich's death. But, other than that, we know nothing of her. She could be a spy for all we know. I think this is great folly, and I wish we had been consulted before you took her into your confidence."

Jarrett bowed slightly in the direction of the old man. "My apologies, Lord Rodanthe, but speed was of the essence, before Marduk had a chance to pervert her."

Rodanthe frowned but made no reply.

Lady Dinar said, "This isn't the first time you've acted without our consent, Jarrett. We value you because of your role in the Palace but you go too far, this time."

"If you had met her," he said, "you would see there is no cause for concern."

"Your faith in her is quite touching, but there is no room for such when dealing with someone as powerful as Marduk." She looked at Bruin. "What do you think of the girl?"

Bruin said, "She was not a spy when I first encountered her, but what she is now, I do not know. She seemed frightened and confused, making her very malleable. Your faith is commendable, Jarrett, but I agree with the others. This is folly."

"If you believe so," retorted the captain, "then why didn't you bend her to your will the other night? You have the ability."

"Because I am not Marduk. I will not resort to his methods."

Jarrett spread his hands before him. "Friends, what is done is done. There is no going back."

"Then what do you suggest we do?"

"Aid Clara in every way we can."

"And how do you propose we do that?"

"Ready the Guard."

The leaders all exchanged concerned glances. The man with white-blond hair said, "That has always been a last resort."

"I know, Jasper, but I think we've reached it."

"If we come out to the Guard, there is no going back."

"I realize that."

"If all fails—"

"Yes, I know. We will die. But I'd much rather die for my freedom than to live as a slave of fear, wondering what could have happened 'if'."

Silence filled the room as they considered his words. Jarrett waited patiently, trying to not twitch or tap his foot in frustration. He remembered the fire in Clara's eyes and the strength in her stance. The idea of Marduk's death was no longer a mere idea. He had not liked Clara's idea but now that he had thought of it, the idea that the reign of fear would end excited him. He took a deep breath to calm his racing heart, watching the others exchange nods.

Finally, Lord Rodanthe said, "Very well. Spread word among the Guard in whatever way suits best. Do you have a plan?"

"I do."

"Then may the Mother and Child go with you."

Gavin sat in the corner of the cell, staring into the dark. He had grown so used to the screams and cries of the tortured, he hardly noticed them. And it was evening. The screams would stop, soon, and there would be silence. But, sometimes, the silence was worse because there was nothing to distract a person from his own thoughts.

Unbidden, Clara's face filled his mind. He had meant to drop some hint to her that he had been lying, that he hadn't been telling the whole of the truth. But Marduk had pulled him aside before they entered the library.

"I'll be listening and watching," he said, "though you won't see me. If you try any way of warning her, you're both dead."

And Gavin believed him, not because Marduk was trustworthy. Of course not that. He believed him because he knew him to be capable of it.

And now it was over and done with. Clara was probably happier now. And if Emmerich came and took over everything, then she could learn the truth then. Maybe she would even forgive Gavin.

But as he sat there, staring in the dark, he knew he would not forgive himself. He had surrendered her to the darkness and there was no undoing that. He had told his greatest lie.

Chapter Thirty-Seven

The War Room sat at the end of what the page referred to as the Hall of Justice. The hall extended from the Throne room to the War Room, with doors leading to small chambers in-between. Clara assumed these to be smaller courtrooms.

When the page opened the door to the room and bowed her inside, she felt relief when her maid and five guards did not try to follow. The door to the room closed behind her.

The chamber itself wasn't much to speak of. Small and octagonal, a large round table dominated the space. An array of maps hung on the walls. Glancing at them, she recognized several places where Emmerich had been, conquering and taking castles.

If the round table had been meant to suggest equality between those who sat there, the effect was ruined by the throne on one side. Marduk sat there, reading a parchment.

When she entered, Marduk looked up and, smiling,

stood. The other men sitting around the table hastened to do the same.

"Lady Clara," he said, "it is good you were able to come."

Clara curtsied.

Marduk gestured around the table. "These are my trusted advisors and my generals. They make up what is known as the Council." He named names but she hardly listened. The paper in his hands gave her a bad feeling.

"Come, sit," he said, indicating an empty chair to his left. She did as bidden and a servant stepped forward with a decanter of wine. Seeing it made bile rise in her throat. She shook her head and the servant backed away.

"I'm afraid," began Marduk, "I have received news of an alarming sort. It had been my hope the now-General Asher would be content with the North, perhaps even send notices of peace. However, my sources report he has marshaled his forces and left Candor City, leaving behind only a meager number of men to maintain it. It is also reported King Precene has sent three companies of men. They are all converging here." He dropped the missive onto the table.

"We must fortify," rumbled a broad-chested general.

"Or, better, send men to meet them before they reach the city at all. We could route the Tierans, or perhaps seek to purchase their loyalty."

"I agree," said another lord. "Do we know where they are now, your Majesty?"

Marduk said, "It is hard to estimate." He stood and leaned over the table, on which had been painted a large map of Lorst. He picked up a long stick from where it sat leaning against his chair and pointed it at a spot a few leagues south of Candor. "I would say there."

"That is quick travel," said the general.

"They're using the river, possibly to them as far as Widow's Bridge. They would have to disembark from the river ships there, as Lyn Tone becomes too shallow and will not deepen again for many leagues."

Another lord said, "That could put them here as soon as two se'ennights. What of the Tierans, your Majesty?"

"I have no information on them beyond that they are coming, though I have ordered my Farseers to look into the matter. They have wizards and there are rumors of portals large enough to transport entire armies. This also brings me to why I summoned her ladyship. My friends, Lady Clara is our new Court Seer."

The men turned their attention to her and Clara fought the urge to look down and away. She straightened her shoulders and lifted her chin.

"My lady," the king continued, "have you gotten any premonitions or visions of late?"

She shook her head, looking down at the map.

"I would ask you to try a technique, if you are willing."

Clara's better judgment said no, but she knew it would be suspicious if she refused. She nodded.

"Please stand, then."

She obeyed, smoothing her hands over the bodice of her cream dress.

"Give me your hand."

She held it out and he took it in his. His hand was warm, dry, and gentle. Unlike Emmerich's there were no callouses. Soft, child-like hands. She thought of the creatures in those cages and swallowed.

He pressed the palm of her hand onto the table and said, "Think of Lorst. Slow your breathing. Let this map dominate your mind. When you have a clear picture of it, stretch out your mind. I will be there to guide you."

She nodded and did as he bid, constructing in her mind's eye a replica of the map before her. When it was perfect and whole, she closed her eyes and stretched out her mind. At least, that was what she hoped she was doing.

Clara immediately felt a presence. Unobtrusive, it tugged on her, reshaped her focus. She felt as if she were flying over the map, which turned from lines on wood to lush forests and meadows, winding rivers and deep lakes.

Clara, whispered a voice so familiar, it almost jerked her out of the moment.

Instead, she tipped forward and darkness consumed her. She fell for what felt like forever and when she landed, it was on her feet. Before her stood Asher and the other captains.

"Where are the Tierans?" demanded one of the captains. "They were promised to us."

"It seems they are delayed," said Asher.

"Without them," said another captain, "we are doomed."

Asher gazed down at something in his hands and did not reply.

The vision shimmered and faded. Clara stood again in the War Room. She slowly took her hand from Marduk's and looked up at him. Never before had she controlled a vision before. With a shiver, though, she wondered if she had been in control at all.

"Thank you, Clara," he said. "You helped beautifully. I would suggest practicing that technique every day so that you can do it without my assistance. Generals, prepare your men. We will meet the Tierans. When Asher's army arrives, he will not be able to stand against us." He rapped his knuckles against the table. "Meeting adjourned."

Clara stared at the map, horror mounting in her throat as the men bowed and left. Looking up, she found herself alone with Marduk.

"It seems we will be moving up that ball," Marduk said. "That shouldn't be a problem, though, hmm?"

She shook her head.

He furrowed his brow. "Are you all right, my dear?"

Clara forced a smile and nodded.

"A little after effect from the vision, I suppose?"

She nodded again.

"Why don't you retire, then? I will call you if I have need of you again."

She nodded and curtsied. Just as she reached the door, Marduk said, "It will all turn out right in the end. Don't worry, Clara. The Academy is here. If a horde of wizards and magicians can't take down a rebel army, then I don't see how we're any use at all."

She turned slightly and nodded, smiling, though she felt sick to her stomach and barely looked around her on the way back to her chambers.

Emmerich allowed himself to be tended and cared for by the Sisters. After a se'ennight of their care, the stitches were removed from his side, though they advised him to continue to rest. That night, he attempted his escape.

He stole bread and water from the kitchen and slipped out the back gate of the garden. The district outside the city walls was the absolute poorest, so he was unsurprised to find drunks and prostitutes loitering in the street beyond. Stepping over a puddle of piss and excrement, he walked down the street.

He got little over a yard down when one of the "drunks" suddenly stood, the ragged cloak falling away to reveal the scarlet tunic of the army.

"Going somewhere?" the soldier asked.

Emmerich stopped, weighing the odds, when a shuffle drew his attention. All of the people on the street were standing and watching. They weren't drunks and prostitutes. They were soldiers sent to guard the House.

Emmerich looked back at the soldier facing him. "No," he said. "I'm not going anywhere."

"Then I suggest you return to the Healing House."

He nodded and retraced his steps back into the house. Dropping the bread and water on the table, he turned to go to his room, only to find Sister Rose standing in the hallway.

"I'm sorry," she said, "but you can't leave until his Majesty sends for you."

"It doesn't bother you in the slightest what he's doing? What he's done to the people here? He's murdered and corrupted. He changes people's bodies to suit his own perverted ends. And this does not concern you?"

"It isn't my place to be concerned."

"Not your place? How is it anything but your place? This is a House of Healing. It is your job to tend and care." The blood fell from his face as an idea formed in his mind. "No."

"If you're thinking that we assist his Majesty in his experiments by finding him specimens with which to work, then you are correct."

"That's monstrous."

"His Majesty wants to create a better world." Her face flushed and something akin to joy filled her eyes. "A world free of pain and anguish, in which people are free to be who and what they truly are within. His Majesty is offering that."

"We encountered those that he supposedly set free. They despised their existence and sought death."

She shook her head. "That is not true. We do such great good here, Emmerich. And we are proud to be a part of it. Now, I believe you need to return to bed. You do not look well."

He didn't argue. Breathing carefully around the agony in his side, he let the sister guide him back to bed, feeling as if the world was breaking up around him and everything was beyond his control.

Chapter Thirty-Eight

Marduk entered the menagerie, Erin following close behind him. The animals in their cages watched him with wary eyes as he passed and the wizards tending to them bowed low. Though he smiled at the workers, Marduk spoke to no one as he went to the ironbound door, running his hand over the lock and muttering the words to open it.

Marduk went to stand at the edge of the circle while Erin closed the door behind them.

"Is everything ready?" Marduk asked.

"The supplies have all arrived, your Majesty."

"And have the students completed the translation?"

"Yes, your Majesty. Our scholars are checking it now but it appears to be accurate."

Marduk took a deep, shaky breath. "I've been looking forward to this day since I was an apprentice. And, now, it is nearly here."

"Your Majesty, if I may be so bold—"

"You know I never discourage boldness, dear boy."

Erin smiled. "Yes. But why her, your Majesty? I've read and re-read the manuscripts but I still don't understand."

"The vessel is inconsequential. I could go pick up a gibbering idiot out of the gutter for all that it mattered. But she can pierce the veil of time at a level few entertain. It makes her more open to spirits and energy."

"So, it's preferring a jar with a wide mouth rather than a jar with a narrow mouth?"

"In a manner of speaking, yes." He began to walk the circle, looking at the chest.

"When will the ceremony take place, your Majesty?"

"Asher's army couldn't have picked a better time. It's given me an excuse to move up the ball. On that night, there will be a star alignment that will aid the ceremony."

"There's a rumor that the rebellion has something planned for that night."

"Let them plan. Let them scheme." He returned to his starting point. "They have already lost."

Chapter Thirty-Nine

The days leading up to the ball passed in a blur. The king decreed it would be a masquerade ball, so Clara found herself having to choose among a plethora of masks and costumes. She finally settled for a deep blue gown and a white mask painted with blue stars and adorned with blue feathers.

She made no other contact with Jarrett beyond speaking with him about her daily routine. He never mentioned their trip to menagerie and she didn't let on to how many nightmares it had given her. Nightmares that made the dreams she had still on occasion, about Dwervin, and her first few months of slavery, look pleasant. It seemed as if every night, she awoke in a cold sweat.

Clara also practiced the technique of using a map as a focus to hone her skills. She once spent an entire hour staring at a map of Tier, trying to foresee what the king there intended to do. But, it felt as if something blocked her, and she succeeded only in giving herself a colossal headache.

And, always right before bed, Clara read aloud to herself in a soft voice. She wasn't sure if she was strengthening it or making it sure it didn't vanish from disuse. She wasn't sure why she hadn't revealed her ability to speak to Marduk. She only felt as if it would be a very bad idea.

The day of the ball dawned bright and clear. Clara stood at her balcony, watching the activity of the city below. Word had come at midnight: to everyone's surprise, Asher's army was a day's ride away. Soldiers were scurrying to perfect the fortifications. No one had heard from the companies sent to engage the Tieran companies.

"My lady."

She turned. Kat curtsied deeply.

"His Majesty wishes to see you," she said. "He is in the hall. May I show him in?"

Clara nodded, following Kat as far as the couch and chairs in the sitting area. Marduk, in his red robes, strode into the room and took her hands.

"You look lovely this morning," he said, kissing her hands.

Clara forced a smile and gestured, inviting him to sit.

She sat in an armchair while he took the couch nearest her.

"My lady," he said, "I must know if you've had any more visions?"

She shook her head.

"That is unfortunate. The generals weren't expecting Asher to arrive so very quickly. We can only assume he pushed his men especially hard."

Clara wrote on her slate, "What of the men from Tier?"

"Still no word. I've had my Farseers search but King Precene has talented magic workers of his own. They've blocked my Farseers. They'll break through eventually but, for the moment, we are blind. This could also explain the speed of Asher's march. Precene may have aided him." Marduk sighed. "There are those who wish for me to cancel the ball. Many courtiers have started to leave, though I assure them that they are safe." He smiled. "You won't leave, will you?"

She shook her head.

"Do you think I should carry on with this ball business?"

She thought for a moment and then wrote, "It would be good for morale."

"It would, wouldn't it? Well, then, I suppose it's settled.

But, tomorrow the fighting will start, no doubt. Listen to Captain Jarrett. Do everything he instructs."

She nodded.

"I must go and oversee the fortifications." He stood and she followed suit. "Do you wish to know what I had done with Emmerich's remains? If you wished to pay your respects?"

Clara nodded slowly.

"I had him cremated. His ashes are in a niche in the Chapel of Penances. We inter all the prisoners there. Perhaps you should go there today?"

She thought about it for a moment before nodding. It seemed appropriate.

"I'll leave you now, then, my lady."

Clara nodded, staring off to the side as she considered his words. She barely noticed his leaving.

"My lady?" asked Katerina. "Is there something I can get you?"

She shook her head.

"Would you like to go to the Chapel?"

She hesitated and nodded.

The Chapel of Penances sat on the far western end of the Palace. Tall double doors covered in silver plates depicting the creation of the world served as the chapel's entrance.

"I'll wait out here for you, my lady," Kat said.

Clara nodded as a soldier pulled open a door for her. Two went ahead of her.

The chapel was dim. Mosaics covered the marble floor. Glancing down, she thought she could make out depictions of souls on their way to the Heavenly Court for judgment. Above, angels and spirits danced amid a violent array of clouds with glimpses of something brighter and greater peeking through. Large windows faced the north, and the worshiper faced east as he entered.

The altar and candles were shrouded in shadow, though several candles had been lit around the giant statue of the Mother holding up the Son. The Child's right hand was raised in blessing and in the left He held a palm branch. At the Great Lady's feet stood a pair of scales.

Clara studied their benign faces for a moment before turning to her right, where countless urns sat in niche after niche from ceiling to floor. Emmerich's sat nearest to the door. A single candle burned in a sconce beside it, no doubt left by an attentive acolyte. She placed a rose in the waiting vase beneath the niche. With tentative fingers, she traced the curve of the alabaster urn.

Her throat closed as the familiar anger burned in her heart. Glancing around, she saw the guards had withdrawn as far as they could, to give her privacy.

Leaning forward, she whispered, "If I let Dwervin die, then what can be so hard about outright killing a man? I'll avenge you, Emmerich. I'm so sorry I left you. But I'm going to make it up to you. I swear it." And she kissed the cold stone.

Why, when he was gone from her forever, did she finally realize just what he had meant to her? This liar, this murderer, this man who had stolen her heart?

"Are you ready?" Sister Rose asked.

It was evening. The sky had turned into shades of blue, purple, and pink. Pink and white clouds streaked across the sky. Emmerich adjusted the belt over his elaborately embroidered tunic.

Everything he wore was black, except for the bright gold embroidery depicting hearts worked into grape vines and leaves on his tunic. He picked up the black and gold full facemask and pulled it on.

"Yes," he said.

"Good." She led him out of the room in the main meeting room.

A wizard awaited them. "Emmerich, my name is Erin. Please hold still."

He raised a hand and intoned words in a low voice. His hand glowed a soft shade of blue as Emmerich felt something lay across him. The hair stood on the back of his neck. The blue light faded and Erin lowered his hand.

"The charm I have just laid will prevent you from speaking, in case you wish to try to warn Lady Clara. It will also keep you from removing your mask. This way, please."

As soon as Erin turned his back, Emmerich tried to remove his mask. Pain, white and blinding, exploded over him. He found himself, shaking and gasping, on the floor. Erin looked down at him with an amused expression.

"Quite done testing the leash?" he asked. "Come along, or we will be late."

Emmerich stumbled to his feet and followed Erin outside to the carriage. With a jerk and a clatter, they began to go down the street.

"His Majesty wishes for you to mingle in the crowd. Dance, if you wish. You may even approach Lady Clara. But that is all. You will be collected when the time is right." Erin adjusted his own costume: a brilliant emerald and yellow tunic and trousers. He picked up an emerald and yellow mask. "Her ladyship will be in blue and white. Her mask is white with blue stars."

Emmerich smiled at hearing that. Clara had chosen his colors to wear. Could it be that she was still for them?

Carriages were streaming into the Palace. They were allowed through the gates with minimal fuss but it still took time for the line to move them to the main gates. Footmen opened the carriage door and lowered the steps. They climbed out.

"I will take you to the ballroom," said Erin, "but then I must leave you."

He led Emmerich through the crowd. It had been a long time since he had last been to the Palace and he saw that little had changed. He even recognized many of the courtiers, lords, and ladies. The crowd wasn't as large as he expected. As he and Erin weaved through the people, he heard several speaking about the great army camped a day's ride away.

Asher had finally come. It made sense, then, if many of the nobles had left. It was very arrogant for Marduk to be having the ball. Or brave, depending on how one looked at it.

The ballroom was long and wide, lit with thousands of smokeless lanterns. A long row of enchanted chandeliers floated above the crowd. On one side was a row of floor to ceiling windows with doors interspersed between them, looking out onto a veranda and formal gardens lit with more lanterns. Erin gave Emmerich a mocking bow before disappearing into the crowd.

Emmerich began to walk around the perimeter of the room, trying to ascertain what Marduk's aim was, bringing him here. Was he mocking him? Torturing him? He stopped beside a marble column, facing a sweeping staircase. He looked up at the top, and waited.

"Aren't you excited?" asked Katerina, breathless. She wore a gorgeous white and pink gown. Her mask had a bird's bill and was decorated with pink and white plumes.

Clara nodded, adjusting her mask yet again. They were walking to the anteroom behind the staircase down which she and Marduk would descend.

Guards opened the doors to the anteroom. Marduk and Erin turned to her. They seemed to have been in deep discussion over something but the slightly anxious look on Marduk's face was wiped away on seeing her.

"Clara," he said, "you look like a vision."

Marduk looked like a nightmare. He wore a red and black tunic over black trousers and the red and black mask he held had fangs. Closer inspection revealed it to be a mockery of a lion's head. He couldn't have looked any more like a demon if he tried. He took her hand and kissed it.

"Well, I suppose with you here, we can begin?"

Erin said, "All of the guests have arrived." He quirked his lips a little as he said it and Clara wondered what was so amusing.

"Then, shall we?" Marduk slipped on the mask and held out his arm. "I'm afraid we're going to be announced, which rather ruins the effect of the masks, but it doesn't ruin everyone else's fun, thankfully."

He led her out onto the landing, bringing her to the edge of the balcony. A herald blew a horn and cried, "Lords and ladies! His Royal Majesty and the Court Seer."

Everyone below knelt as they descended down the stairs. Clara looked over the crowd, her fingers twitching as she remembered the dagger she had secreted into her bodice. As her eyes swept over the people, they landed on a man half-hidden behind a pillar. He wore black and gold and did not kneel.

Who could that be? she wondered.

Chapter Forty

When Clara descended the stairs, Emmerich's mouth went dry. He watched her, following at a discrete distance in the crowd, as Marduk paraded her from one end of the ballroom to the other, so people could bow and curtsy. When the music struck up, he danced the opening dance with her. Emmerich watched with clenched fists.

After that, Marduk went to find other dance partners. A woman in pink and white joined Clara, speaking to her on occasion. A man asked Clara to dance and the woman urged her to take him up on the offer. She accepted and, after that, the offers came one after another.

When the fifth or sixth man came, she shook her head, smiling and pointed to one of the chairs lining the wall. Curtsying, she went to sit while the woman attending her tried to fight her way to one of the punch bowls.

Emmerich had been waiting for this moment, though, and secured a goblet quickly. He took it to her, handing it over with a gallant bow.

Clara smiled from him and took it, nodding her thank you while avoiding his eyes. Emmerich bowed again and walked away, but he continued to watch her. The attendant appeared puzzled when she returned only to find her mistress with a goblet.

Clara was without her slate (on purpose or by accident, he wondered, remembering all the times she had left it in her rooms because she was excited about one thing or another) so she only shrugged or nodded when the attendant questioned her. He hoped she would stand to dance again but Clara seemed content to watch.

Finally, he could wait no more and when the attendant whisked the goblet away for more punch, he strode forward again. Gesturing grandly to the dance floor, he bowed and offered his hand, hoping she understood him. (Was this how it was for her, all the time, hoping people would understand her miming?)

Clara smiled and took his hand.

Everyone was lining up for one of the Northern dances that had moments of popularity at Court. A part of Emmerich was relieved. He wouldn't have known what to do if it was one of those stupid new ones that got created between a group of friends after too much wine.

As the dance progressed, with the partners stepping close then away, holding up hands not quite touching as they circled each other, he tried to catch her eyes. But Clara was suddenly struck with shyness. She never looked higher than his nose.

Finally, the dance allowed him to pull her into his arms and whirl her away. She felt light and wonderful in the crook of his elbow as he guided her through the next series of steps. For a moment, he forgot he was there as part of some private joke of Marduk's, or whatever he planned. Emmerich breathed in her lavender perfume.

He became so caught up in watching the way the light danced over her exposed skin, he wasn't watching where he was going and jostled a couple.

Clara, startled, looked up and met his eyes. Something flickered through them and then there was grief, great and tumultuous. She looked down and away, her body gone stiff and rigid in his arms.

Emmerich couldn't imagine what had gone wrong. Not many men had grey eyes. She had to be reminded of him. Had he read too much in her wearing blue and white?

The song ended and they applauded the musicians. Emmerich expected her to move away but she didn't. The music began again almost immediately. He took her into his arms and she did not fight him. It was one of those riotous numbers based on country dances. Soon, the music quickened and he was lifting and swinging her, his side twinging in pain.

The music ended with a flourish, he spun her, and she tripped. In scrambling to keep her from falling, he pulled too hard and his glove came loose in her hand. He righted her and she smiled up at him awkwardly from beneath her mask. Out of the corner of his eye, he saw Clara's attendant trying to make it through the crowd to them.

Clara's eyes went down to his bare hand and her body went still. It was his left hand. A broad scar snaked below his knuckles. He received it long before he met her as a child.

She looked up at him, recognition filling her eyes. Tears and rage followed quickly behind. She dropped the glove.

"My lady, are you all right?" the attendant asked, finally reaching them.

Clara dropped her eyes and backed away, nodding. She curtsied to Emmerich before returning calmly to her chair. The attendant gave him a good glare before following her mistress. He bent down and retrieved his glove, shoving his hand into it before slipping through the crowd to a quiet corner.

He crossed his arms, trying to understand her reaction.

"I don't think she meant to give it away," said a quiet voice.

Emmerich jerked and turned. The wizard Erin sneered at him from under the mask.

"But she did," he continued, "when she curtsied. She hasn't given anyone but Marduk so much as a bow since her first day." He looked back toward Clara. "She thought you were dead. Now I wonder what she's thinking. I should have charmed your clothes as well, but, no matter. It's almost midnight."

And he left Emmerich to wonder what Erin meant.

Katerina tried to get Clara to go out for some air, but she stubbornly shook her head.

It couldn't have been Emmerich. Emmerich was dead. Wasn't he?

She accepted Kat's offer of a handkerchief and discreetly wiped her eyes under the mask.

But if Marduk was doing such evil beneath the Palace,

what if he had staged Emmerich's death?

She sipped the punch pressed into the hand, tasting something stronger mixed into it. Her nerves began to settle but the rage still throbbed within her.

What if Emmerich had had a different reason for killing Monica than what she had been told?

"My lady."

Clara looked up, meeting Marduk's concerned eyes.

"My lady, are you well?"

She nodded, feeling the anger becoming something cold and lethal. A small smile crossed her face.

"If her ladyship isn't too tired, I would like to ask the pleasure of a dance. Time has passed so quickly: it's nearly midnight." He held out his hand.

Clara took it and, handing the cup to Kat, followed him out to the dance floor. A slow dance began. They wove around the other couples, coming near before stepping away several times before he put his arms around her and they swayed slowly away. During one turn, she glanced around the room. More guards had arrived, stationing themselves around the room.

She smiled sweetly up at Marduk as the song slowly eased into an end. She took his face in one of her hands.

Surprise filled his eyes as she leaned up to press her lips with his.

With her other hand, she drew the dagger and drove it up into his ribs. An explosion burst against her and she flew backward, hitting the ground so hard she saw stars. She gasped for breath. Screams and shots erupted as the soldiers made their move.

Clara's last thought was, *Where is Emmerich?*

Chapter Forty-One

Asher sighed as he read the missive. His generals stood before him in his tent. The shadows of men walking by were thrown against the canvas by torch and firelight.

"What does it say, General?" asked Owen.

"The Tierans were met by Marduk's men. They lost a company of men and have been pushed back several leagues. They will not be meeting us here for at least another se'ennight, if not more."

The captains swore. Captain Turin said, "What are we going to do?"

Asher opened his mouth to answer when a long howl cut through the air. The hair on the back of his neck stood on end.

"What in the nine hells?" muttered one of the captains.

Another howl, this one on the other side of the camp, started up. Soon, the air filled with the sound of howling.

"Gather the men," barked Asher. "Marduk's creatures are about to attack."

The captains charged out of the tent, yelling. One of them grabbed a horn hanging from a pole and blew into it. The army erupted in noise in confusion. Wolves and dogs far too large burst into the camp, slaughtering those they fell upon. Other strange, lizard like creatures, and giant boars, followed on their heels. The men broke and fled like chaff before them.

Bellowing, Asher drew his sword and charged, hoping his men would rally even as he fought.

Emmerich shoved his way through the panicking crowd. Scarlet-clad guards fought one another while wizards in the crowd tried to subdue the rebellious soldiers. Marduk lay in a heap where he dropped after Clara drove a dagger up through his ribs, angling for the heart. She laid several feet away, unconscious.

When he reached her, he dropped to his knees and fumbled at her neck. He sighed with relief at the steady feel of her pulse. Cloth and boots shuffled behind him. Looking over his shoulder, astonishment swept through him as Erin helped Marduk to his feet. His robes were torn and he looked winded, but he showed no other signs of injury. He removed his mask.

"I believe we need a quieter venue," Marduk remarked loudly, tossing his mask to the side. He looked at the fallen Seer. "Clara."

She sat bolt upright, her eyes open but only showing white. She reached up and took off her mask before getting slowly to her feet. The mask slipped from her fingers to fall to the floor.

Marduk held out his arm and she went to him. Emmerich stood, reaching out to stop her, but two soldiers grabbed him from behind. He watched helplessly as she took Marduk's arm. The king winked cheekily at Emmerich.

"Shall we?" he said, leading them through a crowd that parted like water before them even as men fought and nobles panicked.

As they walked through the Palace, it was evident the Rebellion had spread. Skirmishes in halls decked the walls and floor in blood. Women and men fled crying and screaming. Carriages nearly collided in everyone's haste to leave. And they walked through it without someone even so much as seeming to notice.

They entered the complex beneath the Palace and Emmerich looked with disgust at the creatures that stared at him with too-human eyes. The tall cages in the back gave him a bad feeling, though nothing stirred within them.

Marduk opened a door and they entered a circular chamber. Emmerich suppressed a shiver as he looked at the casket in the circle.

"Leave us," Marduk said.

The soldiers released Emmerich and left.

"Emmerich, you remember your old friend?" He gestured to the side.

Emmerich looked to his right. Gavin hung from chains set into the wall. His friend looked at him miserably before casting his eyes back to the ground.

"Oh, and you may remove the mask."

Something snapped, like a belt drawn too tight suddenly popped. Emmerich reached up and pulled off the mask.

"Emmerich," cried Gavin. "You're alive."

"Aye," he replied, saying the word cautiously. But there was no pain. "Marduk, what are you planning?"

"Planning?" asked the sorcerer. "It's planned, my friend. Now is time for the execution. Clara, here, almost ruined it with her ill-timed assassination attempt, but my reflexes are as quick as ever. Are you the one who taught her how to fight so? She's quite marvelous." He kissed her cheek. "I am very proud of her. She turned out better than I hoped. My dear, if you would stand by the wall? There's a good girl."

Clara went to stand at the wall opposite of Emmerich.

"No sense in gazing after her," Marduk said. "She has no sense that you're there. No sense of anything really. She probably thinks she wandering through a forest or something equally foreboding. Erin! How goes it?"

Erin was at the far end of the chamber, arranging vials, bags, and bottles on a table. "It goes well, your Majesty. We are nearly ready."

"Begin by mixing the incense. We must give our friends a proper welcome."

"Friends?" mocked Emmerich.

"Yes." He gestured at the casket. "Elemental spirits, trapped since Creation. Quite mad from their long imprisonment. I'm going to reshape the world, my friend."

"I'm no friend of yours."

"Figure of speech, I assure you."

"When Asher–"

"Asher can go piss in the wind for all I care. By the time he's lined up his troops, this will all be over."

Scowling, Emmerich charged Marduk, but the sorcerer flung out his hand. Wind slammed Emmerich backward and he hit the door with a solid thud. Dropping to the ground, he gasped for breath.

"Stop being a living cliché, Emmerich. It's boring."

Emmerich's body jerked as something unseen dragged him across the floor, pulling him up to pin him to the wall. His arms were yanked upward and manacles clamped over them.

"Now, if you'll excuse me." Marduk gave a mocking bow before going to stand by Erin. The two men began working in separate bowls and spoke in low voices as they mixed ingredients.

Emmerich looked over at Clara, but she hadn't moved since Marduk ordered her to the wall. The realization that she had been under his influence for months made him sick.

"Gavin," he began.

"Emmerich, please forgive me." Gavin looked up at him. "But they tortured me. They said she would be safe if I just cooperated. I couldn't see her get hurt. I love her."

"Cooperated? Gavin, what did you do?"

He began to cry. "I didn't think she would actually

believe me. I wanted to warn her but—"

"What did you do?"

"I told her you murdered Monica in a rage. She already knew you had killed her but you hadn't told her why. It was simple to confirm her worst fears."

He felt the blood fall from his face. "You didn't."

"I'm so sorry."

"You should have refused to your dying breath. How could that be any worse than what they threatened?" He nodded at Clara.

"They were going to kill her."

Marduk interrupted. "Oh, come now, we're trying to concentrate. And, Gavin, really. If I went through all the trouble I have to get Clara, do you really think I would kill her just because you didn't cooperate? I would have had you executed, your head stuck on a pike, and then gone on my merry way. You just made my day a little easier, that is all." He looked at Erin. "Pass me the lindus powder? Thank you."

Gavin began to cry quietly as Emmerich tested the manacles. They were rusted and old. He thought if maybe he pulled hard enough, he could snap free.

Trying to gain a little time, he said, "So, what's Clara

for?"

"You'll see."

"Why see when you can tell me?"

"Impatient?"

"Curious. How long have you been planning this?"

"Since I came across her. Seers of her caliber are rare. And the greater the gift, the more open to manipulation if that gift goes untrained. That child is terribly untutored."

"So? What does that have to do with the box?"

Marduk smiled as he took a bowl from Erin and went around to stand on the side of the circle in front of the casket. He laid the bowl down. "Every spirit needs a vessel."

Marduk waved his hand and the incense began to smoke. Erin came to stand beside him, ceremonial knife in one hand and wooden bowl in the other.

"Don't worry, Emmerich. You'll see the end result of our work. Gavin, I'm afraid you won't. You'll make a fine sacrifice with all that despair."

Marduk raised his hands and began to chant.

Clara opened her eyes. She stood in the room where

she thought she had grieved over Emmerich's corpse. The bed sat empty. She tried to open the door but found it locked.

Slamming her fists against it, she yelled, "Let me out! Someone let me out!"

A sinister chuckle slid over her skin.

She looked around the empty room, searching the shadows. Turning back to the door, she yanked hard on the latch but nothing happened. The chuckle returned and she felt something feather-light brush her shoulder.

Jerking, she turned back towards the empty room.

"Who's there?" she asked. "Show yourself."

No one (or no thing) answered. Slowly crossing the room, she looked out the window. Or tried to. It was completely black outside. She fumbled with the window but it wouldn't budge. Dropping her hands in frustration, her palms brushed her skirt and it wasn't soft silk. Looking down, she realized she wore the dirty tunic and gown from her days as a kitchen slave. Something tightened around her neck as she bent her head.

Her fingers scrambled at her throat and she felt the leather of a collar.

What was going on?

Turning, she ran to the door, banging against it and pulling on the knob. "Let me out! Someone, let me out!"

Wind whispered over her skin and she smelled pine. A voice hissed, "There is no one but us."

And as she turned, the floor opened and swallowed her up.

The shadows lengthened and deepened as Marduk chanted. Erin stared at the casket, captivated as the thing took on a lurid orange glow. Emmerich began to yank on his constraints. Gavin's tears had subsided.

"Don't give up," hissed Emmerich. "Help me."

Gavin glanced back at Marduk for a moment. "I don't see what we can do."

"But we have to try. If you love her, you will try."

He muttered an oath. "That is becoming a very annoying threat."

"Then get loose and fight me over it."

Gavin snarled and began to yank on his constraints as well. Erin noticed and started to walk over but Marduk gave a quick shake of the head. The younger man scowled but returned to his master's side. Emmerich didn't like that.

If Marduk was letting them try to escape, either he knew they couldn't or that it was pointless if they did. Emmerich pushed that thought away as he focused on pulling himself free.

"Clara," Marduk said. He held out his hand.

Clara drifted over to him and took his hand. He kissed it.

"Go to them, my dear."

She stepped into the circle, the air shimmering and crackling around her. Things, twisted creatures with bent backs and crooked limbs, began to appear in the shadows, swaying to unheard music. Wind rose up to tear through the chamber.

Gavin broke free first. Emmerich's came right after. Gavin launched himself at Marduk, Emmerich screaming for him to wait.

Marduk snatched the dagger from Erin and snarling words in another tongue, plunged it into Gavin's throat as he reached them. With a twist of his wrist, Marduk ripped out the blade through the side of his throat and blood fountained over the floor. It fell across the metal circle, where it hissed and steamed. Some splattered over Marduk and the back of Clara's gown. Gavin crumbled to the floor

"We are nearly there," hissed Marduk. "Remove the body."

Erin dragged Gavin's corpse out of the way, the eyes wide with shock and pain.

"Clara," he shouted over the gale, "open the casket."

She raised her hands, reaching for it.

"No," cried Emmerich. "Clara, stop!"

She stopped, her hands hovering over the wood.

Clara landed in a field with a soft rustle from dying stalks of wheat. Stumbling up to her feet, she saw her parents' cottage in the distance. Laundry snapped in the wind as it hung on the line. She ran through the wheat, past the laundry and all the way to the back door into the house, stopping short with her hands grasping the sides of the open door.

The interior was pitch black. Something moved in its depths.

"Clara," called her mother. Her voice was warm and soft. "Clara, my dear. Come to me."

She started to step into the house.

"No."

It was Emmerich's voice.

"Clara, stop!"

She backed away from the door. "Emmerich! Emmerich, where are you?"

And a gale kicked up, tearing at her clothing and hair.

"Clara, leave the circle!"

Circle?

A bright, wild laugh cut through the noise of the wind and her own confusion. The hair on the back of her neck stood on end.

"Clara." The maddeningly familiar voice tugged on her. "Clara, come inside."

The laugh repeated.

"Clara. Darling. Come inside."

"No," she said, gritting her teeth and fought against the wind shoving her toward the cottage.

***

"Clara, leave the circle," Emmerich yelled.

Erin ran toward him, his hands glowing blue. Emmerich swung the chains of the manacles at him. He caught the iron in his hand and it melted. Emmerich backed up, his back hitting the table behind him.

"Die, fool," Erin growled, lunging at him.

Emmerich grabbed the first thing his hand landed on and flung it at the wizard. The green vial broke on landing, splattering its contents over his face. The liquid sizzled and popped. Erin's face began to melt and he fell, screaming.

"I killed your apprentice," shouted Emmerich. "Don't you want to do something about that?"

Marduk's face hardened into hate, but he continued to chant. Emmerich ran around the circle, trying to reach Marduk, but the wind prevented him. The wind seemed to have hands and arms. It shoved, jostled, and struck him, keeping him back. All he could think to do was yell Clara's name over and over.

☐

Chapter Forty-Two

The creatures kept coming. The captains were able to rally some of the men, though there were many deserters. From the screams, Asher could tell they didn't get far. Men fought beast in between tents and out in open areas. Without his armor, he was quickly injured, but he ignored the blood streaming from his shoulder.

They had to hold. They needed to hold. For Emmerich. For Lorst, he kept chanting in his mind. When he fell to his knees, he thought of his sister and stumbled again to his feet.

But it was hopeless. They were dying.

A hawk's hunting scream rent the air. Asher looked up, confused by the sound. His mouth dropped open as scores of brightly plumed, flying lizards stooped from a great height down onto the camp.

"Sweet Mother," he whispered, dropping to his knees, feeling the despair well up in him.

Then, the lizards opened their mouths, and blew fire

upon Marduk's creatures.

Clara's arms ached. Her back arched against the demanding wind. Her calves burned as she fought to pull herself around the corner of the cottage. With a grunt and a heave, she fell forward—into a rose garden.

A lizard, its shoulders coming up to Clara's chest, covered in rainbow-colored feathers, with wings folded on its back, stood before her. It cocked its head, as if studying her.

A soft breeze blew and on it rode a gentle voice, which she felt as if it came from the lizard. "Elemental spirits and wizards. Lies and true love. The stuff of epics. Do you recognize where you are?"

She looked around. "No."

"Go forward."

She did so, passing the lizard, which turned its head to watch her, and the roses dropped away in a burst of scarlet petals and there were only thorny bushes, as far as she could see.

"Where are you, Clara of Bluebell Village? Lady Seer?"

"I don't know."

The voice laughed. It began to sing. "Thorns of hate. Stalks of pain. They twist, they wind. They catch and hold. Revenge is a sword whose edge is dull. It cannot set one free."

Clara gasped. "Is this me?"

"Yes." The voice was near at hand and she jumped and turned.

"Who are you?"

"We are what Marduk did not mean to create. The elementals he has were once creatures of goodness and light. And even though they have forgotten who and what they are, every now and again, a memory comes to them. We are that memory." He stepped past her, sliding into the maze of thorns, but his voice came to her as clear as ever.

"This is your battle, Clara," the creature said. "You have to make the decision."

"What decision?"

"You have to decide what is more important."

The ground suddenly dropped away and she fell through memory.

Her mother dragged her toward the wagon.

Haggard haggled over her price and stood idly by as the slaver checked for her virginity.

Slavers whipped her, called her whore, forbade her to speak.

Loneliness consumed her as she stood in empty kitchen gardens, listening to distance sounds of revelry of a festival day.

Lady Dwervin led her on a leash and called her Mouse.

Emmerich confirmed her worst fears and refused to explain.

All these memories and a thousand others tore through her, ripping at her sanity. Hate and anger filled her until she thought she would burst into flame with rage.

The laughter broke over her again and she longed to embrace it. She wanted the madness to consume her so she could avenge her pain. She wanted to rip her pound of flesh from the world. As she lurched toward the laughter, another sound broke through the dark.

"Clara!"

The laughter turned to snarling.

"Clara, listen to me!"

Who was that? The voice was so familiar.

"Clara, please!"

Emmerich.

She saw him attacking Haggard, yelling for her to run

and save herself.

He taught her how to fight and smiled when she scored a hit.

He cast worried glances toward her when he thought she wasn't looking.

In her sitting room, he nearly kissed her.

In his tent, he swore he would never hurt her.

The anger shattered beneath the weight of the memory, slipping through her fingers like wet sand.

The snarling in the dark became screaming as she tore herself from the darkness of hate and rage, reaching for Emmerich's voice.

Clara stood in a circle, a casket on a pedestal before her. Someone was screaming behind her. She turned in time to see Marduk launching himself at her, dagger in hand.

Catching his arm in her hands, she twisted while she kicked his knee. The joint buckled with a sickening pop. Marduk cried out as he toppled to the side, pulling her down with him. The blade found her, cutting her shoulder deeply.

He tried to scramble on top of her, raising the bloody

dagger. Emmerich appeared as he grabbed Marduk in a chokehold, pulling him back. Clara's hand scrabbled to pull up her gown. She drew the knife she had hidden on a strap at her leg. She had felt foolish putting it there in the first place but that foolishness slipped away as she drew the blade, slamming it into his heart.

Blood gushed from his mouth, flinging drops over her. The sorcerer bucked once, twice, and then went still. Emmerich dropped him beside them.

"Clara," he said. "Look at me. Don't look at him."

Her eyes went from Marduk's corpse to Emmerich. "I thought you were dead."

He blinked. "And I thought you were a mute."

"Things change."

"And death seems to sometimes be a phase."

Relief, sweet relief welled up inside her and she laughed despite herself. "What happened?"

"I must have been a part of Marduk's plan. I'm not sure. Maybe he just wanted to gloat."

Her smile faded. "No. With Monica. Before we leave, and before everyone crowns you a king, I need to know, Emmerich. I need to know what happened. I've had too many nightmares and sleepless nights to not know."

His face turned grim. "Monica was Marduk's apprentice. The night I confronted her, she attacked me. I defended myself."

"Why didn't you tell me?"

"Because the reason didn't matter. The woman I loved was dead and I was her murderer. No reason is good enough to change those two facts."

"The truth wouldn't have hurt you."

"But I still couldn't bear it. I couldn't bear you thinking of me as the monster I am."

"You're not a monster."

He didn't answer for a moment before reaching down to help her up. "We need to leave here."

But on their way out, they stopped by Gavin's body. Clara dropped to her knees. "Oh, why did you lie?"

"He thought he was protecting you. He loved you, Clara."

She sobbed and kissed his forehead before closing his eyes.

"We'll give him a proper funeral, I promise. Come."

She took his hand and allowed him to lead her out.

The menagerie was silent and still. As they passed in front of the large cages, something in the trees rustled and

Clara thought for a second she saw a glimpse of brilliant rainbow feathers.

When they emerged out of the cellar door, they were greeted by dozens of soldiers. Bloody, wearing torn clothing, and most of them wounded, they cheered when they saw the couple.

"King Emmerich!" they chanted. "King Emmerich!"

Jarrett came out of the crowd and in his hands he held a crown. "Stole this from the treasury." He knelt. "My liege."

Emmerich looked ready to refuse but Clara stepped forward and took it from Jarrett. She turned and placed it on Emmerich's head.

"The king is dead," she said. "Long live the king."

And she, followed by everyone else, knelt.

Chapter Forty-Three

"As far as we can determine," said Bruin, "the elemental spirits imprisoned in the casket are able to attach through strong, negative emotion, such as hate. Gavin's death acted as a catalyst. You, Lady Clara, because of your ability, are particularly sensitive to spirits. Marduk saw this and used it to his advantage. If you hadn't let go of your hate, you would have been possessed and would have been his tool to shape the world to his liking."

Clara nodded, watching the aerials winging high above. "Has the king been informed of this?"

"It was in my report. I handed it in just two candle marks ago. But I thought I would tell you directly."

They stood in the Palace's rose garden. Most of the roses were gone and cold wind shook the branches. Winter was coming. It had been three months since Emmerich had been installed as king. King Precene's men, or what had been left of them, arrived three days after General Asher marched into the city with what little remained of his army.

After that was the messy business of rounding up Marduk's supporters and deciding what to do with the creatures in the menagerie. Most creatures killed themselves once the opportunity presented itself. Many others had to be put down. Then someone—a traitor, possibly, they hadn't found yet—released a few still waiting to be put down. They disappeared into the surrounding forest, generating a random sighting and a few livestock thefts.

The aerials, the feathered lizards with their rainbow wings, remained close. They spoke mentally to a few and seemed to only want to sun themselves. No one knew what Marduk had planned for them, or why they had turned on him. Whenever anyone did ask, the aerial only spoke in riddles.

Clara had not told Emmerich about the one that came to speak to her. It seemed too personal, somehow, as if it wasn't meant to be share.

"My lady? Are you all right?"

"I'm well, Lord Bruin. Where is the casket now?"

"Hidden away. We're keeping the location a secret."

"That would be for the best. And what of the Academy? Did the king accept my recommendation?"

"He did. Thank you, my lady, for persuading the king

to allow the Academy to remain open. And I understand you were behind many of the new laws regarding magic. I've been selected to head the new Magical Council."

She smiled at him. "And you will perform admirably, no doubt."

He smiled and bowed slightly. "Her ladyship is too kind."

"No. I'm too honest. Ask my handmaid."

"Where is Lady Amelia?"

"Gone to fetch something for me. How is Lady Katerina?"

"I'm told she's adjusted to life in the nunnery quite well."

"I had hoped she would remain with me."

"Hopes no doubt dashed when she tried to murder you."

"She should thank the Mother every day that I chose to use the hilt of my dagger rather than the blade."

"I'm sure she does." Bruin suddenly cleared his voice. "His Majesty once again extends an invitation for you to dine with him tonight."

Clara suddenly felt heavy and tired at the mention of Emmerich. Learning the truth did not take away how he had treated her and betrayed her trust. Though she was Court Seer and often attended important meetings, she kept to herself, embroidering and making dresses. She visited Gavin's grave every other day and she tried to make sense of her own life, of her place in the world. She looked out on the horizon and yearned, remembering all of the hints that her father may not have been who she thought.

"Tell him I will join him," she said. "If there's nothing else?"

"No, my lady."

"Then I would be alone now."

He bowed and left her as she faced the horizon again. A storm was coming and she watched the rain sweeping down in the distance in dark curtains.

They ate in the king's private dinner chamber off of the main dining hall, the sound of the Court eating muffled by the stone walls.

Emmerich sat across from her as they ate pumpkin soup with crusty yeast rolls. It could have been ashes for all she tasted it.

Emmerich said, "I've noticed the ladies of the Court

wearing your latest designs."

"Does it please his Majesty?"

"It does. It also pleases me, Emmerich. Clara, please don't be so distant."

"You're king now. I shouldn't show respect?"

"You're my friend. In private, we can drop the honorifics." He nodded at the guards. "They won't tell on us."

She put her spoon down. "Fine."

"Why are you angry with me?"

"Who says I'm angry?"

"No one. My keen sense of observation picked up on it."

"I'm surprised. Your keen sense of observation is so often directed elsewhere."

He grimaced. "I'm king now, Clara. I've been busy."

"Is that why you've barely spoken to me since the night of your impromptu coronation?"

"I've been sending you invitations to dinner."

"After the first month."

"Like I said, I've been busy."

"Not too busy. You're out every day practicing with the men."

"If this is about your lessons—"

"It's not that!" The guards twitched when she yelled. Clara took a deep breath.

"What is it then?"

She looked down. "I don't wish to be here."

He didn't answer for a moment. When he did, his voice carried a rough edge. "You are always free to leave."

"I know."

"So why won't you?"

"Because I don't wish to leave you."

"Guards, out. Everyone, out."

She looked up in surprise as the men marched out. Soon, it was only the two of them. "What?"

He stood, walking around the table. "That is such a funny thing, what you just said." He knelt on one knee by her chair.

"Funny? I didn't mean it in jest, I assure you."

He took her hand. "I love how you sound so proper when you're angry enough to punch me."

"Then I must sound proper most of the time."

He gave a short laugh. "That you do. I said it was funny because I don't much like being king."

"I don't think it matters if you like it or not."

"True. But I find myself listening more to Asher than anyone else and many of the decisions I make, they are his suggestions."

"Perhaps. But people look up to you. It wasn't Clara, Lady Seer, who killed Marduk and won the war. It wasn't Asher, brave General and incisive diplomat. It was Emmerich, the hero of the Rebel Army."

"I understand that."

"You can't just leave because you don't want the position."

"Aye, but–"

"What are you think–"

He kissed her. It started off tenderly–soft brushing of tongue and lips–and slowly became demanding as he drew her tongue into his mouth, sucking lightly, before attacking her bottom lip. He held her by the back of her neck, the pad of his thumb tracing her skin. Slowly, he pulled away.

"Clara," he said, "I love you. I want to spend the rest of my life with you. But I'm not cut out to be a king. Do you know why I hated Marduk from the beginning?"

She shook her head, too flustered by the kiss to think of anything intelligent to say.

"Because he killed my family. He slaughtered everyone

in my caravan because we wouldn't help his master, who was ill. We probably could have saved him but Father wouldn't help a magic user. So his master died and Marduk avenged him. The only reason why I didn't die was because I was in the village, drinking with new friends I had made. And when Monica died, I blamed him for corrupting her. This whole war was started because I wanted revenge. That is not a man who needs to be king."

She shook her head, standing. "No, that isn't a man who needs to be king. And that isn't the man who is king."

Emmerich stood. "What do you mean?"

"Emmerich, when you stopped Marduk in the end, when you were in the chamber, were you thinking about your family? Or about Monica?"

"No."

"What, then?"

He shifted a little, licking his lips. "I was thinking about you, of course. I was thinking about how Marduk needed to be stopped. I suppose I was thinking about how everyone was in danger."

"Aye. And that man is king, now. A good, compassionate man who listens to those with good advice and better ideas. You've only been king three months,

Emmerich. You'll learn in time."

He stared at her a long moment. "What are you saying? That you'll stay despite wanting to leave?"

Clara looked down, thinking. After a long moment, she said, "No. I'm saying I will leave. Without you." She looked at him. "You have a duty to the people now. You can't shirk that."

"And you? You're a Seer. Don't you have a duty?"

"I haven't had a vision since Marduk's death. When I'm not at something official, I'm off on my own, sewing dresses for the ladies of the Court. I'm no use to you here."

He grasped her by the shoulders. "Clara, I love you. I want you to be with me because I love you. Not because you have a use." His eyes pleaded with her to accept his words.

It made Clara's heart break as she slowly pulled away. "There are too many unanswered questions about myself. I have to find answers. I have to find out who I am."

"It's suicide for a woman to travel alone."

"I won't be traveling as a woman."

"You can't hold up that disguise forever."

"Well, you can't leave, so what choice do I have? I know I cannot stay here. It feels wrong. I've had three months to think about this, about everything, and I feel as if I have to go." She looked at him, lifting her chin in the old gesture of challenge. "You did teach me how to defend myself, Emmerich."

He sighed, staring at her a long moment. Something sad and lonely filled his expression. "Take Jarrett, then."

"He's the Captain of the Guard."

"Aye. But he has just as much wanderlust as you. He'll be happy to leave with you and I'll be happy knowing you're well guarded."

An uneasy silence settled between them for a long moment. Finally, she said, "Thank you, my liege. I, ah, would like to retire."

He nodded, no longer looking at her. Clara walked past him but when her hand was on the door, he said, "Wait."

She turned to face him. "Aye, your Majesty?"

"Do you love me?"

She almost told him no. She almost told him that there was no point in answering that because she was leaving. But, in the end, she couldn't lie to him. She could never lie to him.

"Aye," she replied.

"But that's not enough."

"No."

He nodded. "I can't wait for you forever. The people need an heir."

"I understand."

"But I'll wait as long as I can."

A small smile tugged on her lips. "Thank you."

"When are you going to leave? It's already snowing in the North."

"There's a caravan bound for Candor, leaving day after tomorrow. I can winter there."

He looked her over, as if trying to memorize her every line. "Will I see you again before you go?"

She licked her lips. "No. I think it's best if you didn't."

For a moment, it looked like Emmerich was going to argue, but, instead, he only nodded, looking down.

The moment had dragged on long enough. Turning, Clara left the room, the door closing behind her with a soft *click*.

Letter to the Reader

Dear Reader,

Thank you for coming along with me on this journey to tell Clara's story. If you enjoyed this novel, then please leave a review! I appreciate all of my reviews and they help me a lot. And don't forget to check out my other books!

Sincerely,

Suzanna J. Linton

Acknowledgements

I want to give a heartfelt thank you to all those who did the proofreading and copyediting that has allowed me to create an updated version of Clara that I can be proud of. A big thanks to Fiona Jayde Media for the cover.

About the Author

Suzanna J. Linton began writing at a young age. At first, she worked on poetry but as years progressed, she found herself drawn to fiction, particularly fantasy. The authors that inspire her are Anne McCaffrey, Robin McKinley, and Charles de Lint. She lives in Florence, SC, with her husband, Brad, and their assorted pets.

Connect Online:
Website: http://suzannalinton.com
Twitter: http://twitter.com/suzannalin
Facebook: http://facebook.com/suzannajlinton

Made in the USA
Columbia, SC
30 June 2019